# PRAISE FOR *SECOND SHADOW*

"An exceptional winner, blending Native American cultural insights with a strong mix of romance and intrigue. Fans of Tony Hillerman and other Southwest writers will relish both the setting and approach of the Thurlos: the mystery is tight and well done, the characters and the added cultural conflicts are gripping."
—"The Bookwatch"

"Fascinating! The Thurlo dedication shows in this suspenseful tale."
—Susan Wiggs

"An insightful, suspenseful and fascinating tale highlighting both the cultural differences between people, and the basic tenets of human natures which make us all similar. A thoroughly engaging read!"
—*Romantic Times*

"A beautiful romance, a credible and well-crafted mystery, and an accurate depiction of two clashing cultures combine to make *Second Shadow* an excellent novel. Anyone interested in the Native American or Hispanic cultures of the southwest United States will enjoy this uplifting, wonderful reading experience."
—*Affaire de Coeur*

# SECOND SHADOW

## AIMÉE & DAVID THURLO

A TOM DOHERTY ASSOCIATES BOOK
NEW YORK

SECOND SHADOW

Copyright © 1993 by Aimée & David Thurlo

A Forge Book
Published by Tom Doherty Associates, Inc.
175 Fifth Avenue
New York, N.Y. 10010

Forge® is a registered trademark of Tom Doherty Associates, Inc

ISBN: 0-812-52381-4
Library of Congress Card Catalog Number: 93-26554

First edition: November 1993
First mass market edition: November 1995

Printed in the United States of America

0 9 8 7 6 5 4 3 2

# SECOND SHADOW

## AIMÉE & DAVID THURLO

A TOM DOHERTY ASSOCIATES BOOK
NEW YORK

This is a work of fiction. All the characters and events portrayed in this book are fictitious, and any resemblance to real people or events is purely coincidental.

SECOND SHADOW

A Forge Book
Published by Tom Doherty Associates, Inc.
175 Fifth Avenue
New York, N.Y. 10010

Forge® is a registered trademark of Tom Doherty Associates, Inc

ISBN: 0-812-52381-4
Library of Congress Card Catalog Number: 93-26554

First edition: November 1993
First mass market edition: November 1995

Printed in the United States of America

0 9 8 7 6 5 4 3 2

To Peggy and Peter Chauvet

Through all the changes in our lives;
houses/homes, city/country,
even ourselves;
the friendship we share has remained the same.

## Authors' Note

The Pueblo rituals described
herein have been abbreviated
out of respect to those whose
religious beliefs depend on the
secrecy of the rites.

And though of magnificence
and splendour, your house
shall not hold your secret nor
shelter your longing.
   For that which is boundless
in you abides in the mansion of
the sky, whose door is the
morning mist, and whose windows are the songs and the si-
lences of night.

—*The Prophet*,
by Kahlil Gibran

# PROLOGUE

IRENE POBIKAN BRUSHED her long ebony hair away from her face, and stared absently across the narrow Rio Grande river valley as the dusty twilight settled over the desert. Ripples of darkness were slowly overtaking the brilliant blaze of red and orange that paid final tribute to the dying day.

As she noticed the empty spot beside her on the window seat, a heaviness of spirit settled over her. Grandfather and she had sat on this adobe *banco* many times, enjoying the last burst of color before night claimed the mesas. Irene's heart ached as the longing to see him again filled her.

Grandfather had been in his seventies when he'd passed on to the land of endless cicada singing. Yet his death had stunned her, for Grandfather had always seemed much younger than his chronological years. Even in his last days, his gentle understanding and alert mind had made him a vital part of their pueblo.

As the tribe's medicine man, or *pufona sendo,* he'd served his people faithfully.

She remembered the last few weeks of his life. He'd been called to the home of a pueblo resident. His patient, an elderly man known for his adherence to traditional ways, had refused medical treatment at the local clinic. Her grandfather had ministered to him for almost a week, but then contagion and a weak heart had exacted its price. Grandfather returned home ill after the death of his patient, and two days later had begun his own journey to the Underworld.

Irene had felt desolate, though surrounded by her family and virtually every resident of their village. His passing had left a permanent empty space in the center of her heart. But it was at times like these, so filled with memories of them together, that she missed her longtime mentor and friend most.

As the cobalt-blue shadows of evening stretched over the piñon-covered hillsides, she caught a flicker of movement out of the corner of her eye. She turned to look at it straight on, but nothing was there. She blinked and stared hard into the twilight. As she strained to see, she discerned the faint outline of a man's body. The moonlight's glow enveloped him in a milky haze. The figure approached her window slowly, then stopped thirty feet away.

Her pulse began to drum frantically as recognition dawned over her senses. The wrinkled, wizened smile, more like the faded imprint on an old photograph, made her heart leap to her throat.

It couldn't be him! Her grandfather was now one with the shrines. It was then she *felt* her name being called. The summons, though crystal-clear, was coming from within herself and made no audible sound. Denial raged through her. Near desperation, she concluded she had to be dreaming, so she reached down and pinched the back of her hand. The pain that shot up her arm was very real!

Despite the protests common sense sent screaming into her brain, the urge to follow the spirit of one so dearly loved became irresistible. She reached for her jacket, slipped it on over her white cotton blouse, and stepped outside into the front yard. She could see the familiar contours of Grandfather's massive shoulders and back as he silently led the way to some unknown destination. He remained several feet ahead of her, never quite out of sight, yet never allowing her to come any closer.

Before she knew it they'd arrived at the base of one of the *Tsin,* sacred hills. As a young man, her grandfather had spent some time in the labyrinths that encircled them. It had been part of the initiation that had enabled him to join the religious society he'd chosen.

The labyrinths were never entered without considerable risk, because going inside the subterranean tunnels meant initiation. There was no guarantee a novice would return from the journey.

Her grandfather stopped just inside the mouth of the labyrinth and turned, beckoning to her with a wave of his hand.

Irene stood frozen to the spot, unable to move or utter a sound. She wanted to follow him, but a bone-chilling feeling of dread held her back.

The old man started to come toward her, arm outstretched, but she pulled back. Terror, deep and primitive, began to build within her. She felt as if a hand were reaching into the pit of her very soul, compelling her to move forward. Irene's throat constricted with fear, making breathing increasingly difficult.

Grandfather finally stopped advancing and shook his head sadly, remaining just out of her reach.

Once again she heard the voice that whispered from

somewhere inside her. It was the sound of his voice, yet not.

"You still don't know when to fight, and when to lower your guard and embrace the possibilities." His image shimmered as he moved away. "Reach into your heart and rely on our ways to give you the courage you'll need. When you see the mountain lion, know that the time of danger is close at hand and be ready."

"Wait," she pleaded as the image faded before her eyes.

Slowly another shape began to materialize. It seemed nothing more than a shadow, low to the ground. As she started to move forward, something incredibly cold grasped her neck and yanked her down. Feeling her skin burning with the icy touch, she struggled desperately against the unseen hands and a moment later, bolted upright and free.

As her own scream filled her ears, Irene came abruptly awake. She glanced into the darkness of her room assuring herself that she was alone in her bed. Perspiration covered her body and flowed down her neck in rivulets that all but soaked the thin nightshirt she was wearing. She threw back the covers and stood, her legs wobbly. Feeling her way to the light switch, she fought the sudden glare with slits for eyes as she walked to the kitchen. Her hands shook as she took a drink of water.

Leaning against the sink for support, her eyes fell on the small cactus resting on the window ledge. Grandfather had given it to her many years ago when she'd graduated from high school. Bittersweet memories crowded her mind, but the pain they created quickly turned into anger.

"Why couldn't you have refused a patient just once! We needed you here with us!" Impulsively she picked up the small pot and threw it across the room. The clay pot struck the whitewashed adobe wall and shattered, sending pieces flying all around the kitchen.

The destruction her temper had caused brought her back to the present and tears began to run down her cheeks. As an immense feeling of loss swept over her, she hugged herself tightly, throwing her head back in anguish. Her grandfather would have been appalled at her outburst. As a Tewa, she had disciplines that sustained her, and anger played no part in them. Self-control was at the heart of all her people stood for. Crying silently, she approached the tiny plant that lay in the midst of the shattered clay. If the roots weren't badly damaged, maybe it could be saved. The desert bred a certain kind of toughness in people and things. So long as the plant had a way to connect again to the soil, it would live.

She shook the small cactus gently, freeing it of what remained of the pot, and quickly placed it in the soil of a larger container. As she began sweeping up the sandy dirt scattered on the floor, she saw it: the fetish that had been misplaced years ago. She set the broom aside and knelt beside it. Grandfather had given the stone carving to her for protection. Then one day, her four-year-old cousin had taken the animal figure to play with. After the little girl left, Irene had noticed its absence. Questioning her cousin had not been productive. Then, as the weeks went by, Irene had given up hope of ever finding her carving.

Now after all these years, the fetish was in her keeping once again. Safe in the bed of soil where the little girl had obviously placed it, the stone had even managed to survive her temper. She held the fetish carefully.

She wasn't sure how long she remained there, caught up in memories, but suddenly she became aware of the rain striking the windowpane. The wind flung the droplets against the glass with barely contained violence. She'd never paid much attention to the belief, but it was said that if one dreamed of the dead, rain would follow. Up to now she'd chosen to believe that it was only an allusion to the tears of the living. Yet as she listened to the storm outside, she struggled between the desire to cling to logic and the need to accept the truths taught by her people.

Sitting by the kitchen table, Irene cupped the stone mountain lion in her palm. As her fingers closed protectively around it, she uttered a strangled cry of disbelief. The warning Grandfather had spoken of in her dream flashed back in her mind with alarming clarity. Her intellect insisted she accept only substantiated facts. Yet her heart and instincts now compelled her to believe something far different.

With her thoughts in a jumble, Irene returned to the bedroom, set the figure on the nightstand, and crawled between the sheets. Severing her connections to the waking world, she drifted off, trying to find peace in sleep.

RENE WALKED ACROSS the nearly empty lobby of the elegant Santa Fe hotel. The red clay tile beneath her shoes made her steps seem too loud, enhancing her feelings of anxiety. She had to land this account; her job and livelihood depended on it. Yet to do that, she would have to turn her back on many of the Tewa ways. The white world demanded a different mode of thinking as the price of survival.

At the pueblo, people were taught to work together. Anyone who tried to stand out above the rest was quickly and harshly criticized. The individual was important, but only in the context of the group. What mattered most was the person's contribution to the unity and quality of the whole.

Now, the situation she was entering would require her to sing her own praises as an architect, and do her best to stand out against the competition. Her stomach twisted into a knot as she forced herself to accept the inevitable. Working on the Mendoza hacienda was just the break her career needed. It would give her the perfect chance to showcase her skills and eventually lead to other career opportunities. Although she'd hoped once to avoid this type of competitiveness, she now realized the impossibility of that.

There was one factor, however, that made it easier for her to bear. She knew she was the best candidate for the job. She had extensive experience with adobe buildings, having worked on the pueblo's aging structures most of her life. She knew the problems and the pitfalls associated with building earthen structures better than any of her competitors.

Most important of all, her heritage had taught her all about birthrights. If Mendoza was the type of person she'd heard he was, she knew what was driving him to restore his home to its former glory. The hacienda was his link to the past, and as a proud "old money" Hispanic, it represented the heritage that gave him and his family distinction in New Mexico.

As she walked down the corridor toward the conference room Raul Mendoza was using, she recalled their first meeting two weeks ago. Confident . . . that was the only way to describe the handsome man in his mid-thirties she hoped would become her new client. He seemed to have the ability to say just the right thing at precisely the right time. The knowledge filled her with envy. Small talk defied her best efforts. The firm she worked for in Santa Fe often held parties for their clients, functions she was required to attend. She always felt awkward, because the conversations she engaged in invariably ended up focusing on her heritage rather than her work. Up to now, however, she'd never felt she had that much at stake in the jockeying for position and posturing that normally went on in the company. Even when the more prestigious accounts were given to others, she didn't complain. But her grandfather's death had acted as a catalyst, shaking her out of complaisance. She'd taken a hard look at her life and had suddenly realized that despite her education, she'd never really been given the chance to do much with her skills.

She'd consistently been passed over for every important corporate assignment, or had been used as an assistant to the architect placed in charge. Now there was a feeling she'd sensed recently in the office that indicated she was about to lose her job. The senior partners had complained that she wasn't aggressive or ambitious enough to remain an asset to the firm.

Irene paused halfway down the short corridor, gathering her courage. The tribe had paid for her schooling. She would not dishonor them now by failing.

She glanced toward the open door near the end of the hall, hearing Raul Mendoza speaking to an architect from a rival firm. Irene straightened her conservative wool suit, brushed away nonexistent lint, and tried to identify the other voice. A moment later, she had the answer. She knew Darryl Baldridge. He'd been a leading residential architect in the area for years. But despite his reputation, she still had the advantage. Baldridge could design and remodel, especially with brick and stucco, but restoration of historic adobe buildings was something he rarely attempted.

Further down the hall sat Jake Myers. He nodded at her, and she smiled back. Jake was a highly competent architect and a real gentleman, but he lacked creativity. She had seen his custom homes, and they reminded her of every other house in Santa Fe. His work was technically sound and frequently attractive, but it lacked imagination and passion. Without that quality, his designs failed to make the leap that would take an average building and turn it into an extraordinary one. Bolstering her confidence with the assessments she'd made, Irene sat down in a tall-backed wooden chair to wait.

A few moments later, Baldridge came out. Seeing her there, he produced a calculating smile. "Might as well go back to your office. This account's mine," he whispered.

She would have normally smiled good-naturedly and shrugged, but not today. "I think you're going to be the one leaving empty-handed *this* time," she challenged back, refusing to let him rattle her.

As Irene started toward the conference room, ready to make her pitch, she casually rolled her hands into fists, hoping to warm them. They felt cold and clammy, and she didn't want Mendoza to think he was shaking hands with a corpse. Keeping her back straight, she went to the open doorway and forced herself to smile calmly at the man inside. He was wearing an expensive gray suit that spoke of success and style.

"Come in, Ms. Pobikan." Raul Mendoza stood and gestured to the empty chair across from the conference table.

"It's a pleasure to meet with you again," Irene said, and shook hands. As it was when they'd first met, she was taken by the clarity of his hazel eyes that now held hers in steady introspection. Within them she could see character and strength.

"After we spoke together at the hacienda you suggested the idea of extensive restoration rather than rebuilding. Now that you've had time to study the blueprints and work up a plan, are you still convinced it's possible within the time frame I've given you?"

"Yes, I'm certain of it. You told me you wanted to recapture the tradition and grandeur the hacienda had when you were growing up. My ideas are going to help you do just that." She unrolled the plans she'd brought along and spread them on the table before him. "These are preliminary drawings, but I have notes explaining each phase in detail. The foundations and walls will have to be reinforced in several places, and drainage improved to protect the walls from deterioration at ground level. Then there's the roof, which we both agreed needed work. Ultimately, my plan is to return the main rooms to their original functions. To maintain authenticity, whenever possible I'll be using hand-carved doors, corbels, and interior woodwork salvaged from other buildings rather than making replacement copies."

"Tracking those down is going to take quite a bit of your time."

She shook her head. "Most have already been located, actually. I've cultivated sources and suppliers here in the state that few others have access to."

He leaned back in his chair and regarded her thoughtfully. Finally he stood and walked to the window.

Irene waited, sensing he was weighing all the possibilities prior to action. She had done some research on him and knew Raul Mendoza's success as a businessman was well deserved. Though innately cautious, he was said to move with vast energy and single-minded purpose once his goals were set.

At length he turned and faced her. "There's one thing I don't understand. You're Tewa. Your ancestors have always been involved in the construction of the Mendoza homes. A century and a half ago, when the existing house was completed, they were used again. The circumstances were never as I would have had them, but . . ." He opened his hands, palms upward in a gesture of resignation. "Are you sure you want this project?"

A coldness enveloped her as she recalled bitter memories held in the tribe's collective past. It was the very subject she'd hoped to avoid, but Mendoza obviously wanted this out in the open. "I'm aware of what the Spanish—including your ancestors—did to my people. We were treated no better than slaves. But if you're asking if my sense of history will make it impossible for me to do the job, the answer is no. I don't blame you for injustices that occurred before either of us was born. But maybe I should ask something now. Does the fact that I'm Tewa bother *you*?"

"If it did, you wouldn't be here. I asked each of the firms I selected to provide résumés of the architects they were sending me. Your experience with restoration projects impressed me. I was looking for an architect with a sense of history. You're uniquely qualified in that respect. That's why I had you take a look at my home last week and prepare a proposal."

Irene smiled. Appearing supremely confident and unshakable took more energy than she'd ever dreamed. "I agree that I'm the architect you need," she said with aplomb. "I can make sure original techniques are used to restore the rooms to perfect condition. I know skilled artisans, specialists in their fields, who are willing to come work on the site if I ask. The kiva fireplaces could be repaired with plaster, for instance, but I propose we use an *enjarradora,* an adobe plaster craftsman, from Taos to resurface them with a color that matches the original. Tewa workers who know how to work with mud stucco can handle the outside walls. Those extras can make a world of difference and will be part of the unique touch I'm prepared to bring to this project."

Raul rubbed his chin pensively. "Meeting the Christmas deadline is crucial. That time of year has great personal significance to both my family and myself. The other architects say that if we use traditional materials and techniques to restore the existing structure, the work won't be completed before the end of January. Both firms want to tear down most of what's damaged, and rebuild using conventional methods."

"If all you want is a modern replica of the old hacienda, any competent architect can do the job. If you want to restore and maintain the style of the home originally built by your forefathers and mine"—she emphasized the latter—"then I'm your only choice." She heard the words that came out of her mouth and marveled at how steady her voice was. Her professional life hung in the balance. Losing her job would destroy the organizing center of her world. Her work structured her hours and lent purpose to her life.

Irene waited, imitating Raul's cool demeanor. This was the hard part. Ambiguity and uncertainty were a one-way road to anxiety and failure. The seconds ticked by slowly. Raul studied her drawings and notes, then finally glanced up.

"The architect I select will have to be on hand to supervise the contractor's work. Having workers, foreman, and architect housed on the job site will ensure that bad winter roads or a two-hour drive twice a day won't delay the renovation. That's why, like I mentioned before, I'll need you at the hacienda for the duration of this project."

"I'm ready to move in when you give the word," she assured.

Raul remained in his chair, his hands resting on her papers. "The other two architects want to scrap the entire west wing and replace most of the interior wood with new, custom-made materials. I don't deny that's probably simpler, but it's not in line with what I have in mind."

"Then I have the job?" She'd blurted out the words

before she remembered the professional cool she'd planned to maintain.

Raul nodded, walked to the doorway, and invited the two other architects to join them. "I appreciate the time and effort you've all put into the project. I've decided to go with Ms. Pobikan and her firm. All three plans are very sound, but her ideas seem the closest to my own."

Baldridge was genuinely surprised. Shaking his head silently, he grasped Mendoza's in a handshake. "My firm will be available when you discover that she's agreed to something that's impossible to deliver."

Myers followed suit with more graciousness. "Should you have any problems, I hope you'll give us another opportunity to submit a proposal."

Baldridge walked to the door, then gave Irene one last glance. There was open contempt in the narrowed eyes that held hers. Irene suppressed a shudder. She'd never liked making enemies, but she had the definite feeling she'd made a new one today. Baldridge, according to rumors, had been having financial difficulties. In his own way, he'd probably needed the job as badly as she did, maybe more so.

For a moment, she fought the recurring impulse to return home and follow the more comforting, traditional life-style she'd known most of her life. There was simplicity at the pueblo that offered security, though undeniably it was a way of life that was slowly vanishing. The pueblo couldn't offer jobs to the young anymore, particularly to those with skills like hers. Circumstances forced many to learn a trade and go out into a world that made little effort to understand them.

Raul Mendoza's voice brought her out of her musings. "I'd like to discuss your plans to restore the circular staircase and interior woodwork," he said. "Can you stay a bit longer?"

"Of course. I'll be glad to go over those with you. Afterward maybe you can tell me more about the hacienda's history. Your recollections will help me fine-tune the details of my work. I'd like to know, for instance, what your favorite rooms were, and why."

Raul nodded slowly. "Would you mind if we spoke outside in the courtyard? I've been in here for three hours, and I need some fresh air."

As he walked beside her to the enclosed patio, she couldn't help but notice the confidence in his strides. They spoke of power, and pride in family position that was as deeply rooted as that of any aristocracy.

Yet it was precisely his wealth and power that made her uncomfortable. She couldn't help but wonder how much of it had been at the expense of her own people. The thought left a bitter taste at the back of her throat.

"It bothers you, the past between my people and yours," he observed, not bothering to make it a question. "So why did you accept my offer? Do you need the exposure?"

His voice was smooth, and the challenge had been delivered so deftly that she found herself answering before she recognized it for what it was. "I'm a fine architect. But not enough people know it yet. An opportunity like this one will give me a chance to prove what I can do."

"Not quite the philosophy I expected to hear from a Tewa," he mused. "Do you find the competitiveness of the business world difficult to cope with?"

Irene found his tone seductive, but she was unwilling to lower her guard again. "It's true that in the pueblo different rules and customs apply. But I have to make a living on the outside."

"Sensible," he answered with a nod of the head.

His comment made her uneasy. She needed no approval from him except when it came to her architectural designs. Though he could not be held accountable for what his ancestors had done, she understood heritage and bloodlines better than most. Deep down, would Raul Mendoza be any different from those who had persecuted her people? His great-great-grandfather had managed the hacienda and the Mendoza mines under a system of forced labor that had been akin to slavery. Without an advocate or the means to resist, her people had been unable to fight back successfully.

Irene remembered a story she'd heard once as a child. It had been rooted in history and had filled her with such horror, she'd been unable to forget it. It had happened around the time of the Mexican War, in 1846.

A Tewa woman had been working for the then Mrs. Mendoza as her personal maid when Mrs. Mendoza's gold necklace was discovered missing. The servant, accused of the crime, was taken outside and flogged. Her screams continued unabated until she'd confessed the crime. A week later, unable to recover from the severe beating, the woman died. Several weeks after that, the mistress of the house learned that her sister, away on a trip to Mexico, had borrowed the necklace. The only tears shed for the Indian woman had been at the Pueblo.

The blood of those who'd committed such crimes against her people coursed through Mendoza's veins. She swallowed, aiding the dryness in her throat. Then again, maybe it was high time for a Mendoza and a Tewa to truly work together and begin the process of healing the past. If their working relationship fostered mutual respect, much would have been accomplished toward that goal.

As they sat down in the courtyard on one of the small *bancos,* or benches, Irene's thoughts came back to the present. She gave Raul the details pertaining to the staircase and woodwork, then continued. "Tell me what you remember about the hacienda. I'd like more of a feel for the atmosphere you're trying to restore."

His gaze focused on a twisted old piñon standing alone in the interior courtyard. "The Mendoza house is called *Casa de Encanto,* Enchantment House. The name used to be appropriate, but not anymore, as you've seen."

His voice dropped and became void of emotion. "Before my father grew ill, our home had the grace and elegance that came from a sense of tradition. It was a source of pride. But then times changed and money became scarce. Though the decline of our home affected all of us, it was hardest on my father. As haphazard or expedient repairs changed the whole complexion of the house, he'd sit for hours telling me how things used to look in his day. It broke his heart to sit helplessly and watch what had once been a showcase home become a handyman's special."

"I'd heard that your family's business suffered during your father's illness . . ." She let the sentence trail.

"Orders for our irrigation systems fell off from lack of buyer confidence. You see, there wasn't anyone on hand to direct the company. My father didn't relinquish responsibility easily, so consequently his vice-presidents hadn't been trained to take over. It might have been different had I been older, but I was far too young to be of any help. That led to hard times for everyone, and *Casa de Encanto* suffered along with us."

"The hacienda's elegance is still there," she assured. "All it needs is a guiding hand and a few months of concerted effort."

"That's why I've hired you. It's in your hands now," he said quietly. "By Christmas I want the hacienda to look the way it did when my father was in his prime and at the peak of his health. Christmas is a time when the Mendozas traditionally come together in unity and strength. You see, that week is also the anniversary of my ancestors' triumphant return to New Mexico. It was the start of a prosperous new era for our family in this state."

She shuddered, remembering the details of the Pueblo Revolt, which Raul had tactfully avoided mentioning by name. The tribe's resentment of their treatment at the hands of the Spaniards had become so great that the Indians united and drove their oppressors out of New Mexico. The Spanish didn't return for another thirteen years. When they finally did, their treatment of the Indians improved.

"I know you want to meet your Christmas deadline," she said, "but autumn in the mountains is not the best time to . . ."

With her words, Raul sat up straight. His gaze, which had been unfocused and pensive, now turned cold and distant. "I don't care how you get the job done, but I won't accept any excuses. I'm only interested in results."

"And you'll have them."

Raul gazed at her for a moment, his eyes revealing nothing of his thoughts. Finally he nodded and managed a trace of a smile. "Maybe our association will mark a new beginning between the Mendozas and your people."

"Maybe, but changes like those will probably come slowly, if at all. Whether or not we like it, our pasts define us." She realized with sudden clarity how trapped they were in their roles by the unresolved pain of those who'd come before.

Raul expelled his breath in a rush. "You might be right, but only the future can determine that for sure." He stood and shook her hand. "Until that time, we both have a great deal of work to keep us busy."

Irene watched Raul walk away. He stood tall and straight, and moved with assurance. There was a fierce pride in who he was that challenged the Tewa in her.

It felt undeniably odd to know that she'd be working for their traditional enemy. Yet for the first time in Irene's memory a Mendoza was treating a member of her tribe with the respect due an equal. If nothing else, that was a sign of progress. Although it was true she'd gone after this job to prove herself to the firm that employed her, there were other integrities involved which in the long run would be far more important.

If she did only one thing for her tribe, she wanted to start the process that would free them to pursue whatever opportunities the future offered. Being shackled by the past had held them in a stranglehold for too long.

Not that they would ever forget the treatment they'd received at the hands of the Spanish. With their religion condemned as heretical, and facing the extermination of their culture and beliefs, they'd learned many hard lessons. Yet the time had come to move decisively forward.

Working with the Mendozas was only one small step of many that would be needed to rebuild confidence, but it was a start. Irene knew she'd face opposition from those she cared about most—her mother and the members of her tribe. She tried to brace herself for the painful confrontation she knew would come, mentally rehearsing persuasive and logical arguments.

Lost in thought, she crossed the empty parking lot, oblivious to the world around her. Then as she drew near her car, she heard running footsteps rapidly approaching. Startled, she whirled around, dropping her keys.

# 2

**D**ARRYL BALDRIDGE CAME to a staggering
halt only inches away, trapping her between
him and the car door. Instinctively she pressed her
back against the warm metal and glanced around frantically for help. Several cars were in spaces nearby, but
no other human beings were in sight. She was about to
yell when Baldridge, probably guessing what she was
about to do, moved back a step.

"You have the Mendoza account for now," he said,
his breath thick with alcohol, "but there's no way
you're going to keep it. You out and out lied to the
man. He just doesn't realize it yet."

Quickly she retrieved her keys from the pavement.
"I have no idea what you're talking about, Baldridge.
I did *not* lie to him."

"What do *you* call it? It's September. You can't possibly meet that Christmas deadline of his if you plan to
restore as much as he wants. How can you oversee

construction, find enough skilled craftsmen, and lo-cate *original* replacements for windows and ironwork during that time frame?" ˙

Gathering her courage, Irene stood up straight. "I have excellent sources I can draw on; you don't. That's one of the reasons I was selected."

"Yeah, right." He made a derisive sound. "You're going to fail at this, woman, and end up costing Men-doza thousands more. After this fiasco, you won't be able to get work designing outhouses. Those wild promises are going to cost you your career."

"I don't believe they are wild." Anger made her body shake. "I can deliver! You just can't accept that I competed with you head-to-head on this account and won it fair and square."

"That's just it. You didn't. You told Mendoza ex-actly what he wanted to hear. Either that was done on purpose, or you have some unbelievable fantasies about your own abilities." His liquor-soaked breath bathed her face. "So which is it, stupidity or dis-honesty?"

Irene hauled back and kicked him in the shins. As he yelped and jumped clear of the door, she dove in-side the car. In the space of a breath, she gunned the accelerator and sped out into the street, tires squeal-ing.

Two blocks later, with her heart still pumping wildly, she forced herself to slow down. She'd done precisely the wrong thing. Baldridge was no threat. He'd meant to intimidate her, that's all.

The episode replayed itself in her mind as she drove back home to the pueblo through the piñon and juni-per foothills north of Santa Fe. She twisted the inci-dent this way and that, dissecting it in a postmortem of events. She should have stayed and argued with him.

He would have understood and respected that. As it was, he'd now see her departure as a sign of cowardice or an admission that he'd been right. By the time she arrived home, she felt totally disgusted with herself.

Acknowledging that it was too late to do anything about it now, Irene opened the thick pine door of her modest adobe home and walked inside. It was a simple place that contained most, if not all, of the amenities found in homes outside the pueblo. Stuccoed in local earth pigments, it fit well into its surroundings, appearing no better or worse than those of her neighbors. There was comfort in the unity sameness created.

Irene walked across the sealed adobe floor and opened a window, enjoying the scent of roasted green chile drifting over from a neighbor's house. She always enjoyed coming home. Sparsely decorated, the whitewashed interior attested to her love of open spaces. Wearily she walked to the kitchen table and unrolled the plans she'd drawn up for Raul Mendoza.

As new ideas came unbidden into her head, she began to modify her sketches. The dividing wall that had split in half the large *sala,* the grandest of all formal rooms in the manor, would have to be removed. The stately grace Raul Mendoza wanted would require the elegance of roomy interiors and careful styling.

Other details that still needed ironing out crowded at the edges of her mind. She'd already made tentative arrangements with skilled restorers from her tribe. Those of her generation were always searching for work and wouldn't mind joining her on the site. Her biggest worry was the approach of winter. She had factored in a certain amount of lost time, but if the weather was more severe than usual, the timing on the exterior project work, which was scheduled first, would be jeopardized.

Doubts assailed her as she thought of Baldridge's words. If she failed, the only thing people would remember was that a Tewa had been given a chance and been proven incompetent. The responsibility weighed heavily on her shoulders.

She stared absently at the drawings. This was no time to allow her own insecurities to undermine her. She had to believe in herself. If she didn't, how could she expect others to believe in her? Irene swallowed back her sudden panic attack. Everything would be okay; she was good at this, and it was certainly nothing new to her. She'd participated in restorations around the pueblo since her teens.

With a smile, she recalled one occasion when they'd all gathered to repair the interior walls of the tribal government center. The pueblo governor had taken off his electronic wristwatch and set it aside, insisting on helping with the labor. Somehow during the afternoon—no one had ever known how—his watch had fallen into the hand-dug pit used for mixing and soaking adobe. The watch had subsequently become part of one of the hand-poured adobe bricks.

No one had given it much thought until the building was opened for use and a new discovery had come to light. Despite being encased inside adobe, the battery had continued to work. Every day at noon it sounded, but muffled by the thick mud it became a tiny chirping noise that seemed to come from behind the wall where the Chief's portrait was hung. The battery lasted two years, much to the amusement of the tribe and the pueblo governor's chagrin.

Irene smiled. The governor's watch had become the pueblo's favorite joke for years. As her mind drifted back, she realized that she'd identified herself as part of a "we" her entire life: part of her village and part of her family. But she was now embarking on a venture that would force her to stand alone and face considerable opposition. She would be taking the risk of disconnecting herself from all the reins that had held her life on a steady course. The prospect was frightening, but there was no turning back.

She tried to push all negative thoughts from her mind and concentrate on the blueprints. Yet despite her best efforts, her fears remained, circling her thoughts like a pack of hungry wolves.

She wasn't sure how much time had passed when she heard a knock. Doors were rarely locked in the pueblo. There was no need. As Irene turned around, her mother stepped inside.

Irene greeted her mother warmly with a hug. Teresa Pobikan's coppery skin was leather-tough, attesting to decades of exposure to the New Mexico sun. Yet the lines that mapped her face softened her expression, allowing the gentle heart within to shine through.

Teresa Pobikan wore a long denim skirt and a simple cotton blouse. The shawl that was wrapped around her shoulders was woven in geometric designs that made use of the earthen tones of the desert. "Tomorrow our *matuin,* our family, will gather here. It's been a year since my father died."

Irene nodded. "I dreamed about Grandfather last night."

Teresa's dark eyes widened. "That shouldn't have been. His soul was properly released after his death."

Seeing the alarm on her mother's face, Irene cursed herself silently. "It was just a dream, Mother."

Teresa shook her head adamantly. "Tell me what happened. You should have gone to the *pufona sendo,* our medicine man, and told him right away."

"It was nothing," she said. "I barely remember."

Teresa's eyes narrowed. "You always remember everything. Don't try to fool your mother. Now tell me."

Irene smiled hesitantly. "I dreamed he'd come to warn me." Irene shrugged and waved a hand across the room. "But as you can see, there's no danger here."

"Warning you against what?" she insisted.

"Something about a mountain lion . . ." Irene shook her head, brushing her hair off her shoulders. "Really, Mother, it was nothing. I'd been thinking about him recently, so when I dreamed, it was natural that he appeared there. If you remember, he gave me a mountain lion fetish, so that's probably how I made the connection."

Teresa nodded. "Most medicine men use carved stone bears, but my father preferred the mountain lion. He felt more comfortable with a fetish that combined healing powers with skills in warfare. He used to say that curing was a battle, and he needed to arm himself for the fight."

"Yes, I remember. That's undoubtedly why I made the connection."

"It rained last night . . ."

"I know," Irene whispered, aware of what her mother was referring to. "But even if it *was* him visiting in spirit, nothing can be done about it now."

"Did you see him clearly?" Teresa insisted.

"No, I didn't. I knew it was him, but there was no substance to see clearly or touch."

Teresa nodded, visibly relieved. "Then the charcoal used on the releasing ceremony has held. It'll be used again tomorrow." She picked up a basket of dried fruit and bread. "I'll take this to the shrine north of the village tomorrow at first light. Then the others will gather here for the final rite."

"It doesn't seem like a year since he left for the place of endless cicada singing," Irene said quietly, referring to the Underworld.

"In some respects, no, but in others yes. I've been seeing you change during that time, *Sohuwatse*," she said gently, using her daughter's secret name.

Irene smiled. Mist Eagle was her Indian name, one that only her mother and grandfather ever used. Her heart wrenched painfully. "I haven't changed, not really," she whispered.

"Once our pueblo was yours too. Yet nowadays you scarcely attend our rituals." Teresa shook her head sadly. "You've been even worse about that since your grandfather died. You spend practically all your time in the Anglo world."

"I'll have to do even more of that in the near future, Mother. I'm very close to losing my job." It was hard to say, particularly to her own mother. What was even worse was knowing her parent's opinion mattered. Someday, somehow, she still hoped to earn her mother's respect for the choices she'd made. "If I'm fired, no one else in this area will want to hire me. That would mean I'd have to move away to find work."

"You were content once just being part of our village. Then you started to change and look to the outside for answers and a sense of purpose." Teresa shook her head again. "And don't tell me it's just a way to make a living. Your heart's divided between our culture and theirs."

"Not divided," Irene argued softly. "I've always tried to find a balance between both. All of us who have to earn our livelihood outside the pueblo do that to one extent or another. It's not giving up the past. It's adapting to the present in order to build a future."

"You can put it any way you want, but the fact remains. You don't participate in any of the rituals of the *Kwiyoh,* our women's society, and half the time you're not even around for our ceremonial dances.

You can't ignore who you are and expect anything good to come of it."

They'd had this conversation before, but once again Irene forced herself to explain. "My goals are more than seeing a comma in my bank balance instead of my credit-card debt," she said patiently. "Why can't I make you see that? If I succeed in the Anglo world, then I'll be in a better position to help the pueblo. Being well known professionally will make it easier for me to get federal funding for projects needed here." She exhaled softly. "There are other ways to help than by being a dancer in a ceremony."

"You're thinking like the Anglos. Unless we maintain our way of life, there's nothing to hold us together. Restoring buildings certainly isn't going to do it, that's just where we live." Teresa stood by the window looking at the Santa Fe city lights, which lay to the southeast. "Don't fool yourself into believing that because you were educated in the Anglo world, you're just like them. Our ways are deeply ingrained into you, though you may not even be aware of it. When things go wrong, or you're in trouble, you'll find that you'll turn to them without even thinking."

Irene dropped down onto the chair and rubbed her dark brown eyes. "I'm not trying to deny my heritage, I'm trying to find my own place within it. To contribute something worthwhile, I have to use my own gifts. The tribe deserves more than an unemployed architect to support. They need a tangible service in exchange for the money they spent on my education."

With a soft sigh of resignation, Teresa stood up and walked to her daughter's side. Curious, she glanced down at the blueprints laid out on the table before Irene. "What's this? Your next project?"

Irene held her breath for a second, then forced a smile. "I'll tell you about that tomorrow. Right now there's other things we have to take care of before sunrise."

Watercolor hues of sunflower and strawberry flowed across the skies as the sun peered over the horizon. The golden rays had just begun warming the desert when the *matuin* began to draw near. Two men approached first, walking down slowly from the north side of the pueblo. They wore heavy silver and turquoise squash blossoms around their necks, large enough to almost weigh them down.

She recognized her uncle, the senior male of the family. He was in his late sixties, or thereabouts. No one ever counted years in the pueblo, so an exact number was difficult to figure. The man beside him was her paternal uncle, and although in his seventies, he was endowed with the energy and youthful exuberance of a man half his age. Both had their hair *chongo* style, fastened like a bun at the base of their necks. Teresa, who'd spent the night with her, greeted them at the door.

Several minutes later, four women close to her grandfather's age arrived. The first wore the traditional long skirt and a delicately made squash blossom. She'd been her grandfather's bride and was of the Zuni tribe. Although in her late sixties, Grandmother's face was almost free of wrinkles. Her hands were small and delicately shaped. Several of her fingers were adorned with intricate petit-point turquoise rings traditional of her pueblo. Teresa showed her inside and then returned to the door to greet her sister.

Alicia Payotsire was a younger version of Irene's mother. Her gray hair was tied in a tight braid fastened at the back of her head. She wore a full, dark skirt which hung to just below the knee. A heavy shawl woven in terra-cotta and mustard hung around her shoulders. "I'm here, Teresa. As long as family surrounds us, neither of us will ever be alone," she said, referring obliquely to their status as widows.

Two more women appeared a short time later, dressed in similar fashion to Alicia. They took seats around the living room, which had been cleared for the ritual.

Irene, wearing a full skirt and long-sleeved blouse with no jewelry, watched the others as she also took a seat. Silently she acknowledged that her mother had been right. She'd lost faith in the old rituals. They now seemed more important in terms of history than anything else.

The mood was somber as food that had been prepared for the occasion was placed in a basket on the floor in front of her uncle, the senior male. Irene joined the others in a ceremonial smoke, forcing her mind to remain on the ritual out of respect for her grandfather.

Completing that part of the ceremony, her uncle went to the kiva-style fireplace, picked up a piece of long-cooled charcoal, and placed it in his mouth. Wrapping himself in a blanket, he went silently out the door.

Her mother followed, then the *matuin.* Irene stood, wrapped herself in a red Pendelton blanket, and proceeded outside with the others. Only one person was needed for this walk to the pueblo's shrine, but her grandfather had been special to many. This final duty was one they all wanted to share as a tribute to him. The walk across the cool, late summer desert was long and demanding, but she'd been prepared. She knew this part of the ritual well. An identical one had been performed right after her grandfather's death. It was repeated now, exactly a year later, as a last farewell. This time the ceremony was more for the surviving members of his family. It was a way of reaffirming the solidarity of the whole tribe in the face of the permanent loss of one of its own.

They followed a small dirt trail to the base of a rock-covered hillside. Their ascent from there was slow, as allowances were made for the elderly, and the uncertain footing the ground provided. Every once in a while, a prairie dog would peer out curiously, then duck quickly into its burrow. As they reached the summit, the shrine came into view. Three large, flat boulders stood vertically, propped up by a circle of heavy, rounded boulders. Traces of prayer meal could still be seen scattered among the rocks.

As they approached, Irene lined up behind her uncle and watched as he drew four lines in front of him with his left foot, symbolizing that death was only four steps from the living. Spitting out a portion of the charcoal in his mouth, he blurred the lines, a sign of separation between the dead and the living. Then slowly he led the way back to the house.

As they reached the front door, her uncle's voice rose in a singsong that entranced all those present. "We have cast shadows between us. Now go, for you are free."

The words weighed heavily on Irene's shoulders. This was the final releasing of Grandfather's soul, but she knew that a part of her heart would never let him go.

As the ritual came to a close, the *matuin* that had gathered began to say their good-byes. Finally only her mother and her aunt remained. Teresa went to the kitchen table and glanced at the rolled-up blueprints that had been placed there. "Will you have to go to work this afternoon?"

She nodded. "This job will keep me away for some time. In late October, depending on the weather, I might be able to come back and visit for a few days, but then I'll have to leave again."

"What's so special about this job?" her aunt prodded, her eyes as alert as Teresa's.

"I'm going to be restoring a historic hacienda near Taos," she said, aware it was time to disclose the truth and face whatever lay ahead. "I had to work very hard to get this job. Several firms in the area wanted it."

"It's logical to me that the job should be yours. You have the experience," Teresa commented. "You've worked on restorations your entire life. The church here, the government center, all have needed work from time to time." Her eyes grew unfocused as her mind drifted to the past. "Your first love was always working on old buildings, and trying to bring back the beauty that was once theirs."

"It still is. That's why this job is so important to me."

Her aunt's eagle-sharp eyes held her. Suddenly Irene felt trapped, like a deer fixed by the headlights of a car. "There's only one hacienda in that area I've read will be undergoing restoration soon." Her words were slow and measured. "You couldn't . . . you wouldn't . . ." she stammered, horror etched in her features.

Irene took a deep breath. She knew with absolute certainty that Aunt Alicia's reaction was a preview of what her mother's would be. "It's the Mendoza house," she confirmed softly.

The flashes of emotions that played on the faces of both women made Irene's throat tighten. There was disbelief, anger, then worst of all, hurt.

Her mother's hand curled into a fist and she pressed it to her heart. "You can't work for that family! Surely you're not serious about this!"

"I've already accepted the job," Irene said, wondering for the first time if she truly had the strength to go through with this. The stricken look on her mother's face was knifing through her. "Even though you don't understand what I'm doing, trust me, please."

Teresa's eyes filled with tears, but she kept her voice steady. "What are you doing? That man's family has committed crimes against this tribe that can't be forgiven. You know his wealth was built on our sweat and blood."

Suddenly dispassionate arguments and logic seemed to elude her. She stared at the floor for a moment, gathering her resolve. "His ancestors were the ones responsible, not him," Irene argued patiently.

"But the same blood runs through all the Mendozas," Alicia affirmed angrily.

"Old hatreds accomplish nothing. We have to put the past behind us, otherwise it'll continue to hold us back."

"Is progress really what you're worried about?" her aunt demanded pointedly. "Let's face it. This is probably a great chance for you to build your career in the Anglo world and that, I suspect, has been your secret goal for a while now."

Alicia picked up her shawl brusquely, then glanced at Teresa. "Talk her out of this craziness if you can. Danger surrounds this move. I can feel it." With a shudder, Alicia walked out of the house.

As the click of the door echoed in the silence, Teresa met her daughter's gaze. "Your aunt is *Apienu,* the head of our women's religious society. She often knows what's going to happen in the future. You've seen evidence of that yourself. Are you going to ignore her warning?"

"I'll admit she's right much of the time. But not always," Irene said gently, desperately staying on the side of logic. "Mother, please don't let her frighten you. That's exactly what she was trying to do."

"No, Alicia's my sister, I know her too well. She doesn't want you to go, but she wouldn't have lied to keep you here." Deep lines of worry crossed Teresa's face as she lapsed into silence. When she finally spoke, her words were carefully measured and uncompromising. "I don't want to forbid you to go."

Irene walked to where her mother sat, and knelt on the floor in front of her. "Please don't make me have to choose between you and what I have to do. I need your support more than ever. Don't turn away, trust what you've raised me to be."

Teresa's cheeks were pinched and her mouth drawn into a white line. The eyes that shone at Irene were hard and unyielding.

"I've always done what you wanted," Irene continued, "but this time I've got to go with what I know is right. I can't spend my whole life defining myself based on what other people want from me."

Teresa's features softened. "I spoke similar words once to my own mother," she admitted. "But despite your view of yourself, you haven't always done what I wanted. You would have married someone from our tribe by now, if you had."

Teresa stood by the *nicho,* a shelf carved into the adobe wall, staring at the burnished black pottery she'd crafted for her daughter. "You're more of a fighter than you realize. I never wanted you to leave the pueblo to go to school, but you persisted and convinced me it was something that would benefit the tribe. But when you returned to our pueblo and didn't marry, I knew that you'd learned more than architecture in the outside world. You wanted to fall in love, not just search for a compatible mate. But look at the way that's worked for those outside. You can't rely on love or anything that's based on desire and emotion."

Teresa shook her head sadly as she turned to face

Irene. "Now I see another Anglo trait in you. Like many of them, you're searching for recognition—with a passion that could destroy you."

"In my heart I'm an artist, Mother. I learned about architecture because I felt the need to create; to make things that would last and that everyone could see and enjoy. That yearning can become so strong it demands you give in to it, but it's capable of doing much good."

"Yes, but it has a dark side."

"Everything exists in two parts, male and female, day and night, even good and evil. To be at peace with myself, I have to use all my skills, and learn to fit in wherever life takes me. But I'm still very much part of this tribe."

"Yes, you are, and the white world will never let you forget that. Old prejudices die hard. You've acquired knowledge they respect, but when they look at you they'll still see an Indian."

"I wouldn't have it any other way," Irene replied resolutely. "But to accept their prejudices as a reason not to try and make a place for myself among them—" She sighed softly. "No—that I can't do."

"Mendoza will use your talents for his own profit, just like his grandfathers did to others from our pueblo."

"He'll be paying top dollar for the privilege this time, believe me. And the construction will create jobs for many here who need the work." She paused, overwhelmed by a sense of futility as she continued to be buffeted by conflicting demands. "Look at it this way. It's taking advantage of an opportunity to do something good, and making use of an old enemy to accomplish it."

Her mother smiled slowly. "I always said you could argue your point well. But I want you to take something with you." She walked to one corner of the house and lifted a section of loose adobe from the corner, revealing a recess containing a small drawstringed bag. "These *xayeh*—the souls of our ancestors in material form—are your life root stones." Teresa held the two pieces of smooth quartz she'd extracted from the pouch. "They've protected you since you were born. Take them with you now, and keep them where you sleep. They may help ward off the danger Alicia felt surrounding you. Your grandfather warned you about that too, remember?"

Irene felt her skin prickle. "Those two incidents are completely unrelated to each other," she said unsteadily.

"Maybe, but even you, with all your logic and white ways, aren't so sure." Teresa pressed the stones into her daughter's hand. "Take them and stay on your guard."

Irene took a deep breath and tried to shift the weight of fear in her heart so she could carry the burden it posed. "I'm only there to do a job. Once I'm finished restoring the hacienda," she continued in a strong voice, "it'll become a tribute to all of us here. People everywhere will know that it was a Tewa from our village who accomplished the work."

Irene drove out of the pueblo shortly after noon. She'd chosen the clothing inside the two soft-sided suitcases in the backseat carefully, trying to blend practicality with a neutral type of elegance. Most of what she'd packed was similar to what she now wore: gray wool slacks, a maroon blazer, and a winter-white pullover. It was easier to blend in when your clothing was non-descript, and since she had no idea what lay ahead for her at the hacienda, that seemed the best course of action. Safely inside her pocket were the *xayeh* her mother had insisted she bring along. The mountain lion fetish she'd left at home on her dresser beside her recovering cactus.

The sun was at its zenith in a blue, cloudless sky as she drove along the dusty graveled forest road north of Taos. This was the first big job she was solely responsible for since joining the firm. It was the chance she'd dreamed of ever since her graduation from architectural school.

Now that it was here, self-doubts filled her mind, clamoring to be heard. What if she couldn't carry it off? Had she been overconfident about her skills all these years? She'd always believed that the only break she'd need was the opportunity to show what she could do. Yet now that she had it, the prospect was terrifying. Fear gnawed at her confidence. In her search for a dream, would she find herself in the midst of a nightmare?

What no one knew, the one secret she'd never told anyone, was that she'd willingly placed her entire life on hold waiting for an opportunity like this. That's why she hadn't married. It wasn't a matter of waiting to fall in love, though she did think that was important too. It was a need to prove her worth to herself before making room in her life for the needs and demands of a mate.

The idea of having a companion who'd travel down life's road with her, sharing a common destiny, was undeniably tempting. In her village there had been two who'd already offered her that security and protection. But she just wasn't ready to merge with another and lose what little she knew of herself in the union.

Yet there was a downside to her decision to remain single. Facing her own limitations could destroy the view of herself she'd cherished and nurtured through the years. She wanted to be a commanding presence that people respected, a success both personally and professionally. Yet the reality was most people fell between the extremes of total success and total failure. The thought that the hopes she'd held on to since her first day in college might end up swallowed in mediocrity made her heart ache. In self-defense, she pushed the dream further down inside her. She'd shelter it there until it was strong enough to stand on its own.

She took a deep breath. It was time to pull herself together and put on the face of the cool professional Raul Mendoza had thought he'd hired. That was the self-image she'd continually held up in her mind's eye, and now it was time to merge with it.

Irene stepped on the accelerator of the late-model blue and tan Bronco, taking the short, straight stretch of dirt road between winding curves with more speed than she usually used. She was now in the ponderosa pine forest, above the piñon and juniper foothills, where thickets of scrub oak alternated with the tall evergreens. Having been on the winding track for over an hour, she knew she was getting close to *Casa de Encanto*.

From the rutted condition the dirt and gravel road was in, she understood why it was so easy to get snowed in during winter. She slowed down slightly, enjoying the contrast between the evergreens and the lightening foliage that attested to the coming of fall. Today was a landmark day in her personal history and she wanted to remember everything. Her firm believed in her, and Mendoza had personally selected her from the competition. She wouldn't let any of them down.

She prepared herself mentally, knowing she'd have to project utter confidence from the moment she arrived. No woman ever had it easy on the work site, and prejudices about her sex and race were bound to come up. If she showed weakness or lost control, she'd also lose the crew's respect and her ability to lead the project.

A moment later, she crossed over the cattle guard and drove through the wrought-iron gates that led onto Mendoza land. The large, multiple-level house would be further up the road, nestled at the end of the driveway in an area thick with trees.

Irene rounded a sharp bend. Suddenly she caught a glimpse of a small figure looming ahead on the inside of the curve. As her senses registered the shape and the hideous markings on the face, she sucked in her breath and instinctively turned the wheel away from the object.

# 3

**A**S IRENE'S CAR careened off the shoulder of the road into the shallow drainage slope, she tried to keep her head. Knowing how easily she could roll the tilted Bronco, she pumped the brakes, resisting the natural urge to try and swerve back onto the road. Metal screamed in protest as the vehicle pitched and rocks scraped against the bottom. Regaining control took some effort, but Irene finally managed to bring the sturdy vehicle to a halt just in front of a stand of telephone-pole–sized pines.

An overwhelming sense of relief made her feel almost giddy. Irene leaned back in her seat and tried to calm down; her hands were still shaking. Angrily she recalled the small two-foot-tall effigy by the side of the road. She'd only had a quick glimpse, but it was hard to mistake. It was half animal, half bird, and sat upon the point of a yucca stick. The icon with two faces, a witch, was the symbol of ultimate evil.

Suppressing a shudder, she reached into her pocket and felt for the pouch with the *xayeh*. As her fingers closed around it, she managed a thin smile. Her mother had been right. Some things were so deeply ingrained, they became second nature at times.

Releasing the pouch, she turned her attention to her predicament and placed the vehicle in gear. She tried to turn back toward the road, but the front wheels sank into the sand of a shallow wash.

"Oh, wonderful," she snapped cynically.

Irene shifted down and engaged the four-wheel drive, hoping for better traction. She was just starting to make progress when a pickup coming from the house stopped uphill from her. She registered the sound of the truck door slamming, but kept her attention focused on the wallowing Bronco.

"Hey, you okay in there?"

The voice sent a stab of memory through her. As she turned to look at the man, distaste clouded her features. This was the last thing she needed! Irene took her foot off the gas pedal.

The tall, sturdily built man approached and stood by the driver's side. "I knew you were coming, but I didn't expect to have to bail you out so soon," he said with a derisive smile.

"You don't," she snapped. He was even less appealing than she remembered. John Cobb was a longtime contractor in their area, a person she'd found impossible to work with, although her culture had always stressed cooperation. His penchant for shortcuts, usually at the customer's expense, had placed them on a collision course once before. Their working relationship, already strained because of his attitude toward Indians, had deteriorated completely after that. "What brings you here to the Mendozas?" she asked pointedly.

"It looks like you and I are going to be working together again. Do you think you'll be able to handle it any better than last time?" Cobb baited. "I'm the contractor in charge."

"What are you talking about? Greg Hughes is the contractor."

"*Was* the contractor. Didn't anyone tell you? Greg had a heart attack Tuesday and will be sidelined for a while. He turned the job over to me as one of his associates, and Mendoza agreed to the change." Cobb held her eyes with a vacant stare. "And while I'm on this subject, I might as well give you some advance warning. I won't put up with you looking over my shoulder."

"I'll do whatever I feel is necessary," she clipped. "And you *will* have problems if you deviate from the plans I've drawn up. Count on it."

"Yeah, right." He chuckled softly. "Try dealing with this work crew without me. I've heard about the Christmas deadline. Screw things up for me here, and I'll haul you down with me. Your best bet is to stay out of my way."

"Right now just stay out of mine," she snapped. "Step back. I've got to get back onto the road."

"What the hell are you doing down here anyway? It looked like you ran off the road for no reason at all."

"There's a figure up there by the curve. No doubt it was placed there as some kind of misguided greeting for the Tewa workers. But it'll have to go. Indian workers aren't going to feel comfortable with that around."

"With what? I don't know what you're talking about. I came from the opposite direction, but the only things near that curve are the cattle guard and the wrought-iron gates."

"I'll show you in a minute," she said, waving him

back away from her vehicle. After a slow but steady climb up the hillside, she parked on the shoulder and walked down the unpaved road to the spot where the figure had been.

Cobb followed her. "What exactly are you looking for?"

"It was here," she said, glancing around in confusion. "It was the icon they use in witchcraft rituals," she added, then described it. "Well, maybe it was a little further ahead." She walked on around the curve for several yards, but finding no sign of the doll, began checking the ground for tracks. After a moment she gave up, realizing the gravel and pine needles that covered the ground would make that impossible.

"You'll be better off leaving your pagan superstitions back at the pueblo," the big man said with a shrug. "The Mendozas aren't going to stand for that, believe me. It's really against their religion."

"I'm aware of their beliefs, and how most non-Indians like you feel about ours," she replied, determined not to get baited into an argument.

"In my opinion," he drawled, "if you keep seeing witches on a stick and running off the side of the road like this, you'll probably last about a week. Then again, maybe that's for the best. I think the pressure's already getting to you. This has to be the biggest job that you've ever had the dumb luck to attempt."

"I know what I saw," Irene answered, ignoring his insults.

"Yeah, so do I—a figment of your imagination, unless you think your wooden statue is capable of disappearing into thin air. Tell that to Mendoza, or maybe *I* should. I'm sure it'll really inspire his confidence."

The thought of John Cobb relating the incident to Raul Mendoza made her stomach lurch. Yet she knew that to show any weakness now would be a fatal mistake. "Back off, Cobb. With your past history, you don't want to start any rounds of storytelling. Just do your job following the specs I've laid out, and we won't have any problems."

Cobb turned and walked back toward his truck, but he managed one last parting shot. "I hope you're better with architecture than you are driving. Otherwise this whole damn place is going to be nothing more than high-priced stacks of mud."

By the time she was back behind the driver's seat, her hands were shaking. She'd seen the witch icon, she was certain of it. What she couldn't explain was its immediate disappearance. Perhaps it was someone's idea of a joke, but it would have had to come from an individual well versed on the Tewa. Yet why would anyone go to the trouble? Kids maybe, hiding nearby to watch people's reaction. Children had a sense of humor that could be extremely cruel. Of course when she'd run off the road, they would have become scared and taken off with the figure.

She continued toward the hacienda, hating herself for having told Cobb about the witch figure. If he said anything about it to the non-Tewa men, she'd become the brunt of jokes. Whether or not the Mendozas heard of the incident, her ability to command the respect of the workers would be seriously hampered.

Irene pursed her lips tightly as she remembered her aunt's predictions and wondered if they'd affected her more than she'd realized. Was she allowing her family's fears to influence her to the extent that she'd mistaken shadows or a trick of her imagination for the witch doll?

Even as the thought formed, she ruled it out. She'd never been the hysterical sort. Something had been there, though it was possible she'd mistaken what she'd seen and equated it subconsciously to something she knew. The explanation was unsettling, but there was no time left to dwell on it.

Reaching the end of the driveway, Irene parked at the side of the house near several other vehicles. There was one big problem she intended to bring up with Raul Mendoza immediately. It was her job to okay the contractors and subcontractors, and John Cobb had not been her choice. She would do whatever she could to see he was replaced as soon as possible.

Irene walked toward the entrance of the adobe multilevel house. Except for the large glass windows, it resembled an Indian pueblo, and was as large as many she'd seen. You couldn't exactly say that it was rundown, for much of its former glory remained. Yet under close scrutiny, *Casa de Encanto* exhibited signs of age and deterioration.

She opened the gray, naturally weathered wooden door that led to a protected courtyard garden. Staying on the brick path, she walked to the main house entrance and used the heavy old iron knocker ingeniously cast into the form of a wolf's head.

An elderly but spry-looking Hispanic woman in a flower-print dress answered the door. Her grayish hair was fastened at the back in an old-fashioned French twist. The style would have been too severe if not for the stray wispy curls that fell softly around her ears. That image of softness was also enhanced by the opulent roundness of her body, which defied any wrinkles to appear on her face.

Irene introduced herself and waited as she was shown inside the foyer. Her practiced eye surveyed the area as she had on her previous visit, confirming that the well-worn brick floor sagged in the center and would need to be carefully leveled.

"I'm Angela, the housekeeper, Ms. Pobikan," the

woman said. "Mr. Raul is expecting you, so let me show you the way to his study."

Claustrophobic passages burrowed through the center of the house while narrow wooden stairways meandered in four directions. Brick floors were laid throughout the ground level, and her boots clacked softly as she walked with the housekeeper toward the heart of the home, where Raul's study lay. *Nichos,* some with special spotlights to illuminate folk art pieces, accented the corridors. The Santa Fe style that spoke of tradition and elegance through the sparse furnishings gave *Casa de Encanto* a distinction seldom equaled.

Eventually they climbed two short staircases and Angela knocked on a heavy set of wooden doors. A voice Irene recognized as Raul's invited them to enter.

Raul stood, walked around his desk, and came to greet her, shaking her hand firmly. "I'm glad you've made it safely. Did you bring in your things?"

"I've got suitcases in the car," Irene answered.

"Good. Angela will see to it that your belongings are taken to one of the guest bedrooms," he said, nodding to the housekeeper.

Irene reached into her purse for the car keys and handed them to Angela. "Thanks for taking care of it for me. I appreciate it."

As the woman left the room, Raul gestured toward an ornate, handcrafted tray resting on a *banco* too high to serve as seating. By combining it with a roughly hewn beam, the *banco* now served as a room divider, sectioning off the large area into two functional spaces. "Have you had lunch yet? Angela makes a very special *empanada.* The spread is from an old family recipe and it's the best I've ever tasted." He held out a small plate for her. "Try one. You won't be disappointed."

The tray, laid out upon a Navajo rug arranged over the *banco*, was filled with the small pastries. The tiny turnovers filled with meat and piñon nuts added an enticing aroma to the room, tempting her. "I'd love one. They smell wonderful."

Irene placed one on her plate, but Raul smiled encouragingly. "Take more. Angela usually leaves me with enough to feed a houseful of people."

She took another, unable to resist the offer, though she knew it would cost her. She was the kind of person who gained weight if she even looked at food for too long. Every day she faithfully placed her bathroom scale on the most advantageous floor slope of her bathroom, checking for any weight that had crept upon her. She could easily put on ten pounds in a month and grow right out of her clothes, unless she kept a close watch on herself.

As she took her first bite and the confection practically melted in her mouth, she smiled. "You're right. These are wonderful!"

Raul helped himself to a plateful and sat down at the other end of the leather sofa, shifting to face her. A pitcher of iced tea had been left on the intricately tiled center of the coffee table to their side.

"I ran into a contractor I know as I was coming in," Irene said casually. This seemed the perfect time to bring up the matter.

"Yes, I was going to tell you about that. I've agreed to have John Cobb take over for Greg Hughes. I don't know if you read the papers, but he had a heart attack and is incapacitated." Raul finished the *empanada* with one final bite. "I've accepted Cobb as his replacement in order to save time trying to find another work crew. Cobb has apparently directed Hughes' men before, and everyone knows everyone else. It'll keep things going smoothly."

"Not so smoothly," she objected, keeping her voice calm. "John and I have had difficulties working together in the past. But even if I discount that, I know he has a policy of bringing in his own subcontractors. That's not going to work here. I've already selected and contacted people who'll be doing the specialty work."

"You're the architect, so he answers to you. Work it out," he said flatly. As silence stretched out between them, he narrowed his eyes and studied her speculatively. "There's more, isn't there?"

Irene nodded. "Frankly I don't trust him. He's been known to cut corners by changing specifications in order to save himself some money."

"He mentioned a job you'd both worked on. He said that you cost everyone time and money."

She glanced up quickly and held Raul's gaze. "Only because things had to be redone. He used low-grade materials, and when I noticed the substitution, I forced him to tear it down and rebuild. Had he done it right the first time, we wouldn't have had a problem."

"I wasn't told about that." Raul paused and rubbed his jaw pensively. "I'll ask him if it slipped his mind when he was telling me the rest. That should serve as a warning that those methods won't be tolerated here."

"The materials he used were legal, don't get me wrong. But they weren't what I'd specified, nor what the client was paying for," she maintained. "Cobb was intending on pocketing the difference, I suppose."

Raul nodded slowly. "I have many people I'm responsible for in my business. I don't pretend to be aware of every detail of daily operations, so I can see how he could have slipped something like that past you. At least you were alert enough to discover what was happening."

He walked around the Spanish Colonial desk. Medallions carved into the front also appeared in the wood throughout the house, giving unity to the decorations.

"Because you know John," he said, sitting down behind his desk, "you'll be on your guard and that will give you the advantage. You and I will keep tabs on him. That will force him to stay in line. He won't give us any trouble."

"Cobb can be very difficult, and could slow things down."

"I have confidence in you. I know you'll meet the deadline and make sure that everything is done right." Raul wore an enigmatic expression. "If you have any problems, or need to talk to me, my door will always be open."

Irene knew she was being dismissed, and the thought rankled her. The problem was, she couldn't figure out a way of gracefully extending the meeting. Since he didn't want to lose time finding another contractor, he'd outmaneuvered her. Unfortunately, at the moment, she had no idea how to counter his argument without seeming to veto his faith in her. "Thank you for your time, and for the opportunity to share your lunch, Mr. Mendoza."

He smiled and fixed her with his exceptional eyes. " 'Raul,' please. No need for formality. You'll be living here under my roof and dining with the family."

Maybe dignity and style became second nature if practiced long enough. Raul exuded a quiet grace that went well with the simple elegance of his surroundings. Yet the intelligence behind the hazel eyes that held hers was a little intimidating. She'd seen how effortlessly he could twist the conversation to suit his purposes. Irene had no doubt that she'd have to work hard just to hold her own around him.

"We'll have dinner at eight," Raul concluded.

"You'll get to meet my family then. If you need anything, Angela will be glad to take care of it."

As she left the study, Angela appeared at the far end of the corridor and came forward to meet her. Irene found herself wondering whether Angela had been dutifully waiting down the hall all that time. "This way, please," Angela said.

The woman escorted Irene through a new maze of stairs, hallways, and rooms of varying sizes, and she took the opportunity to view details she'd only noted briefly before. Portraits of Mendoza ancestors appeared in prominent locations. Some showed stern and somber countenances that looked almost forbidding, while others depicted family gatherings showing little girls in party dresses and young men in dark suits trying to emulate their fathers. Through the images captured on canvas, the sense of Spanish pride and machismo came through clearly. The line of Mendozas seemed to stare down at her in uniform disapproval as she walked past.

"We've given you a room overlooking the mountains," Angela said, interrupting her musings. "It has a pleasing view." Angela stopped by the last door on the right-hand corner of the corridor. "The room next to yours is for our other guest, Mr. Cobb."

Using all her willpower, she managed a question instead of a grimace. "Where will the workers be housed?"

"Four large trailer houses and one small one have been set up beside the apple orchard on the north side of the hacienda's outer wall. You can't see them from here, but that's where the crew will be staying until the restoration is finished." Angela led the way inside the pleasant, simply furnished room, then turned to face Irene. "I've taken the liberty of hanging your clothes in the closet and putting your things away. Your keys are in the top dresser drawer. I placed the small figure of the mountain lion on the dresser."

"The fetish?" she asked, surprised.

Angela stepped to the dresser and picked it up carefully. "This."

Irene stared at the carved stone for a moment. She thought she'd placed it next to the little cactus at home, but somehow the fetish of the mountain lion had fallen in among her things. She took it from Angela's hand. "I'm surprised to see it. I wasn't aware I'd brought it along." She shrugged and placed it in the pouch, removing the *xayeh* and placing them on the dresser. She'd carry the fetish with her. She smiled, thinking her mother would be pleased. "Thanks, Angela."

Irene glanced around the almost monastic decor. The furnishings and their placement had been carefully thought out to create a sense of openness and harmony. The large armoire with its hand-carved doors was Colonial Mexican style, as was the low dresser, but the pine bed frame and the graceful rocking chair were clearly New Mexican, exuding a blend of simplicity and beauty.

"Will you be needing anything else?"

"No, thanks. I think I'll freshen up, then go on outside. There's much work to be done."

Alone in the room, Irene laid the *xayeh* carefully inside her handkerchief. Then, as was the custom, she placed the bundle in one corner of the room. It would be safe and remain undisturbed behind the dresser. After familiarizing herself with what would be her room for the next few months, she went downstairs and walked outside. She wanted to inspect the work crew's trailers to make sure they were adequate. Cobb had also been known for cutting corners at the workers' expense.

As she approached, Cobb came out of the smallest trailer placed there to serve as an on-site office. "You're going to start checking up on me already? We haven't even settled in around here," he said irately.

"I think it's time you and I got procedural things squared away. There'll be fewer misunderstandings later," she replied, her tone brusque and firm. She knew they were both fencing, circling each other, trying to sense weaknesses. If he were allowed to gain the upper hand now, she might never be able to recapture it and that could prove disastrous.

"I already know you've hired your own artisans and they'll be joining my people here," he snapped. "I'd have never consented, but I'll stick by whatever you negotiated with Hughes. Only remember this: anyone who works on that house is part of my work crew. They take orders from me and me alone. We also have several Indians employed here from your tribe, but they're my responsibility. Clear?" His tone made it obvious the question was rhetorical.

"Look, Cobb. They may be dealing with you most of the time, but *everyone,* including and especially *you,* will be answering to *me.* If you have any reservations about that, take the long drive back down the mountain now! You can be replaced in a day, maybe less."

Cobb just stared at her.

"Now, I want to go see the men's and the women's trailers. Then afterward, I want to talk to the entire crew." Irene turned toward the housing area.

"No way. Neither one of those two things has anything to do with you."

"Wrong," she said quietly. "Don't turn this into a confrontation, Cobb, you can't win. You tried to stir up trouble already and it didn't work, so don't waste any more of your time."

"What are you talking about?"

"You told Mendoza about our working together in the past, only you significantly altered the facts."

Cobb smiled slowly. "I call them the way I see them."

"No, what you did is distort the truth in an unsuccessful attempt to undermine me. I won't allow that."

"Yeah, right. I'm really worried," he mocked. "What do you think you can do about it? I've got a contract with Raul Mendoza and he's really squirrelly about that deadline. You can't afford to look for another work crew now. And if I go, most of the workers go with me. They answer to me, not to you or Mendoza."

"Why don't we put it to the test?" she snapped. She was about to say more when loud shouts rose from the far side of the workmen's trailers.

Cobb spat out an oath and rushed toward the commotion. A large Spanish man had pinned one of the Tewa workers to the ground.

# 4

**C**OBB PLOWED THROUGH the cluster of on-lookers and yanked the bigger man off the smaller one. "Carlos, that's enough." Cobb hauled the construction worker to his feet and shoved him several feet back.

The Hispanic man started forward again, but Cobb reached down and picked up a large branch that had fallen from one of the nearby apple trees. He wielded the stout piece of wood like a baseball bat. "To get to him you'll have to go through me," Cobb said very calmly. He angled his six-foot-four frame, never taking his eyes off the man.

Carlos spat on the ground and crossed his arms over his chest. "Hell, I didn't start this. You were the one who paired me with that . . . jerk. I didn't want to share my half of the trailer with him to begin with. On our first night, he covered the living room area with feathers and pollen. I stayed up for hours sneezing, my eyes as big as cue balls. Then today, he brings out the same bags of junk and starts all over again. I told him to get that crap out of the trailer, but he ignored me. So I figured if I introduced his face to the dirt, I'd get his attention."

Cobb's mouth twitched and Irene knew he was struggling not to laugh. The entire incident was ridiculous, but unfortunately predictable. Worst of all, more of these incidents would crop up unless Cobb handled the situation now.

"It's our way and my right," the Tewa man argued, looking directly at Irene.

"Yeah, it is," Irene agreed, though she wasn't unsympathetic to the Hispanic man's complaint. "But there are other rights to consider too." She glanced at Cobb. "Maybe the best solution is to house the Tewas together."

"I'll handle this," Cobb growled. "Carlos, everyone has been allocated a trailer and they've managed to work it out. I suggest you do the same."

Carlos sneezed loudly, and a round of laughter swept through the crowd.

"Give me a break, will ya?" Carlos groaned. "Put me with Manuel, or Steve, or someone who's normal."

"Watch your mouth," one of the Tewa men warned.

"Be quiet. All of you!" Cobb glared at the men. "You're acting like a bunch of"—he turned to look at Irene, then cleared his throat—"old women. Just settle this peacefully and get on with it. I want everyone at my trailer in an hour to look at the work schedule. We're going to begin making some access points for backhoes and such through the courtyard walls this afternoon."

As Cobb strode back to his trailer, Irene saw Carlos talking to another Hispanic while gesturing toward his current roommate. She didn't like this. The last thing she needed was for the men to be at each other's throats.

Several minutes later she finished her survey of the living quarters and stepped inside Cobb's office trailer. "You've only put a Band-Aid on a major wound out there. You can't expect to solve differences that have separated the Hispanics, the Anglos, and Indians for generations with an asinine decree."

"Don't lecture me, lady. I dealt with the problem."

"Some cultures are used to this kind of rivalry, it's a fact of life for them. The Indians have a different mind-set, but we're just as stubborn when it comes to our religion and customs."

"The Hispanic and Anglo women sharing trailers will work it out first. The men will too, after a few busted noses. It all comes with the territory."

She shook her head, realizing she was getting nowhere. "If the men get hurt and it slows down construction, I'm going to step in whether you like it or not."

He fixed her with an expressionless stare and allowed a glassy lake of silence to stretch out between them.

She forced herself not to look away. "I want the crew to start removing that adobe from the south wall as soon as possible—and very carefully. Those bricks will be needed when we rebuild the wall again later. We'll also have to begin some survey work. I need to verify the angles of all the outside and inside walls, and check the elevations and drainage for the entire west side of the hacienda. I also want your crew to dig out very carefully around the foundation of the house in the locations I've indicated on the blueprints. I need to test and make sure it's solid and that water hasn't undermined it."

"I'll get them on it." Cobb walked with Irene to the door of the office trailer. "Hey, I almost forgot to give you some good news. My room is next to yours, so we'll be real close to each other."

"So I've heard. Will you be going home to visit with your wife on weekends?" she asked pointedly.

"I'm divorced. Have been for about a year," he said, his tone suggestive. "Hey, if that's kept you away in the past . . ."

She gave him a look of disgust. "Please, you're making me nauseous."

"I bet a little fighter like you would scratch my back up real bad . . ."

Anger flared through her. "You crude pile of . . ." She stepped toward him, though she really wasn't sure what she was going to do next. Suddenly she heard the sound of heavy footsteps coming up the trailer steps.

A Hispanic man almost as tall as Cobb entered, his gaze taking them in casually as he ducked through the doorway. "*Perfecto.* You're both here. I wanted to see the plans for the *sala,* the formal living room. Raul's told me a bit about the renovation that'll take place in there, but I'm curious about the details." He sat down on the largest chair and leaned back.

Temporarily distracted, Irene glanced at the man, anger giving way to curiosity. He was dressed in jeans and a pullover sweater, but there was a casual smoothness about him that told her he wasn't one of Mendoza's employees. As she speculated, her eyes drifting over his face, she began to see the family resemblance. His features were softer and more rounded than his brother's. It gave him a classical and elegant look that was almost too perfect to be attractive in a masculine sense. "I'm Irene Pobikan, the architect in charge here. Are you Raul Mendoza's brother?"

He gave her a lazy smile. "Gene Mendoza, at your service." He stood.

"It's a pleasure to meet you." Irene extended her hand. She'd heard of Gene. He was a competent, if not spectacular, artist, sculptor, and painter.

He held on to her hand a moment longer than necessary, his coal-black eyes probing hers. "You obviously have special skills as an architect. But to make *Casa de Encanto* truly unique will require an artist's touch too. That means you and I will have to work closely together."

"We have some blueprints here, but they just concern the exterior work," she answered. "My detailed plans for the interior are back at the house. I'd be glad to show them to you, but any modifications will have to be cleared with your brother."

"Raul will agree to whatever I want. This is my home too."

"Of course. I'm sure we'll have no trouble at all," she said quietly.

"But you're still going to check with him," he observed.

"Yes," she replied simply.

Gene looked at her in surprise, then laughed. "Okay, I get the point. Let's go see those plans."

As she started to leave, Cobb hurried around her and held the door open. "Remember that I'm here to make your job easier, so if there's anything I can do, just ask. We'll need to combine our efforts to keep things running smoothly. There isn't much time for delays."

Suspicious of Cobb's change of tone, she glanced up at him quickly. His smile was completely benign as he stood there in front of her. She assessed his expression, searching for an answer that made sense. Then she noticed Gene again, and suddenly realized the truth. In front of others, especially the family, Cobb would remain a paragon of professionalism and kindness. Only when they were alone would she have any problems with him. That way, any complaints on her part would seem unfounded.

She bit back her anger. "If we both do our jobs, the only delays we'll have are those caused by the weather." She glanced at Gene Mendoza, then at Cobb, silently noting Cobb's chunkier, muscular frame. In comparison to Gene, he looked crude somehow, as if he'd been sculpted and formed by an artisan of much lesser skill.

As she strode across the grounds, Gene Mendoza fell into step beside her. "Bad blood between you two?"

His observation surprised her. She could have sworn that both Cobb and she had masked it. "He's not my favorite person."

He said nothing until they approached the gate. "By the way, I'll probably want some modifications made on your designs. I hope you won't find them too difficult."

"But you haven't even seen the plans yet. Maybe my ideas will be right in line with what you want."

"I doubt it. You've relied on my brother's input, and Raul has a different way of looking at things," he replied.

She'd always been able to sense when there was going to be trouble with a client, and this was certainly one of those times. Trying to reconcile the ideas of two people with varied tastes would be next to impossible. "Please try to remember that your brother has imposed a very tight deadline on us."

As they stepped inside the house, Angela appeared from a small doorway. "Mr. Raul has been looking for you," she said to Irene. "He's in the study."

"Let's go see big brother," Gene said, a touch of amusement on his face.

She couldn't quite figure Gene out. He was pleasant, and seemed eager to work with her, but his voice wavered slightly whenever he mentioned Raul. She wondered just how well the two actually got along.

Gene led the way to the study, then stood aside and motioned her in with a casual wave of the hand. "Well, big brother, you get two for the price of one today. What's on your mind?"

"I thought you were going to meet me here an hour ago, Gene." Raul's face showed nothing of his feelings, but his words were very cool.

"I got held up in Santa Fe," Gene answered with a shrug. "But relax, I'm here now."

"Unfortunately, not at the right time for me. I have business to discuss with my architect." The frosty words reverberated with the impact of a command.

"I should be in on this, Raul. You're the eldest, but *Casa de Encanto* belongs to all of us. There was even a time, not so long ago, when according to tradition I would have been expected to marry and bring my wife here."

"There's no question that this is home to all of us."

"Then you understand why I'm going to stay for your conference with the architect," Gene replied firmly.

"Gene, let's discuss this later," Raul answered, turning halfway in his chair to retrieve some papers on the desk extension.

"I'm not your employee, I'm your brother! You're not dismissing *me.*"

Sparks flashed in Raul's hazel eyes as he looked back and fixed a hostile glare on Gene. The effect, coupled with his silence, was dramatic.

Embarrassed, Irene wished there was some way she could leave without them noticing.

"If you want to take an active part in the renovation, that's fine," Raul finally said. "But there's a condition. I want your word that you'll see this through to the end. I don't want to have to track you down because you're too busy with other things, or have lost interest and wandered off to Taos or Santa Fe. This house and the demands of the construction will have to come first in your life."

Gene opened his arms, palms upward, in a gesture of acquiescence. "Then that's the way it'll be." He glanced at Irene, smiling as if the confrontation had never taken place. "So you see? It's like I told you outside. You and I will work together to make sure *Casa de Encanto* retains its unique look and style, and becomes a cultural landmark once again."

Raul relaxed and leaned back, making himself comfortable in the massive hand-carved wood and leather chair behind his desk. "I heard that there was some trouble between the Indian and the Hispanic workers," he said, turning to Irene. "I was hoping that you'd speak to the Indian workers and see if you can help Cobb keep peace."

"What makes you think that it's just the Indian workers who need someone to speak to them?"

Raul shrugged. "I was told that an Indian worker instigated the trouble. He did something that provoked one of the Hispanics. Is this right?"

She hesitated. His tone and manner made him seem perfectly reasonable, but for the first time she wondered how fair Raul was prepared to be. Maybe the prejudices harbored in his family for generations had been passed down to him as well. "It was a matter of religious practices. The Hispanic worker didn't understand, so he overreacted."

"That's what I heard Serna, John Cobb's right-hand man, say. Only he figured that it'll happen again unless you can get the Indian workers to compromise."

She studied Raul's expression, acknowledging to herself she understood practically nothing of what was in his heart. With a wariness rooted in distrust, she chose her words carefully. "Compromises are difficult in matters of religion," she said slowly. "The only answer is to give the Tewa men the chance to room together, something I feel they'd prefer anyway. That way, trouble is not as likely to erupt between the groups after work when they're tired and tempers are apt to flare."

"The lady has a point," Gene said. "The best way to handle this is to diffuse the situation. We're already grouping the workers anyway by housing the five women in their own separate trailer."

Raul glanced up at his brother, then back to Irene. "I just don't like the idea of segregating the Indians."

"It's a way of making things easier on everyone. The workers' housing is all equal so there wouldn't be a question of preferential treatment," she assured, relieved to learn this had been one of his concerns.

"I think it would be better in the long run if they could find a way to coexist." Raul stared at the coffee cup on his desk as if expecting the grounds in the bottom to reveal some vital insight. "It can be done. The fact you're here is proof of that," he added, meeting her gaze.

"Yes, but I have time at the end of the day to do the things I need in the privacy of my own room. My beliefs don't come into contact with yours, so there's no pressure for tolerance and understanding. Without that buffer, the crew's going to have a difficult time."

"I'll speak to John," Gene said. "I know you two

haven't been hitting it off, so he might accept it with less hassle if the suggestion comes from me."

Irene saw the flicker of curiosity that flashed in Raul's eyes and knew she'd just lost credibility. With a few simple words, Gene had suggested that she was already having trouble asserting her authority. Irene looked at Gene, but his expression was one of helpful curiosity. "That won't be necessary," she assured, her tone resolute. "I've already made the suggestion. It's up to him whether or not to incorporate it. The crew is his responsibility. Of course if he fails to handle it, I'll step in."

"If you need help," Raul offered, "don't hesitate to ask either my brother or me."

The implication that she wouldn't be able to take care of the problem without someone to back her up made her angry. "I'll stay on this, rest assured, so please don't give it another thought."

A light knock sounded on the door. "Dinner is served, Mr. Raul. Shall I tell Elena?"

Raul looked toward the door. "Please, Angela."

They went downstairs together to the large dining room. An ornate Spanish-style chandelier was suspended from the high ceiling, illuminating the darkly stained *vigas,* or log beams, that supported the roof. As she glanced around she suppressed a shudder. Within the thick adobe walls were built-in *nichos,* each holding a *santo.* These popular folk art pieces depicted Christian saints in martyrdom. Although she'd been through the room before, the afternoon light had failed to disclose the details. Aware of them now, she had to struggle not to show her distaste.

Raul followed her gaze, promptly misinterpreting the attention she was giving the wooden figures for admiration. "These are all antiques," he said proudly. He went to an elaborate carving of the crucified

Christ. "Look at the detail on this one. It's over one hundred years old. The body of the *Cristo* is all hand-carved, and the eyes are made of glass. The workmanship is fantastic."

Red streaks added authenticity to the excruciating suffering depicted by the piece. She'd never much cared for these and found it difficult to comment. "The agony of the figure is almost too realistic," she said at last.

"Art is about passion, and religious folk art seems to capture that emotion best. It's a shame that the pieces readily available nowadays seem to have lost that special quality. To keep them reasonably priced, speed has taken priority over quality. Many of the modern *santos* look like replicas of an art form that's all but lost. And as far as I'm concerned imitations can't do justice to the real thing."

"That's something Raul and I are in total agreement about," Gene said quietly.

Cobb joined them in the dining room a moment later, coming in from the front of the house. "I hope I'm not late. There was a matter with the crew that needed my attention."

Raul shook his head. "You're right on time, John. Please, join us."

As they took their seats around the massive oak table, they heard rapid footsteps. Seconds later a beautiful dark-haired woman hurried into the room. Elena Mendoza was in her late thirties. Her beauty was arresting, but there was a guilelessness about her face that normally would suggest someone much younger. The men rose from their chairs.

The light brown eyes darted around the table until they came to rest on Raul. Elena smiled, a wonderfully radiant gesture so filled with love it took Irene by surprise. "Am I late?" she asked.

"You're just in time." Raul walked around to his sister's side and took her arm, leading her to the table. "I want you to meet our guests. Elena, this is John Cobb," he said, then waited as his sister shook hands with him.

"It's a pleasure," Elena said in a barely audible voice.

Irene watched Elena. Her shyness made her exquisitely vulnerable. She could see the protectiveness it evoked in Raul, and even Gene's manner seemed to soften as he watched his sister. "And this is Irene Pobikan. They'll both be staying here with us until the repair work on our home is finished."

Elena's eyes met Irene's for a brief moment and she smiled, then she turned back to Raul. "Will that take a long time?"

"Yes, but I promise you, it'll be worth the trouble. It's going to be beautiful," Raul assured.

Elena responded to his gentleness like a flower under the sun. "You'll have to tell me all about it."

A moment later Raul took his seat again at the head of the table. The first course was brought in shortly afterward. The guacamole with thick chunks of fresh avocado was served on a bed of lettuce, with fresh corn chips on the side. A small taste convinced her that it wasn't too hot, just spicy enough to make it even more delectable.

As they ate, Irene's interest was divided between Elena and Raul. Something about Elena's beauty compelled her gaze, but it was more than that. There was an innocence in the eyes that seemed in contrast to her age. Life, with its tragedies and triumphs, had left no definitive mark on her features.

Elena took a sip of water, then glanced at Irene. "Mama always said Indians didn't like the Mendozas. So why would you want to fix up our house?"

Irene stared at her for a second, the directness of the question taking her completely off guard. She could feel everyone's eyes on her as she struggled to find an answer. "It's true there used to be trouble between us, but I think it's time to set aside what happened in the past. Your house needs to be restored, and that's the type of work I love and I'm very good at."

Elena mulled it over as the main course was brought in. "You talk about houses like Gene does about his sculptures. Do you both feel the same way?"

Irene noted how some of the words seemed to wrap around Elena's tongue, making it difficult for her to pronounce them. The light of understanding came to her and she realized that Elena was mentally handicapped, though not severely enough to make it immediately noticeable.

Irene glanced at Gene, who nodded, awaiting her response. "I suppose we do in some ways," Irene said, determined not to talk down to her. "We both turn ideas into something real that people can touch, see, and enjoy."

"Well put," Gene said. As he glanced at Elena she smiled and looked away, embarrassed by the attention.

Irene took a taste of the red chile enchilada that had been placed before her. The sauce was thick and spicy but not so hot that it burned. A thick layer of melted cheddar cheese spilled over onto the tortillas and meat sauce. The side dish of refried beans and Spanish rice complemented it well, as did the *sopaipillas,* fried bread laced with thick brown honey. There was enough before her to feed two others, but it all tasted so good, she found herself overeating and enjoying every bite.

"Elena," Gene continued gently, "if you'd like, you can join us after dinner. Irene is going to show me the house plans. We can explain how things are going to look eventually."

"No, thank you," she replied simply. "Maybe tomorrow. I need to work with my plants tonight."

"Okay. But if you change your mind, you can come down and join us in the den."

Elena shook her head. "I can't. I have to repot some of my plants. I got my special soil today."

"What kind of plants do you grow, Elena?" Irene asked.

"All kinds, but the ones that need replanted right away are the African violets. I like having flowers all year round." She pointed to the centerpiece of burnt-orange mums on the table. "Those came from my plants."

"You should see Elena's miniature roses," Raul said proudly. "She's got quite a collection and they're practically always in bloom."

Elena bit her lip, a worried expression on her face. "But I have to wash them practically every day. The spider mites eat them if I don't." Her eyebrows knitted together. "I can't remember if I did that today." Alarm made her voice rise slightly. "I hope I didn't forget. I don't want to have the leaves turn yellow. They drop off, then the plant dies," she said, her words coming more quickly.

"You can do it after dinner," Raul said firmly. "There'll be time before the day is over."

Elena glanced at Raul, his tone collecting her attention once again. "Okay. I just wish I could remember things."

"We all forget things from time to time," Raul said, his voice softening.

"But I'm always forgetting something," Elena said sadly. "I wish I was like you—smarter."

Irene glanced down at the last of their meal as Angela placed a small dish of *flan* before her. The rich caramel-covered custard was topped with a spoonful of whipped cream. She wasn't sure how she could eat any more, but it looked too delicious to pass up. At this rate, she'd weigh as much as the construction equipment by the time she left *Casa de Encanto*.

"It sure looks like you're smart when it comes to growing flowers, Elena." Irene touched the leaves of the centerpiece gently. "Look how pretty these are. They brighten up the whole room."

Elena shifted in her chair. "I'm good with my flowers, but not with much else. I mean, I could never be like Raul and Gene and get a job away from the house."

"Lots of people work at home. And what you grow brings beauty to everyone around you. You're an artist in that way. You work to achieve something you can share with other people. It seems to me you've already found your talent, Elena. And you're very skilled at it, judging from those mums."

Elena considered what Irene said. "I'll have to think about that," she said at last.

As Angela started clearing the dessert dishes, Raul led them to a cozy sitting room for drinks. Brandy in hand, Irene studied the room. The adobe interior showed signs of deterioration, yet the Spanish-style furnishings and Rio Grande weavings dating back to the 1700s exuded a distinct elegance. The house more than ever seemed like an elderly woman who'd lost her beauty, but not the grace that defined and enhanced what she'd once been.

Irene glanced at the others, her thoughts racing. The members of the Mendoza family together formed an intricate puzzle. None could be easily dismissed, and they'd each make their own demands on her time. She found it a bit intimidating to know that more than she'd even dreamed would be expected of her here. She'd need diplomacy and patience, in addition to architectural skills.

Within ten minutes Elena said good night and left to go upstairs as the others sat down around the kiva fireplace, enjoying the warmth.

Restless, Gene toyed with the brandy in his glass, twirling the amber liquid. Finally he downed his drink in one gulp and set the glass down. "Would you consider parting with the plans until tomorrow morning? I'd like some time to study them," he said, glancing at Irene.

She hesitated. "I'll need my set, but maybe Raul would be kind enough to let you use his . . ." She glanced at Raul and saw him nod.

"They're in my study, in the cabinet behind my desk," he answered.

"Well, then, if you'll excuse me, I think I'll get started on that."

As Gene left, Raul walked to the fireplace and began shifting the glowing logs around with a poker.

Cobb set his brandy glass down and stood. "I'm going to call it a night. It's early, but I have to be up before dawn to get some supplies. Will you excuse me?"

Raul bid him good night, then returned to the large leather chair near the fireplace. "I appreciate the way you spoke to my sister tonight, Irene. She's very aware when anyone talks down to her. I know that it's hard to know exactly what to say or how to say it, but you made her feel good about herself and that's very important—" He paused, then added, "To me as well as to her."

"You're really gentle around her." Irene felt herself warming to him. "When we first met, you seemed distant and almost unapproachable. But you're not at all like that."

"You're in my home now," he said with a ghost of a smile. "Here I'm free to be myself."

"Even with strangers under your roof?"

"Guests," he corrected. "And it's not an unwelcome event." Raul walked over to the fireplace and stared into the flames. "In recent years this house has known too much sadness. And the place itself seemed to change. I'm not just talking about the building or its need for maintenance either. This house has always had a life and a voice of its own, though it spoke in a language familiar only to those who lived here. Sometimes it echoed with the sounds of routines and patterns that divided the day. And during the good times, it was music and laughter that gave it its heartbeat."

He rubbed his face with one hand. "But when the hard times came, there was nothing for it to absorb and reflect back except the sorrow trapped between its walls." As the fire cracked loudly, he stopped speaking and glanced up at her. "Forgive me, I'm tired and rambling on."

"You weren't rambling," Irene said firmly. "You made quite a bit of sense."

Raul smiled wryly. "My brother is the artist, and these kinds of speculations are his province."

"Yes, you're supposed to be the businessman and the realist, but that's the role life handed you. I don't think you're the complete pragmatist you'd have others believe."

"Oh, but I am. Believe me, I'm not a fanciful person. I see things the way they are. Only I know that feelings can be as tangible as objects and sometimes they define our reality." He shrugged. "That's the one thing I could never make my father understand. He could be an incredibly hard man, but then I was the

elder son and he always expected more from me.
When I was seven and broke my arm falling out of a
tree, I remember my father's eyes on me. I was just a
kid, but I was expected to take the pain without a tear.
I did, because I could see the pride in his eyes. Yet
when Gene as much as scraped a knee, he'd howl and
no one would say a word."

Her chest felt as if someone were squeezing it in a
vice as she sympathized with the young boy he'd been
then. "And your mother? Did she also expect that
from you?"

His gaze was unfocused as he stared absently at one
of Elena's plants. "She did, in her own way. She never
really saw me as anything other than a miniature version of Dad." Almost as if he'd suddenly realized what
he'd divulged, he turned to look at her. "I must be bor-
ing you," he added, embarrassed. "I'm sorry. You're
very easy to talk to and I guess it's been a long time
since I've done that with anyone."

She smiled gently. "You're sorry, about what? That
I'm easy to talk to?" she teased, hoping to ease the
sudden tension. She was about to say more when
Elena came into the room holding a small African violet. Elena stopped in midstride, her expression fluctu-
ating between annoyance and jealousy. "I'm sorry,
Raul, I didn't know she'd still be here." Elena shifted
uncomfortably, refusing to make eye contact with
Irene.

"It's about time I went to bed," Irene said, excusing
herself. The look in Elena's eyes had made her feel like
an interloper and as welcome as the plague. "I have to
be up very early tomorrow, so if you'll excuse me . . ."

Raul made no move to stop her; instead he flashed
her a smile and went to his sister's side. "What's this, a
gift?" he asked, noting the bow fastened around the
pot.

As Irene looked back, she saw Elena give her brother a radiant smile. "This one's for you, it's the prettiest. I was able to grow it because of the bags of soil you picked up for me the last time you went into Santa Fe."

Irene climbed up the stairs slowly. The look on Elena's face when she'd come into the room had surprised her. Resentment had shone clearly in the woman's eyes. Elena wasn't used to sharing Raul's attention.

A few minutes later, after taking the wrong second stairway and having to go the long way around, Irene stepped inside her bedroom, glad for a chance to be alone. She was here as an architect, and she'd do her job, but the Mendoza family fascinated her. Each member seemed unique, a little chapter in the Mendoza saga. And Raul was a constant surprise. Every time she thought she had him pegged, a new side of him emerged, challenging her to change her conceptions.

Yet the best and most interesting part of this job was the hacienda itself. Raul was right: the house breathed with a life of its own. Although it still held echoes of the past, that voice was nearly silent now. It was in a time of transition, patiently waiting for the future to take shape before it would be heard again.

Irene crawled between the sheets, her thoughts drifting in lazy patterns. Nestled deep inside the covers, she closed her eyes. The yawning void stretched out in welcome as she surrendered to sleep.

Then someone whispered her name. Her eyes came open slowly and reluctantly. Black shapes against an even blacker background greeted her as her gaze darted around the room. She lay still, trying to let her eyes adjust and clear, almost sure she'd been dreaming.

Then she grew aware of a muffled sound. Graceful, padding footsteps, from either a very athletic human or an animal, were approaching her room. Whoever or whatever it was paced just outside her door, then continued on, only to return moments later.

Irene exhaled softly. Judging from the soft rhythmic movements and its persistence, it was undoubtedly a cat. With a tired sigh, she decided to invite the animal in.

Irene tossed the covers back, opened the door a crack, and peered out. She glanced in both directions, then stepped out of her room looking for signs of the animal, but the hallway was empty. Giving up after a few seconds, she returned to the warmth of her bed, and huddled into the covers.

Irene closed her eyes, her body relaxing as she started to drift. It was then, from the edges of consciousness, that she heard the house calling to her. Was it a greeting, or warning? She tried to listen, struggling to stay alert, but its faint whispers were soon lost in the distance as the oblivion of sleep claimed her.

# 5

RENE SET OUT for Taos early the next morning before the household was up. She'd had a restless night, probably due to a blend of tension and weariness. As her mind drifted to the events of the evening before, she wondered about the Mendozas' cat. She'd make it a point to ask about the mysterious pet later today.

It was shortly after eight when Irene picked up the area's top *enjarradora,* adobe plaster craftsman. She placed the woman's tools in the back of the Bronco and started the drive back to *Casa de Encanto.* Plastering with adobe was almost a lost art, and Anita Sanchez, a Hispanic woman in her early sixties, had established herself as an expert of unrivaled skill.

"You understand that the method I use is one I've learned from elders in my family," Anita said. "I won't allow anyone to interfere with the pacing no matter how much of a rush they're in."

"No problem. You're the best, that's why I specifically wanted you."

"Working with adobe is hard on the body, but the most difficult part of my job is working with the crews. Men generally don't like having me pass judgment on their skill. But I'll tell you, I won't place adobe plaster on walls that aren't right. I have to approve of the work they've done before I start my *alisando* process, smoothing on the colored clay."

"The men have inspected the underlying adobes in the *sala,* and the walls there are structurally sound. Since the materials you requested have already been delivered, I thought you'd appreciate getting started."

She nodded. "I hear the owners want things done very quickly."

"It's not an unreasonable deadline. It can be done in the time they've asked," Irene assured.

A short time later, Irene escorted Anita through the entrance doors. She crossed the narrow corridor until they reached the old *sala,* which now stood in various stages of disrepair. "This was the main formal room once. Nowadays the family uses a smaller sitting room."

The woman looked around, running her hand down the three-foot-thick adobe walls. She looked into each corner, then got down on her knees to inspect along the foundation. "It's solid as good adobe should be. I can start here right away on two of the walls."

"Good, then I'll leave you to your work. I'll be outside most of this morning if you need me. There are exterior walls that will need extensive repair, and I want to give everything another look."

Irene entered the enclosed courtyard at the rear and found a group of men and the few women workers removing the windows and door frames that were too damaged by time to repair or salvage. Each was then carefully replaced by braces to support the adobe already in place.

"If time's so critical," Cobb said, joining her, "you could have just knocked down this back portion of the house and rebuilt it using wood framing and stucco. We wouldn't have had to waste time laying adobes or trying to match styles."

"This is the way the Mendozas want it. It's my job to design it for them and make sure you carry it out according to my specifications."

"I'm aware of my responsibilities," he snapped. His gaze drifted over her lazily, like a lewd caress. "By the way," he drawled, "I noticed you stayed behind with Mendoza after I left. How was it for you two?"

She spun her head around and glowered at him. "Your implications are disgusting, but so worthy of you!" Not giving him a chance to reply, she walked away.

The morning passed quickly, and she didn't see John again, an added blessing. It was almost noon when she went back inside for lunch. As she entered the front of the house, she heard angry voices coming from the *sala*. She hurried toward them as she realized one of the voices was Anita's.

"I don't care if you are the owner. Tampering with that wall is a mistake. I won't work on something that's going to fall down within six months."

"They're just *nichos*. People build them all the time!"

"Not by digging into a load-bearing wall!"

By the time Irene reached the doorway, Anita stormed past her, work tools in hand. "*You* handle this," she said with a quick glance at Irene. "I'm not working with that *cretino*."

"Wait, give me a chance," Irene protested, but the woman was already gone.

Irene strode curiously into the room saw what had happened. Several adobe bricks had been chiseled and chipped out of the north wall, the first step toward making the recessed spaces called *nichos.*

She turned and glared at Cobb, who stared calmly back at her. "What's going on here? This work isn't part of my renovation plans. It's stupid, and dangerous as well!"

"The owner asked that we do this," Cobb said, and gestured to Gene, who was standing back against the far wall looking at her with raised eyebrows. "It's okay, don't worry. It should be possible for this wall to carry the load even with the *nichos,*" Cobb added.

Irene glanced at Gene, then back at Cobb. She was determined to reestablish control over the situation by setting some ground rules. " 'Should be' isn't good enough, John. Get whoever you had do this back in here and replace the adobe—the sooner the better."

"This is the perfect place for me to display my sculptures," Gene said calmly, stepping forward. "My brother has already told you that I'm to have an input in the design here. It's your job to find a way for me to do this."

"I beg your pardon. My job is to implement the changes your brother authorized, according to my best judgment. Nothing, and I do mean nothing, gets done around here without his and my say-so."

Irene scowled at Gene, then turned back to Cobb. "John, as contractor you see me before doing anything that's not on the schedule *I* give you. And Gene, unless your brother instructs me to do something above and beyond what we discussed and agreed to, it won't happen. His name and mine are the only ones on that contract. Raul hired me because of my training and skills. If I agreed to what you want, without even consulting him, and despite my best judgment, I'd be cheating him in every way imaginable."

Gene stared at the adobe wall, his lips pursed into a tight line. He looked over at Cobb next, and the contractor just shrugged. Gene stepped back, thinking about it, and looked at the wall one more time. "If you feel that strongly about it, I guess I'll have to accept your decision and play it your way." He gave her a wry smile. "You've broken my heart, lady. I really wanted to display those sculptures there."

"Why don't you let me help you find another area for those *nichos?* You need a location that will showcase your work and lend itself more readily to special lighting."

Gene gave her a speculative look. "It sounds like you have a particular place in mind."

"Actually I do. How's the entryway strike you?"

He mulled it over for a minute. "Yeah, I like that," he said, nodding. "My sculptures would be the first thing anyone would see when they come into the house."

"We could have special lighting mounted there too and exhibit your pieces like they would be in a gallery."

"I like your idea . . . almost as much as the *stupid* one I had originally," he added with a slow grin.

"Then I'll discuss it with Raul. If he approves, I'll work it into the schedule." Irene could feel her face redden slightly as Gene reminded her of her earlier words.

Hearing footsteps behind him, Gene turned around. As Angela walked slowly past them, struggling with an armful of items from one of the rooms, Gene moved to intercept her. "Wait a second! Where are you going with that?" His tone went instantly from amused to anxious.

Angela stopped, trying to reshuffle the load. "The electricians are going to be working in the sitting room in a few days, and I've got to take everything that was in the armoire so we can move it out of the way."

"That painting . . . Let me have it," he said, his voice taut.

"Mr. Gene, I think I should . . ."

"Didn't I make myself clear, Angela?" he said crisply.

The woman nodded, then began trying to set down the armful of items she carried. As she shifted her load, the heavy painting slipped out of her grasp and went tumbling with a crash to the floor.

Gene let out a strangled cry, almost diving for the painting. "You clumsy old woman!" His loud voice seemed even louder in the confines of the entryway. "This is priceless to our family. "How can you be so careless?"

"Mr. Gene . . ."

"You're constantly misplacing or breaking things. Did you think no one here has noticed? Things disappear from one room and show up in another. Every day I see you sweeping up another heirloom crystal or plate."

Cobb appeared with two of his men near the doorway, hearing Gene's angry shouts.

"Mr. Gene, everyone has accidents," Angela said, her voice breaking. "And that painting"—she gestured toward the oil portrait—"the frame is very heavy."

"I don't care about your excuses," Gene snapped, his hands running reverently over the hand-carved wooden frame. A tiny notch had been chipped off one corner exposing unpainted wood.

They heard a door creak open from down the hall and a moment later Raul appeared.

"Mr. Raul, it just slipped out of my hands," Angela said in a trembling voice.

Raul nodded and held up a hand, his eyes taking in the scene and quickly appraising the situation. "It was an accident, Gene. Nothing can be done about it now," he said firmly.

Gene straightened slowly, his hand curled around the portrait frame possessively. The finely detailed painting was of a beautiful, wonderfully alive young woman clad in an exquisitely jeweled black velvet dress. The lady had her head cocked slightly to the left, flirting with liquid-blue eyes and the faint curve of a smile on full, red lips. "I'll take this to my room, look it over carefully, and see if it's damaged anywhere else besides the corner," he said, his voice taut. "I may keep it there for a while," he added, standing directly in front of his brother, his eyes blazing.

Raul said nothing, but refused to step back, forcing his brother to angle past him to get down the hall. A second later, Raul glanced over at the workers. "I would imagine you people have work to do and places to be," he growled.

As the men dispersed, Irene stared at Raul's expression, not blaming the others for scattering quickly. His features were defined by a cold anger that was truly frightening to behold. His eyes gleamed with a deadly fire she hadn't expected to find in the controlled and cultured man she'd seen just the evening before.

Wordlessly he went back down the hall to the room he'd emerged from. With surprise, Irene heard the door click shut. From the severity of his expression, she had expected him to slam it hard enough to splinter the wood frame.

Angela sighed softly. "The more things change, the more they stay the same," she observed.

"How long have you been with the family, Angela?"

"Since both Mr. Raul and Mr. Gene were in grade school," she replied.

"What was that all about? There was more to this than an oil painting of a beautiful woman."

"It's Señora Reina's portrait. Mr. Gene painted it as a birthday gift for her."

"I didn't know Gene had been married."

"The Señora was not married to Mr. Gene, she was married to Mr. Raul." Angela sighed. "That was a long time ago," she said, then retrieved the items she'd been carrying from the floor. "Now I better get back to work. Mr. Raul doesn't like to see people idle."

Irene thought about what Angela had said. The portrait of Reina had a distinctively sensual quality. Gene had obviously put a lot of insight and feeling into the work. She couldn't help but wonder if there had been some complication in the relationship between Raul, his wife, and Gene. That could explain why the brothers didn't get along very well.

She put the idea aside as none of her business and spent the next few hours working up designs incorporating the *nichos* Gene had wanted. Once finished, she wrote a brief memo to accompany the designs, then took them by Raul's office. He was busy on the phone when she appeared at his open door, but he waved her in long enough to silently acknowledge receipt of the paperwork.

She was on her way outside to check on the progress of the adobe when Gene came down the hall. Hearing her name being called, she stopped and turned around.

"Hold on a sec," he asked, quickening his steps. "Where are you off to?"

"I've got to check on the new adobe they're unloading in the back. I want to make sure it's top quality."

"I'll go with you," he said, falling into step beside

her. He seemed quietly lost in thought as they made their way through the house toward the back door. "I wanted to apologize for my outburst earlier," he said, finally breaking the silence.

"Don't worry about it. We all lose our tempers from time to time. Besides, I'm not the one you should apologize to anyway."

He nodded. "I'll be speaking to Angela soon. I shouldn't have made her lose face like that."

"No, you shouldn't have, but I'm sure she'll accept your apology. She knows we're all human."

As they started through the dining room, they saw several workmen helping themselves to a platter of burritos on the buffet table. Others were already sitting at the table, eating.

Gene stopped and glared at the men. "Who said you could eat in here? This is the family's room. Take that tray into the kitchen. You can eat there with the rest of the staff!"

A few indistinct grumbles sounded as the men left slowly, shooting irate glances at Gene as they strode past him. Irene stared at Gene, annoyed and puzzled by his attitude. "Why did you do that? There's not enough room for all of them in the kitchen. They'll have to eat standing up."

"This room belongs to the family and to our guests. It's not for the workmen," he said simply.

"What about me? I'm part of the hired help, but last night I had dinner here with your family."

"A different category of hired help," he answered with a shrug.

"I don't understand. Like me, they're here to make the hacienda a better place for your family."

"This home has always been sacred to the Mendozas. I don't know if you'll be able to understand this," Gene said condescendingly, "but we believe the hacienda deserves to be treated with reverence. It's more than a house. It represents birthrights and legacies. The staff doesn't eat in the rooms reserved for the family out of respect. I don't want that principle violated by strangers who can't begin to understand the history and the sacrifices that have made our family what it is today."

She exhaled softly. "I understand honoring your home, Gene," she said, trying to control her irritation, "but not by excluding people who are here to perform a service for you. That's just snobbery at its worst."

"I didn't think you'd understand," he shrugged. "It's a difficult concept to come to terms with unless you've been raised with it. You see, we were brought up to believe that everything and everyone has their place, and obscuring those lines does no one any favors."

"I understand what you're trying to say, but those workmen were only taking a lunch break, they weren't intruding on anything. Your family wasn't there."

"But that room should be respected by those outside the family. You wouldn't go into a church wearing cutoffs and eating a hamburger, would you? It dishonors the place and what it represents."

She sighed. "I don't think we're going to see eye-to-eye on this."

"No, maybe not," Gene agreed. "Can you accept something you don't understand?"

The request hit closer to home than she would have liked. It was reminiscent of the criticism she'd voiced about those who lived in the world outside the pueblo. "I can try," she said at last.

"Good. That's a start."

"To what?" Raul said, coming into the room from the hall.

"Never mind, big brother. It would take too long to explain."

Raul ran his hand absently over one of the hand-carved *santos* in the *nicho* on the wall. "By the way, Gene, I looked at Irene's plans for the *nichos* and liked what I saw. I'm glad your work's going to be displayed in the entryway. Your sculptures are going to add just the right personal touch. Which of your pieces do you plan to display?"

The tense wariness on Gene's face vanished. Like a photo print that develops before your eyes, a slow smile spread over his face, redefining his features. "I thought I'd place my Phoenix in the center *nicho*. It goes well with the renovation spirit, don't you think?"

Raul nodded. "I think that's perfect. Let me know if there's anything you need, or any way I can help." He glanced at Irene. "It shouldn't take too long to get those *nichos* in place, right?"

"I'll schedule them in with the work on the *sala,* providing I can talk Anita into staying with the renovation."

"Good. My brother's pieces should be among the first things guests see when they enter our home. They set the tone, do you know what I mean?"

"Of course," she replied.

Gene strode to the door. "I'm going to go upstairs and think about which sculptures to use. I'm glad that you're supporting me on this, Raul."

Raul watched his brother leave, then turned to her with a pleased look on his face. "He's got a temper, you might as well realize that from the start, but he's a good man."

"You work hard at keeping your family together." She flashed him a smile, letting him know she understood he was trying very hard to be congenial and meet his younger brother halfway.

"The family is the most important thing to me," he admitted. "As a Tewa, isn't it that way for you too?"

"Yes, but you also work harder at it than I've ever had to."

"Since I'm the elder son, responsibility falls to me." He rubbed the back of his neck with one hand in a gesture of weariness.

"Nowadays many would say that your only responsibility is to yourself."

He held her eyes, his face a fascinating play of angles and shadows in the semidarkness of the great dining room. "But you wouldn't be one of them. I know you understand the duties of family."

"I do, but I have to admit that's an attitude I've rarely found outside the pueblo."

His mouth tightened. "Then maybe you haven't been looking in the right places." Raul strode out of the room before she could answer.

Irene exhaled softly. She'd stuck her foot in it. Her remark, though admittedly tactless, had been completely innocent. Valid too, as far as she was concerned. But of course she shouldn't have said it. Unfortunately it was too late to take it back without making matters worse. Lost in thought, she stared at the crucifix on the wall. Suddenly hearing someone behind her, she jumped and turned around.

Elena stood at the door. "You made him mad. What did you do to him?" she complained.

"I didn't mean to upset him, Elena, really. But sometimes words get misunderstood."

Elena regarded her frankly. "I don't want people working on the house. Everything's all wrong."

"What do you mean, wrong?"

"You just got started, and already there's lots of noise and guys running all over the yard. Some are even in the house. Gene got angry, and Raul hasn't had time for . . . anything."

"I'm sorry the renovation's taking up so much of

Raul's schedule," Irene said gently. "I know you're used to having most, if not all, of his attention. He's your friend as well as your brother, isn't he?"

Elena glanced up at Irene, then looked away. "Yes. I like friends like Raul because they understand. Away from the house at Taos or Santa Fe it's scary. People come right up to you and won't leave you alone. Here, it's nice. I don't want the house to change. I like things just like they are."

"The house won't really change, it's just getting fixed up. I want to make it just the way it was when your grandparents were young."

Elena walked to the window and looked outside. "But too many people are here, and you brought them." They'd all look at her and think she was dumb. She didn't want to be dumb, but sometimes it was hard to think like other people did. "They'll stare and call me names when they think I can't hear."

"Did one of the crew say something to you?" Irene asked quickly.

Elena shook her head. "No, that's not it." Only Raul seemed to know what she meant no matter how it came out. But lately he was always busy with planning the house. "Everyone should just leave. You're not making things better."

"No, we're not yet; but as we complete each step, you'll start to see how pretty things are going to be. I think you'll agree that it was worth the trouble when we finish."

Why couldn't Irene see that change was never good? When you changed things, people went away. And the ones who stayed behind were never the same. She could still remember the day after her twelfth birthday. The family had decided to change Abuela's room and move her things downstairs. She'd lived there on the first floor for a while. But then she'd gone away.

They'd said she was At Peace, and With God in Heaven. Well, maybe Abuela, her grandmother, was happy there, but she really didn't understand how that could be. Her leaving had made many others unhappy. And Abuela had always tried to make people happy.

Elena looked around the room, wishing Raul were there to hug her. When Raul put his arms around her, it felt good, like being wrapped up in a great big overcoat.

Hearing footsteps out in the hall, and hoping it would be Raul, she went to the door. As her gaze fell on Gene, her heart fell.

"Hello, Elenita," he said, shifting three small sculptures he held in his arms. "Why don't you come with me? I'm going to pick out the ones I want to eventually display in the entryway *nichos*. You can help me choose."

She shook her head and edged away from him. "I'm going to take care of my flowers."

"Don't worry," Gene said, seeing the worried look on Irene's face. "She'll be okay. It's the first day of all-out work inside, and she's afraid of all the people and machines. Elena's led a very sheltered life here."

"Do you think that's good?"

Gene shifted the sculptures he held, making sure his hold on them was secure. "Raul and I have argued about that many times. I'm not sure what the right answers are for Elena. She's happy enough, and I guess that's all that matters."

Irene said nothing. This time she was going to keep her mouth shut and not offer her opinion. The last thing she needed was to start an argument with Gene, particularly now that she had the other Mendozas upset with her. "I better get busy. I need to make sure those new adobes are being laid properly."

* * *

It was almost quitting time for the men when Gene came into the room she'd been given as an office. The small space adjacent to the enclosed courtyard was perfect for her. It kept her near the crew and gave her a place to take care of the myriad of details the construction schedule required.

"I studied the way you're going to renovate the long, building-length porch, the *portal,* at the front of the hacienda," Gene said. "I have some modifications I'd like you to incorporate."

"The designs for that have been completed, Gene, and the work is already scheduled," she protested. "Besides, like I told you before, I'd need to have Raul okay any changes."

"I've already done that. He initialed them and told me to come here for your approval too. Here are the things you'll need to add."

Out of the corner of her eye, she caught a glimpse of Cobb standing right outside the window. At first she wondered if he'd somehow put Gene up to this, but then concluded he didn't have the clout to make a Mendoza do anything.

She studied the sketch Gene handed her, making a point of noting Raul's distinctive scrawl at the bottom. "All right. I'll get the additional posts and corbels you want, but it might take some time to get a perfect match. We might even have to make duplicates."

"That's okay. You can put the *portal* work off for a while and reassign the workers while you work out the details. There's certainly plenty for them to do."

She suppressed a sigh. One way or another, she'd have to make him understand the schedule. Work had to be done pretty much in sequence because many steps were dependent on previous ones. "I'll be glad to add these ideas to the design, but try to remember that your brother's deadline makes things very tight for us."

"Oh, come on. It's not like I'm asking for the impossible," he protested.

"No, you're not," she admitted, "but little delays can add up the costs and end up throwing everything off schedule."

"Don't worry. I'm already aware of that." He leaned back in the chair, stretching his legs out before him. "There's one more thing. Do you plan to do any major wiring work or remodeling in the hall outside the upstairs bedrooms?"

"No, that section's going to stay pretty much the same."

"Good. I'm going to grab one of the electricians for a while and arrange for another lighting fixture there, if it's okay with you."

"Sure. What kind of lighting fixture did you have in mind?" she asked, more intrigued than concerned.

"A small spotlight to accent an oil painting I'm hanging up."

"The same oil I saw earlier?" She saw Gene nod and couldn't resist prodding further. "That portrait has to be your finest painting, it's so beautiful. It means a lot to you, doesn't it?" Irene said.

"Yeah, it does." Gene sank into the thick leather cushions of the chair. "She was the easiest subject I've ever worked with. Her beauty . . . Well, I didn't do her justice." He stared at an indeterminate spot across the room. "Cristina was the most fascinating woman I'd ever met. She was a lady of mercurial moods; one second she'd be carefree and happy, then the next she'd be somber and thoughtful. She was a poet with a fragile soul, and Raul never understood her. She wanted so much for herself and her life, but all of it eluded her."

"Cristina? I heard her called Reina."

"That was the nickname Raul gave her. *Reina,* his queen," he said with a mocking twist in his voice.

Curiosity corkscrewed through her like a current. She didn't want to ask but she couldn't help herself. "Were you two very close friends?"

"Friends?" He chuckled mirthlessly. "She was the woman I loved. I made the mistake of bringing her here for dinner once, and that's how Raul met her." A muscle at his jaw twitched and his expression hardened. "The problem with Cristina was that she would define her worth through the quality of man she attracted. I was too much like her, an artist, an equal in her eyes." Gene stood and walked to the window, staring at the black expanse outside. "But what she saw in Raul was nothing more than an illusion she'd shaped in her mind."

From where she was sitting, she could see Gene's reflection in the glass. Through the distortion created by the room's lighting, the pain etched in his features seemed even more pronounced. Tortuous lines defined the impression on the plate glass, and his face looked drawn and almost cadaverous. "What do you mean? How did she see Raul?" she asked.

"The way most women do: a rock, something solid that they can cling to. But clinging to a rock isn't always safe. If you fall off the edge, it'll just speed your descent." Gene turned around and faced her. "Well, that was a useless walk down memory lane." He ran a hand through his hair. "I think I'll go take care of that portrait."

"It's really a great accomplishment. But maybe you should reconsider the location. Your brother would have to pass by it every day in that hall."

"The place for that portrait isn't hidden away in a

closet. Her memory needs to be kept alive. It's all we have left of her," he said, his voice taut.

"But it could be a very painful reminder for your brother," she countered gently. "I haven't see any other photos of her around."

For a moment Gene was unable to speak. His teeth were clenched and the vein on his forehead bulged. Slowly he brought himself under control, but it was easy to see it wouldn't take much to set him off again. "It's time to change that," he said, his voice frigid.

Irene watched him walk away. As his footsteps faded, an uneasy feeling spread through her. Had her presence and the reconstruction precipitated the trouble here at *Casa de Encanto?* It seemed easier to believe that it had been there all along, hidden beneath the surface, waiting for a catalyst to set the chaos in motion.

She reached into her pocket for the pouch that now held the fetish and found comfort in it. Her heritage gave her a link to the past, and through that she could find peace. But the Mendozas' past seemed to contain much heartbreak and sorrow.

Lost in thought, she wondered if the beautiful home had become a graveyard for lost dreams. Irene flinched as a flash of lightning split the sky, inundating the corridor with its eerie glow. Seconds later, thunder rolled over Taos Mountain in the distance. As the angry rumbling settled into stillness, the plaintive cry of a mountain lion erupted from the valley below.

# 6

**R**AUL SAT ALONE in his study as the clock struck eleven. The rain seemed to go on forever tonight, most unusual for fall. He shifted in his chair, hating the way the cold air and humidity draped around him like a shroud.

Leaning back, Raul turned off the lights, then drew open the drapes to watch the storm. Lightning forked against the tops of mountains and leaped from cloud to cloud. The violence overhead and the dull rumblings of distant thunder matched his mood.

He was weary tonight, and that at least partially explained why his spirits felt leaden. Yet admittedly, there were times when the burden that had fallen to him as the elder Mendoza son seemed almost suffocating. Although he was bound by duty to see to the others, he was also a man with needs and dreams of his own. Many had been neglected, with much regret, for years now.

He swung around in his chair and stared at the portrait of Ramón Mendoza illuminated by the strobelike flashes of lightning. The image that stared back at him from the ebony-framed painting was a good likeness of his father. He was dressed in a black business suit, and his expression bordered on severe. Only the splash of red from his tie, one Elena had picked out for him, reminded Raul that his father had been quite human and loving as well.

Ramón Mendoza had shouldered many burdens and had never shared his worries or his concerns with anyone, not even Raul's mother. He'd been the stabilizing center the family had rallied around until his death.

Now as the elder male, the role fell to him, and Raul didn't much care for it. His father had been unmovable, a tower of confidence and strength, and in comparison he felt like an imperfect replica.

Loneliness carved an emptiness within him that grew with each passing day. Sometimes he felt trapped within his own body, unable to reach out to anyone. He was a stranger to those who knew him best. Then again, it was that distance that had given him time to take charge of his father's company and rebuild it into the profitable venture it had once been.

Gene, on the other hand, never even took part in the business. He was much like a child who needed a father figure to obey . . . and perhaps resent, in order to define himself. Raul couldn't depend on his brother, not even for friendship. That was something their relationship would never include. And then there was Elenita. She needed someone strong to watch over her, a person she could always count on. He was all that stood between Elena and the outside world.

Duty could bind a man and trap him more effectively than chains or a prison cell. He'd tried to find a life for himself here, despite his responsibilities, but he'd failed miserably. He thought of his Reina as lightning silhouetted the tall pine tree that stood like a sentinel over the family's burial plot.

Cristina, his *Reina,* had been as fragile as Elena in many ways. When he'd first met her, she'd seemed a bold, confident woman. But then the façade had crumbled. Inside she'd been nothing more than a little girl putting up a brave front, crying out for acceptance and love. His heart, which had already been hers, remained in her keeping until the day she died. But Reina had never realized that. Unable to love herself, she'd also doubted his love for her, particularly when he'd been forced to spend so much time saving the business.

He pushed her from his thoughts. The wound was still fresh despite the years, and he found only pain in memories. He stood up slowly. It was time to go to bed. Only through sleep would he be able to escape this mood.

Raul left the study and walked softly through the darkened hall, illuminated only by a few strategically placed wall sconces. He'd almost reached his room when Reina's portrait took him by surprise. He stopped, frozen in time as the familiar blue eyes emanating from the gently spotlighted face teased back at his. A soft moan escaped his throat.

"Cristina is family. Her portrait shouldn't be hidden in a cabinet," Gene challenged, stepping out from the doorway to his own bedroom. "I've been standing here watching her. Wasn't she magnificent?"

Raul turned around slowly. "What possessed you to do this? You never stop to think about anyone except yourself, do you? *Your* pain, *your* needs; that's all that matters."

"Her pain mattered to me. You didn't know what

you had. Cristina needed your time and your attention, but all you gave her were a few moments here and there when you weren't busy trying to make more money." Gene weaved unsteadily on his feet and reached out to the wall for support.

For several seconds Raul said nothing, instead taking deep breaths to regain his temper. "You're drunk, Gene. Go back into your room. And take your painting with you."

As Raul started to remove it from the wall, Gene uttered a strangled cry and launched himself at Raul in a clumsy tackle. Raul spun around, pushing his brother away with all his strength. Gene toppled sideways, grasping for handholds in the air as he struggled for balance.

A second later Gene hit the wall hard, dislodging a shelf supporting Spanish Colonial *retablos.* The religious art painted on flat pieces of wood slid sideways or toppled, crashing to the floor. Gene staggered to his knees, his arms dangling limp at his sides. Tears ran down his face. "You took her from me, but you just let her slip away. Why didn't you take care of her? Cristina's death is on your hands."

"Get out of my sight." Raul shook with rage, afraid of what he'd do if Gene didn't leave immediately.

"It's true and you know it," Gene accused loudly. "Damn you, Raul! She would have still been alive if she'd stayed with me. *I* understood her."

"You understood nothing, then or now, that doesn't come from a bottle!" Raul answered, keeping his grief within himself.

"Mr. Raul, we heard a noise." Angela rushed toward them, Irene at her heels. Seeing the *retablos,* Angela moved forward hesitantly and began to pick them up. "I'll just get these out of the hall," she muttered, not looking directly at either brother.

Gene struggled to his feet, then stumbled, and fell back down on his side. Angela barely managed to scramble out of the way, then escaped down the hall with the *retablos* in hand.

Raul went to his brother's side and lifted him gently off the floor. "In many ways you and Cristina were two of a kind," Raul admitted quietly, cradling his brother against his shoulder as if he were a child. "And just like her, you only see what you want."

As Raul turned to lead his brother away, he saw Irene standing there watching him silently and compassionately. Her expression surprised him. As their gazes met, he sensed her understanding, yet she didn't burden her silent show of support with offers of help that wouldn't have been welcome.

"My brother will be fine," he assured simply. "I'll take care of him."

With a nod and a smile, Irene turned and walked back in the direction she'd come, giving him the privacy he wanted.

Raul led Gene to bed, already regretting the bitter words exchanged between them. The gulf that separated them in every way that mattered would widen even more now. Yet despite that, he no longer felt so totally alone. Though Irene had never uttered a word, in those brief moments when she'd stood by, he'd found a friend.

It was a week later, shortly after nine in the morning, when Irene approached the portion of the outside adobe wall currently under construction. This section would support the main gate to the courtyard. She crouched before it, running her fingers over the cracks in the bricks.

"That stretch of wall's almost done," Cobb said, coming up to stand behind her. "Don't start getting picky. Once it's finished and plastered over, we'll re-hang the gate."

Her gaze shifted back to the wall pensively. "The Armijos couldn't have made these adobes. Either too much clay was used in the mixture or they were allowed to dry too fast. There're just too many cracks." She stepped back and kicked the wall with the metal tip of her boot.

The impact went up her leg and corkscrewed through her body painfully, but the small hole it made in the adobe made her smile with perverse satisfaction. She turned around and transfixed Cobb with a penetrating stare. "I warned you before we ever got started about cutting corners. You must think I'm stupid or incompetent. These aren't the Armijo bricks I specified. This is second-rate material."

He smiled slowly. "Yeah, maybe, but they conform to code, and we beat Armijo's price by thirty percent. Quit whining. There's nothing you can do about it now."

"Like hell, I can't," Irene whispered harshly, and started toward the house.

"Mr. Mendoza approved the switch," Cobb remarked offhandedly.

Irene stopped in midstride and turned her head. "Raul approved this without telling me?" She considered it for a moment, then shook her head. "No way. You're lying. I didn't want to have a showdown with you, but you've forced my hand. I will *not* allow you to compromise this project." She continued walking to the house.

"I didn't say it was *Raul*," he added in a bemused tone.

Recognition flooded slowly over her. "Gene had no authority to override me. We talked about this already."

Just then Gene stepped out of the back door and joined them. Irene watched him approach. Unlike his brother's, his clothing, though stylishly expensive, had a more casual air. Today he was wearing a brown leather jacket, an off-white pullover, and jeans that appeared to be faded just enough to fit in with the current fashion.

"I heard you two arguing," he said calmly, then glanced at Irene. "John is right. I okayed the bricks. That's not the same as asking for changes in your schedule or designs. Besides, the price difference will save my brother a bundle."

"These adobes are inferior. Raul approved the cost estimate based on the best, and it's my job to see he gets his money's worth. You shouldn't have gone around me on this." She'd never been big on confrontations, and this one was escalating rapidly. Swallowing back her distaste, she made up her mind to put an end to it. "Next time, come to me beforehand if you get any ideas about changing the materials. That's my decision to make, not yours. This work is now going to have to be scrapped and started over again. It's going to cost time and your brother lots of money, particularly if the unused bricks can't be returned."

"Raul's spending a fortune on the restoration," Gene snapped. "There are plenty of ways you could keep the costs down and you know it. Just because he's got money doesn't mean you have to spend it all."

"I'm doing what Raul hired me to do. Everything has already been spelled out in our agreement. If you have a problem, then I suggest you see him."

"I think we should both go talk to him right now. You're way off base on this, and I'm not going to let you get away with it. Those bricks will not weaken the wall enough to warrant the change." Gene strode past her and went up the stairs to Raul's study.

She stared at him for a second. He knew nothing of the strength of those bricks. Cobb had coached him; she had no doubt about that. Not that it would do Cobb any good. She wouldn't allow him to use Gene to undermine her efforts here. As they approached Raul's study, she grew determined to win this fight.

A minute later she stood with Gene outside Raul's closed office door. They could hear him inside speaking to someone on the telephone. Gene knocked lightly on the door and without waiting for an answer, walked inside.

Irene stood by the open door, uncertain whether or not she should follow. Finally, hearing Raul place the phone down, she entered the room. "Do you have a moment?"

Raul gestured to a chair, then glared at Gene, who had seated himself comfortably. "What's so important it couldn't wait until I finished my business on the phone?"

Gene stretched out his legs and crossed them at the ankles. "Your architect needs to be reminded that she works for us, not the other way around," Gene said, and started to fill him in on the details.

"One minute," Irene said, interrupting. "You're not giving your brother an accurate picture." She explained about the bricks. "The information John gave you," she added, looking at Gene, "is not accurate." She met Raul's gaze with a steady one of her own. "And in this case, saving a few dollars is going to jeopardize the workmanship." Irene took a deep breath. "But most important of all, there's one point you have to consider. If your brother is allowed to arbitrarily overrule my decisions, you're not only undermining my ability to do the job, you're gambling with the final results. To be perfectly honest," she added slowly, "I can't stay here under those conditions."

"Raul, that's a pretty speech she just made, but I spoke to John. He assures me there are lots of ways to cut costs without compromising the restoration."

"Irene presented me with a cost estimate at the beginning of the work," Raul answered. "It was consistent with the funds I was willing to budget, so I agreed to it. I trust Irene to make the decisions on all construction matters. If you want to help, then let our architect do her job."

"But you're wasting money that could be better spent," Gene insisted.

Raul gave Irene an almost cursory glance. "Would you leave my brother and me alone for a moment, please?" he asked.

His voice was soft but held a noticeable edge to it. That told her it wasn't really a request. She left the room and closed the door just as voices erupted from the other side of the thick wooden door.

"What the hell do you think you're doing?" Raul's baritone voice echoed though the pine door, though the thick wood deadened the sound level considerably. "First, you bring my architect in here. Then you give me this unbelievable choice: either jeopardize her authority or make my own brother lose face when I'm forced to side against him. Don't you *ever* think?"

"I'm trying to save us some money. You could use it to invest in my gallery. It's a sound proposition. You'd recover your investment in no time at all."

"I'm tired of your fantasies and get-rich schemes. We each owned one half of the family business after Father died. Yet instead of working alongside me, you asked me to buy you out. You made enough money from the sale to start up any business, but you chose to squander every dollar."

"Even if you are running it, the business rightfully belongs to the family, and that includes me."

"You're entitled to what I give you—nothing more. You've spent your entire life blaming others for your mistakes. Dad and Mom never failed to bail you out, but I won't do that. You'll always have a roof over your head, and enough money to meet your needs. Anything more, you'll have to go out and earn for yourself."

"You've always resented me because I'm not just like you. I chose to be an artist, so you don't think I'm worth much as a man. But manhood isn't something that can be judged by numbers in a bank account. Before you pass judgment on people, take a hard look at your definitions."

Irene was standing a few feet from the door when it burst open. Gene stormed out and, oblivious to Irene, collided against her, nearly knocking her over. Reacting instantly, he reached out and steadied her by the shoulders, then dropped his arms.

She'd never seen such a mixture of emotions in a man's face before. Pain and anger contorted his features, then melted away, reshaping themselves into a mask of resolve. "You came here to make a name for yourself," Gene growled. "You want to make *Casa de Encanto* into your monument. But that's something it'll never be. I feel sorry for you. In the long run, you'll only be one more Indian whose sacrifice and sweat have helped the Mendoza *patrón* attain what he wants."

As Gene brushed past her, she glanced at Raul, who'd come to the door. She'd hoped to find some sign of support from him, but one look at his face made her realize she'd never get it. His eyes were void of expression, making them appear as cold as a January morning. "Do whatever you want with the adobes," he said, then wordlessly returned to his desk.

Though he'd sided with her, she suspected that he

also resented her for the part she'd played in forcing the choice upon him. Irene walked outside slowly. She'd won that round with Gene, but she didn't feel like celebrating. She couldn't afford too many more victories at their current cost. As Gene's words rang in her ears, she wondered how much truth there'd be in them.

Irene crossed the grounds and headed toward the Tewa workers gathered ahead. She needed the company of her own at the moment.

She was almost upon them when she heard one of the Tewa men arguing with the construction foreman, Bob Serna, a burly Spanish man in his late fifties.

"Ask someone else to dig the trench. I can't work there. Why don't you just let me switch with one of the other guys and do their job for a while?"

"Give me a break, will ya? It's just an owl up there, not a vulture. If you don't like the damn bird, chuck a rock at it."

The Tewa man shook his head, and looked up at the rocky ledge about two hundred yards up the mountain, where the owl was perched on a pine branch. "It wouldn't change anything. It's a bad omen. You can't ignore things like that."

"Look, pal, you have a choice. Either do your work or go back home to your pueblo."

"The owl means death. Don't be so quick to discount what you don't understand."

"I'll be even faster discounting you unless you get back to work."

Grumbling, the Tewa man picked up his shovel and reluctantly started to dig along the staked-out line. "You'll see. There's trouble ahead."

In the distance the owl began making a sad call,

halfway between a hoot and a screech. Irene suppressed a shudder.

"Bob, could I have a moment of your time?" She motioned for Serna to join her.

"Now what?" Serna muttered.

"Why couldn't you have one of the other men dig at that end of the trench?"

Serna's face hardened into disgust. "I can't have the workers dictating what jobs they'll do and which they won't." He paused, then added, "Not that I have to answer to you on this."

She'd seen this attitude before. She suspected it wasn't her heritage as an Indian that was at question, as much as her gender. She was a woman with overall authority at a site. The unspoken disapproval of some men who preferred traditional roles sometimes translated into brusqueness. "Their fears could affect their work. If it does, then you'll certainly be answering to me."

"Fine. If it gets to that, *you* can handle it," he snapped.

Suddenly the Tewa worker who'd been digging yelled and flew straight out of the trench, tumbling clumsily to the ground. Serna spat out an oath and walked stridently toward the Pueblo man. "What the hell? You couldn't have hit a power line, you idiot!"

"I told you not to ignore the owl," he replied, scrambling to his feet and backing away, obviously terrified. "I tried to warn you that it brings death."

"What are you blubbering about?" Serna demanded angrily. "You can't dig a straight line either, and now . . ." He stopped short, following the Indian man's line of vision, then cursed softly.

Irene saw the other workmen running up to that section of the trench. Curious, she drew near, carefully edging past those already gathered there. A moment later, she stepped clear of the massive backs and shoulders blocking her view. As she glanced down, her eyes locked on the skeletal hand resting in the worker's abandoned shovel.

# 7

IRENE STARED IN silent horror at the skeletal fingers that grasped the dark earth clinging to the shovel. Long bones she assumed to be part of an arm protruded several inches above the ground like obscene roots. As the screech of the owl filled the air, she shivered and wondered if the person had been buried while still alive.

The Tewa man looked at her, revealing his anger only through his eyes. "I didn't expect them to understand," he said, cocking his head toward the Anglo and Hispanic workers. "But you should have known better. You saw the owl too." He turned his back on the trench he'd been digging, his disgust now flowing freely again. "At seven fifty an hour, I'm not getting paid enough to dig up a graveyard."

Serna spat out an oath. "Jesus H. Christ, just what we needed! Now we have to call in the cops. Damn guy's probably been in that spot since the dinosaurs walked the earth. But now there's no way the police are going to let us dig around here for who knows how long." He scowled at Irene. "You see any way around this?"

"Not really. Just keep the workers from disturbing anything else in the area. Block off access to it and put a tarp over that grave. We have to preserve everything until the cops get here. I'll go inside and tell Raul what's going on. It'd be better if he was the one who made the call to the sheriff's office."

Irene turned and went back to the house. Explaining the situation to Raul was bound to be tricky. He wouldn't be receptive to news that might damage the reputation of any Mendoza, living or dead. And the discovery was bound to lead to some very difficult questions. Since the family plot was around the other side of the house, more than a hundred yards away, the motives behind the burial were, at best, suspect.

A few minutes later, she sat across the desk from her puzzled employer. "The police will have to be called," she said, after explaining what they'd found, "but I thought you'd prefer to do that yourself."

With a preoccupied nod, Raul flipped through a card file, locating the number. Picking up the receiver, he dialed. After Raul had a brief exchange with the person on the other end, he turned his attention back to Irene. For the next twenty minutes, they discussed the find and its implications on the work schedule.

"The sooner the police finish investigating, the sooner we'll be given the okay to continue our work. Do you have any idea who could have been buried there?" she asked.

"None. We bury our dead in the family plot. I wish I could recall something that would explain the location of that body," Raul added. "But it's no secret that *Casa de Encanto* has a checkered past."

"It's also very possible that skeleton goes back a century or more. We have no way of knowing."

"Yeah, and the older it is, the less likely we are to solve the puzzle." Raul reached back and massaged his neck with his left hand, rolling his head wearily from side to side. "How have the workers taken this?"

"Not very well, especially the Tewas," she answered slowly. She was about to say more when a light rap sounded at the open door. Angela stood there, her eyes wide and her face pale as she stared at Raul. "Señor Raul, the police are here. Detective Estevez would like to talk to you. His men are fencing off the garden with yellow tape."

"It's all right, Angela. There's nothing to be concerned about. I'm sure this is all part of something from long ago. An unpleasant business, but nothing that should really bother any of us now."

From her expression it was easy to see she was unconvinced. "Shall I show Detective Estevez into your study, or would you prefer to meet him outside?"

"Have him come in here," Raul answered, then glanced at Irene. "You should stay. At this point you know more about this than I do."

A short, heavyset Hispanic man entered the room a few moments later. His brown houndstooth sports coat was well past its prime, and he had a slightly distracted air about him, but his eyes were eagle-sharp, refuting the former impression. Though he took in the room in one quick glance, he gave the impression he'd missed nothing.

Estevez shook hands with Raul and Irene, then sat unceremoniously in one of the easy chairs. "From what I gathered outside, no one has any idea who the bones belong to or how they got there. Can you shed some light on this?"

"Not at the moment. It might help if you could tell

me how old the corpse is. As you know, the hacienda's past is hardly one associated with the saints."

Estevez grinned. "Yeah, I know a little about the local history, but we'll have to wait for forensics to date the corpse." He paused, then flipped open a little notebook he'd kept in his breast pocket. "The Tewa man who found the body said that he thinks there was another structure in that area at one time. He uncovered painted scraps of lumber and a bunch of rusted nails. Can you tell me about that?"

Raul went to the window and stared outside, his eyebrows furrowed in thought. "Years ago there was a storage shed in that spot. The wood was rotting, so it had to be torn down. We constructed the extra room beside the garage to replace it." Raul fingered the groove on his forehead. "That took place when I was still in college, only I can't remember exactly when."

"Okay, thanks for your help." Estevez stood. "I'd like to speak to your brother before I leave. Perhaps he can remember something."

Raul walked to the window. "His car is here." He paused. "I see him. He's out there with the men." He pointed Gene out to Estevez.

"Thanks," the detective replied. "I'll let you know when we ID, or maybe I should say *if*, we ID the remains. The experts should be able to give you the age and sex of the corpse. Maybe you'll be able to provide us with some more clues then."

Estevez started toward the door when Elena rushed into the room. Her eyes were darting wildly from person to person, the bloodless pallor of her face accentuating her terror. "It was like that movie I saw on television a long time ago, wasn't it?" she said, her voice trembling. "The one that scared me so much! The man kept hitting that woman, then buried her so no one would know. Then bad things kept right on happening to other people for a long time. What are we going to do?"

Raul went quickly to his sister's side, and took her hand gently in his own. "Elenita, I wish you'd never watched that movie," he said sadly. "After all this time, it still frightens you. But don't worry. That has nothing to do with what's happening here now. Someone was buried in the wrong place, that's all. Now their body will be put in a casket and taken to a proper cemetery."

"No, this is just the beginning. Horrible things will start to happen," she insisted.

Irene looked at Raul, guessing about the type of movie. "But Elena, something *good* has already happened. This person's spirit will now be honored with a proper burial."

Elena considered the idea for a few seconds. "You mean that finding the body is a blessing?"

"It is for the person's spirit, and also for this family because a grave really doesn't belong there." Seeing Elena calming down, Irene took the opportunity to change the conversation. "By the way, I've been meaning to ask you about your miniature roses," she said, selecting Elena's favorite subject. "I remember Raul mentioned how beautiful they were. What colors do you have?"

Elena brightened, and motioned for Irene to follow her. "Come, I can show you."

Glancing back as she reached the door, Irene saw the relief that had eased the lines around Raul's face. She was glad to have had a chance to help Elena and at the same time take some pressure off Raul. From what she'd seen of his life, he had enough to worry about from career and family.

They arrived at Elena's room and went inside. At first glance, it looked much like the others in the house, with its territorial and colonial furniture. But there were touches here that made it very definitely Elena's private domain. The wall over the bed was decorated with an enormous collage of dried flowers. The arrangement, set behind glass, added a splash of color to the light sand-tone adobe walls. "Did you make that?"

"Angela helped me, but I did most of it," she said proudly. "All the flowers came from my plants. Let me show you." She walked to the door with a huge poster of the cartoon skunk Pepe Le Pew sniffing a petunia and opened it. The adjoining room was square and large, bordered on opposing walls by massive Mexican shuttered windows. "This used to be a playroom, but it's my plant room now. In the summer, between the gardens below and the flowers in here, it's just beautiful. It's like a fairy-tale place."

The room was aglow in a rainbow of colors that adorned every single inch of shelf and window space. Irene looked at the vast array of flowering plants. In the spots protected from direct sun were varieties of African violets. In the center, receiving direct light, grew miniature roses of almost every color. They'd been carefully pruned and shaped and each was filled with blooms or buds. "Elena, it's just gorgeous in here!"

"I could put one of these in your room, then change it every few days," she said, touching one of the miniature roses. "That way you'd get to enjoy all of them instead of just one kind."

"That sounds terrific, I'd love it. But are you sure it isn't too much trouble?"

Elena shook her head. "I like doing that. It gives me a chance to share my flowers with someone who enjoys them."

"In that case, I accept!"

"How's this one to start with?" Elena asked, picking up a white one with red edgings.

"It's beautiful."

"Good. It's called Magic Carousel. We'll take it over there now."

Irene started out the door. "Oh, I meant to ask you. Should I keep it up high where the cat can't get to it?"

Elena gave her a puzzled look as she walked out into the hall. "What cat? We don't have any pets. Raul asked me once if I wanted a dog or a cat, but I said no. I knew they might dig up my plants. Besides, I'd rather spend time with my flowers than have to feed and brush an animal."

Puzzling over Elena's answer, Irene opened the door to her room. She watched Elena set the pot on the dresser near the window where it would get several hours of light a day. "It's really pretty, Elena. Thanks."

"You're welcome. But tell me what made you ask me about a cat?"

Irene hesitated, not wanting to alarm Elena now that she'd managed to forget about the body they'd just found. One look at Elena's face, however, told her that the woman had already spotted her hesitation. The lines around her eyes and the set of her mouth clearly mirrored her anxiety. "I thought I heard one the other night," Irene said, keeping her tone casual, "but I must have been dreaming. You know how real a dream can seem sometimes?"

Elena nodded. "Yeah, sometimes you even wake up scared. Then it takes you a few minutes to figure out where you are."

"Yeah, those are especially hard to deal with," Irene admitted with a smile.

Elena sat at the edge of the bed and stared at the floor. "Oh, um, thanks for explaining about the person they dug up. I'm not afraid of it anymore," she said quietly.

"Never pay too much attention to movies, Elena, especially the ones that are supposed to scare you. They're mostly nonsense."

Elena shook her head. "Not always," she said. "Sometimes they're just like they say on the news."

"Well, bad things do happen," Irene answered slowly, "but Raul will always see to it that you're never in any danger."

"Yeah, but the girl in the movie was someplace where everyone thought she'd be safe too. And the guy was someone everyone liked." Her words started coming out faster. "Then he just went crazy one day when they were arguing. He grabbed the girl and when she tried to get away from him he hit her. She tried to scream, but he jammed the sleeve of his jacket in her mouth. She fought like crazy, so he pushed her to the ground and hit her with a rock. There was blood and . . ."

"Elena, stop! It was only a movie with some good actors. Remember you saw it when you were a lot younger."

"Oh, but it was so real, at least it looked that way."

"What you have to remember . . ." A knock at the open door interrupted them. Irene turned around and saw Raul standing in the doorway. "Excuse me, Irene, but with John gone on a supply trip, you're needed outside. The Tewa workers are very upset, and the Hispanic men are just making things worse."

Leaving Elena, Irene accompanied Raul outside into the garden. "What's going on? I know you were being vague because of Elena, but I need to know the situation."

"The Hispanic workers started teasing the women, and then the Tewas about digging up more bodies.

Kidding around about it is their way of covering up their uneasiness with machismo, not malice. Can you understand?"

"Tewas take this type of thing very seriously," she said. "It's no joking matter for us."

"I know. But since you're also Tewa, maybe you could explain to them that the Hispanic workers are just blowing off steam. Gallows humor is a way of coping."

"They won't understand. To them it's an affront. But I'll do my best to diffuse the situation if you'll speak to the Hispanic workers too."

"That's being taken care of. Serna's going to handle it."

As they approached the construction area, they saw the workers going through the motions, but something was clearly wrong. The tension that prevailed was a palpable force one could feel thrumming in the air like electricity during a lightning storm.

As subtly as possible, she beckoned one of the Tewa workers aside. Raul, meanwhile, went up to Serna the foreman and began to speak to him in low tones.

The Tewa man, one of the eldest of the workers from her tribe, glowered at her. "You should have insisted that the owl be chased off by one of our *koshare*. You've helped create the problem we now face." Alfonso Sanchez kept his obsidian eyes unflinchingly on hers.

"No. The owl shouldn't have been allowed to create such concern. And what the crew has uncovered is not necessarily an evil. Look at it as the opportunity to right a wrong. If nothing else, the person can now be buried properly, according to custom."

"You've always been good twisting an argument to suit you. I remember hearing that from my younger brother, who was your classmate back in high school.

But this time you can't rationalize what happened. There is something bad here." His eyes narrowed. "If you'll shut out the physical senses and become attuned to the rhythm of everything around you, you'll sense it."

"There is nothing to sense." She glanced around. "Even the owl has gone."

"It was just a messenger, a sign. The evil is already here." Alfonso gestured toward two Hispanics teasing each other as they assembled a metal scaffold. "To them, it's all a joke. And their ignorance will cause even more problems."

"It really isn't a joke to them either," she assured him soberly. "They're also uneasy. Kidding around is their way of covering it up."

"Maybe, but certain things shouldn't be taken lightly. Even to speak of them, unless absolutely necessary, invites more trouble."

"Asking them to show more respect for those of our tribe will do only a limited amount of good. You'll have to make sure that tempers are kept under control. Our people need the jobs. We can't afford to have talk get started saying we're unreliable. Finding employment is difficult enough these days."

"I'll do my best, but believe me when I tell you that there's evil here. Our problems at this site are just beginning."

A moment later she returned with Raul to the house. Silence echoed through the corridors, accentuating the hollowness at the heart of *Casa de Encanto*. "Join me for a drink inside the sitting room before dinner?" he invited.

"All right." She followed him inside.

Raul walked to the bar, poured them both a glass of brandy, then sat across the sofa from her. "How do you think it went with the crew? Do you think it'll affect their work?"

"A bit, but I'll continue to keep an eye on things. The deadline will be met," she said firmly.

"Good." He gazed at an indeterminate spot across the room. "It's a debt, you know, to my father, and what he tried to do for all of us," he added softly.

"You loved him a great deal."

He hesitated. "It's hard to talk about him in those terms. I admired him, and respected him. Those were the only emotions he really wanted from me," he admitted with a deprecating shrug.

Despite the casual gesture, she heard the pain laced through his words, and for a moment felt it almost as keenly as he did. "I think he would have been proud of what you're doing for your family now."

Raul's gaze filled with gratitude. "I'd like to think that. Family has always been at the heart of what we value most. He used to say that as long as we stood together, nothing could really touch us. I believe that too. Only it can be incredibly difficult sometimes." He finished what was in his glass, went to the bar, and brought the decanter over. "Are you close to your parents?"

"My father died when I was six. I don't remember that much about him, except I know he and my mother were very close. She never remarried."

"I'm sorry if I've inadvertently brought up painful memories for you."

"You haven't. My father's death was sad, but I was young then, and my grandfather, my mother's father, stepped in for him. Over the years he was always there for me. He died a little over a year ago. I still miss him a lot at times, but I have my memories of him. And the special love we shared will always be a part of me. In that way, he'll never be far from me," she answered.

Thinking back to her dream, she realized that there was more truth than he'd ever know in what she'd said.

He started to refill her glass, but she shook her head. "No more, thanks. I'm too tired tonight. Would you mind if I went upstairs and tried to get some rest before dinner? It's been a very long day for me."

"I'm sorry. I should have realized that." He stood up. "But I enjoy your company," he admitted frankly. "It's good to have someone like you to talk to."

Something flashed in his eyes, an emotion so vulnerable and human it wrapped itself around her heart and squeezed. "I'll be around," she said, and smiled.

He nodded. "All right. I'll see you later at the table, then."

She thought she saw a glimmer of disappointment in his eyes. Surprised, she stood there for a second and watched him enter the empty room. The duties he shouldered kept him alone and separate. Yet it was through the inner strength that sustained him that his vulnerability came to light. At the very heart of the most self-sufficient man she knew lay an infinite core of sadness.

Dinner seemed more like an exercise in mandatory socializing than a meal. The conversation was too forced to pass as natural, as everyone assiduously avoided the one subject foremost in their minds: the unmarked grave no one could explain.

It was only nine o'clock when she entered her room. She stripped out of her clothes, dropping them onto the floor, and crawled beneath the blankets, grateful the day was finally over. The crisp coolness of the sheets and the weight of the comforter blended pleasantly, forming a soothing cocoon around her.

Irene was already drifting into a peaceful void when

a persistent sound registered through her dream into her consciousness. Too sleepy to come fully alert without protest, she tried to discount it as the contraction and expansion of the old house. But the sound continued, prodding her awake as it rose, then faded several times.

Irene finally opened her eyes and stared up at the dark *vigas* on the ceiling. The sound she'd heard became barely discernible footsteps which fell with muted softness as they crept down the hall. A second later, they stopped and a faint shadow blocked the light from the crack beneath the door.

She held her breath, too terrified to even move. The pounding of her heart filled her ears like the wild cadence of a mad drummer. Then the padding sound started up again, drifting at a leisurely pace down the hall.

Gathering her wits, she went to the door and opened it a crack. It was hard to see anything in the dimly lit hall. She listened for the opening or closing of a door, hoping for a clue. The silence that greeted her instead was deep and encompassing. Uneasiness crept through her, chilling her spirit.

Irene closed her door, locked it securely, and crawled back into bed, determined to stay there until morning. Though she'd hoped to get some sleep, an instinct as primitive as the desert itself kept her mind alert and attuned to danger.

# 8

IRENE WALKED AROUND to the north side of the house shortly after eleven, making her daily rounds. In the past few weeks, Anita Sanchez had done much of the interior plaster repairs, and the other artisans had begun to restore the exterior wooden trim. Cobb and Serna had spent most of the morning examining the roof parapet, trying to estimate the time needed to repair the adobe ledge, which was next on her schedule. Now it was her turn to have another look.

She approached the tall aluminum ladder propped up against the side of the house. After checking to make sure it was secure, she climbed up carefully, inspecting the wall as she went. The long *canales*, pipes set in the adobe to carry the water away from the roof, were still firmly set despite the ravages time had left on the surrounding adobe. At least those repairs, which might have been costly and time-consuming, would be minimal.

Irene hoisted herself over the foot-high parapet, the ridge making it impossible for her to simply step across to reach the roof. For several minutes she moved with methodical precision along the roof edge, checking for cracks and signs of water damage. Finding Cobb and Serna's estimates to her satisfaction, she stepped back over the parapet onto the ladder, ready to climb down. As she placed her full weight on the rung, the ladder suddenly shifted and began to sink to one side, losing stability. With a startled cry she reached for the parapet, but the rounded edges made gripping it impossible.

With only a second to react, she pushed off the shifting foothold and lunged upward, making a desperate grab for the *canale* that stuck out from the wall. As her fingers curled around it, the ladder dropped away and crashed to the ground.

Irene screamed for help, but the sounds of power tools and a backhoe drowned out her efforts. She wouldn't be able to hang on for long, yet no help was in sight. No construction activity was currently taking place on this side of the house.

Her voice started breaking with fear and strain, and terror closed in. Her fingers were beginning to grow numb. She wouldn't be able to hold on much longer. When the sensitivity left her hands, her fingers would just slip loose. As she closed her eyes and uttered a silent prayer to her *po-wa-ha*, guardian spirit, she heard a voice below.

*"Un momentito,"* she heard Angela shout frantically. "Just hang on a little longer. I've got the ladder and I'm trying to place it to your right."

Irene tried to will some feeling into her hands, concentrating on holding out. She heard the ladder scraping against the adobe walls, then Angela yelled again.

"Reach out with your right foot, and you'll be able to touch it."

Irene saw the ladder and moved her foot toward it. Making firm contact with the rung, she reached out and grabbed onto its sides, securing her balance. The sense of relief was so great that for a second or two she could scarcely move. Tears ran down her face, but she quickly wiped them away.

"The ladder is as steady as I can make it. But stay right there until I can get one of the workmen to hold it for you. Don't move, okay?"

It was an easy request to accede to. At the moment her knees felt as if they were made of rubber. She took a deep breath, leaned into the ladder, and tried not to think.

Several moments later, she heard workmen approaching. Peering down, she saw the top of several hard hats. Though their voices were hushed, she could hear bits and pieces of conversation, and knew they were convinced she'd been careless.

Irene climbed down gingerly. As she turned to look at the others, she tried to project an air of authority, hoping to stem any further comments. The eyes that looked back at her held a myriad of responses, but none favorable.

Cobb sneered, then chuckled softly. "I've always known women shouldn't be allowed on a construction site. They're magnets for trouble."

Irene suspected that he'd simply voiced the same opinion held by the others in a half-circle around the ladder. Before she could speak, one of the women workers, a tall, lanky redhead, pushed her way forward.

"Dumb-ass comments like that could get you slapped with a lawsuit," she said, her voice sharp with anger. "I'm sick and tired of putting up with your put-downs and sexist crap. You may think they're funny, but I don't think the Equal Employment Opportunity Commission will agree."

"Oh, for cripes sake, Cora. It's just a joke. You'd think it was funny too if you had a sense of humor."

"Keep on hassling me. I promise you'll be explaining it in court."

"All right, already. You made your point. I'm sorry if I've offended your delicate sensibilities," Cobb mocked.

Irene turned her back on the exchange and examined the ladder carefully. Maybe one of the small metal feet had worked loose or was defective. She crouched by the bottom of the ladder and studied the two leveling braces carefully. The metal feet were not damaged in any way, and neither were the uprights. The soil beneath the ladder was firm enough not to sink on one side, so it couldn't have affected the ladder's stability. There seemed to be no logical explanation for what had happened.

Angela's dark eyes glowed against the pallor of her face. "What on earth happened?"

Cora came forward and stood just behind her. "Didn't you check the ladder and make sure it wouldn't slip before you started climbing?" she asked in a quiet voice.

"It was secure when I went up. I can't explain what happened." She glanced over and saw the wry smile on Cobb's face. "I've been around construction sites too long to be careless."

"Whatever you say," Cobb shrugged. "But ladders don't move by themselves."

"No kidding," she replied acerbically. Refusing to acknowledge his skepticism with any further comment, she strode off.

Irene walked upstairs to her room and sat on the

edge of the bed, trying to compose herself before having to face the others again. When she went back outside, she'd have to be prepared to project impalpable confidence and professionalism. This job was too important to allow anything to undermine her. Though the incident had rattled her more than she dared show anyone, she was determined to set it aside and go on.

Twenty minutes later, feeling in control of herself again, she walked back outside. She continued her rounds, taking in the exterior structure with a practiced, methodical eye. She'd just turned the corner and was heading toward the back of the house when she saw two figures partially hidden behind a stand of junipers.

Curious, she edged closer, trying to figure out what was going on. She approached from the side, something telling her that she should proceed with caution. As one of the men stepped to his right, the shadows that had hidden his face disappeared. She saw Cobb clearly, but from where she stood, she still couldn't see who he was talking to. The conversation was animated. The sweeping gestures Cobb made with his hands made her suspect he was arguing with someone, but she couldn't be sure.

She started forward again when the men parted, each leaving in a different direction. As Cobb's companion turned away, she caught a brief glimpse of his face. For a moment, she could have sworn it was Baldridge, the architect she'd aced out of a job, but that seemed unlikely. He'd have no reason to hang around here. Lost in thought, she started back to the house.

She was a few yards away from the entrance when Elena stepped out from the shade of a tall juniper. She'd been well hidden and the unexpected appearance made Irene jump back with a start. "You just scared ten years off my life!" she managed, one hand over her heart.

Elena's expression was contrite. "I'm sorry. I didn't want to bother anyone, but I wanted to watch."

Irene forced a thin smile. "Are you curious about what we're doing to your home?"

Elena nodded. "But I won't get in anyone's way," she assured. "I'll stay back and they won't even know I'm here."

"I'm sure you will," she replied, aware that Elena's uneasiness around strangers would ensure that. "But it's okay to be curious, you know."

"Angela says I shouldn't come out here because the men will be distracted from their work."

Irene started to reply when Raul came out of the house. "Angela is right, Elena. If you want to look around, then ask Irene, or myself. We'll be glad to show you what's being done."

"Are they going to tear down the balcony? It used to be real pretty."

"No," Raul answered. "By the time they finish with it, you'll be able to go out there like you used to, and watch the sunset."

"I'm glad. I liked doing that. Can I put some of my plants out there in the summer?"

"Sure. You can do whatever you want after it's made safe."

Elena smiled. "Good. Then that's all right."

As she started back toward the house, Raul glanced at Irene. "Can I see you in my study? There's something I'd like to go over with you."

"Sure." She fell into step beside him, wondering about the abruptness in his manner.

A few minutes later, she took a chair across from his desk and waited.

Raul leaned back in his chair, his eyes on hers. "I

don't want my sister outside unescorted when the men are there."

Irene blinked. "She'll be okay. There are a lot of people around."

"No," he repeated flatly. "If you see her out alone again, please make sure she gets back inside."

"I know you're just being protective of her, but . . ."

"You mean overprotective," he countered abruptly.

"Well, you do seem to lean in that direction," she said, struggling for some diplomacy.

"Elena is very sensitive. An unguarded comment can hurt her more deeply than you can imagine. Also, let's face it. It can be physically dangerous out in a work site, particularly for someone like her. There are hazards she could miss altogether."

Irene took a deep breath. Raul's mind was already made up, but she hated the thought of having Elena cooped up like a bird in a gilded cage. "Elena would be perfectly safe as long as she stayed out of the way. And I doubt anyone would say something cruel or nasty to her. Most of these men have families of their own—and they also value their jobs."

"Then you're personally vouching for her safety?" he challenged, his glare cold.

"Well, no, but . . ."

"Then please just do as I ask. I'll be gone the rest of today, and possibly tomorrow, depending on how things go. I have to go to Taos on business. I don't want to have to worry about my sister's safety while I'm gone."

"Your orders are very clear," she replied softly. His imperious tone rankled her, but it was useless to argue. It wasn't any of her business anyway.

Just when she thought she was getting to like Raul, he pulled his commandant-of-the-hacienda routine. But she wasn't going to say a word, even though he needed a few. Biting her tongue, she gave him a curt nod and went to her office.

As usual, her work soothed her until all other concerns vanished, relegated to a hidden corner of her mind. It was nearly three in the afternoon when she saved her drafting files on the laptop computer and left her desk.

Irene put on her yellow hard hat and went directly outside, eager to evaluate the work being done on the second-floor exterior. The hand-carved, deeply stained pine balcony showcased the Southwest style that *Casa de Encanto* had once exemplified. Three different spindle designs combined to give the impression of chapel railings bordering the *balcón*. But the wood had deteriorated so much that it was a risk to even step out to enjoy the view of the Sangre de Cristo Mountains. Everything including the elaborate carved door that led out from the master bedroom would have to undergo repair. But the first order of business was making sure the balcony was secure enough to withstand the weight of the artisans.

As she stood there, a tall crane slowly pivoted, carrying its suspended load of heavy spruce braces that would reinforce the balcony deck. Irene watched it arc around, then slowly come to a halt, its load swaying gently overhead near the balcony. A sturdy metal scaffolding beneath the balcony ensured it couldn't collapse.

A workman came out onto the balcony and shouted instructions to the others below. Soon the crane's engine stopped, and the operator stepped down from the cab. He wouldn't be needed again for a while, since the carpenters would take the wood straight from the suspended load.

"Hard hat!" Irene yelled at the operator, who reluctantly placed the yellow protective gear on his head again. Irene hated to wear the things herself, but it was a matter of safety, particularly around a crane.

She stepped forward and looked up at the balcony. From her vantage point, it appeared the lumber was beyond the safe reach of those who would be retrieving it.

She started to say something when she heard a creak, then the boom of the crane lurched. Suddenly the lumber above began to slide, spilling from its heavy rope harness. Massive beams tumbled to the ground, striking each other as they hit and bouncing wildly. Everyone scattered.

Irene reacted in a flash, diving toward the Caterpillar treads of the crane and losing her headgear in the process. She scurried beneath the monster vehicle just as three massive beams came to rest where she'd been standing.

After the thunder stopped and the dust began to settle, she heard the sound of men running and loud voices raised in alarm. Her heart had lodged in her throat, pounding at a frantic pace. She took several deep breaths, her hands clasped over her face protectively as she crouched by one of the wide steel treads.

"Hey, are you okay?" Serna shouted, peering in on his hands and knees from the back of the crane.

Irene crawled out from under the machine. "I'm in one piece," she joked, her voice too shaky to pass as bravado.

"That was really close. The way those timbers bounced, I thought for sure one was going to nail you!" Offering a hand, he helped her to her feet.

As she dusted herself off, she noticed her hard hat beneath a beam. It was shattered like an eggshell. "I want to talk to the crane operator!"

"That's Ed Reyes," Serna said as a Hispanic man in his mid-twenties came rushing up.

"You saw me get down," Reyes said. "I wasn't even in there when it happened. Either someone released the lever by mistake or it slipped on its own. It sure as hell wasn't me!"

"Show me the controls!" She climbed up into the crane with him and sat in the operator's seat. After a few minutes, she still had no real answers. The lever might have slipped, there was no way to prove it. All that was irrefutable was that the lever was in the release position.

Serna watched her as she got back down to the ground, his eyes narrowed with speculation. "Look, I know Ed. He's real careful."

"I've worked with this crew for three years," Laura, one of the women, added, "and I agree. These guys are not easy to get along with sometimes, but they're good at what they do. Maybe it was the man who's been hanging around since yesterday."

Irene turned toward the small brunette. "What guy? I wasn't aware we had any unauthorized people on this work site," she said, annoyed this hadn't been brought to her attention.

Laura shrugged. "At first I figured he was a neighbor or one of the household staff, but I don't think so anymore. I've never actually seen him near the house itself."

"I know who you're talking about," Pablo said. "I thought he was the boyfriend of one of the women here." He paused, glancing at Laura skeptically. "You had anybody coming around?"

"Go to hell, Pablo. We're here to do a job and that's it," Laura said, glaring at him.

"When did you see the man last?" Irene insisted, bringing them back to the topic at hand.

Laura took off her hard hat and tousled her hair with the free hand. "It was this morning, I think. He was standing right about there," she said, pointing past the trailers. "He wasn't doing anything, just watching."

Irene glanced around. "Do you see him anywhere now?"

Laura took a look. "No, and he's hard to miss. He's tall, middle-aged, and has reddish-brown hair. He's average-looking, and definitely not someone I'd feel threatened around."

Irene mulled over the description. That certainly ruled out Baldridge. For one brief moment she'd wondered if perhaps *he* was connected in some way. Having a total stranger hanging around, however, no matter how harmless Laura thought him to be, wasn't something she was comfortable with. If he wasn't part of the household staff, and she hadn't seen anyone around the house who fit that description, then he had no business being here. Or did he? She'd have to make a point of finding out if he was a neighbor or family friend.

As she returned to her office, her mind drifted back to the shadow she'd seen in the hallway outside her bedroom. Perhaps she was finally starting to find some answers, though at the moment, that only heightened her unease. She knew that it would be relatively easy for someone to use the chaos generated by the construction to sneak into the house during the day and hide. The unoccupied rooms and the organized disorder of the ongoing work would allow him to bide his time and create as much mischief as he wanted later.

Inside her office, Irene leaned back in her chair and stared out at the adjacent enclosed courtyard. Her office, located toward the back of the hacienda, gave her quite a bit of privacy, though the house itself was always filled with people. Slowly and with meticulous precision, she mapped out a strategy. If her hunch was right, her best chance was to catch the intruder when he least expected it. As one of the workmen strode past her open doorway carrying a box of tools, an idea formed in her mind.

She randomly did inspections of the work being done outside and in, but until now she hadn't thought to check rooms in the house currently being used for storage. There'd be little danger. With a dozen men and women around, all she'd have to do is cry out. Yet, despite the logic of that argument, she was reluctant to go. If she discovered someone hiding, she'd be facing an adversary who'd already proven he was willing to harm her.

Grabbing a letter opener from the desk drawer and slipping it into her jacket pocket just in case, she started down the hall.

**9**

**I**RENE SLIPPED INSIDE each of the unoccupied rooms noiselessly, determined to mask her approach, but always leaving the door open in case of trouble. She was nearly finished with the ground floor when she heard a strange sound coming from the last door to her left. The sewing room next to the staircase was being used to store rugs moved in from rooms cleared for restoration work.

For several seconds she stood next to the closed door, listening. The sound was familiar and rhythmic. She smiled, recognizing it at last. Someone was snoring.

Irene turned the knob slowly and furtively. The lock mechanism cooperated, clicking open almost inaudibly. She paused and breathed a silent sigh of relief when the snoring continued uninterrupted. Opening the door just a crack, she peered in.

At first, all she could see was a man's back. He was

lying on a makeshift bed made out of drop cloths spread over a partially unrolled rug. She moved one step further into the room, wanting a clearer look, and immediately saw that it wasn't their redheaded intruder. This man's hair was the color of obsidian, with a trace of gray at the sides.

His breathing remained even, so summoning up her courage, she tiptoed further into the room. Much closer now, she was able to confirm the identity of the prone figure. Carlos, the man involved in more than one confrontation already, was fast asleep.

She'd never had much patience with lazy people. She considered waking him up with a good swift kick, but then decided against it. The lesson he would learn might be more effective if he never knew exactly who'd found him out. That would give him reason to worry. Cobb's way of dealing with those who shirked their work was a very loud public warning, then if the situation wasn't rectified, they were fired without hope of appeal.

Irene picked up his boots and left the room. She strode across the grounds to Cobb's trailer, put the boots by his door, then returned to the sewing room. Peering through the tiny crack in the door, she banged loudly on the wood frame. She saw Carlos bolt upward to his feet and reach for his boots. Not finding them, he crouched down on the floor, searching.

Stifling a laugh, Irene slipped quickly down the corridor and waited. When she heard Carlos emerge a few minutes later, she rounded the corner and feigned surprise at seeing him. "Are you guys starting to work on this section already? I don't think it's on my schedule."

Carlos gave her a startled look. "No, um, I was just looking for my tool belt. I helped move the rugs into this room, and I thought maybe I'd set it down in there," he muttered, watching her carefully.

Irene glanced down and looked back up. "And your shoes too?"

"The guys are just playing a joke," he muttered.

She raised an eyebrow. "Well, whatever's going on, you better get back to work. I've heard that Cobb takes a dim view of wasted time."

She strode past him and headed around the corridor for the front stairs, satisfied with the results. That would take care of the problem. She'd avoided a direct confrontation with Cobb or one of his men, yet still managed to get the point across. Keeping the peace whenever possible seemed a much better tactic.

Irene was approaching Raul's study when his door opened and he came out into the hall. "Well, hello," she greeted. "I wasn't aware you were back from Taos."

"My business finished early. I got in about twenty minutes ago. If you have a minute, will you come into my office? I understand quite a bit happened around here while I was gone."

Irene forced herself not to cringe. She could just imagine the version he'd heard. Cobb would have made sure she'd come out in the worst possible light.

She went inside and sat down. "I'm not sure what you've been told, but we're still maintaining our deadline on the project," she assured, "despite some mishaps." She explained those, keeping her narrative brief.

His gaze made her uncomfortable. His eyes seemed to go right through her, searching, reaching for the truth of her thoughts. "There is one question you could answer for me that would help," she added, giving him the description of the redheaded man. "Do you know who he might be?"

"We haven't had any friends dropping by, and our nearest neighbor is almost eight miles away." He shrugged. "Pablo could be right with his boyfriend theory, even though the women might deny it. But his hair color isn't that much of a clue. It could fit dozens of men in the Taos area."

"I really don't like the idea of a stranger hanging around, particularly in view of the accidents."

"I'll discuss this with Cobb and make sure everyone keeps a lookout. But to be honest, I'm certain the accidents are just that, accidents. No one would try to harm you while you're here at *Casa de Encanto,*" he said, crossing his arms proudly.

She understood his pride. In that, they were soulmates, both fiercely protective of the legacies handed down to them through time. Her tribe was at the heart of hers; *Casa de Encanto* at the root of his.

"Baldridge was here on the property, I believe, speaking to Cobb," she continued. "Have you consulted another architect?"

"No, of course not. I wouldn't do that behind your back." He leaned forward, curious. "Have you spoken with Cobb about it?"

"Not yet. I wanted to mention it to you first just in case there was something you'd forgotten to tell me." She glanced out the window. "Baldridge *really* needed this job . . ." She let the sentence trail, her thoughts wandering far ahead of her words.

"Yes, I've heard the rumors. You think he might be conspiring with John to force you off the project?" His voice hardened. "That would explain the crane and the problem with the ladder, wouldn't it?" he observed.

Irene saw the anger that flashed in his eyes. "I have no evidence to support that theory," she added quickly.

"Let's go see what we can find out," he said, standing up. "If anyone's trying to intimidate or cause you injury while you're in my home, I want to know about it. I won't tolerate that, no matter what the reasons." He strode to the door, his shoulders rigid and set, then waited for her to pass. "There's also the issue of negligence. The crane operator should have been at his post."

"I've already spoken to him . . ."

Raul held up a hand. "If this only pertained to construction, I wouldn't interfere with your authority. But to me, it's a matter of honor that as long as you're in this home you remain completely safe. Can you understand that?"

Irene exhaled softly. "Yes, I do," she said. "I'd feel the same way about a guest at the pueblo."

"I thought you might," he added. "Let's go talk to Cobb."

They went outside together and found Cobb directing the work being done on the balcony. His eyes were as hard as flint as they fastened on Irene, but his expression became more congenial as he noticed Raul. "Good to see you out here," he said to Raul. "The work's progressing nicely, don't you think?"

Raul's stance before Cobb was that of a man prepared for a confrontation. "There have been some accidents, and you're the contractor. What's going on?"

"I accept responsibility for my crane operator, but accidents do happen on a work site," Cobb said calmly. "Other events are a result of carelessness, like the incident with the ladder. Did Pobikan tell you about that?"

Raul glanced at her, then back at Cobb. "I've heard."

"I checked the ladder before I went up," Irene insisted, keeping her voice free of anger. "I'm not completely sure that *was* an accident. The man people have seen hanging around here could be creating problems."

Cobb rolled his eyes. "He's probably just been boinking one of the women."

"You'll speak to the ladies at my house with more respect than that," Raul said in a voice that was deadly quiet.

Cobb backed up a step. "No disrespect intended. I was only trying to point out that *some* of these accidents were the results of poor planning and could have been prevented. I don't think we should necessarily be looking for a scapegoat to blame everything on."

"I understand that you met with Darryl Baldridge earlier," Raul said, abruptly shifting the topic.

Cobb hesitated a fraction of a second. He glanced at Irene, then back at Raul. "You've been misinformed. I've been here practically all the time, and the only meetings I've had have been with the crew. I can't think of any of them who even vaguely resemble Baldridge . . ." He glanced at Irene, his eyes reptilian-cold.

Raul dismissed Cobb's assertion with a wave of a hand that did not reveal whether or not he believed him. "There's also the matter of the crane losing its load. That's clearly something that falls under your jurisdiction." Raul's voice never rose, staying at the same fierce but controlled intensity. "I won't accept any more of those mishaps, is that clear?"

"I'll do what I can, but it's impossible to guarantee that," Cobb shot back. "Everyone involved in construction knows there are risks involved in what we do."

"Some seem to be in greater risk than others," Raul answered.

"That's Pobikan's fault. I won't take responsibility for her."

Irene's body began to shake with anger. Outrage

slammed through her and the reins that had kept her temper in check snapped. She was about to tell John Cobb precisely what she thought, but Raul's response was a breath faster than hers.

He took a step toward Cobb, until only inches stood between them. "If anything happens to her or anyone else due to faulty construction equipment or unsafe practices, I'll get your contractor's license pulled. You'll never work in *this* state again."

Cobb held his ground. "Don't threaten me, Mr. Mendoza. I can't guarantee her safety."

"You're in charge of your men and responsible for their actions. That means their mistakes are yours." His body grew tense and hard, and his voice dropped an octave. "Irene Pobikan is staying at my home, and is under my protection. Make that abundantly clear to your men. I won't tolerate any more mishaps."

His eyes slowly swept over the workers who had paused to witness the confrontation. "You've all heard me. I won't repeat myself."

As Raul pivoted and started toward the house, the men stepped back, opening a path for him.

Irene, stunned by the encounter, stared after him. Raul's temper, up to now shielded by a veneer of civility, had erupted with a vengeance.

Cobb deliberately crowded her. "You started this, trying to cover up for your own incompetence. I won't forget the trouble you've caused for me today, lady. Bank on it."

She stared at him coldly, torn between venting her anger despite the presence of the crew and maintaining her professionalism. "All I told him was the truth. The accidents happened," she clipped.

"You want the boss man's sympathy, is that it? Hoping to make things easier on yourself by generating trouble for the rest of us?"

Anger boiled inside her and she took several deep breaths. She would not let him get to her. It would give him too much satisfaction. "That's not true and you know it. It wouldn't hurt, however, if you kept a closer watch on the construction and your crew," she answered, her voice as hard as stone.

"So *that's* it," he muttered, his eyes narrowing with suspicion. "You're trying to force me aside so you can take over and have complete control. Well, forget it. I'll quit and take my men with me before I relinquish authority to you."

"You have authority, but you're not using the responsibility that goes with it. Keep better track of your men, and don't allow unauthorized personnel to hang around. And while you're at it, make sure your men don't leave equipment unattended while they're in use. Under the circumstances, that's asking for trouble, and neither of us can afford that here."

Not giving him a chance to respond, she turned and walked toward the house. As she stepped through the entrance, Raul came out of the sitting room. "Can you come in here for a minute? I'd like to speak with you."

"Sure."

Raul stood by the window and looked out at the work in progress. "Without any real evidence of wrongdoing, there's nothing more I can do," he said.

"It's already more than I ever expected."

As he turned around, his gaze was icy. "I won't have this home dishonored, particularly by innuendo. I truly believe that what's happened is simply bad luck aided by carelessness. Unfortunately you've been the victim, and that's affected your perception. I've done my best to help you, but now you'll have to do your part. You must not get complacent in the area of safety. Double-check everything, like the ladders, before you use them."

Is that what he thought? Had his pride convinced him that the danger was more imagined than real? Without proof, there was little else she could say.

"You're safe in *Casa de Encanto*," he continued, "but you must remain alert and professional."

Resentment made her throat and chest constrict, and for a minute she could scarcely breathe. She hadn't been anything if not professional, even if he was too dim to see it. "My job performance here is, and will continue to be, above question."

As she stepped out of the room, she saw Cobb standing less than ten feet away. His grin told her he'd already assessed the tone, if not content, of the conversation she'd just had with Raul.

"You didn't exactly win that round, did you? Now he's aggravated with you for making it look like there's a problem here in his precious home. Just think, he might get a bellyful of you pretty soon and decide to protect the reputation of the hacienda by replacing you."

"I wouldn't lose any sleep hoping for that," she snapped.

By the time Irene reached her office her palms were sweating. She was barely behind her desk when Gene strolled inside, knocking on the door frame as he entered. "Big brother's on the warpath. You'd be better off without him fighting your battles for you."

"That was never my intent," she said. "He took this on himself."

Gene shrugged. "This house means the world to him. I think he loves it more than his own family. It's all tied to his concept of duty, honor, and tradition. He won't let anything challenge that. Even if you were telling the truth . . ."

"I always do," she interrupted.

He raised an eyebrow. "Then maybe it's time for

you to learn that there are times when the truth shouldn't be spoken. Voicing it doesn't always solve problems, it oftentimes creates them."

He held her eyes for a long moment, then turned and left the room.

The next several days passed slowly. The weather had cooled, making work with adobe more difficult. Any bricks that hadn't been sufficiently cured would disintegrate in freezing or rainy weather. Today's cold drizzle was doing nothing to improve her bleak mood. To make matters even worse, Raul seemed determined to avoid being around her, so perhaps Gene's words had held true. She'd alienated him by making him face possibilities he wasn't ready to acknowledge.

Having just finished a quick inventory of building supplies, she traversed the grounds at a hurried pace. She'd worn her only blazer over a blue wool turtleneck, and the freezing moisture was penetrating. She was shuddering as she stepped inside the main entrance to the house.

At least it was warmer in here, despite the fact that the furnace had acted up. Raul had asked one of the workmen to take a look at it, but until the part required to fix it was delivered from Albuquerque, the only sources of heat were the fireplaces and a few portable electric heaters around the house.

She walked directly to her office, eager to tackle other jobs that needed her attention. The building inspector had been unavailable, and she needed to work out a schedule with him so inspections wouldn't be delayed, costing construction time. There were also some minor design modifications that would be needed in the library, and would require additional lists of materials and new work schedules.

She went to the drafting table and began to sketch.

The temperature in her office was in the fifties, and after a short time her fingers began to ache from the cold. Irene rubbed her hands together briskly trying to warm them.

As she glanced around the room, searching for her gloves or a sweater, she saw the tiny electric heater Angela had left in one corner. It was plugged in, but it obviously wasn't working, though the dial was in the on position.

Irene crouched by it, trying to figure out what was wrong. She checked the cord leading to the outlet and realized that the plug was almost out of the socket. Glad to see that it was a simple matter, she started to push it back in.

As her fingers closed in around it, an agonizing pain shot up her arm, invading her body. She suddenly flew backward across the room like she'd been shoved by an invisible giant.

For a moment her breath wouldn't come as stars popped and flashed in front of her eyes. Irene lay still, gasping for air, though her chest ached with each breath. As a thin curl of acrid smoke reached her nostrils, she sat up slowly, trying to organize her jumbled thoughts. She grew aware of a burning sensation in her hand that pulsed in sync with her heart. Before she could react, however, she heard a soft cry behind her. Irene turned her head, squinting through tear-filled eyes.

"Stay right there, Señorita Irene," she heard Angela say.

Irene shook her head. "I'm okay. I went to plug in the cord . . ."

Gene ran into the room next. "What the hell happened? The lights flickered, then I heard this crash . . ." He turned toward the two toppled chairs and the small drafting table overturned on the floor. "Did you fall or something?"

"Or something," Irene managed shakily, staring at the angry red skin on her thumb and fingers. She stood up slowly, her head pounding.

"Are you sure you should be moving around?" Angela rushed to her side to steady her. "Maybe we should get a doctor."

"I'm okay."

"What happened?" Gene asked.

"I went to push the plug more firmly into the socket, and I ended up getting one whale of a shock." She knelt beside the cord now lying on the floor and studied it. "Look at this," she said, turning the cord to reveal an area where the insulation had been worn away. "I might as well have touched live wires!"

Gene glanced down, also noticing scorch marks on the wall outlet. "You *were* touching live wires." He turned to Angela. "Did you check those old heaters when you placed them around the house?"

Angela's face grew pale. "I thought I had. And I'm sure I'd have noticed a frayed cord!" Angela wrung her hands, tears building in her eyes. "Mr. Gene, I don't know how this could have happened."

"It's okay, Angela," Irene soothed. "It was my own fault for not checking it more closely."

"No, I'm afraid I'm to blame," Angela said sadly. "I should have plugged it in myself when I brought it here. Then I would have realized something wasn't right before anyone turned it on."

Irene's eyes narrowed. "Wait a minute. You didn't plug it in?"

Angela hesitated. "No one was in the room, so I just left the heater near the wall. I figured you'd place it wherever you wanted it later." Angela's hand went to her chest. "But didn't you say the connection was loose?"

"Yes, I did," Irene muttered, staring at the heater.

"Maybe someone started to plug it in, noticed the bad cord, and went to get some electrical tape," Gene said slowly. "You just beat them to the punch."

"Lucky me," Irene replied cynically.

"I'll go get something for your hand," Angela said, glancing down at the redness that crossed Irene's palm and fingers. "It doesn't look as bad as it might have been, but I'm sure it's very painful."

"It is. I'd appreciate some salve, and a couple of aspirins, if you have any."

As Angela left the room, Irene picked up the damaged heater with her uninjured hand and placed it on top of her desk. "I'm going to have one of the electricians take a look at this."

"I'd say the problem is fairly obvious," Gene commented.

"Yes, but he might have some ideas how it was damaged." She met Gene's eyes and held them.

"Don't you think if someone was trying to hurt you, they would have done more than try to give you a mild electric shock?" Gene pointed out.

"Mild to you, maybe," she shot back. "If this was done on purpose, it brings up some interesting possibilities, don't you think?"

Gene's eyes narrowed. "Before you start searching for answers, make sure that you can live with whatever you find out."

"At this point, I'd say I have a better chance of living with what I find out than staying alive if I don't find answers," she observed wryly.

"You might have a point," he said, and excused himself as Angela returned with the salve, some aspirins, and water.

Irene swallowed back the tablets. "Thanks."

Angela opened the tube containing the salve. "You'll heal quickly with this ointment. It's made with aloe vera."

Irene tried not to wince as Angela's fingers smoothed the cream over the burn. But when Angela tried to place gauze around the burn, Irene drew away gently. "No, let's not wrap it up. It'll be better if there's nothing rubbing against it. The salve will keep the air from hitting it and that's what makes it burn."

Angela placed the tube and gauze down on the chair, then started to pick up the overturned desk and chairs. "If there's anything you need, just call me. You shouldn't use that hand much, at least for a few days."

"Good thing I have two," she said with a ghost of a smile. "I think I'll track down the head electrician."

"I saw him working with some others in the sitting room when I went to the kitchen for the salve."

"Thanks." Irene tucked the small heater beneath one arm and strode down the hall. Deep down she knew this hadn't been an accident, but she wouldn't approach Raul until she had some substantial evidence to show him.

Poking her head in the doorway of the sitting room, she found the man she was looking for. He was standing halfway up on a small Fiberglas ladder, rewiring a light fixture. "Bobby," she called to the electrician, a member of her tribe. "Can you give me a minute?"

"Sure." His long salt-and-pepper hair was braided into a ponytail and passed out the back of his faded Washington Redskins cap. His tool belt, laden with screwdrivers and wire cutters, dangled precariously from his jeans. Bobby climbed down and turned to greet her. "What can I do for you?"

She set the small heater on top of the ladder. "Tell me what you can about the damage to this."

He inspected the cord at the end and whistled softly. "Don't even think of plugging this in," he said, then noticed her hand. "Uh-oh. Looks like you already tried that."

"Yeah." She looked down at her burns and shrugged. "How did you guess?"

"I remembered the lights flickering a while ago. That must have been you. You're lucky, these kinds of heaters draw quite a bit of current." He studied the cord carefully. "This is unusual. I've worked on stuff like this all my life, but I've never seen a cord worn away like this before. It's almost as if someone scraped away the insulation with a knife. Look." He held it out toward her. "See how there are little scrape marks on the vinyl? If it had been wear and tear, the rest of the wire would show some of that too. But that's in excellent condition, not cracked or worn anywhere."

"Are you saying that this was deliberate?"

"Well, I don't know. I was thinking that someone might have wanted to change the plug, started the job, and then decided against it. People often lose their nerve around electrical equipment."

"But why change the plug?"

"Part of it is cracked, here on the side, see it? Like someone stepped on it hard, or dropped something heavy on it."

Of course that could have easily been done on purpose. She was beginning to see just how clever her adversary was. Everything that had happened to her could also be explained away as bad luck or coincidence. But too many things had happened since her arrival for them to be unrelated.

Bobby attached the plug with the help of a screwdriver, wrapped several lengths of electric tape tightly around the cord, then tore the end of the tape from the roll with his teeth. "This'll be safe to use for now, but if you'll let me hang on to it, I'll have it fixed properly as soon as possible." He pressed the end of the tape tightly around the cord.

"Thanks, Bobby. I'd really appreciate that."

A few hours later Bobby presented her with the repaired heater, and she used it to warm her office while she finished the paperwork she'd set aside earlier. Slowly the aroma of freshly made *empanadas* wound its way into her office. Unable to resist the temptation, she followed her nose to the kitchen.

Angela saw her appear in the doorway and smiled. "People from all over this house drop by when I make my *empanadas*," she said. "You just wait. Mr. Raul will come down, and Mr. Gene too," she added. "I'm a very good cook. It's the one thing I do that no one has ever found fault with."

"Well, I've been caught. That's exactly why I'm here," Irene admitted sheepishly. "I couldn't resist."

Angela extended a plate filled with the pastries. "Here you go, help yourself. I don't normally cook a formal dinner on Wednesdays, but I make snacks to take the place of a regular meal."

As Irene reached for one, Elena entered the room. She smiled at Angela, then noticed Irene, who was holding her injured hand against herself. "What happened to you?" Elena asked.

"It's nothing. I just got a small burn."

"How?" she insisted. "On one of the plumber's torches? I've seen them. They look real hot."

Irene hesitated. She didn't want to frighten Elena, but she'd never been much good at lying. "No. The cord on the little electric heater was damaged. I got careless and plugged it in without checking first."

Elena's eyes grew wide. "Your hand's so red."

"Well, it just happened this afternoon, but it feels

much better now. And as you can see," she joked, holding up an *empanada* with her good hand, "it hasn't exactly affected my appetite."

Elena took one of the *empanadas* from the plate. "Things are going wrong. It didn't used to be that way before you and the work people came." She shook her head. "I understand my plants. It's people that make problems. They're always hurting each other, whether they mean to or not."

"You don't have anything to worry about, Elena. No one's going to hurt you. You bring too much happiness to the people here," Irene said gently.

Elena picked up more *empanadas*, put them on a plate, then began walking back to her room. "You're wrong."

It was the simplicity and matter-of-fact tone that captured her attention and compelled Irene to accompany Elena down the hall. "Why do you say that?"

"I've heard things . . ." Elena hesitated. "Someone," she corrected.

"If you tell me what has scared you, maybe I can help," Irene insisted. She was beginning to grow very concerned, but didn't dare convey that to Elena. It was all she could do to keep herself from becoming impatient and demanding a faster reply.

"At night, when the house is quiet, I've heard someone walking around. There's barely any noise at all, but someone's there. Sometimes the person stops outside my room, then keeps walking. Other times they just walk." She glanced at Irene. "I got really scared a few nights ago. I thought whoever it was might try to come in my room. Now I've started locking my door at night. It helps me be less scared."

"If it makes you feel better, then you're doing the right thing," Irene said flatly.

"You believe me, don't you? You don't think it's just dreams?" Elena's eyes widened in an innocent plea for trust.

"I've heard someone walking around too, Elena, but I don't necessarily think it's anything to worry about."

"Okay. Then I won't think about it anymore." She held out her plate of *empanadas*. "I took too many. They say gluttony is a sin. Will you share them so God doesn't get mad at me?"

Irene smiled, unable to help herself. "I don't think God will ever be mad at you, Elena, but I'll accept your offer. These are very good."

Elena smiled brightly. "I'm going to watch a garden show I have on tape, then work with my plants. I'll see you tomorrow."

Irene started back to her room, intending to spend a quiet evening reading. As she walked down the hall, she felt her skin prickle and suddenly a shiver ran up her spine. The feeling that someone was watching her spread through her with an intensity that wouldn't be argued away. She stopped and glanced around, but there were no shadows or stirrings in the silent, dimly lit corridor.

She couldn't see anyone, but she could still *feel* someone there. Her heart pounding, she bolted straight to her room and latched her door shut. Irene leaned against the door, her pulse racing like a runaway train, her breathing coming in shallow gasps. She was safe now. Yet the icy fear that had gripped her had pried through her defenses, touching her on a level beyond logic.

As a Tewa, she'd learned to trust her instincts. Just because something couldn't be explained didn't mean it should be discounted. It wasn't superstition, it was the surety that came from knowing that some perceptions went beyond the capabilities of the physical senses. Instinct told her that tonight someone had been watching—and death hadn't been far behind.

# 10

THE FOLLOWING AFTERNOON Irene stood outside watching a crew finish the repairs on the balcony. The flooring had been reinforced and the railings replaced. Now all that remained was applying the wood stain and preservative. She smiled, satisfied that everything looked so much better already. With the other crews working on the adobe walls and the drainage along the foundation, and the electrical work taking place inside, slowly but surely things were taking shape.

Cobb came and stood beside her. "How's your hand? You know, with all the bad luck you've been having maybe you should consider carrying around a rabbit's foot or something."

She looked him squarely in the eyes. "There's something I've been meaning to say to you. We both know that you lied about your secret meeting with Baldridge or whoever that really was," she said coldly. "I don't know what else you've been up to, but I'm not buying the theory that what's been happening to me is a series of unfortunate accidents. If you and your friends have concocted some plan to discredit me or make me lose my nerve, don't waste your energy. It's not going to happen."

"I guess we can now add paranoia to your growing list of personality defects," he added with a shrug.

"I won't be frightened off—no way." On impulse Irene decided to bait him in hopes of learning more from his reaction. "That also means you might as well stop wandering around the corridors at night, lurking by doorways. It doesn't bother me, but you *are* frightening Elena, and I don't think that's what you had in mind."

"That's beyond low, Pobikan. I wouldn't frighten a woman like her; she's got enough problems. But I don't have to answer to you or anyone else for what I do after hours. If you have a problem with someone walking the halls, then go home or to a motel. And for the record, if Elena's scared, my guess is you're the one responsible. No telling what ideas you're putting in her head."

Anger rose and bubbled inside her, coming dangerously close to spewing over the top. "Just the kind of strategy I would expect from a guilty person," she managed through clenched teeth. "Attack, don't defend. Too bad it isn't a bit credible."

As she strode off, she took satisfaction in the knowledge that his face was as bright as piñon coals.

Angela was out in the courtyard, sweeping leaves off the walk with a battered straw broom as Irene approached. "How is your hand?" she asked.

"It doesn't hurt unless I bump the red spots against something. Thanks for asking."

Angela started to speak, then with obvious difficulty

turned back to her sweeping. Noting her reluctance, Irene leaned against the wall and prodded her gently. "Is there something you wanted to tell me?"

Angela stopped sweeping and looked around the courtyard before speaking in a low voice. "I heard a bit of what you told Mr. Cobb and I thought you should know something." She frowned. "I don't want either Miss Elena or you to be frightened, but this is difficult to tell anyone . . ." She stared at the floor and wiped her hands on her apron nervously.

"I give you my word that whatever you say to me won't go any further," Irene assured, curiosity rippling through her.

Angela's lips pursed tightly, then finally she nodded. "If you think that Mr. Cobb has been sneaking around the house late at night trying to frighten you, you might be wrong. Mr. Gene sometimes has, well, problems, and he stays up real late."

The admission was unexpected, but she'd heard others mention Gene's drinking problem. Maybe she'd misjudged Cobb. It was true that Gene had his own reasons for wanting to thwart anything Raul considered important, like the renovations. She'd overheard their argument after Gene had forced her to go to Raul about the substandard adobe bricks. And there was the matter of Reina. She couldn't help but wonder what kind of woman could have created such a rift between brothers. It would be no surprise to find they were working at cross-purposes.

"Thank you, Angela. It's good to have a friend in the household who trusts me."

Angela smiled. "It isn't always easy to work here. Believe me, I understand."

Promising again to keep their conversation private, Irene went back to her office. Angela's revelation opened new avenues of speculation, but there was no time to dwell on them now. Irene took out her site drawings, ready to update the work already completed or in progress. With practiced discipline, she brushed all other concerns from her mind. There was still so much work to do, and the three-month deadline was tight.

Switching to her desktop computer, she retrieved the file containing the detailed report she'd have to mail to her office. Each phase of progress had to be documented for the head of the firm, and supplemental provisions to the project manual submitted. Revised blueprints also had to be turned in for the records, though her bosses had never commented on them. Sometimes she wondered if anyone really looked at what she sent. Her only instructions from the office had been to make sure Raul Mendoza was satisfied. She was deep in thought when the sound of a man shouting off in the distance jolted her concentration.

Irene stood and stepped to the window. The yells seemed to be coming from the dense forest that encircled the hacienda. Several Tewa workers near the drainage ditch dropped their shovels and headed straight into the circle of pines at a run.

Irene pressed the function key on her computer that saved her work, and hurried outside. Cobb and Serna were at the other end of the hacienda working on a portion of the stepped adobe walls that enclosed the private gardens. With the heavy equipment being used to level the ground there, it was doubtful they'd hear what was going on. As she drew closer, the man's shouts became clearer; the naked terror in his voice made her skin prickle.

A fast runner, she sprinted toward the sound, dodging through the undergrowth and pines. A minute later, she arrived breathlessly at a clearing. The Tewa workers were already there looking around, puzzled.

Carlos, the Hispanic worker she'd caught napping before, was clinging grimly to a branch halfway up a tall ponderosa.

"We can't find any tracks around here with all the leaves and needles on the ground," Henry, one of the Tewa workers, said. "Carlos, are you sure it was a mountain lion and not just somebody's Great Dane?"

"I know a dog when I see one, and a mountain lion too. I'm telling you it was here. The biggest damn thing I've ever seen." He had his feet on a branch about ten feet off the ground, uncertain of what move to make next.

The Tewa men glanced at each other, all wearing broad grins. "I think you've been overmedicating on that cough syrup in your hip flask again," Henry joked, and laughter erupted from around the base of the tree.

Carlos shinnied down the tree quickly, almost falling as he hit the ground. "Henry, you've got a big mouth, you know that?" He tried to shove him hard, but the Tewa man sidestepped and Carlos stumbled forward, tripping over a rock and falling to his knees.

As three other Hispanic workers arrived in the clearing, Carlos jumped to his feet, aware of their presence. "You Indians are always ready for trouble when your friends are around. You want to fight now, then go for it. I'll take you on, one at a time."

The Hispanic workers glanced at the Tewa men, instantly regarding them with suspicion. Carlos' words had the desired effect, and the groups looked ready to square off. Irene could feel the tension building and knew a confrontation was imminent.

"Enough, Carlos!" she snapped. "No one's ganging up on you. These guys came to help, just like I did. You were yelling your fool head off."

"I knew you'd be siding with your own people,"

Carlos spat out. "Now that my *hermanos* are here, things will be different."

Most of the workers had arrived by then, and some of the Hispanics began to fan out around the few Tewas, who took back-to-back positions. Irene tried desperately to think of a way to diffuse the situation before it came to blows. "You all heard the yelling," she insisted, moving between the Tewas and Hispanic men. "Carlos was surprised by a mountain lion, and all of you responded. It's good everyone wanted to help. Now it's time to get back to work. No one's been hurt and there's no need to prove anything."

The three women workers came to stand beside her, effectively keeping both groups of men from getting any closer.

"Oh, this is really bright, guys," Janna snapped. At six feet one, her height gave her a commanding presence; most of the men had to look up to make eye contact with her. "You're all going to beat each other's brains out over something Carlos *thinks* happened. Hell! Most of you wouldn't take his word for it if he swore there were trees in the forest."

A few of the men laughed, finally starting to relax a little.

"Hey, Janna, are you saying I'm making this up?" Carlos demanded.

"No, but you might be getting the details a little screwed up," she retorted. "You're not exactly a rocket scientist."

"Come on, Carlos. It's over," Irene insisted in a quiet voice. "You get involved in a fight and you're out of a job. What will that prove?"

"That he's the baddest, ugliest *vato* in the unemployment line," one of the Chicano workers shouted.

"Hey! After I'm dead three years, I'll still be better

looking than you," Carlos shot back, a grin now tugging at the corners of his mouth.

Irene breathed a silent sigh of relief as the men began to walk back toward their work in small groups, joking and jostling each other. "Thanks for the support," she said to the women who'd stood with her.

"It's like we've always known: the best man for the job is usually a woman." Janna laughed.

"It's testosterone," Sheila affirmed. "I think it slows the thought process down to a crawl."

Irene agreed. "It's just one of those mixed-blessing hormones. Has its uses, but most of the time it's highly overrated."

Irene was walking back toward the house when Gene stepped away from the shadows of a tall pine. "I came to see what was going on, then decided to stick around in case you needed a backup," he said. "But you did okay."

She looked at him speculatively. "Are you disappointed or surprised?"

He shrugged, then fell into step beside her. "It would have been nice to have come to your rescue in the nick of time." He paused, then grinned. "You would have owed me one then."

"Well, I guess it all worked out for the best," she answered, deliberately being oblique.

As they approached the entrance doors Raul came out to meet them. "What was all the commotion about?" he asked, looking at Irene.

She explained briefly. "It's settled now, though. There's nothing to worry about."

Raul went back inside with her. "By the way, I haven't forgotten your warning about John's tendency to cut corners, so I've been keeping an eye on the work. But maybe we should start doing daily rounds together whenever possible. I know you do those as a matter of routine, but four eyes are better than two."

"Cobb's not going to put one over on me. I'm looking right over his shoulder and he knows it."

"We're even less likely to miss anything if we team up," he insisted.

Irene considered his words. He wasn't about to take no for an answer, but why the sudden interest? Had he begun to lose faith in her capabilities? As she glanced at Raul, she saw that what was shining in his eyes was more basic and infinitely more simple. It was the look of a man attracted to a woman. Although the knowledge was flattering, there was another possibility that unnerved her. If he'd sensed her attraction to him, it was possible she was seeing a reaction to a message she'd unwittingly sent.

She forced the thought from her mind, knowing that any further speculation along those lines would only lead to more distractions and major trouble. "All right. How do you want to work this? I prefer to avoid a set time every day. It keeps everybody on their toes wondering when I'll be coming around. Should I stop by your office when I'm ready to go?"

"That would be fine, except I could be stuck on a conference call or away. How about if you tell me the day before, and I'll adjust my schedule accordingly." He glanced down at her hand, but didn't comment on it. "And if I miss you, I'll make a point of catching up with you around the grounds."

"Fine. You can plan on nine forty-five tomorrow, then."

Raul watched her walk away. Irene was all smoothness and confidence, yet his Reina had appeared to be much the same when he'd first met her. That sudden flash of his late wife's memory settled over him like a heavy weight, and he struggled against the feeling. It was time to go on with his life. He couldn't hold on to the past forever, nor would he willingly allow memories to prevent him from ever reaching out for happiness again. Irene was his friend now, he felt. Maybe someday it could become more than that.

He started to go upstairs to his office when his brother came out of the sitting room, only yards from where he'd been speaking with Irene.

"The architect interests you, doesn't she?" Gene observed. "I could hear it in your voice. But what can you offer her? More of what you gave Reina? You think all love entails is the ability to be loyal to one woman. You don't even know how to open your heart."

Before Raul could answer, Gene strode past him and walked outside. Raul's fist clenched tightly as a rage black as night stabbed through him. What did his brother know about opening his heart, and then have someone tear it to pieces? Gene had never totally committed himself to anything in his life!

Raul had shared his hopes for the future, his dreams, his strengths and his weaknesses with Reina. He'd made himself vulnerable in front of his woman, allowing her to see into his soul. He'd never done that either before or since. But Reina had discarded his revelations and the effort behind them as useless. She'd never really understood the cost they'd exacted. But perhaps she'd never stopped to think much about him at all. It hadn't been her way.

He went up the stairs, trying to bring his thoughts back under control. It still hurt, even after all this time. He tried to banish the pain from his mind; it was self-indulgent and pointless. Reaching his office, he strode inside and shut the door firmly. A second later, the telephone rang. Grateful for the interruption, he crossed over to his desk. Business. This was a world he understood.

* * *

Gene waited for Cobb to finish talking to the carpenters. He wouldn't be edged out of the renovation. John at least respected his connection to the family, though both Raul and Irene had done their best to undermine that.

Cobb approached him after a few minutes. "What's up, boss?"

Gene smiled. "Just checking on things. That last flare-up with the workers, the one Irene and the women squelched, had me a little concerned. I wanted to make sure things were running smoothly." He watched the flicker in John's eyes with satisfaction.

"Serna and I were on the other side of the hacienda inspecting the adobe work on the garden wall, and making sure the land was leveled. From the reports we received it wasn't that big a deal," he shrugged.

"That's not the way I saw it," Gene answered.

"Then I guess you interpreted it differently." He met Gene's gaze. "Now, is there something specific I can do for you?"

Gene rubbed his chin pensively, his eyes locked on the workers installing library windows. "She's making us both look bad, you realize that. I'll get over it, but in your profession, news carries. How many jobs have you had since that last project you worked on with her?"

"That's my business."

"I want you to keep something in mind. I'm not willing to discredit her unfairly, but if something comes up, you'll find me a good listener. Everyone makes mistakes, John, even Irene Pobikan."

Cobb nodded slowly. The idea appealed to him, particularly since that's exactly what *she'd* done to him. Maybe his turn had finally come. "I have my eye on her. She's not the only one keeping a close watch."

He paused. "I hear she's had trouble sleeping. Claims that someone's prowling the hall at night. If she gets tired enough, she'll start screwing up. I'll make sure your family is made aware when it happens. It's my duty, after all." He gave Gene a mirthless smile.

"Good."

"What exactly are you working for or against, Mendoza? I can't quite figure you out."

"You don't have to. My loyalties are my own."

Cobb watched him go back into the house. From the smell of tequila on his breath, it wasn't hard to tell Mendoza had already had several drinks. His steps weren't as steady as they should be either, though he covered well.

Cobb ran a hand through his hair. This family was one screwed-up lot. If there was ever proof that money couldn't buy happiness, the Mendozas were it. Not that being poor was a ticket to the perfect family; God knows, his wasn't. His father had drunk himself to death before he turned forty and his mother hadn't given a rip about either him or his younger brother. Pauly had made it, though. He'd always been tough and one of those guys who led a charmed life. Everything he touched turned to gold. He had his own business nowadays, a pair of printshops, and was doing very well for himself.

Accepting that his little brother was doing so much better than him piqued his pride. During the past two or three years, Pauly had repeatedly tried to loan him money to start his own construction company. But he hadn't known about the problems Pobikan had created. She'd nearly destroyed him. Working his way back up had been nearly impossible, and his standing in the business was still on shaky ground. But now it was finally payback time. Discrediting her professionally might even end up boosting his own status.

He grinned slowly. Maybe Gene Mendoza would turn out to be something more than just another rich drunk looking to make himself feel important.

Irene picked out a dark blue skirt and a winter-white angora sweater to wear at dinner that evening. Even dress slacks didn't seem to fit in somehow. Though the men wore casual clothes, they always had an expensive, elegant feel. Cobb had quickly attuned himself to the others, and was very careful about his appearance. Several times he'd opted for a traditional western bolo tie with an ornate turquoise clasp. Elena also went out of her way to maintain the decorum Raul preferred. Although she usually wore jeans during the day, she always showed up in a dress for their one meal together.

Slipping the small mountain lion fetish in the pocket of her skirt, she smiled. *Now* she was ready. She'd been carrying it with her constantly. It somehow made facing all the challenges at the hacienda easier.

Irene left her room and walked downstairs trying to revitalize her energy as she went. She was tired and would have preferred going straight to bed. But this was no time to let others know that the pressure of staying constantly alert was starting to wear her down. The accidents so far hadn't caused any major injuries, but there was no guarantee that whoever was behind them wouldn't escalate the pressure, particularly if they sensed weakness. What worried her most was the thought that others like Elena might get caught in the cross fire.

She entered the dining room and realized immediately that everyone else had already arrived. "I hope I haven't kept anyone waiting," she said, glancing at Raul.

"No, not at all."

As Raul led Elena to her seat, Gene offered Irene his arm. "You look as if you've been working very hard."

"True, but long hours aren't so difficult when you enjoy what you're doing."

Gene watched her speculatively. "You're very dedicated."

They were playing cat and mouse, and she knew it. What was rather unnerving was knowing that Raul's attention was riveted on them. "I'll admit I'm a perfectionist when it comes to my work. But that's the way it should be when you care about the project you're working on and your goals."

"*Casa de Encanto* certainly seems like a career boost for you."

"It is," she admitted. "That's why I'm putting every bit of knowledge and expertise I have into it."

"But all the hours, day and night . . ." Gene purred.

For a minute she could have sworn he was about to call her honey or sweetheart. She arched her eyebrows in surprise. The look on his face threw her; it was one of familiarity and endearment. "I'm a big girl," she said, totally confused. "I'll know when I'm pushing myself too hard."

Gene smiled. "Well, I guess I'll have to defer to your judgment, but I think you should try to get more sleep, at least. Work is good, and so is play," he added, "but you have to schedule in rest time too."

As she sat down, she noticed the odd look Raul was giving them. Then she realized what Gene was up to. He was trying to make Raul believe that there was something going on between the two of them. "I do put in many hours. Sometimes it cuts into my sleep, but it's all part of the job," she said coolly, then glanced at Raul. "I need to work on ideas as they come. A more appropriate design or a solution to a problem may not hit me until three A.M. When it does,

I have to get up and record it. Otherwise, I'll end up forgetting important details and losing the concept."

Raul nodded slowly. "Yes, I've felt that way myself sometimes, though my work is certainly different from yours."

Irene couldn't be sure. Had he understood what she'd tried to tell him? She resented Gene for putting her in a position where her integrity could be questioned. Had they played games like these when Reina had been alive?

Well, she had no intention of letting them use her as a pawn to gain leverage over each other. They'd have to resolve their family problems between themselves. This had nothing to do with her. She avoided speaking directly to Gene again as the courses for dinner were served and cleared.

"I can't believe all the little mishaps you've had, Irene," Gene commented at last, glancing down at her hand. Though it was almost healed, a tinge of redness remained. "But you know, *Casa de Encanto* has always resisted any attempts to renovate it." He picked at his *natilla,* a rich custard dessert, absently.

"What do you mean?" The words slipped out before she could stop them. Blast her curiosity! She could tell from Gene's expression that her reaction was exactly what he'd hoped for.

"I'm surprised you haven't heard the stories," Gene commented. "Years and years ago, my father decided to modernize some of the rooms of the hacienda and build several additions. He hired Alfredo Hernandez, the son of our family lawyer, as architect. Alfredo needed the business, since he'd just opened his architectural firm."

"Wait a minute. I don't understand. It sure didn't look like there'd been any recent work in the rooms I inspected," Irene said.

"Except for a lot of sketches, the renovation work was never done. The story's very sad, really. My dad was busy running the company, so he placed the funds for the project entirely in Alfredo's hands. Alfredo had a good reputation, and his father was a trusted friend, so it seemed a perfectly safe thing to do. But just as Alfredo began to finalize plans and hire crews, things started to go wrong for him. In retrospect, I think it was an omen."

"Oh, for heaven's sake," Raul spat out.

"Well, the facts are the facts, big brother," Gene retorted calmly. "Alfredo was having problems with his wife. Then his sixteen-year-old daughter, Raven, ran away from home. Word had it that his wife blamed Alfredo, and after that, the marriage crumbled fast. As his life unraveled, Hernandez started hitting the bottle. Funny how sometimes it's all the comfort a man gets," Gene added, his voice dropping as he stared at the empty wineglass before him.

"So the restoration was never attempted?"

Gene looked up, the sound of Irene's voice bringing him back to the story. "As it turned out, Alfredo had squandered most of the money. He'd brought in consultants and had dozens of studies made, trying to make up his mind how to go about the work. What was left in the account Dad had set up couldn't have fixed a leaking faucet. My father never pressed charges because Alfredo's dad, Frank, was his close friend. And of course, Frank Hernandez promised to eventually make full restitution." Gene shrugged, refilled his wineglass, and leaned back in his chair. "But the loss of thousands of dollars brought the restoration plans to an abrupt halt."

"That was all a very long time ago," Raul said quietly, his gaze stone-cold as it came to rest on his brother.

"Maybe so," Gene conceded. "I was in high school at the time. But I've got to tell you, I'll never forget the day Dad fired Alfredo. I was in the den when they ran across each other in the hall. They stepped into the *sala* quickly, but from where I was I could still see and hear everything. Dad was in an absolute rage. He wanted to tear Alfredo apart for what he'd done. Alfredo, in turn, blamed Dad for putting so much pressure on him. He accused Dad of being the cause of everything that had happened to him and his family."

"That's unfair," Irene objected. "Hernandez made his own choices and decisions." Gene smiled as if she'd said exactly the words he'd wanted to hear.

"Yes, that's true, but in all fairness, a little pressure applied at the right time can have some far-reaching effects. You never know what can send someone over the edge," he said, his eyes on Raul.

Raul's unblinking gaze focused on Gene until it felt like the temperature of the entire room had suddenly become arctic.

Gene glanced away and continued. "In Alfredo's case, getting fired was the last straw. I think something snapped inside him that day. He swore he'd get even with this family someday, even if it took the rest of his life." Gene dropped his voice. "I'll never forget his voice when he said that. Even Dad's expression changed, and he wasn't one to ever reveal what he was thinking."

"He might come and hurt us!" Elena's voice was thin and shaking.

Riveted by Gene's account, Irene had temporarily forgotten Elena. Now, seeing the mortified look on Gene's face, she realized he hadn't counted on the effect the story would have on his sister.

Raul put his hand over Elena's and gave it a squeeze. "Elena, there's no need for you to be concerned. Your brother sometimes has an overactive imagination, and he likes to tell scary stories like they do on TV." He glared at Gene. "But they're just to entertain the guests."

"You mean like the Indian storytellers we'd see when we were kids going to the pueblo?"

"A lot like that," Raul assured with a nod.

Elena took her last bite of *natilla*. "But there has been someone hanging around. I heard people talking . . ."

Raul winked at her. "Probably just someone's boyfriend, honey. Nothing to be alarmed at."

Irene saw the concern that still flickered in Elena's eyes. "Oh, I forgot to tell you, Elena. The miniature rose in my room seems to be getting tiny insects on the leaves."

Elena glanced at her quickly. "Oh, thanks for telling me! I'll take it back to my room and wash the leaves. Then I'll bring another one to your room, only this time, I'll spray it first. I can keep the spider mites off the plants in my room by washing them every day. But when they're around the house, I have to use a spray that lasts longer."

Raul glanced at Irene and gave her a barely perceptible nod. The smile that touched his eyes didn't reach his lips, but was nonetheless there.

"May I be excused, Raul?" Elena asked. "I have some work to do tonight."

He nodded and smiled. "Good night, Elenita."

As soon as she left the room, Raul glared at his brother. "Next time you get the urge to recount family history, will you spare a thought for your sister?"

"You know I didn't do that on purpose! I never thought I'd be scaring her!"

"That doesn't minimize the damage," Raul shot back.

Gene straightened in his chair. "Well, it might not be so bad for her to be on her guard, Raul. I saw a guy I could have sworn was Alfredo just the other day beyond the circle of pines. After that, I did some checking and found out he's back in town."

Raul pushed away from the table. "I've also seen him across the street a few times in Taos, but Alfredo is harmless. He comes back to try and make sense of the past, I'm sure of it. From what I've heard, he's stopped drinking and has done a fairly good job of putting his life back together."

"What does he look like?" Irene asked.

"He's medium height, with a little bit of middle-age spread, reddish-brown hair, and a longish face," Raul answered. "But what happened between our father and him is ancient history."

"Not to him. He still has to shoulder some heavy-duty memories," Gene said quietly.

It was Gene's tone that made all eyes in the room turn to him. Emotions laced through his words had given his voice a resonance that seemed to hang in the air.

Irene started to point out that Alfredo Hernandez's description matched that of the man who'd been hanging around the day of the accident with the crane. Then she saw the expression on Raul's face and snapped her mouth shut. This was not a good time to bring up more speculations.

Irene looked at the others, then stopped as her eyes met Cobb's. At the moment he was all reserve, a gentleman in the presence of other gentlemen. But it was only a guise. The appraising stare he gave let her know that he was becoming a dangerous adversary. He was searching, waiting, like a predator on the hunt. Uneasy, she glanced away.

Raul stood and led the way to the sitting room, a

routine already established. He poured brandy into glasses set upon a serving tray on the sideboard. "I think this household has been besieged by overactive imaginations."

Irene sipped her drink, then set her glass down. "I hope you gentlemen will excuse me, I'd like to turn in early tonight. We have building inspectors coming tomorrow and I'll have to be up shortly after sunrise to make sure everything is ready."

"I'd like to make rounds with you before they come," Raul said.

She couldn't read anything in the hazel eyes that held hers. Emotions flickered across them at lightning speed, but revealed nothing. "Fine. I'll see you then," she said with a nod.

Irene walked to her room slowly. Raul's pride prevented him from seeing any danger to those in *Casa de Encanto,* but the signs were inescapable. Unless he could face what was happening, he wouldn't be able to defend against it. The storm brewing would rip apart the core of everything he held dear.

RENE WOKE UP shortly after dawn. She'd had another restless night, her dreams twisting the tensions and realities of the household into haunting, macabre images.

Dressed in a long denim skirt and maroon turtleneck sweater, she brushed her ebony hair until it shone, contemplating the day. Finding out about Alfredo Hernandez had really messed up her theories. She'd honestly believed that her troubles at the work site had been directly related to Cobb, but now she wasn't so sure. Hernandez was an unknown element, one she hadn't taken into account.

Prepared for a new day of work, Irene wandered down to the kitchen. She was immediately welcomed by the smell of freshly brewed coffee and cinnamon rolls hot from the oven. "I never liked mornings, Angela, until I came here. Your breakfasts could tempt anyone out of bed."

Angela laughed. "This household isn't much for proper breakfasts, so I've got to do my best to entice them with something good that'll carry them through the morning."

Raul appeared only seconds later. "That wonderful coffee led me right here," he said cheerfully. "And those rolls!"

As he started to grab one from the cookie sheet, Angela slapped his hand lightly. "Sit down at the dining room table, Mr. Raul. *I'll* serve them. You too, Miss Irene."

He laughed as he and Irene walked through to the dining room and seated themselves. Angela followed shortly. "You never change, Angela," Raul said. "That's what I like most about you."

The elderly woman smiled as she set plates filled with warm cinnamon rolls on the table before him and Irene. Coffee followed shortly. "You take time with breakfast, you work much too hard," she chided Raul.

As Angela left, Irene smiled at Raul. "She's very fond of you."

"You know, Angela's very conscious of appearances; it's part of our customs. She only acts this way when she and I are alone. But from what I just saw, she feels completely at ease around you, and that says much for you."

"I like and respect Angela, and she knows it."

"It's more than that. You have a way of making people feel comfortable around you. It's a very special quality."

"Thanks," she said, looking away.

"Now I've embarrassed you," he said with a tiny grin.

"Try not to look as if you're enjoying it."

"I'll give it my best shot." Raul eagerly attacked

two rolls, then finished his coffee. "So tell me, is the construction outside progressing the way you want?"

"We've had a few setbacks, as you know, but nothing that's put us behind. If the weather stays mild, we might even consider ourselves a few days ahead."

Finished with breakfast, she stood and walked out with Raul. She led the way around the house to where the men had restuccoed part of the south wall.

Raul pointed up at the new layer. "Why is that so dark? It doesn't match the existing color."

Irene tried to ignore the uneasy feeling his observations gave her. Did he think she was incompetent? "I realize that, Raul. The new stucco will lighten up in a few weeks when it's fully cured, and it'll bleach out even more as the sun beats down on it. Remember that this is a south wall that will be constantly exposed to the winter sun. In a few months, the color will match so well you won't be able to tell the new from the old."

He looked at the wall a bit longer. "Yes, I follow the logic. Have you had experience with this before? I mean you're certain it'll really work?"

"Of course," she replied, forcing herself to remain patient. "And if you can detect a difference after it has had time to dry, we'll redo it. Our goal is to make sure that the workmanship here is second to none." She gestured to the *portal*. "That's turning out very well, don't you think? The extra carving and beams Gene wanted to add look very nice."

As he drew near, his eyes moved to the posts that were stacked to one side, waiting to be erected. "Those don't look quite right, Irene. I think they're just a little too thick around the middle. Take a close look."

She smiled. "They're less than an inch thicker in the middle. You've got a good eye. But trust me, they'll look just right once they're up. The Greeks found out after they'd made a few temples that unless they constructed the pillars just a little thicker in the middle than at the ends, the pillars actually looked thinner at the halfway point. It's an optical illusion, but to look aesthetically correct and visually pleasing, sometimes you have to compensate."

Raul smiled. "My hat's off to you. Maybe I should stop questioning so much and let you do the rounds alone."

"Not at all, you're the boss. Ask away." She smiled wryly. "Besides, it really can't hurt to have both of us keeping an eye on Cobb's work. The best indicator of what a person is going to do in the future is what he's done in the past. I just don't trust him not to undermine my efforts."

"He doesn't exactly hold you dear to his heart."

"That's the understatement of the year."

Raul stood beneath the corbels, studying the carving just out of his reach. "These don't quite match."

"I noticed that yesterday. The pattern isn't cut deeply enough into the wood. Cobb sometimes hurries the artisans, complaining that they work too slow. I think what we're seeing here is the end result of that."

"Matching the original design takes a steady hand, a good eye, and patience. I know I've pressed you for a tight deadline, but I don't want this type of work compromised."

"I feel the same. I intended to talk to Cobb about this later today. I'll make sure the artisan comes back and finishes it up right."

She watched Raul out of the corner of her eye as they circled the house. When she did her rounds, her mind was always clicking at a million miles a minute, her body under tension that struggled to show itself. Yet though Raul had been as alert as she was, he managed to appear relaxed and confident. Certain people had that quality, one she'd always envied. It was a talent that allowed them to maintain an image that made them seem superior to their actions, no matter what they were doing at the time. It was an elegant blend of style, grace, and confidence that was impossible to acquire; you either had it or didn't.

Unfortunately she didn't. When she was nervous or under pressure, she looked it. This was definitely not a plus outside the pueblo where poker faces prevailed in the world of business. But she was getting better—at least she hoped so. The thought that she might be as ridiculously easy to read as ever was too depressing to contemplate.

"Why don't you let me talk to John about the craftsman? He might take that better if it comes from me," Raul offered.

Irene knew he was just trying to help, but the suggestion was annoying nevertheless. "I'll handle Cobb. I never wanted him here, but since he is, he's got to learn to answer to me. Your interference, even if it is well intentioned, will only set me back." She saw Raul's expression turn cold, and realized that as usual her lack of tact had created a problem. "Raul, I know you're trying to make things easier for me as your architect, and that you're concerned about the workmanship," she started.

Raul turned to face her. "It's becoming more than that, and I think you know it."

He made no move to touch her, but was so close she could feel the warmth from his body. She had no idea what to say, and fumbled for the right words. "This job . . . I mean, I . . ."

Raul held her in speculative study. "Is it really so hard for you to believe that I'm interested in you?"

She didn't want this complication. The physical attraction she felt for him was already too strong. "We can't pursue this. It would only lead to disaster and we both know it. We are products of what came before. Too much history stands between your people and mine."

"Yes, but the fact you're here means the healing has begun."

His words were soft and compelling, but she knew that in his culture words and actions didn't mean commitments. The machismo code allowed for lots of latitude. Offhand, she couldn't think of anything more damaging to her professionally or personally than to allow any romantic relationship to develop. The crew would soon get wind of it, and in their eyes, she'd become the *patrón*'s woman. It would be a plus for the *patrón*, but a very big detriment to her credibility or ability to command respect.

"Raul, your efforts to help me and make things easier could backfire in a major way," she said hesitantly. "It's hard enough being a woman architect sometimes. Do you understand?" This was her best shot at diplomacy. When tact wasn't your strong suit, it was better to mince words.

He nodded. "But I think you know I would never compromise you in front of the others." He placed his hands inside his coat pockets as a chill wind blew from the north. "Don't fault me for trying to help. It's in a man's nature . . ."

"No," she said gently, "it's in *your* nature, and that speaks well for you."

Hearing a pickup coming up the drive, she glanced over. "Here's the inspector now," she said, disciplining her thoughts back to business. "It's time for me to do what you hired me for." As she walked toward the county vehicle, she couldn't deny feeling a twinge of disappointment that their talk had been cut at that precise moment. But then again, maybe it was for the best. She fingered the small fetish in her skirt pocket.

The mountain lion was a hunter, but it also knew when to back away. That was the quality she appealed the fetish to endow her with now.

As she accompanied the inspector through the hacienda, she felt the unshakable self-confidence that came from knowing that her skills as an architect were second to none. The inspection tour proceeded as smoothly as she'd hoped. Everything done so far had well exceeded the demands of the building codes. When it was over and the inspector had gone, she went to her office, ready to file a report to her firm.

She was at her computer when Cobb walked inside. He sauntered across the room and dropped into the chair nearest her desk. "Okay, what's the word? Any problems with the inspection?"

"Not at all. But you and I have to discuss the carving on the *portal*."

"That guy you found, Ray Cata, was taking forever. That work he did will look okay once it's stained and sealed, but you've got to find another artisan for the stuff we've got planned later on. He's just too slow."

"Ray needs to take his time, but he's the best. He stays," she replied flatly. "I'm going to ask him to go back to his carving and get a better matchup. I don't want you to rush him either."

"With the deadline the Mendozas gave us, we can't afford all this detail work," Cobb spat out angrily. "Look, I've done my best to push the men because that's what's needed to finish on schedule. This 'Indian time' bull isn't going to cut it here. We need someone who can carve that wood quickly, and still do a good job. I know you've caught Raul Mendoza's eye, and that might make things easier for you right now. But if you botch this job, he'll lose interest in a hurry, believe me. You're going to be knocking on doors looking for your next job just like the rest of us. So start thinking, get off your high horse, and set some priorities. We both have something at stake here."

She was holding the edge of the desk so hard that her hand began to shake. This man could make her lose her temper faster than anyone she'd ever met, but she would not give him the satisfaction now. "The man I hired stays," she answered coldly. "You'll work around him."

"For all your soft-spoken words, you're on a power trip, lady. It's understandable in a way, I suppose. From what I've heard, this is a make-it-or-break-it job for you too. You're not exactly popular at your firm right now. But if I walk out with my crew, you might as well pack it in. You need me, keep that in mind."

"Don't make threats. They have the opposite effect on me."

"I wasn't threatening, just pointing out a few facts." Cobb grinned slowly and lowered his voice. "You could make our work here a lot more pleasant for both of us if you'd just be a little nicer to me." He reached across the desk and cupped her chin.

She swatted his hand away. "Don't you *ever* lay a finger on me—not unless you want to pull back a bloody stump," she said, swallowing back the revulsion his touch had sent through her.

"You're making enemies, little girl," Cobb declared, his voice low and slow. "It's bound to catch up to you."

Gene walked into the office, knocking on the open door as he passed through the entrance. "I heard the inspection went well, and that we're actually ahead of schedule."

Cobb smiled at Gene, then fixed Irene with a patronizing smile. "That we are. Your brother hired the right architect. Irene knows how to get the most out of the crew. That's why we've been able to maintain the quality of the work." Cobb stood up. "I'm glad this job's given us the chance to work together again, Irene."

That statement could have greened up half of the lawns in New Mexico. It was clear Cobb would be nothing but a paragon of courtesy around others. She'd never been very good at these kinds of games, but she wanted Cobb to know she wasn't intimidated or rattled by them. "We both have our professional integrity. That's why I'm sure things will continue to run smoothly." Having said it without gagging, she felt tempted to touch her nose and make sure it hadn't grown a foot or so.

Gene gave her a curious look, then placed some sketches on her desk. "I'm glad you're dedicated to making *Casa de Encanto* a showcase home. In the spirit of that, I've got a few more modifications I'd like to have you make in the *sala,* assuming you get Raul's approval."

Irene suppressed a groan. She knew all too well she was making enemies, and if she didn't control her temper, things would only get worse. She tried to console herself with the thought that only a fool could go through life without making enemies, but somehow it didn't help. "Okay, let see what you've got for me here."

It was close to eleven by the time she was ready to quit for the night. Incorporating Gene's drawings had meant having Angela bring a dinner tray and eating at her desk. Not that she was sorry, she'd desperately needed some time alone. Her attraction to Raul and the feeling that she was surrounded by enemies had combined, making her feel as trapped as a mouse that had ventured under a tree full of owls.

As she rose from her desk, Elena strolled inside, holding a small African violet. "I brought this for your office. I thought you needed something extra in here, particularly if you're going to start eating dinner here." She shrugged and shook her head. "Sometimes you're just like Raul."

"You think he works too much?" Irene asked with a faint smile.

"Everyone but him thinks so."

Irene chuckled. "Work isn't all bad, you know, not when it's something you like. Look at all the time you spend with your flowers. Some would call what you do very hard work. You have to wash the plants, repot them, water them, prune them, and so on."

"Oh, but I love doing that!" Elena protested quickly, then stopped and smiled. "Okay. I see what you mean." She lapsed into a thoughtful silence as she positioned the plant on the side of Irene's desk closest to the window. "Can I ask you something?"

"Sure, go ahead."

She hesitated. "Maybe I shouldn't. Mother would have said I was being imper—tinent," she said, struggling with the word.

"Nah. We're friends and I've already told you it's okay." Irene turned off the lights to the office and went with Elena out into the hall.

"You don't have any photos you've brought from your home. I know you're pretty, and that others think so too. I've seen the men look at you when you're not watching." She paused. "So how come you don't have a family?"

"I do. I have my mother, my aunt, my uncles . . ." She stopped, seeing Elena shaking her head.

"No, I mean kids. If I was more like you, I would have found a husband by now, so I could have lots of children."

Irene laughed. "Well, it's not that simple. I do want children someday, but that's one of those things you can't just rush into."

"Oh no, you should. I saw it on television a few days ago. They said that the clock ticks away fast for women, and before you know it it's too late. Aren't you afraid you'll wait too long?"

Irene looked at her, then laughed. "Elena, I'm not *that* old."

Elena looked surprised at first, then laughed too. "Yeah, but just think of all the fun you could be having! Little kids are so cute."

Elena was leading up to something, but at the moment Irene couldn't tell what. "They're also lots of responsibility."

"Women think Raul's a good catch and they always want to marry him. Is that what you want too?"

"Me?" Irene's voice rose slightly. "Raul's my employer, Elena. Besides, I'm not ready to marry anyone."

"Good," she replied simply, "because I don't want Raul to marry again either. When he was married to Reina, he never had time for me. Well, no, that's not exactly true," she admitted after a brief pause. "He had time for me once in a while. But it's better now that she's gone."

"He loves you very much, Elena. His feelings for you would never change no matter what the circumstances. Surely you know that."

"You weren't around when he was married to Reina. Everyone was unhappy. Gene and Raul couldn't be in the same room without fighting. Reina spent most of her days complaining and making Raul sad." She sighed. "I don't think married people go with this house. My mother and father weren't really happy together either."

"Different people have different experiences, Elena. It has nothing to do with *Casa de Encanto.*"

"Maybe." Elena shrugged, unconvinced. "I would still like to be an aunt someday," she added thoughtfully, "but only if Raul and Gene don't get married. Kids would be fun, but not with wives living here too."

Irene found herself unable to think of something to say.

At that moment, Gene stepped out of the sitting room. He grinned at Irene. "My little sister has raised some very interesting possibilities," he teased. "How do you feel about that? I must say, I think this is something definitely worth looking into." He gave her a rakish grin.

Irene wanted to crawl into the woodwork. She'd never been good at this kind of flirting, but with Elena's feelings at stake, the situation made her even more tongue-tied than usual. "Well, I suppose one answer is to set up a day-care center here. You'd have kids and no extra wives living in the house."

"You're no fun," Gene muttered sadly. "There are other ways."

"I think I'll let *you* explain it to Elena, then," Irene said.

"Explain what to Elena?" Raul asked, appearing at the top of the stairs.

Great. Just what she needed. "You two should discuss this by yourselves. It's a family matter," she added with a smile. "In the meantime, it's time for me to get some sleep."

"Aw, that's too bad," Gene teased, his voice barely audible.

She shot him a hard look, but seeing the mischievous sparkle in his eyes, chuckled. "Forget it. I'm too tired for a battle of wits, and I wouldn't settle for a loss or a tie."

She started down the hall, and Elena joined her. "I don't understand what you two were talking about, but I'm going to bed too." Elena yawned, then glanced at Irene. "Are you still hearing it?" she asked, her voice lowered.

Irene's body tensed. "You mean the person who has been wandering the hall?" She saw Elena nod, and continued. "Yeah, I have, but I've tried to ignore it."

"So do I, but I still get a little scared. Even though my door is locked, I'm afraid to go to sleep sometimes. I keep getting up to make sure it's still locked."

"Elena, tell me something. Do you remember ever having this happen before?"

Elena shook her head. "Gene gets up sometimes at night, but his footsteps are loud, and I mean *loud.* And if he trips, he starts saying all those bad words. I know Gene."

Irene considered it. Yes, she'd know her brother's footsteps, unless Gene was deliberately trying to disguise what he was doing. But that didn't make sense . . . or did it? She took a deep breath. The time had come for her to stop speculating and start taking action. "Don't worry, Elena. If anyone or anything ever threatened you, Gene and Raul would be at your side in an instant."

Elena considered it. "Yes, you're right. If I screamed, they'd come running."

"In a second. Count on it." As they stopped by Elena's door, Irene gave Elena's shoulder a reassuring squeeze. "You'll be just fine. And if you ever get scared and want to talk, I'm just down the hall. You can always come to my room."

"You wouldn't mind?"

"Not in the slightest."

Elena smiled. "Okay, but you know I think I'll sleep just fine tonight." She stifled a yawn. "I really am sleepy."

"Good night."

Irene waited until Elena latched the door, then continued walking to her own bedroom. Enough of this, she wasn't going to allow anyone to terrorize poor Elena in an attempt to unnerve *her*. She hated going on the offensive, but this was her only option.

Irene took a spool of transparent nylon thread out of the sewing kit in her drawer, and unwound several yards of the sturdy line. Carefully she tied one end to the leg of the heavy armoire in her room. After making sure it was tightly fastened, she peered outside into the corridor. No one was in the hall. Passing the thread between the door and the jamb at about six inches above the carpet, she looped it around the leg of a Mexican hand-carved pine chest against the far wall. Finally she walked back to the armoire, fastening the loose end tightly to the same leg as before.

Tonight, when their mysterious wanderer made his way down the corridor, he was going to find a nice trip wire waiting for him. With a smug smile, Irene closed her door and turned off the light.

It was shortly after midnight when she heard the faint footsteps. The hallway was almost dark at night. Unless you were specifically looking down for the strands of clear thread, you'd never see them. She reached for the pouch containing her fetish, walked noiselessly to the door, and waited. Whoever was out there lurking was about to get a very big surprise.

# 12

IRENE PRESSED CLOSE to the door and listened. As the heavy footsteps drew closer, she held her breath, fingers tight around the mountain lion fetish. If the hunt went well, she'd find her answer tonight. Only one worry nagged at the back of her mind, the thought that she might end up tripping Gene or Raul. But their rooms were at the other end. It didn't seem likely they'd be wandering around aimlessly. And by now she'd had it with whoever was playing games with her.

The armoire suddenly jerked six inches away from the wall as if alive, startling her. There was a heavy thud and a muttered oath. She threw open the door, simultaneously switching on the light in her room. The soft glow bled the dimly lit hallway. The first thing she saw was the back of a man as he struggled to his knees. A heartbeat later she had her answer.

"Hello, Cobb. Out for your midnight stroll?"

"What the hell is going on?" he demanded, turning his head to see her.

"I've had enough of your wanderings. I told you, they're scaring Elena. I won't put up with this."

He struggled clumsily to his feet. "No one tells me what to do after hours, lady, especially not you. I could have broken my neck. If I had, I could have sued you for everything you own, and then some."

"Somebody thought of protecting the clumsy years ago. There's extra padding beneath the carpet runner. You're not hurt."

He muttered something under his breath. "So what did you prove?"

"That you're wandering around the hall at night, lurking in front of bedroom doors. Learning that you've been scaring the heck out of Elena isn't going to sit too well with either of the Mendoza brothers. They'll probably take a dim view of having a pervert living in the same hall as their sister."

"I haven't done a thing to that woman, and that includes trying to frighten her."

"Fine. I'll just present Raul with the facts, and let him decide."

The fixity of Cobb's stare bored through her. "You'll be taking a chance too, and don't you forget it. I would assure them that I was just on the way to my room. Then I'd blame your nerves on all that tribal superstition you grew up with. I wonder how the Mendozas would feel if they knew about that little incident the day you arrived," he said, eyebrows raised in speculation. "But the long and short of it is that Raul Mendoza would have to choose who to side with, and one of us could get fired. Then everyone would lose. The renovation needs both of us here to be completed by Christmas. How long do you think Mendoza would listen to your sweet talk if you failed him on that?"

Irene fought the urge to kick him as hard as she could in the shins. "You're right about *one* thing. If the job doesn't get done, no one wins. But my main concern is for Elena. She doesn't deserve to be caught up in your stupid games. You're frightening her by wandering around the hall late at night. And I'll tell you right now, I'm not going to allow that."

Cobb took a step closer to her. "What would you have me do, get a note from my boss every time I decide to leave my room?"

"How you handle it is up to you," she said with a shrug. The scent of a woman's perfume still clung to his clothing, giving her an indication of where he'd been. That, in an odd way, gave Cobb's words a touch of legitimacy. He was either innocent of what she was accusing him of or an accomplished liar.

"Are you sure Elena's fears aren't something you've created?" he challenged. "You're afraid of something and she knows that. She might be reacting to you more than anything else."

She slipped the trip wire off the table leg and wound it up, glancing absently down the hallway toward Elena's door. It was partially open. Something told her that Elena had heard much of what happened. "Elena's brighter than you give her credit for."

Cobb started toward his own room. "Yeah, sure. I should trust your word for it." Shaking his head, he opened his door and went inside.

Irene waited a few seconds to make sure he was exactly where he was supposed to be, then walked down to Elena's room. Seeing the door was closed once again, she knocked softly. "Elena, it's Irene."

Elena unbolted and opened the door, inviting Irene to come in. "I saw what you did," she said, her eyes bright with excitement. "That was a good idea."

"Yeah, but it doesn't prove anything. The best we

can hope for is that it might worry Cobb enough to keep him from creeping around in the dark anymore."

Elena sat at the edge of her bed, reached into a drawer of her nightstand, and pulled out some chocolate mints. She silently offered them to Irene.

Irene took one, watching Elena's thoughtful expression. "What's bothering you?"

Elena hesitated, nibbling on the mint. "I know Gene's steps and I can always tell when Raul's coming because he walks so fast. I've known all along it wasn't either of them. But Mr. Cobb's footsteps were wrong too. I mean, I know what he sounds like when he walks; he's got those big boots. The person I've been hearing out in the hall at night walks with softer steps, so light you can barely hear them. It's like he's just in his socks."

Irene considered Elena's words. "You're absolutely right," she conceded slowly.

"So, do you think you caught the wrong person?"

"Now that you mention it, yes. And if the one really responsible was anywhere close by tonight, he'll be on his guard from this point on." Irene sighed softly. "We've lost the advantage."

"Maybe not. If someone did that to me, I'd try and behave myself, at least for a while."

The words were simply put, and in one context made a great deal of sense. But the problem was that there was no telling if her enemy would react that way or not. If he didn't, she'd be up against an even craftier opponent. Yet there was no sense in pointing that out to Elena. "What do you say we get some sleep?"

Elena nodded. "I think I'll still keep my door locked at night."

"Can't hurt." As Irene walked back to her room, she realized that people had underestimated Elena all through her life. The woman had good instincts and judgment—strong points many so-called normal people were sorely lacking.

The following morning Irene stood by as Janna used a radial-arm saw to size heavy spruce two-by-twelves that would be used to repair portions of the roof. "I've rechecked my figures and we're still within the weight parameters," Irene assured Janna. "These beams will be more than adequate when tied in to the rest of the roof."

"So, I should continue?"

"Sure. Although these aren't the grade of timber I originally ordered, they're knot-free and kiln-dried. They'll do fine where they're going to be used."

Cobb approached her. "Let me guess. Looking for more trouble?"

"No, not at all. These resawn beams will do just fine," she said, more convinced than ever that she'd caught the wrong person last night. The possibility that she'd wrongly accused him made her feel incredibly guilty. Even Cobb deserved better than that. Leaving him with a puzzled look on his face, she walked back to the house. Gene was watching the work on the *portal* and waved as she approached the main entrance.

"What happened last night?" Gene asked. "I was coming home late and heard someone fall. When I got to the top of the stairs, I saw you arguing with Cobb." He grinned. "He was on his knees and you were standing, so I guess we know who won that round."

More than just annoying, his cavalier attitude made a twinge of unease spread through her. "Someone's been wandering the hall, stopping by my bedroom door, and sometimes by Elena's. I got tired of those games." She held his gaze.

"By Elena's door?" His voice grew hard. "Does Raul know?"

"I have no way of proving what's going on, and Elena keeps her door locked. Mentioning this to anyone else at this point seemed . . . well, premature."

Gene exhaled softly. "Knowing my brother, holding back until you've got more facts isn't at all unreasonable," he conceded. "What did Cobb have to say about being there?"

"Not much. He claims it was a coincidence. He might have been telling the truth."

"Or not," Gene observed with a wry smile. "You know, things have become very interesting around here since you arrived."

She was about to defend herself, then decided against it. Instead, she maneuvered past him and headed for her office.

Irene immersed herself in her work for the remainder of the workday. Every time a distracting thought intruded on her concentration, she firmly brushed it aside. She felt good about the work she'd managed to accomplish, and about herself.

Sitting back, she rubbed her eyes. The first time she got a chance to go to her pueblo, she'd ask her aunt for some herbs to help her sleep. She needed several good nights of rest if she was going to be able to keep working at the pace she'd set for herself.

"You look exhausted," Raul commented.

Irene jumped. "I didn't hear you come in!"

"Sorry. I didn't mean to startle you. I just wanted to remind you that Wednesday is Angela's night off. If you want her to leave something special for your dinner, you have to let her know by five."

"Thanks, but I thought I'd just go to the kitchen and make myself a tortilla peanut butter and jelly sandwich. Afterward, I'm going to hike up the mountain. I need to get out for a bit."

"Excellent idea. Why don't you let me go with you? I know a trail we can follow."

The idea was tempting, too much so. "I appreciate the offer, but I need a little time by myself—if I get finished with some of these reports, that is."

Raul nodded, his expression hard to read. "I'm beginning to think you'd rather avoid me altogether after hours."

"No, and yes," she admitted candidly. "But you already know the reasons."

"All right. I won't press. But honestly, all I wanted was to spend time with a friend. It's something I don't get to do very often."

She saw the sadness in his eyes and felt a response forming inside her. His need was real, and the silent plea of his heart reached hers. "You know, I've been wondering, Halloween is coming up in a little over two weeks. Does your family do anything special?"

"We used to have a big party when my dad was alive, but we haven't done it since then. Nowadays, Gene and I carve pumpkins for Elena; she really enjoys that. Since we're fairly isolated we don't have kids coming for trick-or-treats, so it's a quiet evening." He glanced out her window. "The crew might feel differently."

"Probably. There'll be some pranks played and some partying, I'm sure."

"Do your people celebrate Halloween?"

"Not really. It isn't part of our culture. That's not to say that we don't go to parties that our Anglo or Hispanic friends throw, and have a great time." She smiled.

"Maybe you can help me carve the pumpkin?" Raul

asked. "I always have a terrible time. Gene's are masterpieces."

"Who selects the pumpkins?"

"Gene and I do, and then we keep it from each other like a couple of grown-up kids." Raul laughed.

"Well, I'll be glad to help you carve, but I warn you, I have no experience with that."

"Trust me. Experience in this case doesn't make up for lack of skill." He stood up. "I'll let you get back to your work."

As he left, she looked around for her calculator. The thing was always getting misplaced. It was small and handy, but that also made it easy to bury under the tons of paperwork that covered her desk at any given time. After several minutes of careful searching, she leaned back in her chair. It wasn't there.

She tried to think back to the last time she'd had it. For a while no answers came, then suddenly she remembered using it when she'd been talking to Janna. Maybe she'd dropped it near there.

Irene went outside. The radial-arm saw was not being manned at the moment. Most of the crew was on the other side of the house either working on the roof parapet from the top of the scaffolding or involved with the *portal*.

Irene glanced around, figuring she'd dropped it on the ground somewhere, but after searching several minutes, gave up. As she started to go back inside, she noticed it on the saw table.

Irene reached for it, then pulled back quickly as a cold breeze made a shiver run up her spine. An intense, almost irrational fear spread through her. Standing rock-still, she studied the saw and the calculator. It took her a few seconds, but she finally realized what had alerted her, though admittedly on a subconscious level. The saw's red power switch was in the on position, and the heavy-duty tool was plugged in. She started to push the switch off before reaching for the calculator when the blade suddenly whirred to life. A second later, she heard an abrupt screech as the blade pulled the plastic calculator into its teeth.

Her heart at her throat, she looked across the way at the pole that held the main electric panel and power switches. It was near Cobb's trailer. She took off at a run, determined to catch whoever had turned on the machine. She covered the ground in seconds, but even so, it wasn't quite fast enough. By the time she arrived she was only able to catch a quick glimpse of someone in a work jacket ducking behind the crew's housing.

Irene followed, determined to find out who'd set her up. But the late afternoon shadows had deepened, and her adversary was making full use of them. She heard him slip into the forest, then his sounds stopped.

Unwilling to give up, she continued into the wooded area, searching. After an uneventful fifteen minutes, she reluctantly turned back. She hated to admit failure, and these circumstances made it even worse. The moment she stepped out into the clearing she saw Cobb standing beside his trailer, watching her. She suppressed a groan. This was not what she needed right now.

"You're certainly peculiar at times. I've been looking at you dart around trees and run through the bushes like you're training on an obstacle course. I hate to be the one to tell you this, but I think you're flipping out."

"Cobb, someone just shredded my calculator with the radial saw. I was lucky my hand wasn't part of the bargain. If you've seen someone in a denim work jacket around here, then give. If not, try to keep from advertising your ignorance."

He stared at her. "What happened?"

She explained, then added, "Since the main power switch is near your trailer, I ran here as fast as I could. I almost had him too."

"Yeah, like you had me last night? God only knows what poor jerk you would have tried to lynch."

The words stung, but she tried not to show it. He had a point. She'd torn across the grounds, ready to do battle. Was the figure she'd seen the culprit, or just an innocent bystander?

Before she could say anything, Serna walked up. "It's about to hit the fan, boss," he said to Cobb. "Half the crew is ready to tear the other half apart. We're going to have to do something." He glanced at Irene. "You might want to hear this."

"What happened now?" she asked. Serna's attitude worried her more than anything he'd said. He wasn't the kind who would have included her in the discussion unless something was critical.

"We've been pushing the men, making them work at top capacity. Most of them have been bearing up well, though it's been tough on them. Then the wood-carver took all that time on the corbels that border the *portal.* Comments started up about the Tewas being slow and lazy, and some of the guys complained that they'd have to work two shifts a day just to make up for the Indians."

"You should have squelched that kind of talk fast," Cobb spat out. "Why didn't you split up the trou-blemakers and load them down with work so they'd be too busy to gossip? That would have given them something else to worry about."

"It wouldn't have worked. Things are *way* past that. It's like a powder keg out there, and a toss-up which side blows up first. The Indians are now bitching that the Hispanics are hurrying along, doing a half-assed job. Said they had no pride in themselves or their work."

Cobb swore softly. "I'm surprised somebody hasn't started throwing punches."

"It's been close. For now, I've managed to keep the lid on, but the situation is deteriorating fast. We're in for major trouble and once that happens, the work schedule, our crew, and everything will be jeopardized."

"You've got to talk to the men and deal effectively with their complaints," Irene said.

"You don't *reason* this kind of stuff away, Pobikan. It doesn't work like that."

"You can't outmacho it either," she argued.

"You handle the architecture and stay the hell out of my way with the rest," Cobb said, then brushed past her as if trying to make the warning as vivid as possible.

Irene watched him stomp across the grounds to the other side of the house. Violence was in the air, and his aggressiveness would only fuel an already explosive situation. Century-old hatreds were about to rip the two factions apart, and she had no idea how to stop it.

John Cobb entered Raul Mendoza's office and sat down. He had no other option. There was no way he was going to give Pobikan the satisfaction of knowing she'd been right. He should have squashed any signs of dissension immediately, instead of allowing the men to work things out. Getting Mendoza involved now would at least cover him partially in case things went sour fast. Mendoza would have to offer an opinion, and that would mean he'd share some of the blame if the situation got worse.

Raul leaned back in his chair and regarded Cobb. "I think I know why you're here. I overheard one of the workmen, Pablo Contreras, talking today. He was right beneath my window running off at the mouth about the Indian workers."

"It's tense out there. It's not just cultural differences, it's this deadline. Everyone's feeling the pressure."

"If the crew couldn't handle it, you should have told me a long time ago. Now it's your responsibility to deal with it. I won't tolerate excuses at this date."

"No excuses are being offered, I'm just telling you what's happening. I thought you had a right to know."

"What are you going to do about it?"

Cobb saw the intelligence in Mendoza's eyes and knew he'd been outplayed. Raul was waiting for him to make his own decisions; he wouldn't share the blame. "Since you're Spanish and your family has been in this state for generations, I thought you might have some suggestions. I've never encountered problems this severe between Indians and Hispanics on the job. I really think the deadline pressure is bringing things to a head."

"Have you spoken to Irene? She might have some insight on this."

"No, I haven't. She might want to talk to my men and I believe that would make things worse. I really don't think the men would trust her to be impartial. No matter what she did, they'd assume her sympathies would be with her own people. The only person besides me they'd respect and listen to is you."

Raul knew that there was truth in what he was saying, but to bypass Irene's authority would be to undermine her ability to lead the project. "Let's go find her and see what she says. Then we'll decide how best to solve this."

Raul led the way to her office, but found it empty.

Hearing someone out in the courtyard, he walked to the window. Irene stood just a few yards away, surrounded by a mixed group of workers.

Cobb came up and muttered a soft oath. "Looks like she's taken matters into her own hands . . ."

Raul held up a hand, interrupting him. "Listen. I think she's got the right idea."

Irene's voice carried clearly to where they were standing. "Not all jobs can be done at the same speed. Certain specializations take longer. But the only way this project will get done is if you all pull together and work as a team."

"Listen, you're a great cheerleader, but that Indian carver's been at it for days, and he still hasn't completed what needs done."

"Now wait a second," Anita Sanchez interrupted. The sixty-year-old *enjarradora*'s voice was strong, and commanded instant attention. "Do you think Michelangelo used spray paint on that church ceiling? I go as slow as molasses when I'm replastering with adobe. That's just the time it takes to do the job right. I'm Hispanic, like you, but nobody tells me how to do my job. And I sure as heck didn't carry on when you guys had to tear out those adobes because nobody noticed the *canale* had been set in backward. I just figured that some mistakes are expected, and that redoing it was part of what it took to get it right."

"That's my point precisely," Irene maintained. "Whatever results we achieve here will speak either highly or poorly of us. Unless we allow each other the breathing space we need to complete our jobs, this project will be an embarrassment for every person involved here."

"This home is in the history books and my children are proud I'm working on it. The hacienda is part of our heritage too, not just the Mendozas'," Paco said slowly. "If my sweat's going to become part of the work here, I want things done right." He stared hard at Bobby, the Tewa man. "I don't always agree with the way you guys think, but in this case, we're on the same side. We all want quality work." He cleared his throat. "But do you think your group can try to work a little faster? I mean, sometimes you're so laid-back it puts the rest of us to sleep just watching."

Bobby grinned. "We wonder how you can work at all, putting so little of yourselves into it. Let's just stay out of each other's way and get things done."

"I think that's the closest we'll come to agreeing," Paco answered. "I say we take it as a win and quit for the day. I hear a beer calling me."

As the men dispersed, Irene realized that her hands, hidden inside her trouser pockets, were shaking. She slipped them out and slowly flexed them, taking a deep breath. She felt like the star in a deodorant commercial. At this point she would have extolled the virtues of dry underarms despite the pressures.

Irene turned around, ready to walk back to her office, when she noticed Raul smiling at her from her office window. She smiled back. She wasn't sure how much he'd heard, but from the look on his face he was suitably impressed.

Pride gave her new confidence. She had a great deal of professional respect for Raul Mendoza, and it meant much to know that she had his as well. Raul might have considered her attractive, and liked her as a woman, but professional admiration was something he'd give only if it had been earned.

As she reached her office, the look in Raul's eyes warmed her. But as her gaze shifted to Cobb, the heat turned to cold. There was malice in his eyes. She tried not to flinch, but found that took effort.

"You had no right to do what you just did. The crew is my responsibility."

"I was there at the proper time, you weren't. I was coming back to the house when I saw the men about to square off. The situation needed to be handled right then. Had you taken care of this problem before it escalated, my interference wouldn't have been necessary."

"All you've done is put it off again. This will resurface, don't kid yourself."

"Maybe, but I've bought us some time. For the moment that's the best we can expect."

"Would you come to my office? I'd like to talk to you," Raul said cryptically.

Irene studied his expression, trying to guess the direction his thoughts had taken, but his eyes revealed nothing. Glancing at Cobb, she saw the malicious edge that tainted his expression and instantly wondered what he'd said to Raul. She had no doubt that he'd be at the bottom of whatever trouble lay ahead for her.

# 13

**T**HEY ENTERED RAUL'S office a minute later. Irene took a chair opposite his desk as he sat down. "I think you should know that Cobb came to my office earlier. That's what we were doing in your office. I'd gone there to look for you."

"What was the problem?"

He recounted the events. "I think he had no idea how to handle his own crew. But what you did proved that you're more than up to the job."

"I don't think *he's* impressed," she added cynically. "Cobb was furious with me."

"Does it matter to you?"

"Yes, but only because I've made him even more dangerous. You can bet he'll do whatever it takes to undermine me from this point on."

"There's something to that." He didn't like to see Irene worried. She seemed so alone here in *Casa de Encanto*. She was a woman used to the support systems in the pueblo. Yet despite that, she'd fought her battles skillfully. He was sure, however, that her self-confidence didn't go as deep as it merited.

"I don't like having enemies," she admitted. "But at least if you know who they are it's easier to press your back to the wall when they walk by," she added.

"*I* am your friend. Can you accept that?"

She held her breath for a moment, his words circling in her mind. "I know that you won't let Cobb or anyone else damage my professional reputation unjustly . . ."

"It's more than that," Raul interrupted gently. "Can you understand, or at least try to? We're part of the present and the future. What happened between your people and mine in the past shouldn't stand like a permanent wedge between us."

Her heart was tearing in two. As their eyes met, she knew her pain had touched him. "It isn't just the past; look at what's happening between the workers right now. We're all part of what came before. You can't run from that."

"I've never run from anything in my life." Raul walked around his desk and took her hands, pulling her to her feet. He stood inches away from her, his hands clasping hers. "Don't tell me you don't feel anything."

His breath touched her cheek like a feather-light caress. "Feelings aren't enough," she answered, stepping away. "I don't really know *you*. The distance you keep from people makes seeing the man you are inside very difficult. Without that, trust can't grow, and without trust, there's no basis for anything."

"I didn't think I was being particularly secretive with you."

Irene ran a hand through her hair. "I don't think it's conscious, but it's there. For instance, I know you were married before, yet you never speak of Reina. The only time her name was mentioned here was in a moment of anger between you and your brother."

"That's something I just don't talk about. She's gone, and there's nothing I can do to get her back." He turned away from Irene. "That shouldn't concern you."

"You still love her, or it wouldn't tear you apart like this."

The struggle inside him knifed at his guts. "The circumstances of her death made it difficult to say good-bye or put her memory behind me. But it's over." He forced himself to face Irene squarely.

Irene shook her head. "No, you still haven't released her spirit. Until you do, neither of you will be free. You're tied to your own past, Raul. There's no sense in trying to deny that." She walked to the door.

Raul saw her hesitate, and knew part of her wanted him to stop her, but he didn't. Her observations had been right on target. It was hard to mount a defense against the truth. What Irene didn't realize was that his feelings for Reina did not prevent him from also having feelings for her.

Irene saw him as a tower of strength and confidence. Though it was flattering to see himself through her eyes, what she saw was only an image he'd learned to project through the years. He could be hurt like any other flesh-and-blood mortal. Alone, and weighed down by responsibilities he was honor bound to uphold, his life all too often tasted like dry ashes.

To be able to explain and make her understand would have meant the world to him. But this wasn't something he could ever talk to Irene about. Baring his soul wasn't something he did well—not anymore.

He shut the door to his office and went to his room. He wouldn't get any more work done tonight; maybe he'd listen to some CDs. There was passion in Spanish music with its lyrics and beat. Yet it was a safe kind that allowed him to feel, but not to hurt.

Irene walked to her office. She was too keyed up to get any sleep now. Somehow, she had to find a way to master the crazy kaleidoscope of feelings that went through her whenever she was alone with Raul. Moments of exquisite tenderness were followed by panicky second thoughts. And all too often they convinced her she was in a lemming-like rush that would hurl her off an emotional cliff.

She sat behind her desk and saw the small bowl of fresh apples that had been placed on the corner. At least Angela was her ally. With her around she'd never have to worry about starvation. She took a deep breath and let it out.

Shifting her attention to her laptop computer, she decided to use her time productively. Irene switched it on, then sat back and waited. A few seconds later an error message flashed on the screen. Scowling at it, she tried again, but the results were the same.

It didn't take long for her to figure out what had happened. Anger ate into her with each passing second. Both her computer's hard drive and the utility disk had been completely erased. The chances of that happening by accident were nonexistent.

Irene leaned back in her chair. Her enemy had surprised her, but by keeping backup copies of everything, she still had her ace in the hole. She reached for a box of labeled disks inside her file cabinet. This was a minor, time-consuming inconvenience, nothing more. She wouldn't let it get to her.

As she tried to start up the restore program, another error message came up on the screen. Puzzled, she went through the checks, then slammed her hand down on the desk. Her restoration program and backup diskettes had been erased as well. Her adversary had been determined to destroy all the work she'd labored over for months. All files about the project were now lost, not only to her computer but also on the backups.

She took a deep breath, and managed a grim smile, wishing the skunk who'd done this could see her expression. Despite the thoroughness of his job, she was still ahead of him.

Irene packed the laptop inside its canvas bag and walked upstairs to her bedroom. In the bottom drawer of the dresser, beneath her sweaters, was a box of unlabeled diskettes. She'd kept an additional set of backups here as a precaution. This time when she booted the small laptop with her backup program, things finally went right.

Getting everything loaded back into the hard drive took quite a while. As she worked, she tried to figure out who might have had the time and opportunity to sabotage her computer. That's when she remembered leaving Cobb alone in her office while she'd gone with Raul to his study.

She exhaled softly, knowing that didn't prove anything. It was possible it might have been done before that time. She was trying to remember who else she'd seen around her office today when a knock sounded at her door.

Irene went to answer it, but kept her foot wedged against the door. Until her laptop was fully operational again, she wasn't taking any more chances. As she peered out, Elena's innocent face greeted her.

"I came to change your plants," she said, holding a new miniature rose. "This one's bright yellow, and that signifies friendship. I thought you'd like it."

Irene felt the tension flow from her body. "Thanks, Elena. Come in." She opened the door.

Elena glanced at the disks on the bed and gave her a puzzled look. "You brought all that up here to work? How come? Were you getting too many interruptions in your office? I know Gene went there looking for you earlier, then one of the work people stopped by."

"You mean this afternoon?"

She nodded. "I heard you inside Raul's office and I didn't want to interrupt you if you were busy. I decided to just let myself into your office and change the plants. I hope you don't mind."

"No, of course not," she assured. "But tell me, did you see anyone messing around with my computer?"

Elena looked at the laptop, thinking. "No," she said at last. "Mr. Cobb was standing by the window, staring outside. And Gene came in, asked where you were, and left after I told him." She chewed on her bottom lip, her eyes narrowed in pensive silence. "Oh, and Angela came by and left you a small bowl with apples just as I was leaving."

Irene placed the last of the disks into the laptop's drive and waited for it to load. "Thanks, Elena."

"So, is *that* why you're working up here? Are there too many people bothering you? You could do what Raul does. He closes the door to his office when he doesn't want to be disturbed. All of us know to keep out then."

"I'll have to remember that," she said, dodging the question, "but it's not so bad in here. I can get comfortable and wear a grubby sweatshirt while I type away."

Elena picked up the plant that had been on Irene's dresser. "Well, I better let you get back to work."

Irene placed the loose diskettes back into the box, but left the box on top of the bed, unwilling to reveal its hiding place. She hated herself for distrusting

Elena, but she couldn't quite let her guard down. "Thanks, Elena," Irene said, and held the door open for her.

As Elena walked to her room, Irene wondered if the constant pressure was finally starting to get to her. Distrusting Elena was beneath contempt. Disgusted with herself, she closed the door and went back to the computer. At least now the hard drive was back to normal.

Brushing everything from her mind, she started to redo the latest reports. Today's work hadn't been backed up except on the now-erased disks downstairs, and was therefore irretrievably lost. Still, she'd minimized the damage that could have been caused. Consoling herself with that thought, she began to type in the missing data again.

It was nearly two the next afternoon when Raul stopped by Irene's office. "Are you anywhere near a break? I wanted to talk to you about Elena. I've been a little worried about her."

Irene saved her file and turned off the computer screen so she could give Raul her undivided attention. "What's wrong?"

"I may be concerned for nothing, I do that a lot when it comes to Elena. But has she said anything more to you about the body that was discovered?"

Irene shook her head. "She hasn't mentioned a thing. If you ask me, I think she's forgotten all about it. Our conversations lately have been mostly about her plants."

"Good, that's what I'd hoped you'd say. It's been almost a month now. Since we haven't had more cops around, I'd prayed she'd put it out of her mind." Tension seemed to ease away from Raul's shoulders, and he sagged a bit into the chair cushions.

"Have the police said anything else about the body?"

"I called the station this morning. The detective was being very closemouthed for now. The bones had to be taken to Santa Fe for further testing, and he wants more facts, like an accurate dating, before saying anything. But the labs in Santa Fe, according to him, have a waiting list and are impervious to pressure."

"When they come back with more questions, and I'm certain they will, that could frighten Elena again."

"I'll take care of it." His gaze drifted aimlessly over her desk in a pensive gesture. "I wish I'd insisted that Elena go to our aunt's home in Phoenix until the work here was completed. She really hated the idea of leaving, but in retrospect it might have been the best thing for her."

"I've noticed how very seldom Elena leaves home, Raul. Do you think that's good for her?"

"She's not being coerced in any way," Raul answered. "I hired a companion to take her places years ago, but that just didn't work out. She hated the outings. We found out that she was happiest here working with her plants, so I stopped pushing her."

His doleful eyes sent a stab of sympathy through her. He loved his sister a great deal, and it was clear that he was doing his level best with her. "She's reclusive because she lacks self-confidence. If you encouraged her to become more independent, her life might become fuller."

"I'm not so sure. That world isn't always kind to the innocents. And if I allowed anything to hurt her, I'd be failing myself."

"Neither you nor Elena will ever know how much she's capable of until you give her the chance to test herself. Isn't that part of taking care of her too?"

Raul stared down at the desk for a moment, then

looked up again. "I don't know if I can take the risk. She's not as strong as you think."

"Maybe. But believe me, she's not as weak as you make her out to be either."

Raul walked to the window. "Look at her, Irene," he said as he saw Elena walking back from the rose garden. "She's terrified of even making eye contact."

Irene saw Elena deliberately take the long way around a group of men erecting a scaffold. "Oh, come on," she teased. "If I wasn't the architect I'd take the long way around some of these guys too."

Raul didn't crack a smile, his face remaining somber. "Something's not right, though. Her attitude's changed. Before, she'd show enough curiosity to try and edge in closer to the construction areas. Now all she wants is to get away as far as possible."

"Could it be that she's trying to please you? She must have sensed your uneasiness before."

"That's one possibility, I suppose," he said slowly.

She watched Elena hurrying along, keeping her eyes focused on the ground in front of her feet. She didn't look to either side. Uneasiness spread through Irene. Something *wasn't* right. "Would you like me to talk to her? Maybe all the noise from the heavy equipment has frightened her. Whatever it is I could try and help her through it."

Raul nodded. "That's a good idea. Will you let me know how it goes?"

"Sure. I'll go see her now. I was about to go on a coffee break anyway."

"I'd appreciate it."

Irene walked out to the gardens and met Elena coming around the walk. "What are you up to?" Irene greeted.

"I wanted to plant some bulbs that I got through a catalog," Elena answered, her eyes darting around nervously. "I did it as fast as I could. It's not much fun today."

"How come?" Irene fell in step beside her.

"Too many people watching," Elena said with a shrug, then looked at her wristwatch. "Oh, good. It's almost time for Angela to set out the *merienda.*"

Irene knew the Spanish word for tea. Since the Mendozas dined around eight, they often had a snack prepared at four. Like an English tea, it consisted of small sandwiches and coffee, or some other beverage. "Are you hungry? I am a bit."

Elena nodded. "I want some of the deviled ham and cream cheese sandwiches Angela fixes." Elena's eyes grew wide as a worker passed by them. Subtly she edged in closer to Irene.

Irene's earlier uncertainty gave way to conviction. There was definitely something going on. But experience had taught her that she'd have to take it slow to get answers from Elena.

As soon as they reached the sitting room, Elena seemed to relax. "We're the first ones here." She walked to the small African violet on the table near the window and began speaking to it softly.

Irene listened, trying to make out the words. It seemed to be a simple poem. "What is it you're saying to the plants, Elena?"

" 'Water and air give you your life, but sunshine is your soul.' I learned it a long time ago."

"I think that's beautiful. You know, Tewas also tend plants with lots of care. Every spring we have rituals to ensure that our crops will be blessed. What you're doing for the benefit of the plants is along the same lines, particularly because it's done with love."

Elena smiled. "Tell me more about what it's like on the pueblo. When you're away, like now, do you get homesick?"

"A bit, I suppose. I miss my family, my mom and aunt especially. They're a lot of fun to be around. They're best friends but they're always playing tricks on each other."

"That sounds mean," Elena said hesitantly.

"Oh no, not at all. Everything's done in fun. I'll give you an example. The pueblo sometimes has cooking demonstrations for the tourists. One time my aunt added a whole bunch of cornstarch to the flour my mom was using to make fry bread. The more water my mom added, the thicker the dough became until it was practically a solid lump. She couldn't even roll it out to fry. Meanwhile my aunt kept making light, beautiful puffed-up pieces of fry bread, one after the other. Finally someone told my mom what was going on, so she decided to turn the tables on my aunt. She had someone come tell my aunt that my grandfather needed her. While my aunt went to see what he wanted, she switched the dough. My aunt knew what had happened, but they had a good laugh about it. Afterward, they split the money they'd made from the good fry bread that day."

"Does your mom play tricks on your aunt too?"

"Oh yes! My mom loves to tease my aunt. About a year ago my aunt bought an economy car that was supposed to have wonderful gas mileage. My aunt would drive it around, and the gas gauge would go down each night, but then the next morning, the tank would be almost full. My mom told her that it was the heat and expansion of the gasoline and that she was very lucky her car got such great mileage. My aunt was so proud of her smart buy she bragged to just about everyone." Irene laughed. "What was really happening, of course, was that my mother was sneaking in every night and refilling the tank. Everyone in the pueblo went along with the joke, chipping in for the gasoline and convincing my aunt that it was practically a miracle. We had her going for weeks before she figured out what was really going on!"

Elena smiled. "Raul and I did things like that to each other when we were kids. We'd play tricks on each other a lot."

That was a side of Raul she'd never suspected. Irene grinned. "I can't believe Raul was ever mischievous."

"Oh yes, he was always getting into trouble with Dad and Mom! He loved playing pranks. One year Dad bought a beautiful ivy for me. I really took special care of it. I'd check on it every evening after dinner. Then I started noticing how fast the plant was growing. There were new, big leaves every day. I thought maybe it was the fertilizer I was using, so I kept it up, and the plant kept getting bigger and bigger. The long green-and-white striped leaves were easily a foot and a half long. At least a half dozen little miniature 'airplanes' shot out on runners in every direction."

"That must have been some fertilizer! Plants don't grow that fast."

She smiled. "Well, Angela noticed and asked me about it. I told her that it was the fertilizer, but she talked me into hiding in the bathroom with her one evening after dinner. We saw Raul come in with a bigger plant and switch them."

"Did he get into trouble?"

"No, Angela wasn't like that. She helped me fool Raul back. The next night when we were all together in the *sala,* I told Raul that my fertilizer was really working. He thought it was very funny. Then, right in front of him, I started putting the fertilizer on Mom's tiny airplane plant. Well, every morning before we got up, Angela would switch it with a bigger one. Angela and Mom and Dad were all in on it. We really had

Raul going there for a while. He sure felt silly after he found out what we'd done."

"It's hard to imagine either Raul or Angela being that playful," Irene admitted with a chuckle.

"Both of them used to be lots of fun. Things didn't change just because Raul grew up or Angela got older either," Elena said quietly. "It wasn't until Reina came that everyone here started acting differently."

"How did you get along with her?"

Elena shrugged. "She was hard to like. She'd get really jealous whenever Raul wanted to spend some time with me. Then she'd yell at Raul and twist things around until she made everyone miserable. Raul and she would fight a lot. After she came no one was really happy here anymore. Raul shouldn't have married her." Elena paused, then shook her head. "I don't want to talk about Reina, okay?"

Elena looked at the window quickly as one of the workmen came into view. For a second, her face contorted with fear. Then as the workman passed, she relaxed.

"What's wrong, Elena? You should be used to the crews by now. There's no reason to be afraid."

Elena stared at the floor, then edged sideways around Irene. "I just don't . . . like having them around."

Before Irene could say anything else, Elena hurried out of the room. Quickly gathering her wits, Irene started to go after her. But as she ducked out the door, she practically collided with Angela.

Angela shook her head. "You might as well let her go. I've seen her like that before and it won't do you any good to try and talk to her right now. What happened?"

"I don't know," Irene answered honestly. "She got

really scared when one of the workers went by outside."

Angela's brows knitted together. "Maybe it's all the confusion around her right now. The circular stairway's been braced with supports, the *sala*'s had one wall knocked out, and the billiard room is having new flooring put in. It's noisy and dusty almost everywhere. All that happening inside her home at the same time probably has her on edge."

"Could be, but I think there's more to it than that."

"I don't know what else to suggest." Angela cleared the side table, preparing it for the *merienda*. "But I do know that she'll eventually ask for help if she can't handle something. You can count on that." Angela picked up a tray with coffee that had been there since lunch, and walked out.

Irene sat down and mulled things over. Something was very wrong. She could feel it. As she stared across the room, her gaze settled on the television set inside the partially open entertainment center.

The movie that had frightened Elena so much had been about a woman who'd been attacked. A new idea formed in her mind as she recalled Elena's vivid depiction of the fictional events. Perhaps what Elena had seen hadn't been a movie at all.

# 14

S HE CONSIDERED ELENA'S reaction to the workmen in view of this new possibility, but before she could give it much thought, Angela came into the room.

"Your mother is on the telephone," she announced.

"Thank you, Angela." Irene picked up the extension on the table next to the sofa. "Hi!" she greeted. "I've missed you!"

Her mother's voice was guarded. "Can you get away later today? Your aunt convinced me it would be a good idea for us to drive into Taos if you could take some time off."

Irene took a deep breath and let it out. As usual her aunt had a sixth sense that was amazingly accurate. "Could we make it an early dinner?"

"Sure. Why don't we meet at Gomez and Company at six?"

"I'll be there."

Hours later, after making sure she wouldn't be expected for dinner at the hacienda, Irene changed clothes. Wearing a denim skirt and a chambray blouse, she started the long, dusty drive out of the mountains. The glow of autumn had long since passed, and a clear, cold sky reminded her it was nearly winter in the valleys as well. Fortunately no snow was forecast, and the drive was uneventful.

The minute she saw her family, it felt as if spring had arrived. They were the world she knew and loved. "It's so good to see you both!" she said, embracing her mother, then her aunt. Both women were dressed in brightly colored cotton dresses. Alicia wore a hand-knit cardigan sweater over hers, but her mother had opted for a more traditional embroidered shawl.

Teresa Pobikan held her daughter at arm's length, her gaze drifting over Irene gently. "Alicia said we should come."

Irene tried to give her aunt a stern look, but couldn't carry it off. "I should be angry at you for upsetting Mom, but I'm too happy to see you."

Alicia smiled. "I got the feeling you needed us. From the looks of it, I'd say I was right."

They seated themselves in a booth at the far corner of the restaurant. Soon afterward, the waitress came, took their order, and left. The moment they were alone, Teresa placed her hand over her daughter's. "How are things going for you at the hacienda?"

"It's been very hard work, but once it's done it'll all be worth the effort." She told them about the renovations, filling in the details.

A few moments later, their simple dinner arrived. Platters of *chiles rellenos*—green chile peppers stuffed with cheese and chicken, dipped in batter, and fried—were placed before them. As they ate, Irene grew silent, only half listening to the latest gossip from the pueblo.

"You're very distant. Something's bothering you," Teresa said at last.

"I'm sorry. I've been listening, really," Irene assured.

"You've encountered the danger I told you about, haven't you?" Alicia said quietly. "It's the beginning of what's yet to come."

Irene tried to keep her expression neutral. "I'm handling the situation," she assured them.

"But you're troubled, I can see it," Teresa insisted. "Talk to us. If you can't trust family, who can you trust?"

Irene nodded. "Things are very tense at work right now and I'm under an incredible amount of pressure," she admitted. "For one thing, I'm working with John Cobb, and he's creating as much trouble for me as he can."

"I remember him. You've had problems with this man before," Teresa said.

"Yes. But the person I'm most worried about is Elena Mendoza," she admitted slowly. "I think she needs help, and I'm not sure how to give it to her."

"She's different, not like the rest of us," Alicia answered, misunderstanding, "but she has her own part to play in the lives of others around her."

"I'm talking about far more than her handicap, Aunt Alicia." Irene explained about the workmen and Elena's difficulties around strangers. "When Elena first told me about that movie, I didn't think much about it. Now I'm inclined to think that Elena might have been attacked when she was younger. Crediting her memory to a movie might be her way of coping."

"You must tell Raul Mendoza. He's the head of

that household and he has a right to know," Teresa said adamantly.

"I'm not sure how he'll take something like this, particularly since it's just a theory."

"Your duty is still to inform him of your suspicions."

"But I'm not sure I'll be doing anyone a service," Irene said slowly. "If I'm wrong, then all I've done is given Raul a reason to worry needlessly about his sister."

"Wait until you're certain that what you're doing is the right thing," Alicia counseled. "Acting on impulse now can only lead you into situations you're not prepared for."

Something in her aunt's tone made Irene look up. There was a veiled warning laced through the words. But her aunt couldn't have known about her feelings for Raul. She'd said nothing to give herself away.

"Think before you act, and stay alert," Alicia added. "You have many enemies at that place."

Was it possible that her aunt had heard about the accidents through some of the Tewa workers? If she had, then perhaps her references hadn't alluded to Raul at all. "I'll stay alert. But my main concern is for Elena."

"She has others to take care of her, you don't," Alicia insisted. "Many temptations are going to be crossing your path, and you need to concentrate on yourself," she said, her fingers tracing patterns over the frost on the iced-tea glass before her.

"I'll watch my step, don't worry about me," Irene answered, wondering just how much her aunt had really managed to guess.

While Teresa paid the bill, Alicia took her niece aside. "The danger to you is real, so be very careful."

She paused, then in a barely audible whisper added, "With your heart too."

As they walked out to the parking lot, Irene decided to change the subject. "Would you like to come to *Casa de Encanto* and see how the work has been progressing?"

Alicia and Teresa exchanged glances. Finally Teresa answered. "We're interested in your work, Irene, but that's one place we could never go. That kind of progressive thinking belongs more to your generation than ours."

Irene nodded, understanding. "All right. I won't insist." She stuck her hands into her coat pockets to keep them warm. "But don't ever think that the Mendozas have escaped their own tragedies. That's a troubled house, Mom. That family has known their share of sorrow too."

Alicia glanced up. "One of the young women from our tribe worked there for a short time last winter. She said that Raul Mendoza mourned his wife deeply." She fished her car keys from her purse. "I understand he still does."

"I don't really know. He doesn't talk about her. Actually, if anyone wants an argument with him, all they have to do is bring up her name."

Alicia nodded. "Then he still harbors strong feelings for her," she said, and lifted her gaze to meet Irene's. "Strange. From everything I've ever heard, the woman brought trouble wherever she went."

"Yes, I've heard that too," Irene conceded.

"It's time for you to start back to the hacienda," Alicia said, looking up at the sky. "Those mountain roads can be tricky after nightfall. But get in touch with us immediately if you need anything."

"I will, so stop worrying," Irene said, hugging them both.

Irene watched her aunt's car go around the curve and disappear from view. In frowning silence, she went to her own vehicle and started the long drive to the hacienda. Her aunt never ceased to amaze her. She couldn't quite figure out whether Alicia really did have special powers, or whether she just had access to every shred of gossip that ever reached the pueblo. Her warnings, though, hadn't fallen on deaf ears.

By the time she reached *Casa de Encanto,* Gene, Raul, Cobb, and Elena had gathered in the sitting room. Elena, who'd brought in several blooming mums, was trying to find the best places for them around the room.

She smiled as Irene entered the room. "Look! I've learned something new! I can put glitter on the mums and make them sparkle."

"They're beautiful," Irene said, joining her. "How did you get the idea?"

"Angela suggested it. She bought the glitter for me." As Elena placed each of the potted plants around the room, she repeated the same little poem Irene had heard her whisper before.

"Do you recognize the words, Raul?" Gene said, his voice hard.

Irene looked at Gene. His eyes were bloodshot, and from the way he was standing she could tell he'd been drinking again.

"Do you, Raul?" Gene insisted. "Or have you forgotten even that?"

Fury blazed in Raul's eyes, but he held his body perfectly still. "Drop it, Gene."

"If you could, you'd erase her from everyone's memory and make it as if she'd never existed. You don't even want Elena to use the poem your 'Reina' "—he spat out the name—"taught her. You don't honor her even in death."

"She was my wife and I loved her, Gene. Why do you find that so hard to accept?" Raul's tone was too controlled to pass as natural. His face held a tinge of redness that betrayed his feelings, despite the image of calm he was trying so hard to project.

The vein in Gene's forehead bulged ominously. "I would accept it if you'd ever given me reason to believe it," he answered, his voice rising slightly.

"Not now, Gene."

Irene saw the savage pain that stabbed through Raul's control. He held himself rigid, scarcely moving a muscle as he remained in his chair.

"Gene," Irene said quickly, "this isn't you doing the talking, it's the brandy. Come have some coffee with me." She started to pour some from the carafe into a cup.

Gene spun and faced her. "You're the last person I need making excuses for me," he hissed. "You have your own reasons for wanting Raul to forget."

Raul rose to his feet slowly. "I've had enough of this, Gene. You're embarrassing our guests, and I won't put up with that."

Gene turned to his brother. "Do you think I'm blind to what's happening? You want to bury Reina's memory and start over. Renovating our home is all part of that."

Elena left her chair and came to stand between the two brothers. "I hate it when you two act like children." She turned her head and looked directly at Gene. "You want to tell everyone what they should think and what they should feel. But how can you know what's best for anyone? You don't even know what to do with your own life."

Irene struggled hard against the impulse to go up to Elena, pat her on the back, and congratulate her. Elena's observation had been right on target.

Gene stared at his sister, his face crestfallen. "Elenita, you don't understand."

"I understand that we're family. We should stick together. Reina's gone, but we're still here. Instead of worrying so much about Reina, maybe you should start thinking about us."

Raul stared at his sister, a mixture of surprise and pride on his face. Irene watched the three Mendozas frozen in silence, knowing that Elena had done what no one else in the room could have. Through heartfelt emotions and simple words, she'd stopped the anger from escalating.

Gene reached out and tried to take Elena's hand, but she recoiled almost instantly. "Elena, I didn't mean to upset you. I'm sorry."

"Then show it and stop picking on Raul. You hurt all of us when you do that."

Gene nodded once, then turned and left the room.

Elena grabbed Raul's hand. "I'm sorry, Raul. I know you don't like me butting in, but I couldn't let you two fight like that."

"I'm not mad at you, Elenita." Raul's voice was hushed.

The corners of Elena's mouth turned up in a faint smile. "I'm glad." She stifled a yawn. "I'm tired. Can I be excused now?"

"Sure you can, honey. Good night." Raul kissed her on the cheek, then watched her walk out.

Cobb, having hidden behind his goblet of wine during the Mendoza's confrontation, shifted from foot to foot nervously. "I think I'll hit the sack too." He didn't just leave the room; it was more like an escape.

Irene sat down and remained silent, sipping the cup of coffee she'd poured for herself.

Raul regarded her thoughtfully. "And you, Irene?

Don't you have some fast excuse to get away from this embarrassing situation?"

"Is one needed?"

Raul sat back down in his chair with monolithic dignity. "No, it isn't," he agreed. "Do you know me so well that you're already that comfortable around me?" A ghost of a smile played on his lips.

"In some ways."

"Some of what Gene said is true, you know," he said, his eyes touching her with exquisite gentleness, not lust. "It's time for me to close the door to my past."

She said nothing for a moment, her heart lodged at her throat. "And Reina?" she whispered, unable to refrain from asking.

"She's gone."

"But the feelings in your heart remain."

"I'm capable of many kinds of love. A part of my heart belongs to Reina, but you have a place in there too." He crossed the room, took her hand, and lifted her to her feet.

The temptation to yield and step into his arms was great. But too much was at stake to indulge in things that could only cause pain. Using all her willpower, she stepped away from him. She wouldn't share a man who still belonged to another. "I came here to do a job, not to start something that will end up in heartbreak." Her hands were trembling so badly, she stuck them inside her pockets to hide them.

"You've brought me a very special gift, Irene. You've shown me that even though my heart's been scarred, I haven't lost the ability to care deeply. You helped me see what's been missing in my life, though I've tried to hide that even from myself. Don't ask me to just let you walk away from me."

"What you feel for me is only the comfort of friendship. You're able to be yourself around me because you know I won't pass judgment on you."

"There's more than that between us. You know it."

His words reverberated in the silence of the room. Nothing seemed in sharp focus except the man before her. Her heart yearned for the promise of warmth he held out to her. She shook herself free. Romanticism was impractical, and the last thing she needed in her life. It would lead only to expectations reality could never match, and disillusionment. "No. Passion can't play a part in what I have to do here."

"And love?"

"That's a word that can have a million meanings, or none at all. More often than not, it only represents a yearning for something undefinable, a lack many people feel in the center of their being but aren't sure how to fill." She shook her head sadly. "What it isn't is a road to happiness, or the secret to dreams fulfilled."

"But it can be," he said, then paused. "No, I don't want to try and persuade you to see this my way. I want you to need me and want me, but that's something that has to come freely from you. If I try to force it to happen, then it's no good."

Seeing this feeling of helplessness in a man used to being in control touched her soul. He was openly acknowledging his vulnerability to her. He was letting her see how alone he stood in the face of emotions that couldn't be mastered through will alone.

A groundswell of feelings swept over her, and emotions she didn't dare name formed within her. She wanted to comfort him, to take away his regrets, and the shadows of a past that hung over him like dark storm clouds.

Instead, she found herself tearing her gaze from his and walking out the door. Despite her grandfather's warning, some things were better left untapped. Not every possibility was meant to be explored.

It was shortly after lunch when Angela came into Irene's office. "I know you're busy, but if you could find a moment . . ."

"Come in, Angela. Sit down," she said, waving at the empty chair in front of her desk. "What can I do for you?"

"It's not for me," Angela said slowly. "I don't know if you've noticed, but Miss Elena hasn't been down for either breakfast or lunch."

"Isn't she feeling well?"

"I don't think that's it," Angela said slowly. "I've seen Miss Elena like this before. I think she's trying to avoid something."

"Like what?"

"I don't know. If it was just the workmen or the confusion, she would have done this long before now. It's got to be something else." Angela stood up. "I thought that you might be able to persuade her to come out of her room, or at least talk to you. I can't seem to get anywhere. I even offered to make her piñon fudge. She loves helping me fix it, and until today she'd never turned me down."

"Let me see what I can do," Irene said. "I have an idea what might work." As soon as Angela left, Irene finished transposing the measurements of newly delivered antique window frames into the computer, made two backups, and then slipped one inside her jacket pocket.

It was time for her break, and she intended to put it to good use. Irene left her office, walked upstairs to Elena's room, and knocked lightly.

Elena opened the door a crack. As she saw Irene, a smile lit up her face. "Oh, it's you! Come in."

"I have a better idea," Irene countered with a smile. "Take a walk outside with me. It's a beautiful day and we both need some fresh air." Sensing that Elena was about to refuse, she continued quickly. "You said that there's a garden of bulbs and some other plants you tend during the winter months. I thought you could show me what you do there."

Elena hesitated, obviously torn between complying and staying there. "I could show you, if you want," she said slowly. "But there's really not much to see. Plants only bloom during the winter if they're inside."

"I'd still like to see it. Maybe I can learn something from you. I have a small garden in the pueblo, but during the winter I don't do anything with it except water my onions."

"Oh, that's not right. That's the time to prepare," Elena said. She grabbed her jacket from the closet. "Come on. I like teaching others about making a garden, but around here no one's usually interested except Angela. Oh, my brothers enjoy the flowers, but they don't pay attention to how they're grown."

Elena walked alongside Irene, staying very close, and avoiding the part of the house where construction noises were coming from. As they reached the hacienda's entrance, Elena hesitated. Her eyes studied the workmen outside warily. Glancing back at Irene, as if making sure she was still close by, she overcame her reluctance and went out the door.

Irene struggled against the urge to come right out and ask Elena what was bothering her, but that had never worked well in the past. She had to bide her time. "Is your garden very far from the house?"

"No, it's just on the other side of the courtyard. It's a sunny clearing away from the evergreens. Pine needles smother anything beneath them, including grass, so I picked an area that would stay free of them."

Elena led the way across the grounds to a narrow trail bordered by stones. "This path is lined by daisies in the spring and summer. I plant them in all colors and it really is very pretty. Right now, it just looks sad and empty," she said.

"No, not sad. Your plants are resting, and the earth with them. You have your rest period, sleep, just like them. Our people believe that everything in nature works in two parts like that. This is the season of harmonizing, because without rest there couldn't be activity. It's such an important time that our Chief does rituals every fall to assist in putting nature to sleep."

"I don't understand. That happens anyway," Elena said.

"So who's to say that it's not working?" Irene answered, giving Elena a wink.

Elena smiled. "Right!"

The path branched off, but Elena kept to the left. "It's this way."

"Where does the other trail lead?"

"To our family plot, where the graves are. Mom and Dad and all the dead Mendozas are buried there. I don't like going that way, but in the spring I put tulips around the graves. I do it for Raul, though it's supposed to be for Reina. She loved peach-colored tulips, and it makes Raul happy."

As they arrived at a clearing, Elena waved a hand around the area. "As you can see, I work hard to keep the weeds pulled. And this is the time when I add the most to the compost pile."

"To feed the earth," Irene said, and nodded in approval. She started to say more when she saw a figure up on the hillside beside a spruce. The man seemed to be watching the construction, and hadn't seen them. Irene fought the impulse to try and catch up to him as he began moving away. It might have been just a neighbor curious about the work going on, but it made her wary.

"Let's start back to the house," she suggested. "I should be getting back to work."

Elena glanced up and caught a glimpse of the man just before he disappeared into the trees. Her expression changed, the friendliness gone and replaced by anxiety. "Yeah, I think we should go too."

Elena led the way, frequently glancing back to make sure Irene was right behind. Finally, as they neared the house, she slowed down. "Did they ever find out anything about the body the men found?"

"No, but investigations like that take forever. Remember, whoever it was had been there a very, very long time." Irene saw the color drain away from Elena's face. "Are you still thinking about that movie you saw?" she added gently.

Elena nodded. "After I saw that, I was so scared I wouldn't come out of my room for weeks. Daddy was worried, and Mom would come up to my room just to talk. I really didn't want to go anywhere."

"But why, Elena? It was only a movie."

"I was afraid that someone would sneak up on me like the bad guy in the movie had and I wouldn't be able to get away either. I don't know what it's like to be dead, and I don't want to find out."

The statement took Irene off guard, and she smiled. "I think that's perfectly normal, Elena. I feel the same way."

"So you understand," Elena said finally. "Good."

"Can I ask you something—as your friend?" Seeing Elena nod, she went on. "Lately, you haven't wanted to come out of your room. You're acting like you did after you saw that movie. How come? Has something scared you?"

Elena avoided Irene's eyes. "You're my friend," she

whispered. "If I was going to tell anyone, I'd tell you, but I can't!"

Before Irene could reply, Elena dashed into the house.

Something inside Irene twisted and churned as she saw Elena run up the stairs. Elena's world was a simple one, but someone or something had come into it, leaving confusion and fear behind. Anger against whatever had threatened Elena formed inside her.

Making up her mind to act, she walked straight to Raul's office. Whether or not he wanted to hear it, this was something he had to know about.

As she reached for the door to his study, a chilling possibility occurred to her. What if another family member was responsible for Elena's problems?

# 15

━

**A** FEW MOMENTS later Irene was seated inside Raul's study. She hesitated, wondering if perhaps she should have waited until she knew something more about what was going on. Raul's hazel eyes mirrored control and logic. Yet he also possessed an undercurrent of volatile emotions that lay hidden below the surface. She'd seen that side of him firsthand. Still, she had to do something about the situation with Elena, and she trusted Raul the most.

"What's wrong?" he prodded gently.

"It's about Elena," Irene said after taking a deep breath. She told him about the person who'd been wandering the hall at night and pointed out the recent changes in Elena's behavior. "I don't know if this is connected, but I thought you should know."

"You said you actually caught Cobb?"

"Yes, but in retrospect I don't believe he's the one who's been doing this all along."

"But since you tripped him, have you had any more problems with this"—he fumbled for the right words—"night stalker?"

"No, not really."

"Then I'd say you've handled the problem."

She bit her lip pensively, measuring her words. This is where she had to tread very carefully. "You know that movie that frightened Elena so badly?" Irene saw Raul nod, and went on. "Her fears about coming out of her room now, seem to parallel what happened to her after she saw that movie."

"I better figure out just how much this night stalker has frightened her. She has to understand she's safe here in her home."

"Raul, there's something I'd like you to consider." She had to be more direct. Raul's pride was keeping him from seeing the point she was trying to make. "Is it possible that Elena wasn't frightened by a movie at all?" Irene spoke quickly, afraid she'd change her mind. "Could she have been attacked when she was younger, and then convinced herself it was a movie in order to cope with it?"

Raul bolted to his feet so fast that his chair was sent flying backward. "If someone had hurt my sister don't you think one of us would have noticed immediately? Do you really believe the family pays so little attention to her that something like that could have escaped our notice?" His voice was remarkably even for someone so full of anger. "No one has *ever* harmed Elena!"

She'd expected a strong reaction, but not like this. He'd taken it as a personal affront; an insult to his ability and that of his family to take care of their own. "Raul, I was only suggesting a possibility I thought you should be aware of."

Raul held up a hand, interrupting her. "You're practicing armchair psychology. In the future, please

spare me your efforts." He stepped around the desk
and went to stand by the window. "As for your night
stalker, I'd be willing to bet it's my brother, Gene.
He's always running out of booze and going downstairs to restock the supply in his room. It's been a
long time since he was able to fall asleep without first
passing out." He turned to face her. "My family has
its problems. But to suggest that Elena has come to
harm, and in that particular way—" He shook his
head. "I won't hear of it. That's the sort of ugliness
that rumors feed on. My sister has enough problems,
she doesn't need a cloud like that hanging over her
too."

"It was only one possible way of explaining her behavior; an unsubstantiated theory, that's all."

"You're speculating too much. Maybe that's a result of the accidents and your heightened paranoia.
You're seeing problems where none exist."

She pressed her lips together, trying to keep from
blurting out something that would create irreparable
harm. "Fine. I'm glad you know what's best. I won't
bother you anymore."

"I know what I need to about my family and *Casa
de Encanto.* Don't doubt my ability to watch over the
Mendozas. It's a trust that was passed on to me from
my father, and one I've always discharged," he said
flatly.

She'd injured his pride in the worst way, but her intent had only been to help Elena. From now on she'd
know better than to approach him with anything other
than solid facts. "I better go back to my office. I've got
a lot of work waiting for me."

The rest of the day went by slowly as minor interruptions gnawed at her patience. Then the crew discovered that a section of the hacienda's exterior west
wall had been seriously eroded. An earlier examina-

tion hadn't revealed any weak spots. But now, in light of this new discovery, the best they could hope for was that they wouldn't have to tear out all the adobes and rebuild that portion completely.

Cobb appeared in her office around midafternoon. "We've done what you asked and dug out an area about a foot from the wall. I don't think you're going to like what we found."

"Let's go see," she said.

She accompanied him outside and around to the west wing of the hacienda. Five men stood beside a trench that revealed the circular foundation of something resembling a pond. "That wasn't in the plans."

"I spoke to Angela. She said the elder Mrs. Mendoza had a fountain there once. Unfortunately it leaked, so they eventually tore it down to ground level."

Irene crouched by one of the cracks that ribboned through the exterior stucco of the wall. "I'm afraid the internal damage is going to be extensive."

"There were flowers lining that wall."

"Great," she muttered softly. "Many adobe buildings after World War II were covered in portland-cement–based stucco. Mud plaster on adobe had to be renewed every three to five years, and it was so labor-intensive that people decided they didn't want to fool around with that. When they switched over to stucco, they didn't realize the harm it would cause poorly drained walls. Unfortunately that's exactly the case here."

"Well, stucco didn't hurt anything right away," Cobb commented, "so that fooled people into thinking it was okay."

"Yeah, stucco does have a life of about twenty years before it starts to crack. But from the second that begins, the adobe beneath deteriorates at an alarming pace."

Raul came out, Gene at his side. "What's wrong?" Raul asked. "I overheard one of the workmen say there was a major problem."

Irene explained. "The cracks in the stucco channeled in water, but the texture of the stucco prevented moisture from evaporating out again. The adobe walls within got saturated with water, and now they're crumbling away."

"Shall we weigh the cores the crew removed from the bore holes?" Cobb asked.

"Yes, then bake them dry, and weigh them again." She turned to Raul and explained. "That'll allow us to calculate the percentage of water that's seeped into the walls." She reached inside one of the holes drilled into the wall and extracted a small handful of dust. "This is what we call *tierra muerta,* dead earth. This brown dust is what's left of a solid adobe brick."

"Is the entire wall in danger?" Raul asked.

"We may have to remove and rebuild sections of it, but I don't think the entire structure has been compromised. Of course the cement stucco that's still here will have to go. We want to do what we can to speed up the drying process. Walls this thick are going to take a couple of years to dry out completely. Recovering it with mud plaster, though, will give it some protection while it does."

"But I suppose you won't really know the extent of damage until the cores are baked dry," Gene said.

"True," she replied. "I wish one of you had remembered the water fountain. There was nothing about it in the plans I received."

Raul nodded. "You're right, it wasn't there, and I just didn't think of it. That goes back to when I was in grade school. My mother had a small flower garden right there next to that wall."

"Maybe that's why the utility room on the other side has always smelled of mildew," Gene said. "No matter how thoroughly Angela cleaned, it never went away."

"I'm sure that's it," Irene answered.

"What can you do now?" Gene asked. "And what will it do to the deadline you're committed to meet?"

She glanced up sharply at him. "I'll meet the deadline. Admittedly, this'll force us to put in extra hours when we divert one of the crews, but it shouldn't affect our overall rate of progress."

"Do whatever you have to," Raul said. "I trust your judgment and expertise." He started to walk away, then stopped and turned around. "By the way, I want you to understand that I take full responsibility for this. It was up to me to check those plans."

As Raul and Gene returned to the house, Cobb exhaled softly. "Considering the boss man's temper, you're lucky he likes you. If anyone else had been the architect, that poor sucker would have been nailed to the wall."

"No," she replied calmly, "that's your style, not his."

Cobb glared at her for a second, then laughed. "Oh my, and we defend him too." He paused, raising an eyebrow. "Raul must be on your mind a lot. This is getting serious."

"Who are you jealous of Cobb, me or him?"

Cobb's mouth fell open, but before he could respond, she strode away. That round was hers.

It was late by the time Irene left her office and walked upstairs to her room. She was tired. She'd recalculated her estimates, trying to come up with several repair options depending on how much of the wall had to be torn down. No matter what their tests showed, she'd be ready with quick, alternative plans.

She crawled into bed, glad that the day was over. Her eyes would barely stay open. She fell almost immediately asleep after her head hit the pillow.

Irene didn't know how much time had elapsed when a soft shuffling sound right outside her door woke her up. At first, she wasn't sure she'd heard it. She lay still and listened, wondering if perhaps she'd dreamed the entire thing. As she started to fall back to sleep, she heard it again. It was the soft padding she'd almost become used to before.

Irene crept noiselessly to the door, then in one fluid motion swept it open. She looked both ways down the empty hall, but only silence greeted her.

With a sigh, she returned to bed. Old houses made strange noises. No one could have disappeared down the corridor that fast without making some noise. Maybe Raul was right. It was a case of pressure and too much imagination.

Despite the logic, the sensation that something was out there persisted. Forcing it from her mind, she drifted to a troubled sleep.

The next morning Irene woke up slowly. It was Saturday. No work would be going on today, though they'd all worked late yesterday. Monday, after the arrival of more adobes and the test results, they'd be ready to tackle the damaged section of the west wall.

The sounds of birds chattering in a nearby tree soothed her, and she turned on her side and listened. She could linger in bed as long as she liked. The agreement she had with the Mendozas stipulated that whether or not she was a guest at the hacienda, weekends were her time off. She wanted to enjoy this day too because if they got behind schedule, they'd soon be working weekends.

The household was still quiet, and no sounds drifted through her closed door. She checked her watch. Barely seven-thirty. Today she'd treat herself to something she'd been wanting to do since her arrival. The forest around the Mendoza hacienda was extensive and she'd been hoping for the chance to hike around at her leisure.

Irene got up and put on a pair of jeans and a wool turtleneck sweater. Opening the blinds, she looked outside. It was the perfect time of day. The sun was almost up and the air would be cold and invigorating.

After grabbing her jacket from behind the chair, she moved down the hall noiselessly. As she went past Elena's room, she heard the door open. Elena glanced at her in surprise. "I didn't know anyone else would be up this early on a Saturday!"

"I was going out for a walk," Irene said. "Would you like to come? I've been wanting to hike around the property."

Elena nodded. "I've missed doing the same thing. No one's around today and I wouldn't have to . . ." She stopped speaking abruptly and glanced down at the floor. "It's just not fun when there's too many people out there."

Irene decided not to press. "When it's quiet like this it's also much easier to see the wild animals who're out in the morning."

Elena's face brightened. "Yeah. I like to watch the rabbits and the deer. I saw a fox once too."

"Come on, then. We'll go together."

Irene led the way down the stairs and through the house, but once they were outside Elena took the lead. "Have you been on that ridge?" she asked, pointing to her left. "You can see for miles. There's a little stream that flows down, and if you listen it's really pretty. Lots of animals go there."

"Sounds like a beautiful place. Let's go."

Elena walked silently through the brush as if she'd done this hundreds of times before. "You know how to be quiet out here," Irene whispered, "like a practiced outdoorswoman." She was rewarded by a beaming smile from Elena.

"Raul showed me how. He used to bring me here when we were kids. We used to sit behind a big rock and just watch the animals. This was his 'think' spot." Her expression grew troubled. "But we don't come here together anymore. Raul spends almost all of his time in his office or going on business trips. Angela says that he's forgotten how to play."

"Maybe he has," Irene said gently. The hillside was steep and rugged with lichen-encrusted rocks jutting out of the ground. She had to be careful not to trip as she threaded her way through the thick evergreens.

"At first I was afraid to come here alone, but Raul always had something else he had to do, so one day I just went and it wasn't scary after that."

"You could go anywhere you wanted to, Elena. You shouldn't be afraid. Would you like to go down to Taos shopping with me later today?"

Elena thought about it for a while. "No. I don't think so," she said at last. "When you're not like other people it really makes a difference," she added. "It's hard to explain. I want to go, but it's scary out there. There's too many people and things that come at you all at once. I don't know how not to be afraid then. It's not like coming out here when no one's around." She shrugged. "I can't explain it any better. It's a feeling I have inside."

"But if we were to go together . . ."

Elena shook her head. "No, I'm afraid I might like

it. Then I'd start to think about things, like what I'm missing, and how good it would be if I were like other people. That won't make me happy, I'll just want something that I can never have. Sometimes it's better when you don't think too much."

"You make a lot of sense, Elena," Irene replied softly. She tried to think of a counterargument, but before she could get her thoughts together, Elena held her index finger to her lips and cocked her head to one side.

Irene followed her line of vision. Up ahead, in a narrow, thickly wooded draw, was the bubbling stream Elena had mentioned. Drinking from it, framed by the golden rays of sunlight that filtered through the large pine to the east of him, was a large, powerfully built mountain lion.

The golden-brown cat turned its head and looked at them, then resumed drinking the icy water, unthreatened by their presence.

"He's beautiful." Elena's whisper melded with the breeze that rustled through the pines.

The animal sat back on its haunches, yawned, then lay down in the sun, watching them. Irene stayed frozen in her tracks. Her heart beat madly as she waited and watched, although she knew intuitively that they were in no danger. There was something familiar about the amber eyes that fixed on her as the beast got up slowly, stretched, then walked off into the wooded area, disappearing instantly.

Elena clasped her arms around herself. "He was wonderful! I've never seen one of those!"

"It's a mountain lion, also called a cougar. They're not so rare around here, but I must admit I didn't expect to find one this close to a house," Irene said, exhaling softly.

"This place is filled with surprises. That's always been one of the best parts about coming here."

"Well, the cougar certainly fits the bill today," Irene said.

They stayed there a while longer, but as the sun got higher in the sky, Irene stood and brushed the soil and pine needles from her pants. "We better start heading back. I don't want the household to worry about us if they find we're gone."

"Angela will know where I am, but she might wonder about you," Elena said. "Let's go." She stood up and began to lead the way back down off the ridge.

As they entered an area thick with man-high red-and-orange-leafed scrub oak, Elena glanced back reassuringly at Irene. "This isn't the way we came, but it's a shortcut. Don't worry, I know my way around here. Be careful not to let the oak scratch you up."

"I'm okay, and I'll stay right behind you," Irene answered.

They were almost to the next clearing when Irene heard a rustle and the sound of twigs snapping. Before she could warn Elena, a man appeared in front of them. He was a middle-aged Hispanic with reddish-brown hair and a long, sad-looking face. Wearing a green and blue flannel shirt, jeans, and old lace-up boots, he looked at home in the forest.

Elena took two steps backward. Then, like a deer frightened by headlights, she stood rock-still and stared at him.

"I'm sorry, Miss Elena, I didn't mean to scare you." Giving Irene a nod, he turned and went back the way he had come.

# 16

◆━━◆

ELENA DIDN'T MOVE, but kept her eyes on him until he disappeared through the thicket.

"Who was that?" Irene asked.

"Mr. Hernandez. His daughter Raven and I were friends once." Elena shrugged. "I didn't really like her much. The only reason she wanted to come to the house was Raul. *He's* the one she was interested in. That used to make me really mad."

"Why?"

"Because the minute he came into the room, she just ignored me. It was like I wasn't there anymore." Elena made a face. "Then one day, she just ran off to Santa Fe or somewhere. She never came back, or wrote a letter saying where she was, or anything."

She remembered Gene telling them about Hernandez. The man had vowed revenge after being fired. A cold chill ran up her spine. He shouldn't have been hanging around in the woods near the house. Maybe

Gene had been right, and their troublemaker wasn't a member of the household or work crew, after all.

"I don't like Mr. Hernandez," Elena admitted. "He scares me. I know Raul says he wouldn't hurt any of us, but he's strange. He comes by a lot and just watches."

"You've seen him around before?"

She nodded. "He never says much, he just looks at the house." Elena brushed her short black hair back away from her face. "Do you think we'll see the mountain lion if we come back tomorrow?"

"I doubt it," she answered, glad that Elena had shifted the focus of her attention. "They don't keep to a schedule," she added with a teasing grin.

"I can't wait to tell Raul! We never saw one of those when he was with me."

Irene hesitated. "Maybe you shouldn't tell him, Elena. He might worry, and you and I both know that the cougar didn't mean us any harm."

"It looked as tame as a house cat!" Elena said enthusiastically.

"But it isn't, you know. That's very important for you to remember. Don't *ever* try to approach it. It's a wild animal, and could be very dangerous."

"It wasn't even interested in us."

"It knew that it could get away. If you cornered it, or if it felt threatened, that would change. I think it would be a very good idea for you not to come out here alone, but if you tell Raul, he might forbid you to come at all."

Elena nodded. "Yeah, that sounds like him. He always worries."

"Whenever you want to visit this spot, just let me know. Then, if we continue to see the cat, we'll tell Raul. But as long as all he does is come here in the

morning for a drink, it seems a shame to run him off.
He's part of this land too."

Elena nodded. "I don't want them to hurt the lion.
I'd like seeing him again sometimes."

"To those of my tribe, the mountain lion is very special." Irene fingered the fetish in her pocket, but decided against showing it to Elena. There was no way of
predicting how she'd react to something that was not
in tune with her family's religious beliefs. "Mountain
lions are very secretive and that makes them good
hunters. They're brave fighters too. They have just the
right blend of grace and physical strength and they
bring a blessing by harmonizing the balance of nature.
Cougars eat smaller animals and keep them from
overpopulating. So even when they hunt, they have
their purpose."

They were just approaching the house when they
saw Raul coming back from the path to Elena's garden. Elena quickened her steps and hurried to join
him. "I haven't seen you up this early in a long time!"

"I couldn't sleep," he said with a shrug, then
glanced at Irene. "What have you two been up to?"

"Hiking," Irene answered nebulously.

"I showed her the special spot we used to go to,"
Elena answered.

"The grounds around our home are filled with special memories," Raul said, glancing around. "Dad
built Gene and me a fort just down that slope. We
used to play there for hours."

"Show it to me?" Irene asked.

"Sure, but wouldn't you like to have breakfast
first?"

"I would," Elena answered, then glanced at Irene.
"But it's buffet style on weekends, so you don't have
to come in right away unless you want to."

Irene smiled. "In that case, let's look at the fort,

then we'll have breakfast. It looks like we might be in for a morning rain soon." She glanced overhead at the gathering of clouds.

Elena waved at them and continued toward the house. "I'll see you two later, then."

Raul watched his sister, love gentling his gaze. "You've managed to get her to come out of her room. I'm grateful."

"It was her decision. I just did some very subtle cajoling," she said, following him down the hillside.

"She's not the easiest person to persuade. Maybe I should be more on my guard. No telling what you'll talk *me* into," he teased.

"I think you'll be able to hold your own. I can't imagine you being *persuaded* into anything."

"Try," he baited with a grin. "Please?"

"I'll tell you what. I'll keep that request in mind. Who knows when I'll need to make use of it!"

Raul chuckled and pointed ahead. "There. That was our fort."

The tiny log cabin could only have been considered a "fort" by boys with big imaginations. Raul hunched over to go inside the door. "It's still safe. You can come in," he said through a small window opening, and waved her inside.

She didn't need to bend over, and smiled sheepishly at him. "The advantages of being petite," she muttered.

"I used to rule this place like my own personal palace. A small group of my friends would meet here regularly during summer vacation. It was our clubhouse. Gene was two years younger than us, so we'd change the password just to drive him crazy." He grinned. "Those were the good times."

A peal of thunder shook the skies. "It looks like we're in for rain sooner than I expected. It's too warm for snow. At least today it can't interfere with the crew's work."

He sat on the dusty, leaf-covered concrete floor and gestured with an open palm. "Sit, there's plenty of room. Forget about work, at least for now." A low, dark gray cloud drifted over the mountain, darkening the sun.

She did as he asked and leaned against the sidewall. "This place could use an architect," she quipped.

Raul's gaze drifted around the tiny cabin. "What it could really use is a couple of kids who'll use it and give it back its life." He rested his arms on his knees and looked at a tattered image on the wall. Water stains and years faded an old black-and-white poster of John Wayne in cowboy gear. "He was my idol," Raul said. "The last of the good guys." He gave her a wry smile. "Someday I'll get another one of those for my kids."

"And they'll look at you and say, 'John who?' "

Raul laughed. "Probably." His gaze took her in slowly and thoroughly. *"Casa de Encanto* needs to be as happy as it once was. When I was ten and Gene eight, this was truly a home. Then a few years later, Dad started having heart trouble. He'd get better for a while, then get worse again. Things were never the same." Lightning cracked above, followed by a sudden quaking of thunder. The fort itself seemed to shudder under the impact of the expanding air.

"Maybe we should start going back."

"Naw, the roof's still okay. See? There's no water stains on the floor." He ran his hand over the remains of a long board that had once served as a table. "Someday this hacienda will become a real home again."

"The renovation can be a very firm step toward the future."

"I think so too." He glanced up. "Would you mind if I asked you something personal?" He saw her shake her head. "Have you ever been married?"

"No. I've always thought that I should know myself and learn what I was capable of accomplishing on my own first." She studied his expression. "Why did you ask?"

"I don't know, curious, I guess. I'm surprised at your answer, though. I expected you to say something like you'd never found the right man to fall in love with."

She smiled. "I'll admit that concept has influenced me, but it's something that carries much more importance to those outside the pueblo." She fingered the fetish in her pocket. "I used to think my ways were just like the ones of the white world; I went to school on the outside and I've learned how to adapt. But I'm finding that some of the beliefs I grew up with are very much a part of me. I'm not as progressive as I thought. I reach out for the things I know and hold on to them without even thinking, especially when I'm away from the pueblo."

"It's the same with anyone. We cling to what's familiar to us—culture, patterns, life-styles, because they give us a sense of order."

"The Lifeway is that, and more. It's the basis of everything we think and do. Being Tewa is a culture and a religion all rolled into one."

"But surely there's still a place within that framework for love, the kind that happens between a man and a woman."

"It's something we believe comes in time if the important factors like compatibility, mutual respect, and common goals are present." She shrugged. "My problem is that I've lived in the white world for a long time and like most of my generation I'm a product of two cultures. I want to fall in love, but then I also believe that when the time is right, I will. It's not something you can rush, no more than you can force open the petals of a flower. Unwillingness to wait results in the destruction of the goal you're trying to reach." She shifted to face him, disregarding the darkness and raindrops that were altering what had started as a relatively pleasant morning.

"But enough about me," she said, smiling. "Tell me more about how it was when you and Gene were children."

His expression softened, growing pensive. "Our father was gone a lot," he admitted. "He had to spend a great deal of his time away on business. And Mother . . . well, she hated that. The minute he'd leave, she'd closet herself in her studio upstairs to work on her watercolor paintings. That was her own private world, one she kept closed to everyone else. As kids, we were always under strict instructions not to bother her whenever she was in there."

"So much like the comfort Reina found in her poetry," Irene commented almost to herself.

Though her words had been barely audible, Raul heard and nodded. "That was *her* escape. She could sit for hours with a yellow pad and a pen, staring at the garden looking for inspiration. Dreams were her reality. In a way, she was ill equipped to deal with life. She needed to be protected, but didn't know how to let go and allow that. She was always in search of something she couldn't quite define, so naturally it eluded her grasp."

"What happened to her? How did she die?"

Raul's eyes became agate-hard. "She drowned in a boating accident during a vacation."

Irene felt the coldness that had turned their rapport into a cloud of silence. "Tell me more about your parents," she said, trying to recapture their earlier spontaneity. "Were they close, despite the demands of his work?"

"That's the strangest thing. I never thought so, but after my dad died, my mother grew despondent. She wouldn't draw or paint, and she spent all her time alone upstairs. Months after Dad's death, we learned she'd developed cancer. She died ten months later."

"Couples have their own way of working things out. Appearances don't always tell the truth."

He considered her words. "You might be right, but it always seemed to me that they lost so much time. Dad literally worked himself to death." He watched what remained of a spiderweb in the corner. "I don't want to make that same mistake. I know the business is important, but it's meant to serve us, not the other way around."

Irene waited, expecting him to mention Reina, but he lapsed into a long silence which she didn't interrupt.

"I won't neglect the business, like Gene has chosen to," he continued after a bit. "It provides the material resources all of us need to survive." He shifted and lay on his side, oblivious to the thunder and rain continuing just outside. "But the one thing I want most for my family is not something I can buy. Elena's had the best teachers and tutors, but she's gone as far as she can. I really want to do more for her; she desperately needs a sense of self-worth. But I'm not sure what I can do to give her that."

"Elena has her plants, and a legitimate green thumb. Why don't you allow her to raise plants to sell to nurseries in the area? You could even build her a greenhouse."

He gave her a despairing look. "She has no sense of

business, Irene! I'd be taxing her capabilities and turning what she enjoys most into a burden."

"Or maybe giving her direction and a source of pride and satisfaction." She paused, selecting her words carefully. "It's true that you can't bury her with bookkeeping or other things that are beyond her abilities. But you could hire someone to keep the records while she does the gardening. She'd then be able to channel her love of flowers and plants into something that will make her feel constructive. It'll boost her self-confidence, and a little push like that in the right direction can make a world of difference."

"I don't know," he said slowly. "But I'll think about it. Especially the greenhouse. Maybe you could draw up some plans for me?"

"Sure."

He smiled and moved closer to her side. "It feels good to have you at the hacienda—and with me."

"You're surrounded by people, but you're more alone than anyone I've ever met," she said gently. "I'll be here as your friend whenever you need me."

He pulled her to him, gathering her into his arms, then brushed her forehead with a kiss. As she sighed and buried herself against him, he rained soft kisses all over her face, then covered her mouth with his own.

His kiss was tender and persuasive, both qualities she'd expected in the man she'd come to know. As his tongue penetrated her in a loving and intimate caress, she wrapped her arms around his neck and pressed herself into his kiss.

Suddenly a gust of wind blew a stream of rainwater through the door opening, splattering all over them. The coldness of the water jolted them, and they quickly scrambled out of the way.

"I guess it isn't as waterproof as I thought," he commented as the spray continued.

"There's no water stains because the water just runs right back out the door. Look at the way it's sloped," she said, pointing to the newly formed stream that cascaded out of the cabin. "Unless you have a sailboat handy," she teased, "we better make a run for it back to the house."

He glanced at the puddles of mud that surrounded the entrance to the cabin already. "Angela isn't going to be thrilled to see us."

"That's a sure bet," she said with a chuckle, "but we'd better make a run for it now before it gets worse."

As they ran across the grounds, sticky red-brown mud clung to their shoes in thick globs that made it hard for them to pick up speed and still maintain their balance. The tiny rivers of running water they traversed splotched their clothing with even more of the gooey mixture.

Raul kept her hand firmly in his. The warmth of his grasp was like a feeling of home, and for those precious seconds it was as if a vital part of her had found a place to reside. Neither the cold nor her wet clothing had anything to do with the sudden trembling that shook her body.

They arrived at the long *portal* a few minutes later, completely soaked and breathless. Gasping for air, they stood there for a moment, sheltered from the cascades of cold rain. A crack of lightning flashed horizontally across the sky between clouds, and was almost simultaneously followed by the peal of thunder.

Raul released her hand and wiped the water from his forehead, clearing his eyes. "You okay?"

"Sure." She felt the warmth of his touch fade and was suddenly very cold once again. "Let's have Angela bring us some towels. Maybe we can dry off here instead of tracking it in."

"We can't. We'll freeze." Raul rapped the iron wolf's-head door knocker firmly.

A second later, Angela was at the door. "We've been so worried! I don't remember when it rained like this so late in the year. And Miss Elena said you went to the old fort? Surely that's in no condition to provide shelter!"

"It wasn't," Raul said, laughing as they stepped into the warmth of the foyer.

As they stood on the brick floor, dripping wet, Gene emerged from the sitting room, his wineglass nearly empty. "So, big brother, having a little fun?" He swayed unsteadily but managed to recapture his balance by leaning against the door frame. "It surprises me that you're interested in such mundane things." His glance shifted to Irene. "Then again, you're quite tempting, though your motives, like your wet blouse, are a little transparent."

"What do you mean, my motives?" Irene demanded, wrapping the towel around her. She should have made allowances—Gene was clearly drunk—but she found it impossible to let the remark pass.

"Do you think we're fools? You're doing everything you can to become part of my brother's personal life. Your interest in Elena, and even your interest in Raul, has nothing to do with either of them. It's just your way of getting your hands on our money. That's why you're working so hard to erase Reina's memory from my brother's mind. You want to take her place."

Raul stepped between Gene and Irene. "What you've said is an insult to everyone here, including yourself. Apologize to Irene right now. You and I will have this out later."

"You poor idiot," Gene goaded, not backing away. "She's got you so mixed up you don't even see what's going on! Is your ego so fragile that it can't face up to the truth?" He stepped up to Raul, daring him to do something about it.

It was a fighting pose if she'd ever seen one. Irene wedged in between them, making the men shift their attention to her. "You want to goad Raul into a fight so you can prove you're as much of a man as your brother is," she said, keeping her voice soft and extremely calm. "But you'll never be that as long as you act like a spoiled child. Your actions are immature and beneath you."

Gene stared at her, the import of her words weaving through his alcoholic haze. "What I think of you isn't worth fighting for." He took a step back and glanced at his brother. "But I am worried about you, Raul. She's changing you, whether or not you see it." Gene turned and walked stiffly back into the sitting room.

Raul started to go after him, but Irene placed one hand on his arm. "Settle it later when anger won't play so prominent a role," she said softly. "No matter what he says, he's still your brother."

Raul pressed his lips together until they formed a thin white line. "That he is." He took the clean towel she handed him.

"Come on, let's dry off," she encouraged. "You're a mess and so am I. And Angela's really going to bless us when she has to mop up this floor," she teased.

He smiled grudgingly. "Okay, you've got a point. It's time for a hot shower and a change of clothes."

Irene managed to make herself scarce the rest of the day. She spent most of the afternoon in her room working on the corn-husk doll she intended to give her neighbor's daughter on her birthday next spring. The hobby always relaxed her. The doll-making craft, a skill she'd perfected over the years, required very few supplies. Some string, glue, yarn, and bleached corn husks were all that were necessary and she'd brought what she needed in her big purse. Corn being the primary crop of the pueblo, husks were always in plentiful supply. And when she was ready to start another project, she'd easily be able to get more from the kitchen here.

It was eight-thirty at night when she finally put the materials away and walked downstairs to the kitchen. She noticed Angela was still around as she approached the dining room.

"Have you had anything since lunch?" Angela asked, her face a polite mask. "I can fix something for you now if you're hungry."

"Thanks, but no, Angela. Just a glass of milk, perhaps. I think I'll go back upstairs and goof off for the rest of the evening. My boss sent me a computer game in the mail yesterday, and I'd like to try it out in my laptop."

"I'll never understand the attraction people have to playing with those things. For work, I can see it, but for play?" She shook her head. "There's too many other things I'd rather do."

"The games can be lots of fun, and since they force you to concentrate, it takes your mind off everything else. That's a great way to unwind, particularly when I've had one of those days when everything goes wrong." She smiled wryly. "And those do seem to happen around here."

"Yes, to all of us," Angela observed. "This family is almost like my own, but they aren't easy to work for."

"Well, if you ever want to try out any of my games, come upstairs. I'll be glad to teach you."

"Me? No, thanks," Angela said quickly. "But I'm glad you asked me anyway."

In good spirits, Irene went upstairs to her room with the glass of milk and loaded up the game. Outside, the wind was high. She could hear the gusts slamming against the window.

She stood up, and cupping her hands against the glass, peered out into the darkness. The stars and the moon were hidden under a thick layer of fast-moving clouds, enshrouding everything in a gray gloom.

As she returned to her chair, a shrill scream from inside the house rose above the whine of the storm. Irene bolted out the door and caught a glimpse of Elena as she flashed down the stairs, oblivious to everything around her.

"Elena, wait!" Irene ran after her, but before she could catch up, Elena threw open the heavy front door and raced out into the night.

# 17

**R**AUL RUSHED OUT of the kitchen into the foyer, a sandwich still in hand. "What the hell happened?"

"Was that Elena?" Gene appeared from inside the sitting room at almost the same time.

By then Irene had reached the bottom of the stairs. "Something frightened Elena, and she ran out of the house."

Raul tossed the sandwich on a table. "Gene, go up to her room and see what scared her. I'll go outside." He grabbed a coat from the closet in the hall, then turned and collided with Irene. "Where are you going?" he demanded.

"To help you find Elena," Irene replied, reaching past him to grab a spare jacket. "You're going to need me. I'll go to the right, you take the left. I don't think she'll go too far from the house in this storm."

"Neither do I. Try the garden. There's a toolshed

there she could be in. I'll search the grounds behind the house and the courtyard. She's always liked it back there."

"Here," Angela said, appearing from out of the kitchen. "You'll need flashlights on a night like this." She handed one to each of them. "I'll look too."

A cold, wet gust slammed against Raul as he stepped out of the house and he muttered a curse under his breath. Elena had never acted like this before! What the hell was going on? The possibility that someone had hurt her in the past still preyed on his mind. He'd come down on Irene hard, but the reaction had been defensive. The implication that he'd somehow failed his sister had enveloped him in pain and guilt.

He struggled against his fears now as he seriously weighed the chances that Irene might have been right. He had done his best with Elena, and would continue to do so. But he was just a man, and men could make mistakes.

"Elena!" He shouted above the wind, determined to be heard. She would come if she could hear; Elena had always felt safe with him. The prospect that he might not have been worthy of her faith in him made his gut twist.

No, he hadn't failed her. Elena was just going through a tough time because of all the strangers she'd been exposed to, and she needed reassurance, that was all. "Elena!"

He buttoned up his jacket and faced into the wind, hunching over to keep warm.

Gene rushed up the stairs, threw the door back, and burst into Elena's room. He looked around hurriedly, searching the closets, checking behind doors, and looking under the bed. If there was some pervert hiding there, he'd take great pleasure in shoving his teeth out the back of his head. But the room was empty. It didn't make sense. His sister wasn't the hysterical sort. She was a gentle creature, seldom aware enough of danger to feel fear.

He walked to the window and looked outside. There was a scaffolding directly outside her window, but no one should have been out there at this time, and in this weather. Then again maybe one of the workers had decided to have some sick fun. Elena was a child inside, but physically she was a beautiful woman.

Gene studied the ground around the scaffolding, but it was impossible to tell anything from here. He left the room and went downstairs, aware that the adrenaline had driven all the effects of alcohol from his system. Raul and he had many differences, but when it came to protecting Elena they'd always presented a solid, united front. And when they stood together, they became a formidable force, strong enough to defeat any adversary. He pitied the person who'd threatened the weakest Mendoza. They were about to discover that strength and ruthlessness came naturally to any Mendoza forced to fight.

Irene made her way slowly toward the garden, sweeping the flashlight back and forth across the inky blackness. Like thick oil, the darkness flowed back away from the beam, coalescing the second the light was withdrawn.

"Elena!"

There was no answer; only the wind heard her cry. Her nerves felt raw. If someone had harmed Elena, she would be as much to blame as anyone. She should have taken a firmer line with Raul, pressing him to investigate the source of Elena's fears, past and present.

His pride was one thing, but it didn't stand up when compared against the safety of an innocent person.

Frightened, her fingers clenched around the small mountain lion in her pocket. "You're a hunter, help me now," she prayed.

She stood still for several moments, but no answers came to her. Suddenly she heard footsteps behind her.

"It's just me," Angela said, joining her. "They haven't found her yet. The few workmen who are still here are starting to check up on the hillside, but they've been asked not to approach if they see her. They're just to call one of us."

"Good."

Angela aimed her flashlight around in an arc. "I can't imagine her staying out here, not in this weather. She'd be too frightened."

"Where do you think she'd go?"

"I don't know. I've been racking my brains trying to figure it out."

An indefinable feeling compelled Irene to turn back toward the house. "If I were her, and something frightened me in my room, I would have run out too. But then once out here, I would have tried to go someplace where I felt safe, where I thought I could hide." Her intuition leaped into sharper focus, guiding her. "Let's circle the house, staying very close to the outer wall."

Angela followed her lead, watching her curiously. Irene felt the woman's gaze on her. She couldn't really explain it in any way that would make sense, but she knew she was on the right track.

"Maybe I should search the grounds again while you do this," Angela said.

"Do whatever feels right to you," Irene encouraged. "I'll finish checking here, then go join the others."

She was just to the northern corner of the house

when her flashlight revealed barefooted prints in the mud beside the building. Irene bent down for a closer look when the beam of another flashlight cut across her own.

"Have you seen any signs of her?" Raul asked. His voice held a taut edge that attested to an ever-growing fear.

"Come here," she said, gesturing before her. "Look."

He saw the footprints, then followed them with the light toward the outside door to the kitchen.

Irene added her light to his, and saw mud on the walk. The kitchen door was open a crack.

"Elena!" he shouted, running to the door. Irene followed, and they entered the kitchen almost together. Traces of mud led across the floor toward the cellar door, which was closed. The sliding bolt on the outside was unfastened. Raul flung the door open and gazed down into the darkness.

"Elena!" he yelled, fumbling around for the light switch on the kitchen side of the entrance to the basement. The single dim bulb wasn't much help, casting long shadows around the cluttered room.

"Your voice might be distorted by the echo in this room and frighten her even more. Let me go down first."

"Elena?" Irene heard a rustling in a corner and suppressed a shudder as she eased down the steps. "Elena, please, I hate places like this. If you're down here, say something."

"I'm not going back upstairs. The man's there." Terror edged her words as Elena very slowly stepped clear of several trunks that had been stacked in the tiny half-basement.

Raul moved toward the steps leading down from

the house. At the sound, Elena ducked back behind the trunks with a startled half-cry.

"Elena, no." Irene reached out her hand. "It's just Raul. He's been very worried. The entire household has been looking for you."

"Elenita, what happened?" Raul's voice gentled as he reached for his sister and gathered her into his arms.

The tenderness Raul showed Elena made Irene's heart melt. His love made him vulnerable, yet through it, he became a tower of strength for Elena. Her heart filled with longing for something she dared not define.

With effort, she pushed the thought aside. She had to see Raul for what he was, a man with good points, yes, but some bad faults too. It was possible his pride had been at the root of the problem they'd faced tonight.

Her thoughts shifted to Elena. "You said something about a man, Elena. Do you mean Hernandez?"

"What's Hernandez got to do with it?" Raul interrupted.

Irene gestured for Raul to wait, then nodded to Elena. "It's okay to tell us, honey."

Elena shifted, and Raul eased his hold. "Come on, Elenita. This is important," he said firmly.

Elena's eyes, bright with tears, contrasted with the pallor of her face. "I don't know who he was. He had a handkerchief over his face and was standing right there, outside my window."

"But honey, you're on the second floor," Raul said quietly.

"There's a scaffolding," Gene said, coming down the stairs. "I went to take a look. There are footprints all around it. But of course, there would be."

Raul turned Elena over to Angela, who immediately

wrapped a quilt around her. "Take care of Elena," he said, his voice suddenly taut.

"I'm not going back to my room," Elena said quickly, moving away from Angela. "I'm not."

"Then why don't you share a room with me?" Irene suggested. The smile Elena gave her was so full of gratitude that a lump formed in her throat.

"Then it's settled," Raul clipped. "You'll stay with Irene." Raul glanced at Cobb, who'd appeared at the top of the stairs. "You're here. Good. You and I have matters to attend to."

The fury she saw in Raul's eyes chilled Irene to the bone. She glanced at Gene, hoping to enlist a calmer influence, but his expression was tainted with a viciousness that took her by surprise. "We should call the sheriff's department," Irene suggested loudly.

"We'll handle this matter our way," Raul said. "Let's go upstairs."

Irene followed the group to Raul's office. The tension in the air hung over them like a loose power line that snapped and cracked, moving in unpredictable directions. She felt as if she were sleepwalking through a nightmare. "You have no idea who that person might have been. It's not good to go off half . . ." Raul turned his head and with one look, disclosed the intense blackness of his rage. Confronted with that, the words suddenly lodged in her throat.

After the group had entered his study, Raul closed the door. "Tell me about Hernandez," he ordered Irene.

She told of seeing the man, then added, "But he wasn't close to the house, he kept his distance. He was also extremely polite to Elena. He seemed genuinely sorry to have startled her."

"It could have been an act," Gene warned.

"Maybe not. As far back as I can remember, Alfredo went out of his way to be kind to Elena." Raul's voice was as flat as if he had refrigerant pumping through him instead of blood. "I tend to think it was one of the workmen, maybe even one of the men who put up the scaffolding."

"I know this crew," Cobb protested. "I can't think of anyone who'd do something like that."

"But if there is one who might, there's a chance the others would know about it," Gene added thoughtfully. "They've been living in close proximity now for some time."

"Good point, Gene," Raul answered. "Cobb, get the workers who are still on the property together, and I'll meet them outside."

"You can't summon those men as if they were criminals or your slaves, and then hurl blanket accusations," Irene protested. "You're going to create an intolerable situation that will backfire on you." Irene glanced at Cobb. "Back me up here. You know what I'm saying is true."

Cobb nodded. "They're going to really resent it, and that's going to make them difficult to work with."

"I don't plan to accuse them. Just do as I asked," Raul snarled.

Cobb shrugged, then turned and hurried out the door. Though disappointed Cobb hadn't helped her try to diffuse the situation, Irene didn't blame him. There was a savage purpose fueling Raul's control that frightened even her.

"Gene, I want you outside with me," Raul said.

"You couldn't keep me away." Gene was tight-lipped.

"Raul, your sister is safe," Irene said, hoping to diffuse some of the anger. "Keep in mind that all she saw was a figure on the scaffolding. That doesn't mean that person necessarily meant her any harm."

"Then why cover his face? You're forgetting a few crucial details."

Raul's answer made her heart start pounding. There was nothing left of the warm, tender man who'd comforted Elena. In his place was this stranger bent on revenge.

"There *is* a quick way to find out who's responsible," Gene suggested. "We could bring each one of the workers before Elena. Even if she can't recognize him, the man might give himself away."

"That would terrify Elena. I don't think she could handle it." Raul glanced at Irene. "That's also the reason I'm not calling in the police. Elena could tell them nothing, and it wouldn't get us anywhere. We'd just make things more difficult for her."

Cobb came back inside a moment later. "The men are outside. Shall I have them come into the *sala*? It's freezing out there."

"No, let them be uncomfortable," Raul growled, and walking past Cobb, led the way outside.

Raul stood and stared at the work crew. In a clipped tone, he summarized what had happened. "My sister is handicapped, and the man who did this is beneath contempt. In the olden days, the person responsible would have been hung from his wrists and flayed until there was no skin covering his bones. Justice is no longer that primitive out here, but I guarantee you the man responsible will wish he never laid eyes on my sister. I'm the owner of this house, and the women within it are under my protection."

He met the gaze of each man, going from one to the next. "Although only one of you is guilty, the rest will soon know or be able to guess the identity of the person responsible. I'll be very grateful to whoever brings me information that will help me find him. And you'd all do well to remember that a Mendoza never forgets a friend."

"We don't know who's responsible, but we have no intention of letting this pass," Serna said. "This puts all of us in a bad light."

"Yes, it does," Raul replied in a voice too calm to pass as genuine. "But rest assured, I *will* learn the truth." He paused, then enunciating each syllable, added, "And then that man will regret the day he ever set foot on this land."

The moment Raul turned and walked back inside the house, soft murmurs became urgent as the men started arguing among themselves. Irene watched in silence, knowing that Raul had stirred up the proverbial hornet's nest. She would have given anything to have kept the situation from taking this turn.

She walked back to the house slowly and joined the others in the sitting room. A fire had been made, and the flames were quickly taking the chill off the air. "If any of the men come to you with something that will shed light on this," Raul told Cobb, "I want to know immediately."

"Count on it," Cobb assured.

Angela came into the room and set a tray before them. "I made some hot cocoa for Miss Elena, and thought the rest of you might also enjoy a warm drink about now."

"That's very kind of you, Angela," Raul answered. "How's my sister?"

"She's much better. She's looking forward to staying with Miss Irene. To her it's almost like a slumber party. I think she's determined to forget what happened tonight."

"Good. For now, that's probably best," Irene said. "Since tomorrow's Sunday, I'll be able to spend some time with her, and make sure she's going to be okay."

"I hate to have our family problems intrude on your plans," Raul said quietly, "but I won't forget the kindness you've shown Elena."

"It's my pleasure." She met his gaze with a level one of her own. "Elena's view of life has already taught me a thing or two."

Raul nodded, a shadow of a smile playing at the corners of his mouth. "She has a way of helping all of us see the most ordinary things in a new light. My sister is remarkable in her own way. I'm glad you've taken the time to get to know her."

With a nod, Irene walked upstairs to her room. Elena was already there. "I've brought some of my most special flowers in here. I hope you don't mind."

"No, that's great."

Irene took off her jacket and tossed it on the back of the chair as Elena closed the door. "I'm tired. Are you?"

"A little. I mean my body is tired, but I'm not sleepy."

"Yeah, I know what you mean."

"I'm glad you and Raul came after me. When I heard your voice I wasn't so scared anymore. And then, once Raul was there, I knew neither of us had anything to worry about."

"You have a lot of faith in Raul."

She shrugged. "I know that when he's around, he takes care of things. No one has to worry."

Irene thought about the burden of responsibility Raul shouldered on behalf of his family. Perhaps he needed his pride to help him carry the weight that circumstances and tradition had placed on him. She realized now that she'd judged him far too harshly. "He does try very hard, doesn't he?"

"*Tries?*" Elena considered the idea. "No, that's what I do. Raul *succeeds* with things." She paused.

"But I don't think Raul has ever figured out what to do about me."

"What is it that *you* would like to do, Elena? Have you ever thought about it?"

"I like the way things are now, I guess. I'm happy growing things, and I'm good at it." She smiled slowly, secretively. "I've never told anyone—it might seem kind of silly—but I've always wanted to have one of those big hothouses like the plant shops have. I could grow lots of flowers in there without ever worrying about finding enough sunny spots for them. My flowers make people happy, and if I could sell some, then I could buy more plants without always having to ask Raul for money. He never minds," she added quickly. "And he's never said no, but it would be nice not having to ask."

Irene nodded slowly. "I understand you perfectly, Elena. Believe me."

Elena threw back the covers on one side of the big double bed and snuggled deep between the blankets. "I'm glad I don't have to sleep alone tonight and that we're friends."

"So am I, Elena. You're the only person I feel completely comfortable with around here."

The next few days passed slowly. The identity of the man who'd frightened Elena had not come to light, and Raul's mood had darkened even more. The tension among the crew manifested itself in frequent confrontations between the men. Inside the household, everyone seemed on edge and wary, as if no one was really sure of what would happen next.

Dinners were couched in silence, and Gene hadn't bothered to show up twice in a row. Irene had heard him in his room, but short of a few forays to the wine cellar after dinner she hadn't seen much of him.

The day the scaffolding was finally moved, Elena's spirits seem to brighten considerably. Irene went upstairs to retrieve some papers and found Elena in the room gathering her things.

"What's this, bored with my company already?" Irene teased.

Elena's eyes widened. "No, that's not it. I thought . . ." She fumbled for words.

"Elena, I was just teasing you!" Irene reassured quickly. "It's okay. I know the scaffolding was moved so I figured you'd be going back to your own room soon."

"I have to get back to my plants. I haven't been taking care of them like I should. They need to be washed and sprayed for insects, and watered, and talked to."

"Sure. Don't let my kidding upset you. We're friends. It's okay for us to tease each other."

"Teasing is okay," she said, obviously relieved. "Oh, did Mr. Cobb find you? He came looking for you just a little while ago."

"No. I haven't seen him. Did he say what he wanted?"

Elena shook her head. "He just seemed really upset about something."

Irene gathered her papers and tucked them under one arm. "I better go find him, then."

Elena picked up one of the pots from the windowsill. "He's out there by the courtyard wall. I can see him from here."

"Thanks." Irene glanced over Elena's shoulder. Something was going on. Too many workmen were gathered there for it to be anything but a sign of trouble.

# 18

STOPPING ONLY LONG enough to drop off her papers, Irene hurried outside. Cobb saw her coming and went to meet her. "We've got a big problem with the wall over here. The calculations, materials, or workmanship must have been faulty. The blasted thing just crumbled overnight. It'll have to be torn down to the foundation and rebuilt completely in some places."

"There were no mistakes made on this. We both went over everything too carefully. I know it's been cold, and normally that would affect the adobe, but we covered ourselves by using bricks that have already been cured. This shouldn't have happened."

He shrugged. "Take a look. It starts with a crack about three feet ahead of you, then progresses to the crumbled mess ahead."

Irene walked down the length of the damaged wall. Cobb's assessment was accurate, but it didn't make sense. This wasn't another case of faulty plans and *tierra muerta*. This wall was brand-new and built exactly to specifications. She'd even watched some of the adobes being laid and knew the masons had done their job right.

Cobb came to stand behind her. "Shall I have them tear this entire section down, or just the damaged areas? I've got to tell you, if we have any more delays, there's no way we'll be finished by Christmas."

"Give me a minute to check this out. I can understand what happened to the wall bordering the courtyard and the house. There were things there we didn't know about. But this is an entirely different matter. I want an answer that makes sense."

"Maybe your very expensive adobe bricks aren't up to par?"

She glared at him, then focused back on the wall. "We'll talk in a few minutes."

Irene worked her way down the wall slowly. As she arrived at the point of greatest damage, she stopped and inspected the adobe carefully. Moving a few aside, she exposed the area beneath and discovered that someone had strung a wire between the bricks. It was barely visible between two at the bottom, but was attached to a very distinctive tool still protruding from the edge closest to the ground.

"John, come over here," she snapped. "Look at that."

Cobb crouched by the wall and scratched his chin pensively. "A 'come-along,' the kind used for tightening wires in fences."

"Exactly. Someone weaved a wire back and forth through this wall either while the adobe was still wet or shortly thereafter. Then he came back before it set and tried out the come-along. The leverage he got with the wire stretcher caused the structure to collapse."

Cobb stared at it, lost in thought. "It doesn't make sense to me. No one wants to create more work for themselves around here. They don't need or want the overtime."

"Maybe the intent was to discredit my design specifications, the workers, or the people who provided us with the adobe." She challenged him with a hostile glare. "Any guesses who's responsible?"

Cobb held her gaze. "I don't need to resort to vandalism to discredit your role in this project. Eventually you'll do that all by yourself. All I have to do is stand back and wait."

"What do you mean by that crack?"

"Oh, the term 'conflict of interest' comes quickly to mind. I mean if stuff starts falling down, and the boss man's too distracted . . ." He grinned slowly. "But I'm sure you know exactly what I mean." Before she could answer, he continued. "There is, of course, the possibility that this trouble was created by someone from the outside."

Irene swallowed back her anger. He would *not* get to her. "You mean Hernandez?"

"Well, he *is* part of the equation, from what the Mendozas said."

"Yeah, and it's something that needs to be looked into."

She walked inside the house and went directly to Raul's office. "We have a problem. There's some vandalism going on." She told Raul about the wall and the come-along and then waited.

Raul said nothing for a while. "I'll check out Hernandez again, but I think our problems are closer to home." He stood near his father's portrait, his hands clasped behind his back, and faced her. "By the way, I've moved my things to the bedroom at the end of the hallway so I'll be closer to where you and Elena are.

It's just a precaution. But if there's trouble again, I want to be in a position to counter a threat to anyone here in *Casa de Encanto*."

"That's fine, but I really think we need to do more than a cursory check on Hernandez. This situation makes me uneasy."

"I hired an investigator to discreetly look into his recent activities. I want to make sure it's done with tact, since I believe he's probably innocent, and I don't want to jeopardize his standing in our community. I've also put the word out to the businesspeople in our area and let them know I'm very interested in learning who's creating problems for the Mendozas. Our name carries considerable weight in this county, and many will look around just in the hope of earning our favor. We'll get results, and in the meantime, I intend to personally make sure nothing dishonors my home by threatening those who live here."

Irene said nothing. She understood what was driving him. Someone had challenged him on the most basic of levels: his ability to safeguard the people under his own roof. He would do whatever he felt was necessary to protect all of them.

As the day wore on, she was unable to escape the feeling that the worst was yet to come. It was like waiting for thunder after having seen the lightning—bracing yourself for the concussion that you knew was inevitable. It grated on her nerves. From the hushed silence of those inside the house, she knew others shared that feeling.

It was shortly after eight when she decided to go upstairs to her room. Earlier, she had picked up a sandwich from the kitchen, informing Angela that she'd be skipping a sit-down dinner. She could do no more work tonight, and desperately wanted a few hours alone to sort out her feelings. The emotional undercurrents that alternately bound together and alienated the Mendozas from each other affected her deeply. There seemed to be no permanent harmony for the residents of *Casa de Encanto,* only lulls in the storm. For the time being the Mendozas had been united by adversity, but there was no telling where this would lead, or how long it would last.

She sat on the floor and laid out the materials for a second corn-husk doll. Angela had donated the husks and corn silk as leftovers from the kitchen, and Irene had dried them between layers of newspaper for two weeks. She already had the other supplies she needed.

First she rolled five husks together and tied them securely at the center. Peeling the top half down, Irene tied the husks again about an inch from the top, forming the head. She was preparing a quarter-inch strip of husk to hide the thread when she heard a soft, scratching at the door.

She turned, unsure of what it was, and remained motionless for several moments, scarcely breathing. When silence stretched out uninterrupted, she dismissed it from her mind and focused on the doll, tying the strip at the back of the head. Then unexpectedly, she heard it again, and set the doll down.

Irene started across the wooden floor when the board beneath her foot squeaked. In a flash, soft, running footpads echoed down the hall, fading quickly away.

Irene threw the door open and glanced around. Elena was already at her door, looking in the same direction as she. "What was that?" Elena asked in a whisper.

Irene held a finger up to her lips as she sneaked away from her door. She was about to turn the corner when she caught a glimpse of a low shadow, like someone lying on the floor.

"What's going on?"

Startled by the loud voice behind her, Irene spun completely around. Raul had left his room and was striding toward her. She gestured for him to be quiet, but when she turned back toward the shadow it had already vanished. "Aw dammit," she whispered under her breath.

"What happened?" Raul asked, glancing at his sister.

"I heard soft footsteps outside my door," Elena said, "but when I came out to look no one was around."

Raul looked at Irene as if expecting answers, but all she could do was shrug. "I saw a shadow, then you came out. When I looked back, it was gone."

"Let's search the top floor," he said, unconvinced. "Elena, why don't you go back into your room and lock the door? I'll come back and check on you in a few minutes."

Irene accompanied him on a thorough search that included every unoccupied room in the top floor. "What exactly did you hear?" Raul asked.

"First there was a scratching noise. Then a different kind of sound, like someone running in socks. But the footsteps were light, like a small but very coordinated child would make."

He rubbed the back of his neck with one hand. "You're an architect and you know about the sounds of wood creaking and the settling noises houses make from time to time. If it can't be explained that way, I'm out of suggestions."

"Could someone have brought in an animal, perhaps a pet?"

"You mean is Angela hiding a cat or a dog somewhere?" He smiled. "She did that for me once when I was a child because my mother wouldn't let me keep a pet." Raul smiled at the memory. "Angela would do that now for Elena, but my sister could have any kind of pet she chose and not have to hide it." He smiled and shook his head. "So the answer's no, there's no pet around here." He paused and considered the issue. "And if by some remote chance an animal from outside had somehow managed to get into the house, Angela would have found signs of it almost right away."

"Then I'm afraid I have no other explanation," she said as they walked back to their rooms.

Hearing them, Elena came out. Raul gave her a reassuring smile. "You don't have to worry, it was a false alarm. You're all right."

Elena gave him a calm smile. "I wasn't scared this time. It didn't feel like something I had to be afraid of."

Curious by her reply, Irene studied Elena's expression. The woman seemed truly unafraid, showing a poise neither Raul nor she felt. She fought the impulse to ask Elena to explain, deciding this wasn't the right time.

Raul said good night to his sister, then accompanied Irene to her door. "I'll be right down the hall if you need anything. And don't worry, I'll stay alert to anything that sounds out of place."

"You know, it's now become a matter of pride for me as well as safety. I want to find out what's going on in this house," she said.

"You and me both, and our reasons aren't so different either." He smiled, then continued to his room.

The following afternoon shortly after four, Raul came into Irene's office. "Remember when you offered to help me carve the pumpkin?"

"I think I was volunteered," she corrected with a smile.

"Okay, but you agreed, and tonight just as soon as the sun goes down, both Gene and I bring out the pumpkins for Elena."

Irene stood up, glad to leave the reports stacked on her desk. "In that case, let's get busy."

Raul led her to the pantry. The small table there had been covered with paper sacks. A pumpkin as large as a full-sized ceremonial drum had been placed in the center. It had already been cut open at the top, and the pulp inside cleaned out. "Angela has everything already set up for us."

Irene stared at the massive pumpkin. "Geez, it certainly is big!"

"I buy them as large as I can," he said with a sheepish smile. "It's easier to cover mistakes that way." He handed her a carving knife. "Can you start it?"

"Do you have any idea what you want it to look like?"

He paused. "Yeah, decent."

"Do you think you could be a little bit more specific?" she asked with a grin.

"I dunno. I'm not good at this," he muttered.

Irene tried not to laugh. He was the head of the family, used to crushing responsibilities, yet this simple task for his sister left him stumped. She picked up a marking pen from the table and drew a face on the paper sack. "Okay. What do you think?" She sketched it with several sharpened teeth protruding from a wide grin, and big triangles for the eyes and nose.

"Can we give it some eyebrows?"

She drew a jagged line that arched. "How about that?"

"Yeah, now you're ready. Go ahead. Start carving. You're doing great."

"Wait a second. This is a joint project."

"I'm all thumbs." He exhaled softly. "I have no artistic talent."

Irene used the marker to draw the face onto the pumpkin itself, then handed him the knife. "Here you go. I may be better drawing than you, but that's the extent of my expertise."

Even with her help, it took Raul until sundown to finish, but the results pleased him. "It's the best one I've ever done." He glanced at her and winked. "Okay, we'll share the credit, since you helped."

Irene laughed. "You don't have to."

"Trust me, they'll know," Raul answered with a chuckle. Placing a small candle in the interior, he carried the giant jack-o'-lantern to the sitting room. Halfway there, they met Gene as he came down the hall. His pumpkin was covered with a cloth, waiting for the right moment to be unveiled, but his unabashed smile assured them he was very pleased with his creation.

Elena was already inside the room, waiting for them. Angela was there too, setting out a dinner buffet on the long table next to the wall. Irene realized that this was a tradition this new generation of Mendozas had established for themselves. Knowing she'd been included in their family gathering filled her with a special warmth.

The second Elena's gaze fell on the jack-o'-lantern Raul was holding, she glanced at Irene and smiled brightly. "You helped."

Irene nodded, but said nothing.

"It's a wonderful Halloween pumpkin, Raul; I love it!" she said, taking it from his hands. "Thanks for making it for me. And for your help too, Irene." She placed it on the table by the window. "I know it should face outside, but I wouldn't be able to see it, and I want to enjoy my jack-o'-lantern."

"Good," Irene answered softly, knowing how much effort Raul had put into it.

"Now mine," Gene said. He placed the smaller pumpkin in front of Elena and pulled the cloth off.

Elena's eyes grew wide and she smiled. "It's beautiful!"

Gene's face beamed with pride at his sister's reaction. Irene glanced at Raul, wondering if this would create more tension between the two brothers. Yet the look on Raul's face reflected only the love he felt for his family.

Irene stepped up to take a closer look at Gene's pumpkin. It had been skillfully carved. Nothing about it fit the crude jack-o'-lanterns she'd seen over the years. The eyes were circular, and carved with pupils that were hollow at the center and would reflect the light. The nose was shaped in a "U" and only the sides were hollowed out so that one could actually make out the bridge of the nose. The mouth appeared to grin, and between the carefully fashioned lips was an uncarved center that gave the illusion of a tongue. "Wow! That's some pumpkin!" Irene said at last.

Elena placed it on the fireplace mantel so that it also faced them. "Perfect! Will you help me light them, Irene?"

Seconds after both had been lit, Gene turned off the lights. The pumpkins glowed eerily, and Elena laughed. "These are the neatest ones ever."

Angela smiled. "Dinner is ready. I know you'll all enjoy the pumpkin pies; they're fresh and so's the whipped cream." She glanced at Elena knowingly, then at Raul. "Make sure Miss Elena eats some of the main course, not just the pie, even if it is her favorite. The tamales are very, very good, and there's plenty of tacos and coleslaw."

"Will John be joining us?" Gene asked.

"He said he and Serna would stay close to the crew this evening," Raul answered. "I agreed it was a good idea."

They sat around the room, plates on their laps, enjoying their meal. Their only light came from the candelabra Angela had placed on the table for atmosphere, the glow of the fireplace, and the pumpkins. This was by far the most casual and pleasant meal she could remember since her arrival at the hacienda.

Irene's gaze strayed leisurely over the group. They actually looked like a regular family tonight. Elena hadn't bothered to wear a dress this evening. Instead, she'd worn jeans that appeared brand-new, but comfortable. Raul's thick fisherman's knit sweater looked elegant against dark blue corduroy slacks, but he too seemed more relaxed. Gene's casual sweater, worn over an oxford-cloth shirt, made him look at peace, and that was a real first.

"I've never been big on coleslaw, but this is great," Irene said, helping herself to seconds. She glanced at the tamales, then gave in to temptation and placed another on her plate. The cornmeal and the spicy chile-laced pork made them delectable. Worried the others would think her a glutton, she glanced over at Raul and Gene. One look at their plates convinced her it would never occur to either. Their helpings looked positively mountainous.

As the moon rose high in the nighttime sky, the food heaped on their plates began to dwindle. Soon they began to hear catcalls and hoots coming from the crew's trailers. Elena tensed visibly and became restless. Her eyes darted around the room, her face pale.

"It's okay, Elena," Gene said quietly. "They're just celebrating Halloween in their own way."

She nodded automatically, but quickly finished the slice of pie she'd stuck next to the half-eaten tamale on her plate. A moment later, she approached the window hesitantly and blew out the candle inside Raul's pumpkin. "I'm going to take this one to my room for tonight, Raul. I'll leave Gene's down here for all of you to enjoy."

"You're going upstairs already?" Raul asked, surprised.

She hesitated, then nodded. "Do you think you'd all like to come upstairs with me and see what both pumpkins look like in my room? It'll be quieter there, and we'll have plenty of room to sit and talk. We can take the pies up too."

Raul studied her pensively. "If that's what you want."

Elena picked up Raul's pumpkin, then turned to Gene. "Can you carry yours for me?"

"Sure."

As the two left the room, Raul glanced at Irene. "The fool who climbed that scaffold really scared her. He won't get away with that."

The words were simple, and his voice had been scarcely more than a whisper, but the determination and power behind them were deafening. Suppressing a shudder, she followed him upstairs.

The next afternoon after Raul left on business, Irene walked the grounds, again checking the progress of the work. As she approached the wall that was now being rebuilt, she saw Gene talking to John Cobb. Her first impulse was to avoid both of them. Then, changing her mind, she continued her course. The last thing she wanted them to think was that she was hesitant to be near them when Raul wasn't around.

"How are things progressing here?" she asked Cobb.

"We'll stay on schedule, unless something else happens. I've hired extra workmen from Taos for this, but the budget's going to go through the ceiling if I have to do that very often."

"Point taken," she said with a nod.

Gene cleared his throat. "Look, if you have a few minutes, I'd like to speak with you."

"Sure." She felt her body tense up. His expression told her she could expect unpleasantness of some sort ahead. "Would you like to go to my office?"

"No, let's continue on around the grounds for a bit."

She fell into step beside him, a bit uneasy. Silence stretched out between them, but she didn't press. Finally Gene spoke.

"You and I haven't been on the best of terms, and it's been mainly my fault. I think it's time we put our bad feelings aside."

"I never had any quarrel with you, Gene," she said honestly.

"I know. You just got caught in the middle of something that has stood between my brother and me for a long time. But Elena's in trouble now and I think we all have to do our part to decrease the tension in the house. How about you and me starting by giving each other another chance?"

There was no way she could refuse, particularly since she knew it would make things easier for Raul. "Consider it done," she replied, and smiled.

"Elena talks to you quite a bit," he commented as they headed back. "I know she trusts you, so there's something you may be able to help me with. I've been worried about her staying in her room so much, even now that exterior construction's moved away from that part of the house. Can you think of anything I could do to help her?"

"Not really," she said after a moment's thought.

"But you might like to know that Raul and I have discussed the possibility of building a greenhouse for her."

"That's a wonderful idea! Have you considered a location for it yet?"

"No, at this point no definite plans have been made."

"Maybe I can help you pick out a spot. It'll need just the right exposure to the sun. There are areas on the property that would be perfect, though you wouldn't see them at first glance because of the way trees are clustered around here."

"Well, my plan was to have it attached to the house. That way she'd never be too far away from other people."

"You might have a point there." He waved Cobb over, and told him of Irene's idea before she could stop him.

"Wait, you're going to build a greenhouse? As site foreman I'm supposed to know about these things!" he demanded angrily.

"It's still in the planning stage, and isn't something that necessarily has to be added to the present work schedule. It's just something Raul was interested in having done, either now or sometime soon."

"I suppose we could erect something out in the clearing just past the rose gardens," Cobb speculated.

"I'm thinking of a site that will be adjacent to the house."

"You're thinking of an attached structure?" He looked at her incredulously, then glanced at Gene. "Will you excuse us for a moment?"

Cobb led her aside. "Look, Pobikan, this place is almost a historical landmark. Once the work is done, every builder and major property owner in New Mexico will know who had a hand in shaping this place. If it looks great, that will translate into more work for everyone. But if you attach a greenhouse to a pueblo-style home, we'll be the laughingstock of the Southwest. You can't add something like that without detracting from the basic design structure of the hacienda."

"I'm aware that there are pitfalls, but the primary function of the hacienda is to serve those who live here. Elena shouldn't have to work off by herself. This property is very isolated. I just have to make sure I come up with a design that'll maintain the integrity of the hacienda while serving as a functional greenhouse."

"That would take a miracle and you know it. Get serious. You're going to trash all the work and planning we've put into it."

"I disagree," she said coolly. "But either way, it's Raul's decision. You can present your objections to him."

"Count on it. I'll fight you tooth and nail. Raul's proud of this place, and I'm going to make sure you don't do something that'll jeopardize everything he wanted it to be."

"Do whatever you feel you have to. I certainly intend to." She walked to where Gene was standing, and joined him as they made their way toward the house. "By the way, don't mention this to Elena yet. I want to make sure that it's feasible and that Raul approves of the plans before she learns about it. I'd hate to disappoint her."

"You know, you should figure out a way of asking Elena where *she'd* want the greenhouse to be. It's possible she'd rather not have it right next to the house. Of course the tricky part would be finding out without letting her know what you're doing."

"Yeah, but you're right about leaving the choice up

to her." She considered it. "Let me see what I can do."

"Keep me posted," Gene added. "And I'm behind you one hundred percent. I think this is something Elena would love, and she deserves whatever we can give her."

Irene was on the way to her office when she saw Elena sitting alone in the dining room. "Elena, is something wrong?"

She shook her head. "No. It's just that when everyone's busy, like today, I wish I could be more like other people. I can't 'be useful.' "

"Who said that? One of the crew?"

She shrugged. "I heard the men working outside talking. One man said his wife just would not get a job. He said a woman should 'be useful and earn her keep.' " She paused. "I don't have a job either. Do you think that's bad?"

"In some cases, it is. People need money to pay rent and buy food, but you have a family who loves and takes care of you. And you make this house a real home for them." She saw Elena relax and she breathed a sigh of relief. Elena had enough to contend with already without worrying about things like that. "By the way, I remember you told me that you wished you had a greenhouse. Only you never said where you'd put it. Have you ever really given it serious thought?"

"I did when people first started building things around here, but I'm tired of having strangers in my house all the time. I want things to go back to the way they were, and soon. A greenhouse would mean more building, more noise, and I don't even want to think about that. I want it to be over."

"Well, you could order a kit and maybe get a handyman to erect it for you. Those are basically glass houses you could set up anywhere on the property."

Elena grimaced and shook her head. "It's better to

have a room in the house for just my plants. I don't want to be off by myself someplace. I wouldn't know what to do if I was all alone and that man . . ." She shuddered, then turned away from Irene.

"Do you mean the one outside your window?" Irene prodded.

Elena's face grew pale. "I'd better not talk about this. Very bad things could happen then."

"Why do you think that, Elena?" At first she thought that Elena was alluding to the pueblo belief that to speak of evil was to attract it, but that didn't seem likely. In a way, though, maybe she was. "Has something else happened?"

Elena rushed to the door. "I'm going upstairs. Don't say anything."

"About what? Elena, don't go away. Talk to me!"

Elena's eyes darted around the room. "No, hush. Too many people are here. Irene, promise. No more questions." Not giving Irene a chance to reply, she rushed down the hall.

Irene felt a shudder race up her spine. Something was very wrong, and she had to get to the bottom of it. Corruption that exceeded the *tierra muerta* within its walls had taken root inside the hacienda and was weaving a stranglehold around the one person least able to fight back.

She had to get answers fast. John knew the crew and was in a unique position to help, but the thought of going to Cobb for anything made her skin crawl. She took a deep breath. This was for Elena's sake, not her own. Bracing herself, she decided to give it a try.

# 19

IRENE WALKED TO Cobb's room and was about to knock when Gene came up the stairs. "If you're looking for John, I just saw him walking across the grounds toward the crew's trailers."

"Thanks," she said. "I need to talk to him."

"Would you like me to walk over there with you?"

"No, it's not necessary, but I appreciate the offer anyway. Did you happen to notice which trailer he headed for?"

"The next to the last one on the right."

"Thanks, Gene."

The crew had already quit for the day, and she could hear the discordant sounds of televisions tuned to different channels. As she approached the trailer Gene had pinpointed for her, she heard loud voices inside that were not part of any programming. Cobb's words were indistinct, yet there was no doubt in her mind that the deep, resonant tones were his.

The woman's voice was very loud, so distorted by anger that she couldn't quite recognize which of the women workers it belonged to. "You better start giving me some kind of break around here instead of all the crappy jobs. I'm not going to put up with it. The way things stand now, I don't have to anymore."

She heard the low rumble of John Cobb's voice, but madeout only a few words. "Who asked . . . Chill . . ."

"Don't try to put me off, John, it's not going to work. Either cooperate, or I'll blow the whistle on you."

The words made her skin prickle. She'd suspected off and on that Cobb had been behind all the accidents and sabotage. This seemed to substantiate that. Still, in all fairness, the snippets of conversation she'd overheard were scarcely conclusive.

Realizing that the voices inside had grown silent, Irene ducked behind a tree. She had to get out of here fast, before someone discovered her. The information she now had might give her an advantage, but only if Cobb didn't know she had been listening.

Irene backed into the shadows, certain this was no time to approach him about Elena. She headed instead into the old apple orchard and stayed near the tree line until she cleared the area where the trailers had been placed. Finally, moving cautiously, she came back out into the open.

The sound of twigs snapping behind her made her turn on her heels. Irene froze and waited, hoping to catch a glimpse of whatever was back there. Nothing moved, so she continued on her way, trying to boost her courage. A heartbeat later, she heard the soft rustling of leaves.

Someone was there, stalking her. She waited for a second, her hand reaching deep into her pocket and gripping the mountain lion fetish.

She wasn't sure how long she'd stood there, peering into the darkness, when she heard the sound of men's laughter. Two Tewas were heading away from the trailers and toward the house.

Spotting her, the men approached. "Is something wrong?" the older one, Juan Ortiz, asked. "You remind me of someone hunting a rabbit. You know what I mean—waiting, listening, and watching for movement."

She forced a smile. "Actually I thought that maybe there *was* an animal in the bushes back there and I was curious," she answered, unwilling to tell the truth. If they searched for someone and came up empty-handed, her credibility would suffer again, and it had taken enough blows lately.

The Tewa men regarded her story with open skepticism. Finally the other, Ricardo, spoke. "Why don't you walk with us? We were just on our way to the house. Isn't that where you were headed?"

"Yeah, I was," she admitted.

"Good. Then we'll keep each other company," Ricardo said.

"How come you two are going over there now? Did you leave something behind?"

Ortiz grinned. "The housekeeper, Angela, makes little *empanadas* the crew can come by and get if they want an evening snack."

She smiled. "I've tasted them. I'm surprised there isn't a line at the kitchen door."

"There usually is. We're late, though. I hope there's some left."

Juan stopped in midstride and held up his hand, motioning for them to be quiet. He listened intently for a few seconds, then shrugged. "I think I'm beginning to see why you stopped to listen. I *feel* something around us, though I can't really hear it." He shook his head, as if he'd tried to come up with a better explanation but had been unable to find the words.

She nodded. "Yes, that's exactly the way it hit me too," she said, her fingers again wrapping around the mountain lion fetish.

"Come on," Juan said. "I'll feel better once we're clear of these trees."

They were nearing the courtyard gate when the sound of rapid footsteps erupted from along the wall to their left. John Cobb appeared from behind a stand of junipers and strode toward the gate. He hurried past them wordlessly, brushing roughly against Ricardo as he did.

Ricardo started to protest, but saw Juan shake his head.

"What the heck got into him?" Ricardo demanded a second later as Cobb reached the entrance and went on inside.

Juan stared ahead pensively. "I don't know, but I figured you'd better let it pass. He looked like he was itching for a fight."

"So what? He has no right to run over me that way. I should have grabbed him."

"No. I've seen Cobb ticked off before, but not like that. He's really angry." Juan scratched his chin absently. "Confronting him now would have been a very bad idea. You don't need that kind of trouble, and neither do the rest of us."

"Maybe he was the one following us all that time," Ricardo said.

Juan zipped up his work jacket and shoved his hands inside the pockets. "No, he was coming from the wrong direction, and Cobb really isn't the kind to bother sneaking up on anyone."

Irene stood on the *portal* by the entrance and smiled

at both men. "Well, I really appreciate the escort service, fellas," she said with a tiny smile.

"No problem, boss lady. Glad to help," Juan said.

As she went inside, she thought how lucky she'd been that the two Tewa men had happened to come by. She wasn't certain that she'd been in danger, but their presence had certainly made her feel better. As she pulled her hand out of her pocket, she felt the tiny fetish brush against it. She smiled, a warm feeling settling over her. Her mother would have said that the power of the mountain lion was at work.

Raul didn't return from his business trip until after dinner. Irene was in her office loading her laptop into its case when he appeared at the door. "I'm glad you're here, Irene. I've been looking for you."

"Is something wrong?"

"Angela is very worried about Elena. She said that Elena spoke to you earlier and had run out of the dining room very upset. Since then Elena hasn't come out of her room."

Irene set the tiny computer down and returned to her seat. "Why don't you sit down too? There's something I really should tell you." She tried to explain what had happened earlier. "I really think someone's been giving her a hard time. It's one of the workers, I'm sure, but there's no way of figuring out which one it is without her help. And she either can't or won't say who it is."

The muscles in Raul's jaw clenched and his expression twisted into something merciless and hard. "Find Cobb for me. I want him in my study right now, and you too."

"Maybe you and I should try to figure out what's going on first, then we can approach Cobb with a firm plan of action." She didn't like Raul's demeanor at all.

His face was as red as a dusty sunset. For the moment he had the lid on his temper screwed on tight, but it wouldn't take much to set him completely off.

"Just do as I've asked, please. I don't want to argue with you. This matter involving Elena is going to stop, or I'll have heads rolling."

Normally that would have only been an expression, but in Raul's current mood, she suspected that it was right at the edge of wishful thinking. "I'll see if he's in his room."

"If you see Gene, bring him too."

She realized as he walked out that she'd been practically holding her breath. Inhaling deeply, she tried to feed oxygen into her starved lungs. This situation kept getting worse, but although she was concerned about Raul's temper, nothing worried her more than the harm being done to Elena.

As she was climbing up the steps, she met Cobb coming down the stairs. His face was set, and his strides purposeful as if he was in a rush to get wherever he had to go. "Cobb, Raul wants us in his office. There's been some trouble again."

"My men?" he clipped.

"One of them. And Raul's sister."

Cobb spat out an oath. "Once I find out who has been frightening that woman, Raul's going to have to wait in line until I'm done with him."

"Have you seen Gene?"

"Someone looking for me?" Gene came out of his room. The redness of his eyes was indicative of the amount of alcohol he'd already consumed that night.

"Raul wants to meet with us in his study. It's got something to do with your sister," Cobb said.

Gene had appeared tipsy when he'd first emerged, but at the mention of Elena he straightened his back and removed his hands from his pockets. "Did something happen to her?"

"That's what we're about to find out. Come on. Let's go," Cobb answered.

As they walked to Raul's office, she could see alertness in Gene's eyes. It was as if the effects of alcohol had suddenly vanished. But she knew better. The effects, though masked, would still be there and could make the situation even more volatile.

Raul met them in the hall, waved them inside his study, then shut the door. He quickly recapped the story about Elena, then glared at Cobb. "They're your men. If I don't find out who the guilty person is, then I'm holding you responsible. You'll never get another contract in this state again. I guarantee it."

"You can't be serious. There's a crew of sixteen regulars out there and other specialists brought in constantly for detail work by your architect. I can't watch each and every one of them after hours."

"They answer to you, you answer to me. That's the chain of command, and if you can't furnish me with the name I need, then it's your failure. When you brought the crew here onto my property, you were in fact vouching for them. Find out who it is, or pack your suitcase."

Cobb turned to Gene. "For God's sake, reason with your brother. I have no idea who it could be."

"I find no reason to question Raul's decision. Think of this as incentive," Gene added with uncharacteristic calm.

She stared at Gene and Raul, realizing that despite the differences that had separated them, they'd stand completely united against anything that threatened a Mendoza.

Cobb turned to Irene. "And what about her? You

put Irene in charge of everything. None of this reflects on her?"

"It's *your* crew. She didn't want you here to begin with. I overrode her decision," Raul replied. "Now get out of my office and get to the bottom of this. I'm anxious to greet this piece of slime with a two-by-four."

"I'll find him," Cobb said, not too convincingly.

"And Cobb," Raul added. "Make sure you control the rest of your men. One more incident and I'll fire every one of them along with you."

John Cobb's hands curled into fists so tight that his knuckles turned a pearly white. "I'll talk to every man tonight and let them know their jobs are on the line. This time of year, work is scarce. They have families to worry about and their own inflexible code of ethics. You'll have your answers, but this'll create dissension and the work is bound to slow down. Be prepared for that."

"Just do what you have to, Cobb," Gene snapped. "Grab your *cojones* and act like a man. Whining doesn't become you."

Cobb's eyes darkened with rage and he took a step toward Gene. Irene stepped between them. "Okay, that's it. Enough. The purpose of this is to find out who has threatened Elena, not start a stupid fight." She glanced at Gene, then at Cobb. "So keep your minds on the objective. Find the sleaze who's after Elena."

Cobb's face remained purple. With one last glance at Raul, then Gene, he headed out the door.

Raul glanced at his brother. "You might have handled it a bit better, but I share your sentiments."

Irene looked from one to the other, then threw up her hands. "Forget it. I can't deal with this male/macho stuff. It's a contest and I don't understand the rules."

Raul shrugged. "You're not a man."

. She glared at him, then sighed. "Thank God."

"Was that a crack of some sort?" Gene commented as she walked out.

Shaking her head slowly, she continued down the hall.

Irene couldn't sleep, no matter how hard she tried. Keeping the lights off, she sat on the windowsill and stared outside at the moonlit night. Slivers of light filtered through the trees and dappled the ground, creating a myriad of interesting patterns that shifted and swayed on the ground.

It wasn't long before her thoughts focused on Raul. He had a dangerous edge to him when provoked, but he was also capable of great tenderness. The attraction she felt for him was there, and was deepening with each passing day. There was something intensely sensual about the raw maleness he coupled so easily with elegance and civility. But there was no future for her here, so musings like these would get her nowhere. She stood up slowly, listening to the creaks and groans of the old house. Pain enshrouded many of the residents of *Casa de Encanto,* and that oppressiveness was an almost tangible presence that lingered within the spirit of the house. Maybe not having a future here wasn't such a bad thing, after all.

She had started toward the bed when she heard someone walking past her door. The footsteps weren't muffled like those she'd heard on previous nights. Wondering who would be about at that hour, she cracked the door open and peeked out into the hall. Irene caught a brief glimpse of Cobb as he turned the corner and disappeared down the hall. Curious, she tightened the belt of her robe and followed him.

When she reached the end of the hall, he was nowhere to be found, but she could still hear footsteps ahead. She quickened her pace, following him downstairs. As she neared the kitchen she realized he was heading for the old cellar.

Irene checked her watch. It was three A.M. There was no legitimate reason she could think of for him to be going down there now. She continued to follow, determined to find out what he was up to.

The door to the cellar was open by the time she reached it, but the downstairs light wasn't on. Puzzled, she went to the top step and peered into the darkness. She wasn't going any further unless she was sure it was safe.

Irene stood there for a second, listening, when suddenly someone shoved her forward hard. Thrown abruptly off balance, her feet tangled in her floor-length robe and she tumbled down the stairs with a startled cry.

# 20

IRENE LAY STILL at the foot of the stairs, gasping for air and enclosed by the darkness. As she waited for her eyes to adjust, she tried to assess her injuries. Though the staircase was scarcely more than twelve wooden steps, every inch of her body hurt from her fall onto the adobe floor. She tested her legs and arms. Then, untangling the clothing that had wrapped around her, she fumbled for the stair rail and rose slowly to her feet.

Okay, nothing major was broken. She hurt like hell, but she'd live. She glanced around, trying to get herself oriented, but it was pitch-black except for the faint glimmer of light coming from beneath the door. To make matters even worse, it was clear there was no one down here. In the total silence, she would have heard someone breathing. Based on the open door and a stupid assumption, she'd walked right into a trap.

Angry, she felt her way back up the stairs. The door

was shut; whoever had shoved her probably hadn't wanted the noise she made as she tumbled down to wake up anyone. How considerate. Forget that she could have broken her neck.

Irene's hand closed around the knob, but when she turned it, it failed to click open the mechanism. Wondering if it was jammed, she pushed against the door, then realized she'd been locked in. Fury pried into her. On top of everything else, the only light switch was on the other side of the door.

Stuck down here, there was little she could do about whoever had trapped her. The thought made her seethe, fueling her resolve not to give up.

Irene started banging against the door as hard as she could, yelling at the top of her lungs. She continued relentlessly until her fists throbbed from pounding the thick pine door and her throat started to ache. Coughing, she sat down on the step. She'd known that adobe absorbed sounds, but she'd never expected it to work quite so well.

If only she had a few simple tools, getting out would be a cinch. As a thought formed in her head, she smiled. It was possible that the crew had stored some of their equipment down here. Or if not, maybe the staff or family had.

Irene searched around by touch in the darkness, but gave up after an hour. All she'd managed to find were jars of canned goods, wine bottles, and innumerable boxes and trunks containing clothes and what felt like linen. Her shins and knees, meanwhile, incurred a further series of bumps and scratches.

Accepting defeat, she resigned herself to waiting until the household woke up. Then she saw a shadow moving past the door, obscuring the light on the other side. She went to the door, banged on it loudly, and yelled out. To her surprise the shadow continued pacing back and forth, ignoring her efforts.

She suppressed a shudder. Whoever it was knew she was there and wasn't going to let her out. The thought that someone was lurking just on the other side began to turn her anger into fear. Why was he waiting? Was he hoping she'd fall asleep so he could come in and take her by surprise? She hadn't been sleepy before, but now she knew there was no way she'd doze off.

Irene felt her way back down the stairs, then took a large bottle of wine from one of the racks. If he came after her, she'd make sure to give his skull something to remember her by. She turned, planning to find a secure hiding spot, then as an afterthought, went to the racks and took two more bottles. She set them on different steps, carefully laying them on their sides. Nothing like a little sabotage to give her an advantage.

Feeling a small nook between the wall and several crates, she sat down in the darkness and waited. From here, she could see the light beneath the door and the shadow pacing back and forth. She took a deep breath and let it out slowly. Her *tasendo,* grandfather, had taken her hunting many times and she'd learned to remain still and wait. She thought of the tiny fetish, still upstairs. The lion was a master hunter who knew how to utilize patience to achieve its goals. She appealed to it now.

Time passed slowly. She'd stopped seeing any signs of the shadow on the other side of the door. Everything was silent. Expectancy of danger that never materialized left her demoralized, but darkness still enveloped her like a protective cocoon, and she was no longer frightened. Intense fear was impossible to sustain, she decided. Eventually it exhausted the mental capabilities, leaving only a weariness.

She leaned back and shut her eyes for a second. She

was a light sleeper; always had been. No one would be able to open the door and sneak down the stairs in the dark without her knowing about it. If they didn't trip over the bottles she'd left to surprise them, the boards would creak and give them away.

As she settled back, she found her thoughts drifting to the fetish and the *xayeh*. She wondered what her mother and aunt would have said if they knew that she'd found herself in this predicament without the aids they'd given her for protection. She smiled wryly, knowing full well what the words would be.

She had to admit that having her fetish with her now would have given her some comfort. In a cry from the heart, she invoked its power with a prayer. "Share with me the essence of what you are," she whispered in the dark. "Give me your strength, your wariness, and your skill to survive."

Irene became more convinced than ever that the plan hadn't been to harm her, though she doubted whoever it was would have shed tears if her fall had resulted in broken bones, or worse. She thought of Cobb. Although she'd been following him, there was no telling if he'd actually pushed her down here. Of course she hadn't seen anyone else, so he remained the best suspect.

She wasn't sure when she finally fell asleep, but in the dreamscape that unfolded she became aware of her grandfather's presence. Although she couldn't see his face, his voice was unmistakable. "Be at peace, grand-daughter. You are in no danger now."

She felt her heart begin to hammer. "Am I in the Below?" she asked, referring to the Underworld. Had she died and not known? The thought frightened her.

"No, you are not with us yet. I've come to warn you that you have reached a dangerous crossroads in your life. The choices you make now will lead you either to the fulfillment of your dreams or to your worst night-mares."

"But how will I know which choice to make?"

Before her grandfather could answer, there was the sound of the door squeaking open and the basement was suddenly bathed in light. She squinted, trying to adjust to the abrupt change, her mind slowly leaving the dream state she'd entered.

It occurred to her somewhere in the back of her mind that an enemy wouldn't have switched on the light. And that's when she remembered the bottles. As she bolted out from between the crates, she saw Raul about to step on her first booby trap.

"No! Stop!"

Raul jumped, startled. Seeing her, he studied her speculatively, trying to decide whether she was in her right mind or had helped herself to a couple of bottles of his special reserve. Suspecting it was neither, yet knowing something was wrong and she needed help, he started down the stairs.

Like a step onto glare ice, Raul lost his footing in-stantly as the bottle rolled. With an oath, he fell to his buttocks and bounced noisily down the remaining steps on the seat of his pants.

Irene rushed to his side. "I tried to warn you! Why didn't you stay still?"

"What are you doing down here this time of night, and why are you trying to kill me?"

"I was just trying to defend myself. Someone pushed me down the stairs, then locked me in here. I was afraid they were going to come down after me, so I set traps and hid."

"Locked you *in?*" He stood up slowly, rubbing his behind with both hands. "That door was closed, but it certainly wasn't locked."

"I tried it several times. Believe me, it was locked."

He gave her a sympathetic look. "You tumbled down the stairs? No wonder you got rattled. That's enough to disorient anyone."

"Raul, I left my room to follow Cobb. It was late and I thought it odd that he was wandering around at that hour. I came downstairs, couldn't find him, but saw the cellar door open, so I peeked down. Next thing I knew, someone shoved me down the stairs."

"John Cobb might have only been going to the kitchen for a snack," Raul reasoned. "You don't know. It isn't fair to accuse him of something like this, particularly when he's not here to defend himself." Raul placed his arm around her protectively. "And believe me, Irene, that door wasn't locked. Stuck maybe, that's all. It's also ridiculously easy to fall down these stairs in the dark. I've done it myself, and so has Gene and just about everyone who has lived in the house." He glanced at her hands. "Come on, we've got to get you upstairs and cleaned up. You're all scratched and bruised."

His insistence that she was confused and the incident had been nothing more than an accident irritated her. But the concern in his eyes was genuine. Grudgingly annoyance gave way to softer feelings that response evoked. "You're not exactly unscathed yourself. I think we should help each other."

He grinned slowly. "I have a better idea." He lifted her off the floor, one arm cradling her shoulders and the other tucked beneath her knees. "Superior strength has to count for something, right?" he teased, seeing the look of surprise on her face.

"Raul, you just bounced down these steps. You're in no shape . . ."

"Let me keep some of my macho image intact, okay?" His hazel eyes gleamed.

She chuckled. "It's hard to argue when you're so humble."

Raul easily carried her upstairs. "Now we need some antiseptic. There's some in my medicine cabinet, so I'm going to take you to my room."

"Your line's original," she teased, "but I question your motives."

"I give you my word, I will not compromise you in any way," Raul whispered as he crossed through the house silently. "Unless, of course, you give me permission. A gentleman always tries to please a lady."

"No, no permission given," she said. "But I will gratefully accept something for the cut on my arm."

"Rejected again! How can a man keep his fragile ego undamaged around a woman like you?" he quipped, entering his room and setting her down on the easy chair near his bed.

"Hope?"

Laughing, he returned from the bathroom with a warm, dampened washcloth and an antibacterial spray. "Here you go. Guaranteed not to sting. Shall I take care of it for you?"

"I think I'll do the honors myself." She took the cloth and cleaned the cuts and scratches, then accepted the plastic bottle from him.

Irene had wanted to keep it light, but here in his room the atmosphere between them became charged with unspoken needs. As an awkward silence descended over them, Raul seemed to become the only clear and distinct object in the room.

It was desire, she told herself, and biology; neither wrong, just part of nature. But the attraction was more than that because she wanted so much more from him. It was that realization that made her pull back into herself. "I better go."

Raul didn't make any move to stop her. "Why don't

you take the day off tomorrow? You've been through a lot tonight. Leave the hacienda," he said softly. "Go someplace where you feel safe and take time for yourself."

His words surprised her. On some level, he must have finally begun to believe that the threat to her had been real. That was the message laced through his words. "I think I'll do just that," she answered, then quickly left.

A few moments later, she was locked in her own room, safe beneath the covers. Rain fell gently outside her window, lulling her to sleep. Her rest was peaceful, born of exhaustion. She didn't wake until well after dawn. As sunlight peered through the cracks in her blinds, she got dressed and left *Casa de Encanto.*

The air was crisp and cold, making her turn up the heater in the Bronco. She drove slowly down the mountain, through Taos, then southwest to the pueblo.

It was good to have time alone to think and relax. She remembered what Raul had once told her about *Casa de Encanto.* He'd claimed it had a soul and a life of its own. She was beginning to believe him. She'd felt it drawing her in, demanding and taking more from her than she'd ever expected to give. The people there and their problems, instead of alienating her, simply added to the pull it exerted.

Time after time along the twisting and turning road, she reached for the fetish nestled in the pouch inside her pocket. Everything she'd ever believed about herself and her people was being tested. Was there protection in the fetish, or did her belief create an illusion? In this case, an illusion of protection could prove fatal.

She arrived at her home in the pueblo shortly after ten. The cornfields were empty, and one could see the Rio Grande clearly now, narrow in its cool winter ribbon of silver. The oldest section of the pueblo, where flat-topped adobe apartments stood two stories high, framed a central plaza. The ancient circular kiva occupied a spot near the village center where vehicles were forbidden.

Irene's house was one street away from the plaza—a single dwelling rather than apartment style—and was less than fifty years old. A few children were in the dirt road playing soccer, and she waved as they scurried to one side, recognizing her vehicle. Except for a neighbor chopping wood, no other adults were visible outside.

Leaving the Bronco parked near the front door, she walked inside and dropped onto the couch. It felt good to be back, if only for a little bit. Things made sense here.

Her mother came out of the back bedroom and smiled. "You've come. Your aunt said that you might, so I dropped by here today to do a little dusting, just in case."

Irene walked to her mother and gave her a long, snug hug. "Things are so difficult at the hacienda. I'm not sure of anything any more."

Teresa Pobikan held her daughter tightly. "You've bruised your cheek and the back of your hand. How did that happen?"

Her aunt appeared from the kitchen. "She's bruised more than that," Alicia said quietly.

"Yeah, maybe I have," she admitted.

Leading the way back to the couch, she recounted the strange events she'd encountered since her first day at *Casa de Encanto,* omitting nothing. "They seem like accidents or coincidences, and no one can prove any differently. But I know someone has targeted me as their enemy. There's something very wrong at the heart of that house. It seems to eat away at the people living there."

"It's the people that corrupt the house, not the other way around," Alicia said. "But their problems have nothing to do with you. I realize that you want to try and help Elena, but remember that ultimately she's one of them and their responsibility. You're only an outsider, no matter how Raul Mendoza has treated you."

"I know that I'm just an employee there. But I want to help them. There's so much bitterness and sadness at the hacienda."

"I'm not worried about the Mendozas," Teresa said resolutely. "I'm worried about you. How can you possibly protect yourself against the kind of accidents you've told us about, and the person stalking you? You can't!" she added, answering her own question. "You have to leave there. Get away for good."

"No," Alicia said. "She's started a chain of events that she has to see through." She glanced at her niece, then with a rueful smile looked back at her sister. "But this discussion is pointless. We both know Irene won't back away now, no matter what the cost." Alicia met Irene's eyes with a penetrating gaze. "I'm right, aren't I?"

"If you're asking me if I'll quit, the answer is no. I accepted the job, and I intend to see it through." She paused. "I dreamed of grandfather again last night."

"Your *tasendo* is there watching over you. You were always his favorite, and he loved you very much," Alicia said quietly.

"That's all well and good, but I don't want to test his powers against this threat to my daughter," Teresa said stubbornly, looking at her sister. "I still say she should leave there as quickly as possible."

"No, that's not the answer. But you are absolutely right about seeking help," Alicia said. "I think we should visit the *pufona sendo,* the head medicine man of the Fire Pufona. He is the oldest man in our puèblo, and the wisest. We'll go to his home and ask him what you should do to protect yourself further."

Irene didn't relish the thought of going; there was something about the old man that had always frightened her. Jose Awino had some remarkable gifts. Once he achieved the proper trancelike state, he was able to foresee events with disturbing accuracy.

Her aunt's gifts and those of a few others had never quite convinced her in the same way. She had a tendency to discount prophecies that could be based on logic, for instance that the President of the United States would remain white for the foreseeable future. But Awino's prophecies were different. She'd never forgotten how he'd foreseen that one of the villagers' sons would be declared missing in action by the Army, then found perfectly okay in one of the white man's hospitals later that same week.

As they headed toward Awino's home, Irene saw that a few tourists had already made an appearance in the plaza. They were busy taking photographs of the pueblo residences and the tall, austere Roman Catholic church.

Alicia circled the low above-surface portion of the central kiva, checking to make sure no outsiders had ventured too close. Visitors were forbidden to draw near, and anyone caught on the stairway leading to the rooftop entrance would be fined and expelled from pueblo land.

Assured there were no trespassers, they continued to the oldest occupied dwelling in the pueblo. As her aunt knocked at the *pufona sendo*'s house, Irene's stomach tied into knots. Awino answered a moment later. Though in his eighties, he stood tall, and his wiry frame was still remarkably strong. The desert and the rigors of life at the pueblo had etched its history in the lines that framed a gentle face. Eyes that shone with the bluish opaqueness of cataracts still held a mental alertness that neither age nor time had dimmed.

Her aunt exchanged some words quickly with him, and Awino showed them inside. As her mother joined in the accounting, Awino shook his head. "No more, you've told me enough. You want me to tell you if it is all right for her to return or whether the risk is too great. For that we'll have to prepare my family kiva, then go inside and seek answers."

Teresa glanced at her daughter warily. "Now we'll see where the truth lies," she said softly. "Keep your mind open, Irene, and don't prejudge based on what you've heard in the white world. There are things you could learn from your own tribe too."

"Once, I might have questioned the good this would do, but no more. I'm beginning to learn that just because I can't explain it doesn't mean it isn't true."

Her mother smiled and nodded. "Maybe you're finally beginning to understand."

They followed the *pufona* outside, crossed the small backyard, and stopped before the partially roofed, adobe-lined pit. Normally women weren't allowed inside except during certain rituals. Irene could remember and count the times when she'd been inside a kiva.

Teresa stepped closer to her daughter's side. "I can't go in with you. Your aunt is special so she'll be allowed, and you're the one in need of help. But I have to remain here."

Irene squeezed her mother's hand reassuringly. "I'm sure he'll just confirm what we already know. If I wasn't meant to go back, Grandfather would have made that clear."

"Remember that you're searching for ways to protect yourself. Get the answers you need."

"I will." Out of the corner of her eye, she saw her aunt motion for her to hurry.

Irene followed Alicia down a narrow wooden ladder that led into the heart of the small kiva. By the time she reached the bottom and sat on a low wooden bench, Awino had already started a fire, chanting as he worked. When the flames began to warm the small interior, he picked up a pipe, filled it with herbs, and began to smoke. Her aunt chanted softly as he prepared himself.

The chanting continued for several minutes and then stopped, encasing the kiva in a tomblike silence. Awino's eyes became unfocused and he seemed to look right past Irene. His expression indicated he was seeing things visible only to him.

After a long while, Irene saw his body relax, and he shifted, sitting up to face her more squarely. "Your aunt was right bringing you to me. Danger encompasses you on all sides, and there are those who want to harm you. But it isn't you so much, as what you represent to them."

"I don't understand," Irene said, hoping to learn what lay behind all the mysterious occurrences at the hacienda.

He shook his head. "I saw shadows pressing, trying to overwhelm you. They were cunning, but there is one presence on your side that is strong and wise in the Lifeway. He is your *po-wa-ha*. He will not abandon you."

"But can he keep her safe?" her aunt insisted.

"That is unclear, but he will *not* abandon her. And he is extremely powerful, that I'm certain of. His presence stood out above all the others." Awino hesitated. "There *is* something else. I felt that she had to go back. Her destiny is linked to whatever she does . . . or doesn't do . . . there."

"I agree," her aunt said softly. "But how can we protect her? Will she need more than the mountain lion fetish and the *xayeh*?"

"When she leaves the pueblo, have her take the bowl used in her naming ritual, and some cornmeal." He glanced at Irene. "Feeding the mountain lion fetish inside the bowl each night will make it grow even stronger. But much will still depend on you. You have the knowledge of our Lifeway, but you must allow the ancestral spirits in the *xayeh* to protect you, and give the mountain lion the power to act on your behalf. It's your belief that will awaken the fetish and open your heart to hear its counsel."

Irene held her breath. "Thank you, *pufona sendo*," she answered respectfully.

As she climbed up the ladder to where her mother stood, she wondered if her belief in something as intangible as the Tewa Lifeways would ever be that strong. Belief had been known to accomplish things that were not otherwise possible. Yet even though her survival was at stake, placing her trust in powers that couldn't be seen or touched didn't come easily to her.

She glanced down into the kiva, realizing that the *pufona* hadn't come up with them. Puzzled, Irene looked at her aunt and saw the woman shake her head. "Leave him," Alicia said. "He needs time now for other concerns."

As Irene stepped off the ladder, Teresa Pobikan placed an arm around her daughter. "I see from your expression that his counsel didn't make things easier for you."

Alicia joined them. "We need to give Irene the bowl used at her naming ritual."

"She'll have it," Teresa said quickly. "Now my daughter and I need to talk alone."

Alicia nodded, then glanced at Irene. "I have duties

this afternoon as *Apienu*. I won't be able to see you again this visit, but I'll do all I can to make sure you receive strength and wisdom."

Teresa watched her cross the plaza, now much busier, with tourists and residents entering and leaving the shops or their homes. "Her prayers are very effective. But I'm still worried about you. I wish you'd stay here with us where you'll be safe."

"Mother, I work under contract. If I don't go back . . ."

Teresa held up her hand, interrupting. "I know all that, but I feel here," she said, tapping her breast, "that there's more to this than you're saying. I think it's the family that draws you back; maybe one member in particular, and I'm not referring to Elena. Am I right?"

"I'm attracted to Raul Mendoza," she admitted hesitantly, "but I'm not foolish enough to believe there can ever be anything between us."

"You say that, but why is it that I sense your heart isn't listening to your logic?"

Irene said nothing.

"So I *am* right." Teresa sighed. "That family has never known happiness because through the years they've done their best to attain it at the expense of others." Teresa considered the matter silently. "All right, then," she said at last. "At least stay in Taos at night. Don't consent to live at the hacienda anymore."

"I can't do that either. It's too late. All the terms were already negotiated. Besides," she said, dropping her voice to a whisper, "I feel some responsibility for what's happening there."

"You've always followed the lead of your heart, but in this case, you're making a terrible mistake." Teresa stared at the ground absently as they walked to her house. "That man can give you nothing but misery."

"He's not the hard, cruel man you'd expect if you judged him solely on the basis of his ancestors. He's just someone who's very much alone and tied down by honor and duties. He carries a lot of pain inside him, but no one helps him shoulder the load. I can't help but respond." She followed her mother inside the house, which was similar in layout to her own home.

"But your feelings go beyond that," Teresa observed shrewdly.

Irene drew in a deep breath, then finally nodded. "Yes, they do."

"The Mendozas have never thought much of our people. To them we're something not quite worthy of their respect."

"Raul's not that way."

"Hear me out. Sometimes prejudice burrows beneath the surface, but history has proven over and over again that it's never truly buried. Pick a mate here, from those who understand you. You need someone who'll support what you value while you pursue your future."

"I've never been much for risk-taking, but this time I can't back away. Before I can think of my own future, I have to face whatever lies in store for me at *Casa de Encanto.*"

Teresa went to a cabinet in the living room and extracted a small, beautifully made black pottery bowl. "This was used at your naming ritual." She took a small pouch from the shelf and poured the contents of it into the bowl. "And this is blue cornmeal; I ground it myself. It'll nourish those that protect you. But please, be very careful. You've never encountered evil, at least not the kind that will destroy whatever's in its path. Whether you realize it or not, that is exactly what you're facing there."

Irene gave her mother a long hug. "I have to go

back now, but I'll be on my guard, I promise. Try not to worry." She walked outside and across the dusty street to her own house, where the Bronco was parked.

Moments later, she drove past her mother's house. Standing on her porch, Teresa Pobikan waved goodbye to her daughter, worry clearly etched on her face. It tore at Irene's heart to see her that way. Bracing herself to follow the course she'd set, Irene kept her eyes straight ahead as she crossed the pueblo.

Two women she recognized were removing loaves of bread from a *horno* oven. Irene knew the women must have been cooking since sunrise. The domed stone and adobe oven had been heated with a cedar fire for hours. The bread being removed now by long wooden spatulas was only one of many loaves that would be baked and sold today.

A long, uphill drive stretched out before her as she headed back to the hacienda. Deep in thought, she glanced at the small pottery bowl on the seat next to her. She wasn't sure how effective her fetishes and the Lifeway would be against the very human adversary she faced.

She shook free of the thought. In the final analysis, her wits would be the best weapon she possessed. By staying alert, she'd be watching after herself and doing all she could to help those in *Casa de Encanto*.

The next few days were uneventful, except for normal day-to-day challenges associated with any big job. She was beginning to wonder whether her visit to Awino had somehow managed to put an end to the problems that had beset her at the hacienda.

Her ritual bowl was by her bedside, and the fetish was fed whenever she came back to her room for the evening. She knew the protection they provided would be with her regardless of what was to come.

Irene strode across the grounds feeling more secure than she had in weeks. As she did, Cobb waved and came toward her. "The gas lines are in. They've been inspected and checked for leaks, and we're ready to cover them over. Did you want to take one more look before we do that?"

Even Cobb's manner was changed. There was no sign of the antagonism that had existed between them. "Sure. Let's both go," she said, hoping that this was the beginning of an easier working relationship.

Cobb fell into step beside her. "I took a look at our progress this morning, and believe it or not, I think we're still ahead of schedule."

"Good. That'll give us some leeway if the weather holds us up later on."

"Well, time is still tight; I don't want to mislead you," he warned. "Remember that we still have most of the interior work to finish. We haven't even begun on that front staircase. We've made plans to reinforce it, and will do so right away, but there's a major effort still ahead of us."

"Yeah, but the weather's going to turn sour before long, and that'll be the best time to be inside. That's why I scheduled the more complicated interior work last."

Cobb heard someone shout out his name and glanced up. "I better see what Serna wants. I'll be back in a minute."

"Sure." As he left, she couldn't suppress a feeling of triumph. Things *were* working out. Maybe all she'd needed to do was outlast whoever had been making trouble for her.

Her mind absently registered loud voices in the distance, but her thoughts were elsewhere as she continued toward the trench that held the gas lines. It wasn't until she heard a low, deep rumble and felt the earth shaking that she snapped her head around.

Horrified, she saw the large dump truck used for hauling sand only a few dozen feet away, rolling rapidly toward her!

# 21

MAKING A SPLIT-SECOND decision, Irene spun around and dove into the deep trench. Reaching out to her *po-wa-ha* in a silent plea for help, she closed her eyes tightly.

A heartbeat later, the massive vehicle lurched and heaved itself into the trench, its huge tires poised halfway into the hole. With a crash, the body of the truck came to rest directly above her. Large chunks of dirt calved away from the sides of the trench and tumbled down on her. She curled into a fetal position, protecting her head until the cascade of dirt stopped.

Irene remained immobile for a while longer, making sure there'd be no sudden surprises. Finally, sputtering and spitting out dirt, she looked around anxiously, trying to find the safest and quickest escape route.

"Hey, are you okay?" Cobb yelled.

"Yeah," she managed in a very shaky voice. "But you'll have to tell me which way to get out. The truck loosened dirt on both sides, and I don't want to be buried alive."

"Or have the truck drop down another three feet," Cobb muttered to himself. "Let me take a quick look."

She'd heard his words, but was determined to ignore the fear that gnawed at her confidence. It was then that the tremulous purl of an owl rose in the air. She shuddered with a deep, ingrained distaste for what it signified. As she waited for Cobb, she tried to shut out the voices coming from above. The Tewa workers had heard the owl too, and their reaction was predictable.

"Pobikan, don't move to the west side. That took the worst of it, and the wheel looks like it's ready to slip some more," Cobb warned. "Crawl east about ten feet. That's the direction the shadows point. The ground's solid enough there, and I can haul you up."

She didn't argue; her one goal was to get out of there in one piece. Then she'd find out who was responsible for the truck. If the accident had been due to anything except equipment failure, she'd personally see to it that the driver was fired immediately.

As she edged back carefully, trying to squeeze her body through the narrow trench, she slammed her knee against the pipe twice. Then she heard Raul's voice over the rest.

"Irene! Come on, you're not that far now."

She turned her head and looked up. She was less than two feet from where he crouched, arms extended down toward her. Relief swept over her, boosting her morale. A second later, she reached up, grasped his forearms, and allowed him to pull her straight up.

"Thanks," she managed in a shaky voice. Giving herself a few precious seconds to gather her wits, she tore her gaze from his and brushed the dirt away from her face and hair.

Raul appraised her carefully. "You're okay," he said, exhaling softly. "Now let's go find who's responsible for that truck."

The gathering of men and women stepped back as he turned around and glared at them. "I want some answers now. Who's the driver of that truck?"

Cobb glanced at Serna, who checked a work list attached to a clipboard. "Carlos!" he yelled out after a moment.

There was no answer. Anna, a small brunette at the back of the gathered crew, worked her way forward. "Carlos got sick and went to his trailer. *I* took over for him. But I parked that thing after hauling two loads of fill, and I haven't been near it since nine o'clock this morning."

"Where did you park it, and how do you explain what happened?" Irene demanded.

"I parked it there." Anna pointed to a spot beside the backhoe. "And there's no way I can explain why it all of a sudden started rolling down that slope!" She paused, biting her bottom lip pensively. "Unless . . ."

"Unless what?" Irene prodded.

She glanced over at Serna, who looked at the ground a few seconds before answering. "We've been having some problems with the truck," he admitted. "I thought I'd fixed it . . ."

"What problems?" Cobb roared.

Serna cleared his throat. "Well, the emergency brake wouldn't hold, so I adjusted it myself yesterday."

"Why the hell didn't you have the company send someone over to fix it?" Cobb bellowed.

"It was a minor repair; I've done it a lot of times before, and the brake held when I tested it. Had I called for a mechanic, it would have taken two or three days just to have it worked on. But the truck was needed here to haul gravel and sand for the drainage canals around the west side."

"Your quick fix almost got someone killed!" Cobb growled, his expression deadly. "This is on your head."

"Now wait a minute. That emergency brake worked, I'll swear to it. You can't pin this mess on me." He strode toward the truck. "I'm going to back that thing out of there and check it right now."

"Wait. I don't want two accidents on my hands." Cobb barked an order, and one of the men rushed to another of the heavy vehicles.

It only took five minutes to pull the dump truck out, using a small bulldozer and a stout chain. Then after making sure the dump truck was on secure ground, Cobb slipped into the driver's seat and checked the controls. "Hey, the brake's not set, and the gears are in neutral."

Anna jumped up onto the running board of the truck. "No way I did that, Mr. Cobb. I'm not the careless type. I *always* put it in gear—in this case reverse—then set the brakes."

Cobb gave her a long pensive look. "You've worked with my crews for years. I believe you."

"So you're saying that someone deliberately caused this?" Irene demanded, wanting him to put it in plain words so Raul wouldn't be able to refute it.

"No, not at all," Cobb protested. "Maybe someone sat in here just to get out of the cold and bumped the wrong thing. Or it could be they reached inside to get something and knocked the gear into neutral. But after what happened, no one is going to admit it was their fault; I guarantee it."

Irene gave him an incredulous look. "So you're going to do nothing?"

"Look, I don't know what happened here, and neither do you. If you want me to go around firing everyone who was near the truck, that's going to leave us real short of manpower," he snapped.

Raul's gaze was as icy as the wind that had started coming in from the north. "You don't seem to have much control at all over what happens here. Maybe the problem would be resolved if we replaced you."

John Cobb challenged him with a steady gaze. "You can do that, but the crew goes with me; that's in the contract." He squared his shoulders. "I had nothing to do with this, and you'd be hard-pressed to prove that any of my crew did either. What about that guy people have seen hanging around?"

"Hernandez," Irene said quietly.

Raul nodded. "I doubt very much that he's responsible."

"Look, I'm going to offer my two cents here," Serna interjected. "I think if there is a problem, it's focused on our architect. You attract bad luck, lady. Why do things always seem to happen around you and no one else?"

"It isn't her fault," Frank Tatasawe protested. "Listen to the owl's message. We warned you before the body was found that the bird brought only misery, but none of you would listen."

"Oh, right!" Serna spat out sarcastically. "It's the bird again. Now he can drive a dump truck. Never mind that the woman is the one who's always in the middle of the problem."

"You're always quick to blame anyone from our tribe," Tatasawe affirmed. "Your prejudices blind you."

"All right, cut it out," Cobb snapped. "There's work to do. Get to it."

Irene glanced at Raul. "If you don't mind, could we talk inside for a few minutes before I go and change from these dusty clothes?"

Raul walked with her back to the house. "I don't like it, Irene. If this type of thing is someone's idea of a prank, it's a deadly one. You could have been killed. If it's negligence, then we have to take some action."

"Agreed, but it isn't right to penalize all these men and women for what one of them may or may not have done."

"We can't just let this pass."

"No, we can't. I'm going to have to pressure Cobb into keeping a closer watch over all his men. In turn, I'll keep an eye on him. Cobb has lots to hide, believe me. His concerns extend well beyond his job." She explained about the fight she'd overheard at the women's trailer. "There's also that meeting of his with Baldridge."

"Well, his business with the woman could be personal. Unless she's harassed or threatened, neither one of us has a right to interfere." He rubbed his jaw pensively. "The meeting with Baldridge is another matter. I found out that Baldridge has traveled to Las Cruces and is working as a consultant on a New Mexico State University project there. As it happens, Baldridge is working with Cobb's boss at that site. My guess is Baldridge dropped by to discuss some business with Cobb, and Cobb decided to make it a secret just to bug you. There are times when he seems determined to do whatever he can to unnerve you."

"That's very true."

"You have to find a way to handle him. If you need my backing from behind the scenes, just say so. We can work out a plan together."

It was the way his voice resonated when he added the last part that captured her attention. He would protect her any way he could, but without undermining her self-confidence. The gesture and the feelings behind it made a great rush of tenderness swell inside her.

"Let me give it some thought. I'd prefer to handle this on my own, but if I can't, I'll give a yell." She smiled. "Listen to us. Time is working a change in us as well as this house. You've moderated your tendency to take over, and I'm willing to accept some help."

He smiled. "Yeah, maybe we're both learning something."

Irene left Raul's office feeling her heart yoked to the man inside. Understanding and mutual respect were strengthening the bond that already existed between them. Stubbornly she refused to name what was at the core of those emotions. Yet in the quiet reaches of her mind, her heart continued to whisper the truth.

The day went by slowly as she tried to come up with a plan to rectify the situation with Cobb and the work crew. The more she attempted to force an answer from herself, though, the more muddled her thinking became. Finally, in desperation, she retired to her room.

Working alone on a corn-husk doll helped her unwind, and the tension slowly left her muscles. The piece was coming out well. Now the husks she'd used to fashion the garment would need to dry again. Before she worked with the pieces, she always sprinkled them with water and kept them in a plastic bag overnight to soften. Tomorrow, dry, the skirt would flare out and look more natural.

Placing the doll aside, she refocused her thoughts on the problem with Cobb. She didn't know to what extent he was involved in what was happening to her, but she was certain he had a hand in it somehow. Still, no solutions came to mind.

Turning off the lights, she sat down on the window-sill and stared outside. Sky Old Man was clear tonight. She smiled as she remembered relaxing on the window seat back home with her grandfather, watching Moon Old Man. That seemed so long ago, but his guidance was with her still. She glanced at the fetish nestled inside her birth bowl, its shape showing up dimly in the darkened room. The cornmeal would have to be replaced from time to time, but for now, what was there would do.

As she shifted her gaze back to the gardens, a flicker of movement caught her eye. A darkened figure, nearly hidden by the gray shadows, seemed to be looking straight up at her room. With her heart lodged in her throat, she watched it turn and disappear into a stand of ponderosa pines.

# 22

◼️

IRENE RAN OUT into the hall. It wouldn't prove much, but she intended to see if Cobb was in his room. She knocked loudly on his door, but got no response. She was about to knock again, just to make sure, when out of the corner of her eye she spotted a long, gray shadow just around the corner. It was large and low to the ground, the kind one might expect from a giant hound.

But there were no dogs in the hacienda. She started to walk toward it, then stopped, courage abandoning her. A fear more powerful than any she'd ever known gripped her. She didn't want to know what was there.

Gathering her wits, she forced herself to walk toward it. Her eyes were fixed on the shadow when Gene emerged from his room. Irene jumped, and so did Gene. "What are you doing out here?" he asked.

She swallowed, trying to find enough saliva to complete the process. Her mouth had gone as dry as sand.

"Gene, will you come with me? I think there might be an animal inside the hacienda."

"What kind of animal?"

"A very big dog." She paused. "No, on second thought, it was much too quiet. Maybe a wolf?"

He gave her an incredulous look. "A wolf?" He grinned. "Hey, have you been helping yourself to the brandy?"

She glared at him. "It was there. Now, will you come with me or not?"

He shrugged. "Sure."

He walked just ahead of her, old work gloves sticking out of his back pocket and flapping at her in a mock wave with each step he took. As they reached the corner, he gestured down the empty hall. "Wolf, huh?" As a mouse scurried along the baseboard and into a closet, he chuckled. "Mouse, maybe?"

"What I saw wasn't the shadow of a mouse! Not unless he had one major thyroid problem."

"Well, maybe he was crawling next to the light bulb," Gene said, a smug grin on his lips.

She wasn't going to win. "Listen to me, Gene. There's something peculiar going on."

"Whatever you say." He gave her a wink. "Don't worry. I won't mention 'the mouse incident' to my brother. I wouldn't want you to lose face."

At that moment she wanted to rearrange his. "You really think all I saw was that little guy? Do I look crazy to you?"

"Is this a trick question?" He glanced down at her, taking in her favorite old corduroy shirt which had seen better days a decade ago. Her jeans weren't in great shape either. They had holes at the knees, not in an attempt to be fashionable, but because they'd been worn through. The clincher seemed to be her socks. She was wearing one green sock and one pink one.

Somewhere in her drawers, she knew, there was another pair just like them.

"Forget it." Seeing the look on his face, she started walking back toward her room.

"Oh, come on," Gene said, laughing. "I was only teasing you."

"Well, the joke wasn't appreciated." As she turned around, she noticed he had dropped one of his gloves. She picked it up. "Here."

"Thanks." He took the glove and shoved it back into his pocket. "I helped Elena earlier with her plants."

Irene went inside her room, then noticing he was right behind her, stood at the door, blocking his way. "Thanks for the help." She paused and added, "Such as it was."

"Are you angry because all we found was a mouse, or because I pointed it out to you?"

"Both," she admitted.

He grinned. "Well, no one can fault your honesty." Gene turned and walked back to his room.

Irene locked the door and crawled into bed, wishing she'd never said a word about the shadow. But at least she knew one thing. The figure she'd seen lurking outside couldn't have been Gene, and since Cobb didn't answer his door, circumstantial evidence still pointed to him.

She closed her eyes, determined to sleep. After several minutes of tossing and turning, she shifted and stared at the whitewashed wall. Shadows cast by moonlight upon the evergreens played there, making a kaleidoscope of bobbing shapes. Watching them, she finally drifted off to sleep.

The next morning as Irene started to go downstairs, she heard the sound of an unfamiliar voice coming from Raul's study. Curious, she listened as she made her way down the hall. From what she could make out, the man was a policeman.

She was passing by Raul's open door when he called her inside. "Detective Estevez has some new information about the body discovered on the grounds. You might want to hear this too."

The detective waited until she was in the room, then continued. "The body was that of a man named Ricardo Vigil. Do you remember him?" he asked Raul.

Raul considered it, his eyebrows knitting together. "Name sure sounds familiar. Give me a second."

"He worked for your family more than a decade ago. He was a gardener."

Comprehension flooded over his features. "Right. This was back when I was in college, but I do remember that the guy supposedly packed up and just left one day. My mother was absolutely furious! She'd just received a shipment of roses, and there was no one around to plant them. Ricardo did something to the soil—he never did say what—that made roses grow like crazy."

"He didn't just pack up, he packed it in. The coroner says he was struck hard from behind, murdered. His skull was bashed in pretty good. Did your family ever find any of his personal possessions?"

"I think I would have heard if they had. Could they have been buried with him?"

"Our boys did a thorough job at the grave. All we found were a few items that probably came from his pockets." Estevez stood and walked to the door. "This is a pretty isolated house, and people don't just drop by. Who was living here at the hacienda at the time of the murder? Do you happen to remember?"

"My parents, brother, and my sister. I just came to visit on holidays. And of course, there's Angela."

"Your housekeeper?"

Raul nodded. "If you want to talk to her, she'll be in the kitchen this time of the morning."

"I think I will. You won't mind if I speak to the others?"

"No, but please not my sister. Her testimony wouldn't help you, and I don't want her upset. From her reaction when the body was uncovered, I can guarantee she doesn't know anything about it."

"I'll agree to that for now, Mr. Mendoza, but there might be a time when I'll have to speak to her."

"I'll have to rely on your discretion, then. You know she's . . . special."

Estevez nodded. "I'll do all I can to keep her out of my investigation, but as I'm sure you can understand, I can't promise that."

"Do your best," Raul replied, seeing him to the door. "I do want this murder solved, if possible. It's a cloud that might settle over my family, and not something I want there."

"I'll do everything I can. Will you compile a list of employees who worked for your family around the time the gardener disappeared? And try to give me a date that would approximate when the gardener disappeared."

"That was a long time ago and both my parents are gone now." He took a deep breath, determination changing his expression. "I'll find a way to get it done. Shall I call you when I have it ready?"

Estevez picked a business card from his pocket. "You can reach me through the station anytime."

"Why don't you help yourself to some breakfast downstairs in the dining room? It's buffet style and there's always plenty of food set out," Raul invited.

"I'll do that, thanks. And Mr. Mendoza, I appreciate your cooperation."

Raul returned to his chair after Estevez left. "When they found the body I was afraid something like this would happen. Sooner or later in the investigation they'll want to drag Elenita into it with a bunch of questions. Of course, they'll scare her half to death in the process."

"Maybe not. Estevez seems sensitive to the problem," Irene answered quietly, then continued after a pause. "You know this new discovery does bring up some very interesting possibilities."

"I don't follow you."

"These so-called accidents around here might have been engineered by the murderer."

"Why? Once the body was found he would have had no further reason to try and stop the construction or target the architect in order to do that."

"Unless there's some other damaging evidence hidden here someplace. What if the gardener's belongings are buried someplace where it's likely they'll be uncovered during the work?" she suggested.

"Okay, suppose you're right and he had left something else around. Wouldn't he just dig it up and get rid of it?"

"It's possible there are too many workmen around for him to have the time and opportunity to do that. Or it could be he can't find the exact location."

"I don't think that's very likely. He could search at night when the workmen are in their trailers. And as far as the location, well, the grounds surrounding the house haven't changed much over the years."

"Still, with people around, he's not exactly free to go skulking around, and digging noises would attract attention. He'd be taking a big risk because the chances he'd get spotted are good." She remembered the figure she'd seen from her bedroom window, but decided against mentioning it now.

"And trying to stop construction by sabotaging equipment and terrorizing you is less risky?" he countered, shaking his head. "No, you're off base on this one. If there is a connection, we haven't found it."

Just a thought. Could the footsteps Elena and I heard out in the hall at night belong to the gardener's killer? What if he's searching for something inside the house instead of outside?"

Raul smiled. "I think this theory is along the same lines as the giant shadow of *El Lobo* that turned out to be a mouse."

She felt her face burning with embarrassment. So Gene had told his brother, after all. "What I saw had nothing to do with that mouse."

"I know that architects are supposed to have imagination," he teased, "but I never suspected yours was quite so vivid."

She hated being made fun of, even if it wasn't malicious. "Maybe the problem is that yours is limited."

"Oh, my imagination isn't limited at all. Try me sometime."

Great, she'd walked right into that one. "Yeah, we'll play King's Booty on my computer. Let's see how good you are."

He grinned. "I'm not much for games."

She was getting out of here. This was going from bad to worse. "I better get back to work."

"That's probably wiser and safer," he answered in a barely audible voice. "You don't need the problems I can bring you."

Hearing the depths of sadness in his voice, she stopped by the doorway and turned to face him. "Raul, you've shouldered a lot of disappointment and sadness in your life, but sooner or later you're going to have to let go of the past." She paused, choosing her words carefully. "You've got to learn to forgive yourself."

"What have you been told?" His eyes darkened with anger. "Did Gene relate his version of my life with Reina?"

Now she knew for sure. Though the grave separated them, Raul's guilt shackled him to Reina. Until he resolved whatever haunted him, he'd never really have a life of his own. "Gene hasn't told me anything. You have," she said softly, "in your own way."

He pressed his lips together and gave her a curt nod. "Be careful, Irene. It's dangerous to make judgments based on incomplete knowledge."

He was cautioning her about feelings. For a second she couldn't even think straight. What they were seeing mirrored in each other's eyes was too basic for either of them to mistake.

It was like being on the edge of an experience, or standing in front of a closed door that could hold answers to questions she'd never even dared ask about herself. Every shred of female intuition she possessed assured her that the man before her, though an enigma in many ways, could show her a new level of intimacy and open the door to a world she'd never seen. But finding intense joy often meant finding intense sorrow.

"We both have our own demons to wrestle," she said softly, then turned and left the room.

Raul watched her leave his office, his heart hammering. She wasn't right for him. Relationships were hard enough without adding the complications already built in between him and Irene. And he wasn't a teenager, able to brush aside as unimportant whatever stood in the way of what he wanted.

Gene walked in unannounced and took a seat

across from Raul's desk. "What are you going to do about her?"

Raul stared hard at his brother, but the challenge or criticism he'd expected to find there was absent. "Not a thing. She's here to do a job. When that's completed, she'll go."

"Please," Gene scoffed. "Don't tell me you plan to forget her just like that." He snapped his fingers in the air.

"I won't."

"So why haven't you made a move on her?" he asked.

"I have no plans to make a move on anyone," he answered, his eyes on Gene. "Is that what you wanted to hear?"

"You have to live with your past," Gene said, his voice void of emotion and humanity. "I think that's punishment enough."

"I'm getting sick of your insinuations, Gene. Maybe you should focus on straightening out your own life for a change. Your work's cut out for you."

Gene's face turned a shade paler. "At least I don't try to pretend I'm a paragon of virtue. It's the great *patrón* of *Casa de Encanto* who worries about the image he wants to maintain."

"That's *mierda* and you know it," he growled.

Gene leaned back in his chair. "This is pointless. We should be discussing how best to protect Elena from what's going on in this house. Was that Estevez I saw leave?"

"Yeah, he came to tell me about the body." Raul recounted the events. "I think if we can come up with a date, and enough names on that employee list he wants, he'll be too busy to talk to Elenita."

"Let's give it a go, then."

They brainstormed for an hour, but managed to

come up with only a rough estimate of when Vigil disappeared and a list of five people. One of them, their father's butler, had long since passed away. Raul stared at the names. "This isn't much for the police to go on."

"Let's face it. We never had that many servants. The few we had stayed over the years until they retired. And Angela's still here."

"I know that girls from town came in to help with housekeeping from time to time, but I can't remember a single one of those names."

"I'll bet you Angela does. And my guess is that Estevez already has them," Gene said.

"You realize this is going to mean we're in for another round of gossip about this family in the Taos eateries and post office. It'll affect all of us in one way or another, but I'm not worried about you and me."

"Elena seldom goes into town. I don't think we have anything to be concerned about," Gene answered.

"The workers could get to be a problem with smart-ass remarks."

Gene stared at the small cactus near the window for a long time before replying. "You've always tried hard to protect Elena, but be careful you don't smother her in the process. It's a mistake to shelter her too much, Raul."

"I don't want her hurt."

"Neither do I, but I want to see her develop some self-confidence. To do that, she has to test her own strengths, and face adversity from time to time."

"There might be something to that," Raul said after a moment. "But it's hard to see someone you love in situations like that. It's all part of letting them go, I know, but that's something I never even considered with Elena until recently."

Gene exhaled softly. "Even a wounded bird has the right to attempt to fly."

Irene sat inside Elena's room on an easy chair. She agonized over her decision to come here today, but instinct told her she couldn't put off what she had to do any longer. As long as Elena tended the flowers, she seemed relaxed, and she hated the idea of upsetting that. Yet fear for what Elena might know and the danger it could place her in forced her to continue. "Do you ever sit at your windowsill just to enjoy the view?" Elena's old room had overlooked the shed and the place where the gardener's body had been found.

Elena considered it. "I used to, but then I stopped. I can't remember why. Maybe it was when I started getting my own plants in here to take care of. There's always something to do when you're taking care of flowers indoors."

Irene watched her carefully, intent on finding out if her hunch was right. "Elena, do you remember that movie you told me about, the one where the man killed a woman?"

Elena nodded, her eyes wide. "It was an awful movie!"

"Where did the murder take place, do you remember?"

Elena bit her lip, her expression one of concentration. "I just remember that it looked like our garden outside. Lots of flowers, roses, and grass. Maybe that's why it was so scary."

Irene felt her heart hammering at her throat. What they needed was a link in time between the gardener's murder and Elena's movie. Though the gardener had been a man, maybe Elena had changed that detail to fit with her movie's fictional theme. "I don't think I've ever seen you watching TV. Did you watch it more when you were younger?"

Elena shook her head. "No, not that I remember. I do watch the Christmas specials and that Channel 5 garden show, but for the most part I get bored in front of the television."

"How long ago did you watch that movie?"

"Oh, it was a *long* time ago. Raul had just come home after his first year in college. Dad was so proud of him, he hardly had time for anyone else. Gene was still in high school and always complaining that no one paid attention to him." Elena shrugged. "But no one paid attention to me either. I was the oldest, and not in school, so my life wasn't as interesting as my brothers' were. Mom had more fun planning stuff for them."

Irene frowned. So the movie could have been Elena's gambit for attention, rather than the result of something she'd really seen. She was less sure of the truth now than she'd ever been. A knock at the open door kept her from continuing to press for information.

Elena turned to the open doorway and beamed Raul a wide smile. "Come look at my newest plant. It's a lavender miniature rose that looks almost blue!"

Raul walked with her to the bench near the window. "It's beautiful. Is it supposed to be that small?"

"Yes, it's bushy but not stalky. That's when they're prettiest."

Raul exchanged a few pleasantries with her, then turned to Irene. "May I talk to you in private for a minute?"

"Sure." She walked with him out into the hall and noted that he closed Elena's door behind him.

His expression changed in an instant. "I couldn't help but overhear part of your conversation as I passed by. What are you trying to do, stir up trouble? I think she's got more than her share already," he added in a harsh whisper.

"Raul, that's unfair. I was trying to find out if Elena had actually witnessed the death of the gardener. The movie she talks about that scared her so much might have been an interpretation of events she saw through her window. Keep in mind that she's bound to over-hear the police questioning people around here. That might trigger memories she's not equipped to handle, and you've got to be prepared to deal with that if it happens."

He ran a hand through his hair. "Elena is my re-sponsibility. You should have come to me."

"I've gone to you before, and you usually dismiss everything I say. You require hard proof before be-lieving anything that doesn't suit you."

Raul's eyes darkened. "Maybe I'm not as quick to jump to conclusions as you are."

"I haven't jumped to conclusions. I've arrived at theories based on facts."

"You can have all the theories you want, but *not* at the expense of my sister."

"Is that what you think this is all about? Or is that your pride talking?" She forced her voice to remain gentle. She didn't want a confrontation; she wanted him to help by keeping an open mind.

He leaned against the wall, his hand curled into a fist, and avoided her gaze by pretending great interest in the curtains at the other side of the hall. Finally he spoke. "Come back in there with me, but let me handle my sister the way I see fit." He took a deep breath. "And whatever happens in there stays between us. I don't want the police involved unless I say so."

"You can't hide evidence of a crime, Raul. Be rea-sonable."

"I can keep it from becoming public until I get a

doctor qualified to see Elena through this. Fair enough?"

"Definitely." She stopped him before he reached the door. "One thing," she said, recounting what Elena had already told her. "Is it possible the movie was something she made up to get attention?"

Raul considered it. "She wouldn't have that kind of imagination, not when it comes to a brutal murder."

"Maybe she compiled it from different things she heard on the news."

"Let's find out," Raul said. He knocked, then entered the room when Elena invited them inside.

At first Raul kept the conversation light, talking about the gardens in the spring, and her houseplants. Slowly he shifted the conversation to the topic that was on his mind.

"Do you remember the party Mom and Dad had for us here?"

"Yes, you guys got to stay up, but I was told to go upstairs early. Dad didn't want me around your friends. I don't know why, they all liked me and were very nice."

"They'd had too much to drink and you're very pretty," Raul said gently. "Dad didn't want anyone to upset you."

"But I *was* upset. I had to go upstairs to my room even though I was the oldest. I was so bored! I watched television that night in Mom and Dad's room. They said it was okay. But it wasn't the same as being downstairs with you guys."

"I remember you liked going into Mom and Dad's room when they weren't there. I never could figure out why. It was right next door to yours."

Elena smiled. "That room is the only one in the house that has those funny curved windows with a padded *banco* beneath. It was comfortable sitting there. Whenever Mom had parties, I'd sneak into their room and just watch. People would always walk out into the garden. In the darkness no one ever saw me."

"What kinds of things did you see?" Raul asked gently.

"People wearing pretty clothes. A lot of times men would bring women out there and they'd kiss. It was like watching a really romantic movie."

Raul glanced at Irene, but then focused his attention back to Elena. "Did you ever see something that upset you, Elena, or maybe see something bad?"

Her eyes grew wide and she dropped the small potted plant she'd been holding. "I don't know what you're talking about," she said quickly. "Look what you made me do! Everything's a mess!" She scooped up the soil with her hands and tried to put it back into the pot. "I have to fix it now. I don't want to ruin the roots. Just go, okay?"

"Let me help you, Elena," Raul offered, bending down and sweeping some of the soil into a small pile.

She shook her head. As she glanced around, her face was filled with fear. There was a trapped helplessness about Elena that wrenched Irene's heart. "No, just go. Both of you. Please?"

Raul stood and walked to the door, uncertain what else he could do. "It's okay, Elena, we're leaving. Don't worry about your plant. I know you can repot it."

"I can't always fix things that are broken. If it's hurt bad . . ."

"It won't be," Irene assured softly. "Just do it quickly."

Elena nodded, and as she picked up the pot, her hands were trembling. "Please go." Her voice rose slightly.

Irene closed the door and glanced at Raul, her head shaking. "She saw something."

"Maybe."

"What do you mean, maybe? How can you doubt it after the way she acted?"

"I've seen Elena unravel like that before when something happens to her plants. You haven't. That's why you're misinterpreting the signs. She was nearly hysterical once when her favorite azalea died. It took Angela and me days to get her to come out of it. She wouldn't even let anyone throw out the roots. When things go wrong, Elena's always had a tendency to fall apart emotionally."

"Raul . . ."

"Look, Irene, you've seen her around here, and you know that sometimes she can't even handle a little crisis. How do you think she'd handle police questioning? Face it, her testimony would never be seriously considered in court."

"You're probably right." She looked steadily at him. "But something's troubled her for a long time, Raul. I don't know what it is, but it goes beyond her handicap."

Leaving Raul, Irene walked to her bedroom. So many of the mishaps that had happened to her around the house, like getting locked in the cellar and the witch doll near the entrance gates, had the earmarks of a kid's prank.

Elena's innocence seemed genuine, but did she truly recognize right from wrong? And what was frightening her? Had she seen something, or maybe inadvertently caused something to happen?

The questions were endless, but one thing troubled her most. By confronting Elena, she could end up harming the woman irreparably. She brushed her fingertips against the miniature rose on her nightstand, and the tiny flower disintegrated into a shower of petals that cascaded onto the carpet.

# 23

RAUL WAS IN his study when Gene sauntered in. "An idea occurred to me a little while ago. You know when we were trying to compile that list of employees?"

"Yeah, we didn't do so well," Raul said.

"I was thinking about it, then I recalled Mom's ledgers. Remember how Dad made her keep them? She had to keep track of all the household expenses in there and show him where the money went."

Raul nodded slowly. "Yeah, that's right." He glanced around. "I kept them too, because they really reminded me of her. She would write the strangest little notes to herself in the margins. I remember one where she was reminding herself to try and fix us up with some girls."

"Who?"

"Jenny and Tara Santeiro. Mom used to think they'd make the perfect wives for us."

Gene held up his arm, as if warding off something. "They hated us, especially me. I'd tormented them on the school bus for years!"

"But their mother was Mom's best friend. And Mom always saw the girls as tough enough to stand up to us."

"Yeah, Tara could sure kick. When she got off the bus in junior high, I always got my hair pulled and a kick or two in the shins. Then there was Jenny's boyfriend from Taos, Tivo."

"Primitivo. What were his parents thinking of when they gave him that name?"

"Are you kidding? It was perfect for him. It fit. He was big enough to pull off our arms and legs and put them back in interesting new ways if he'd wanted."

Raul laughed. "That he was." He opened a cabinet door at the bottom of a bookcase and looked through the stacks of folders and other records there. "I think these might be it," he said at last. Raul pulled several warped fabric-covered ledgers out of a cardboard box and blew the dust off the first one. A thin cloud bellowed in front of him and he sneezed. "These were up in the attic at one time, but I brought them down."

"In their original state," Gene added, rubbed his nose, then sneezed himself. "Come on. We'll split up the work and get the names we need faster that way."

Raul placed one volume on his desk as Gene moved to the couch with another.

Hours ticked by slowly. The notes on the side reminded them of past events, everything from birthday parties to lists of medications that chronicled their father's illness and death. Finally, after having spent most of the morning searching fruitlessly, Raul placed the last volume back inside the box. "These are a mess. I don't know how she ever kept anything straight."

"Three quarters of her numbers don't even add up."

"She never was one for math."

"I remember the screaming fights Mom and Dad used to have. Dad had a jackrabbit temper, but so did Mom, and she always stood up to him. I used to side with her, thinking Dad was too hard on everyone. But now that I've seen these ledgers, I'm beginning to think Dad had a point, at least every once in a while."

"Did you look at the notes in the margins? She might have been trying to record numbers, but her mind was always on us. I never knew how much she worried."

"And how strongly she believed in Elena." Gene smiled, memories replaying in his mind's eye. "I remember her telling me once that Elena would become the center of this family someday and keep all of us together."

Raul leaned back in his chair and stared at the oil painting of his parents across the room. "She was right. Elena's even managed to get us to set aside our differences."

"That's because it's our duty to protect her," Gene said, then shook his head. "No, it's more than that. She's so innocent, and we both love her. Wanting to protect her comes as naturally as breathing."

"Everyone thought Mom was scatterbrained, but you know, in her own way she was smarter than all of us. She could see things we'd miss altogether."

"You and I are a lot like Mom and Dad; it's just that their qualities are mixed inside us in different proportions. I'm the dreamer, like she was. Logic isn't as important to me as the way I feel inside. Logic takes the front seat with you, but the dreamer is also there just waiting for the right time to be let out."

"Maybe." Raul felt the stirring the truth usually evoked. Restless, he stood and walked to the window.

It was best not to dream. If you didn't have expectations, then you wouldn't feel pain.

Irene sat down with Benito Penya, the oldest of the Tewa carpenters on the job. Benito had acquired a reputation for his knowledge of local lore, and many of the historians from the universities often came to consult with him.

"Do you remember anything about Raul Mendoza's parents? He never talks much of them."

"Ramón Mendoza had a fierce temper, but so did Lupe. It was said by those who visited on weekends that when they fought, the adobes trembled," he said.

"What was it like to work for them? I know that through the years many from our tribe were employed here in one capacity or another."

Benito nodded. "Mostly doing the upkeep. Ramón Mendoza would always give you a job, but he expected you to work hard. Of course there was the big renovation that never happened. Hernandez was the architect. Some of the men here today were part of the crew back then too. Did you know? Even John Cobb. He hadn't started working for himself yet."

"No, I didn't realize that."

The crew's break ended then, interrupting their talk, and Irene thanked Benito for his time. As the Tewa man went back to his work, Irene stood there alone, thinking. So the case against John Cobb grew. Perhaps Cobb knew something about the gardener's death, or was working in conjunction with someone who did.

Hearing footsteps coming up behind her, she snapped her head around and saw Baldridge approach.

"Sorry. I didn't mean to startle you," he said.

"What brings you here?" she asked bluntly, uncomfortable to see him.

"I had to meet with Cobb. I'm working with his boss down in Las Cruces, and since Cobb will be joining us when he finishes here, I keep him up to date."

"I've noticed you around before."

Baldridge smiled. "I heard what happened. Don't let Cobb and his games rattle you. I don't." He led her away from the others. "Little minds need little pursuits." He waited until a group of several workers went past. "I hear you've been having all kinds of trouble here."

"Not all kinds. The trouble has been of a very specific nature," she said obliquely.

"Listen, I know this crew. And I also have more experience than you. Why don't you hire me to serve in an advisory role? It sounds to me like you need some help."

"No, I'll handle this on my own, but thanks anyway," she said, unable to bring herself to trust him.

His whole demeanor changed abruptly. "Don't you realize you're about to blow it? Take a look around here. You're not in control of this project; you're just reacting to whatever happens." Baldridge's voice was filled with contempt. "I've offered my help, but I won't make that mistake again."

As he strode off, Cobb came toward her, a grim expression on his face. "We've got *major* problems, and I'm out of my league when it comes to superstition. Naturally that's right up your alley."

Her eyes narrowed. His words held an edge that accentuated the insult. "What's going on?" she asked coldly.

"It's the Indian workers and that same old owl. Serna offered to shoot the damn thing, but they won't hear of it. We're at a crucial stage in the work; the weather's almost too cold already to work with adobe. We need to finish the exterior fast, but the Indians are refusing to pick up the pace. They want the place cleaned first."

"You mean cleansed."

"Okay, whatever. They think the owl brought bad luck, that's why we've had accidents around here. They also claim it's that little bug-eyed bird's fault that a body was found."

"Before you put down our religious beliefs, I suggest you take a closer look at your own. You'll find a fair number of hard-to-explain metaphysical events in it too," she snapped.

"Yeah, but mine haven't interfered with work," he shot back. "Now, I can fire the lot of them, but if I do, we're going to have the civil rights people all over this place. I don't need that kind of trouble, and neither do you. If the state or special-interest groups start investigating and creating trouble, our project deadline's going to go right down the old chemical closet."

"The only solution is to invite a medicine man out here. It doesn't take long to have that rite performed."

"Yeah, but even if he accepts, will he come to the hacienda right away?"

"I don't know, but I'll find out."

It took getting her Aunt Alicia to intercede, but after several lengthy telephone conversations, the *pufona sendo* finally agreed to come out that same evening. Irene relayed the news to the others, who'd refused to do any more work until the situation was resolved.

"Will the *Towa é* also come?" Bobby asked.

"Of course. They're the guardians of the *pufona's* ritual. They will serve as his lookouts and protectors."

"I just wanted to make sure this would be done properly, not just quickly."

The insinuation bugged her, but seeing the concern

in the man's eyes made her soften her response. "Please don't worry. Things will be done according to our customs." She glanced at the wall. "But you have to go back to work now. It serves no one to have hours wasted needlessly. You know the *pufona* will be here and that'll be your protection."

Reluctantly the men returned to work on the adobe wall. She watched for a minute. "I'll let you know as soon as the ones from our tribe arrive and preparations for the ritual begin," she said, and started back to the house.

Raul met her near the entrance. "I've been following what happened. I'm glad you were able to handle it so effectively."

"Thanks, but it was all a matter of understanding what was at the root of the problem. To Cobb, their fears aren't real. To the Tewas, they are."

"What if the owl doesn't leave?" he asked.

"The evil that hangs over this place will still be cleansed," she answered simply. "They won't like the owl being there, but they'll take courage and comfort from knowing the rite was performed."

"Everyone needs courage and comfort from time to time. But some of us find it in other places," he said, brushing her face lightly with his palm.

Feeling herself responding to him, she quickly brought herself back in check. If she let emotions like these get out of hand, she'd end up offering to bear his children, or at least keep trying until they got it right.

"Don't run away from me," Raul pleaded gently. "Friends don't do that, and I'd like to think we're at least friends."

"At the moment, I'm your architect, and the time clock's running. So if you'll excuse me, boss," she teased, trying to lighten the mood, "I've got to get back to work."

She worked on greenhouse plans the rest of the afternoon, refusing to think about Raul. Had she been Hispanic or Anglo, the attentions of a drop-dead-gorgeous bachelor like Raul might have turned her knees to Jell-O. But she was Tewa, and that changed everything. And of course he wasn't exactly offering the promise of lasting love and security. The project would come to an end in another month. Then if nothing else, their life-styles would pull them apart.

It was nearly sunset when the *pufona sendo* and two *Towa é* arrived. Raul stood at the entrance ready to greet them, but they declined the invitation to come inside the house. It wasn't unexpected, and Raul's expression remained cordial.

Irene went outside and spoke to the elderly medicine man, who was clad in wool trousers and a homemade shirt. He wore his hair long, bound into a *chongo* at the nape of his neck. A blue kerchief served as a headband, and instead of a coat, the medicine man had wrapped himself in a colorful blanket.

His companions were dressed in similar fashion, except they wore jackets. Their hair was short, and they both wore tall black Stetsons.

"What can I do to make things easier for you while you're here?" His eyes held hers with an intensity that made her want to glance away, but she forced herself not to.

"Make sure we're not interrupted. I am here now as a favor to your aunt. Speed, so the workmen could return to their jobs, was not my concern," he said firmly.

"I know, and I appreciate you coming. The others from our tribe are also grateful. Families back at the pueblo depend on the wages they earn here."

Jose Awino nodded and signaled one of the *Towa é*. "We will prepare."

She started to tell Awino about the witch doll she'd

seen upon her arrival at the hacienda, then changed her mind. Raising the subject now would have meant risking the other workers would find out, and that would have created even more problems. The cleansing was supposed to take care of all the negative influences. She'd rely on that. There was no need for her to do more than was already being done.

Awino sat on the ground and began preparing a mixture of herb medicines. Removing a pottery bowl from a large leather pouch, he cleaned it ceremonially with his thumb, then set the bowl on the ground before him. He half filled the bowl with water from a pottery jug, also taken from his medicine pouch.

Muttering a low prayer, Awino took pinches of herbs from three deerskin pouches, crushed them one at a time between his finger and thumb, then sprinkled them into the bowl.

Meanwhile, the *Towa é* each took a stone fetish and held it up to the cardinal directions. Scarcely aware of them, the *pufona sendo* stared deeply into the bowl before him as if he were peering into the heart of another world.

Raul came up to join her. "What's he doing?"

"He's supposed to be able to see and locate the source of the problem that way. The Navajo medicine men sometimes use quartz crystals for the same purpose."

Holding several sacred eagle feathers, Awino began walking resolutely toward the trailers, chanting prayers in his native tongue. The *Towa é* remained with him, guarding as he went around the housing and through the grounds much as their ancestral counterparts had protected the village during important rituals. The cleansing, an exorcism of a kind, progressed methodically, but the Indian men waited inside their trailers for the rite to end.

It was late by the time the *pufona sendo* completed his work. His eyes were sunken in, and the lines that framed his face had deepened. He found Irene and took her aside. "I've done what I can, but the danger to you is still here, I feel it. You have to rely on your *po-wa-ha* for your protection. He and your guardians are now stronger than ever, so you can face what comes with courage."

She suppressed the shiver that ran up her spine. "I'll be fine, Uncle," she said, using the term to signify respect, not kinship. "Please assure my mother of that."

His eyes were filled with compassion. "You are much like your *tasendo*. I see him in you."

"I'm glad," she said, humility in her voice. "I've tried to become someone he would speak of favorably."

"You have succeeded, then."

A moment later, Angela arrived, carrying a large picnic basket and a kettle. "Mr. Mendoza wishes to convey his gratitude for your services."

With Awino's nod, Angela spread a blanket on the ground and laid out servings of hot green chile stew, freshly baked bread, and steaming coffee. All three men sat down on the blanket and began to eat.

Irene, standing to one side, motioned to Angela. "How did Raul know to do this?"

"He asked one of the Tewa workers what form of payment was customary." Angela smiled. "I think we're all learning a lot more about other cultures here today."

Later, Irene stood by the side of the road as Jose Awino and the *Towa é* drove away in an old, beat-up pickup. Then the sounds of someone hammering nearby broke her thoughts, and she turned around.

Serna stood near one of the trailer doors glowering at a Hispanic worker. "What the hell are *you* doing?

Don't tell me we have to guard against vampires now too."

Pablo glanced at Serna and shrugged. "Go ahead and make fun if you want, but this crucifix stays right where it is."

As she approached the trailer, Irene saw the small wooden cross attached to the door.

Pablo saw her coming. "And I don't care who minds."

"What's going on?" Irene asked.

"Your Indian guys all think there's something spooky about this place. We tend to agree. But the Indian ritual doesn't do much for us. We feel more at ease with a crucifix nearby."

"You think it'll do any good?" Serna countered.

"I don't know, but it sure won't do any harm," Pablo answered, then looked at Irene. "I hope you're not planning to give us a hard time about this. I mean none of us squawked when you brought in your voodoo priest."

"Medicine man," she said coolly.

"Yeah, that. You have your way of dealing with it, we have ours."

"That's perfectly reasonable. I have no qualms about that."

"We're just hedging our bets," Pablo said in a calmer tone. "Let's face it, strange things have been happening in this area for a long time. There's been talk about the restless spirits of those who died here for as long as I've been around. Longer, actually. My grandfather told me some of the stories."

Alberto Cruz joined them. "Hey, it's part of our history, like *La Llorona,* the ghost lady who wanders around the ditch banks looking for her drowned kid or whatever. Surely you've heard stories like that," he said to Irene.

She nodded. "Children outside the pueblo use them to scare each other," Irene conceded. "But we believe our rituals are effective wards."

"Well, we trust our ways more, so the cross stays," Pablo said. "And don't be surprised if you see lots more of these around."

Irene started to go back to the house, but then changed her mind and walked to the courtyard instead. Though it was cold, it was a clear and beautiful night, and she didn't want to go inside just yet. She sat down on the *banco* near the side of the house, ready to enjoy Yellow-going Old Woman, the Evening Star. In legend she was said to pursue Morning Star, her spouse. As Irene relaxed, she became aware of two men talking somewhere close by. She remained still, and listened as she heard her name being mentioned.

"Mendoza's getting hungry for the Indian woman. Have you seen the way he looks at her?"

"So what? He's a man with needs just like the rest of us. It don't mean anything."

"Get real. You see his face? He's not just looking to play. He's serious."

"Man, you're crazy. There's no way a Mendoza's going to *marry* an Indian. He was raised to practically choke on that medicine man stuff the same way we do. It's pagan ceremonials and lots of superstition, not a *real* religion. He'd never allow an Indian to bring thinking like that *inside* to his family."

The words settled over her heart like a heavy weight. Racial barriers were still as strong as ever. Despite her accomplishments, to those in Raul Mendoza's world she'd never be more than an outsider looking in.

# 24

IRENE SAT IN her room, her fingers busy fashioning the body of a second corn-husk doll: a male Tewa warrior to go with her corn-husk maiden. The workman's words still preyed on her mind. Though she knew Raul had never treated her customs with anything but respect, she wondered how he would have reacted had he been more exposed to the rituals that were part of her everyday life.

She set the doll down. He'd undoubtedly see this corn-husk figure as an example of colonial folk art shared by his own ancestors, but there were other things he might not have viewed with such tolerance. She took the pouch from her pocket, removed the mountain lion fetish, and placed it inside her birth bowl. She'd just started sprinkling fresh blue cornmeal over it when she heard someone knocking. Leaving the small pottery bowl on the dresser, she went to answer the door.

Elena stood there holding one of her plants. "It's time to change the miniature rose in your room. How do you like this one? It's called Petticoat. It's white in the summer, but the colder it gets, the more pink it'll become. See the color around the edges of the petals?"

"It's beautiful."

Elena walked to the dresser to place the plant down, then saw the bowl with the fetish inside. She stared at it for several seconds, a puzzled look on her face. "Are you trying to *grow* something?"

Irene smiled. "Well, in a way, I guess." She hesitated, then decided to answer Elena's question more completely. "Tewa beliefs say that the spirit of the fetish needs nourishment. Pollen or cornmeal is placed around it so that its spiritual essence can feed the fetish."

"Pollen?" Elena's face brightened. "My flowers have that. I never knew they could 'be useful' too. That's wonderful!"

Irene smiled. "I've always told you that what you did was important."

"Tell me more about these," Elena said, pointing to the fetish. "Is it like one of our statues of the saints?"

"I don't think so," Irene said slowly, searching for the right words. "But it's hard to compare things based on different religions." She explained the general significance of the fetish, then added, "It was given to me by my grandfather a long time ago."

"Does it really help you?"

"I believe it does," Irene answered.

"Different animals mean different things?"

Irene nodded. "Like the animals they represent, they all have different qualities they're supposed to bring out in the owner of the fetish."

"I'd love to have one. But you know, others here might not like that. We're taught that things like this don't work, and that God doesn't like it if you believe in them."

"We all follow different *poeh,* or life paths. I believe the important thing is to make sure everyone acts according to their highest concept of what's right."

"I don't understand."

"You do the most good you can, and be the best you can be."

"That makes sense." Elena smiled. "You know, I think people would be much better off if they kept things simple."

Irene awoke the following morning to an unusual quiet. Sunlight streaming through cracks in the curtain made her realize that she'd slept late. She yawned and stretched, enjoying a lazy Saturday. A quick glance at the clock on the nightstand revealed it was almost ten. Most of the workers would be home for the weekend by now. Yet something about the stillness outside seemed more than normal for a Saturday morning.

She went to the window and parted the curtain slightly, seeing clearly what had created the silence. A thick blanket of snow covered everything. The hacienda and the surrounding forest had been transformed overnight into a beautiful fantasyland that took her breath away. Ice on the tree branches captured the rays of sunlight and sparkled with dazzling intensity. Snowflakes swirled to the ground in slow arcs that reminded her of those water-filled paperweights that simulated falling snow when you shook them. Feeling good as the warmth of the house enveloped her, she dressed and walked down the hall. She was passing by Raul's study when she heard loud voices inside. The intensity of the argument ensuing behind the closed doors shattered her blissful mood.

She continued downstairs, eager to leave the discord behind.

Raul slammed his hand down on his desk. "We've been through this already, Gene. I will not subsidize you anymore. You've done nothing to earn my trust or my confidence."

"All I'm asking is that you go in with me as a partner and pick up half the monthly rental of the gallery. If I'm going to get this off the ground, I need to be right in the middle of Santa Fe. That's where the people who can afford my prices will be."

"The owner's asking an exorbitant rent. You shouldn't even consider paying it."

"Don't you understand? That's a *prime* location. I could double my drop-in business just by being there."

"I suggest you work up to that, then. When your business grows to the level where you can afford it, you won't need my help."

For a second Gene was unable to speak. "You want me to fail, don't you?" His voice was a fierce whisper.

"No, I don't. But by not forcing you to depend on yourself, this family has hurt more than helped you. Get your life together, Gene. Stop drinking and feeling sorry for yourself. If you can show me something that inspires confidence, I'll be proud to back you."

Gene's fingers were clenched tightly into fists. "I'm not asking for charity, just a loan. See me through the first six months by splitting the costs with me."

"No." Raul remained in his seat, doing his best to keep cool despite Gene's goading.

"You like the power that comes from controlling the money, but I won't feed your ego by begging." Cold, hard anger filled his voice, and he spat out each phrase as if it left a bad taste in his mouth.

"Good. Because my mind is made up. Show me that

you can make it, that you'll really stick to your goals this time, *then* I'll help you."

Gene gave his brother a contemptuous stare. "Meanwhile, here you are spending money hand over fist on the renovation. Don't you realize that just a few cuts in the remodeling could save enough to finance my gallery for years!"

"Forget it. The work on the house is going to go as planned."

"What if I could prove to you that money is being deliberately wasted, that your faith in the Indian woman is not warranted?"

Raul stood up, walked to the door, and held it open. "Gene, leave now. We've argued enough for one morning."

Gene stepped out of the office, head held high. His brother might want to bring him to his knees, but that would never happen. He was a Mendoza too, whether Raul chose to remember that or not. Gene considered his options. He still had one advantage. He knew Raul well. His brother would never purposely waste money, even on a project as dear to him as the renovation. When he wanted something done, he was willing to pay top dollar, but he expected his money's worth.

That's precisely what he wasn't getting, but Irene Pobikan had blinded him. It was to be expected: his brother had been without a woman for far too long. He smiled slowly, thinking of what Raul's reaction would be once he saw Irene for what she really was. Not the noble architect, but someone out to bilk him out of every dime.

The plan forming in his head lifted his spirits remarkably. All he had to do was keep track of every cent Pobikan spent. Cobb would be eager to help. Whistling, Gene went down the stairs.

* * *

Elena sat in one corner of the breakfast room, eating alone. As Irene strolled in, she glanced up but didn't smile.

"You okay?" Irene asked, taking a warm tortilla from a chafing dish, then filling it with scrambled eggs, potatoes, and green chile.

"I don't like it when the weather's like this on weekends. Both Gene and Raul stay home, and then they fight all the time. They've already started. I could hear them clear down the hall in my room."

Angela brought in some fresh buns. "It'll pass, Elena, it always does."

"I know, but I still hate to see them fighting. Gene always hurts Raul's feelings."

"The boys will work out their differences by themselves," Angela said firmly. "Don't you worry."

Gene walked into the room as Irene finished filling her plate. He served himself from the buffet, then sat down beside her. "What are your plans for today, Irene?"

She shrugged. "Originally I'd intended on going home, but the weather doesn't make that possible. So I'll just relax and take it easy around here."

"You certainly deserve your time off. It's high time you had the chance to sit back and enjoy the results of your work. The interior seems to be really taking shape. The *sala,* I noticed, is virtually finished, and the game room only needs a few more things. From the looks of it, I'd say it won't be much longer before the renovation is finished."

"We've made good progress, but there's still quite a bit of work left. The front stairs and stairwell, for instance, will be a major undertaking. There're also miscellaneous repairs that need done in virtually every room and the final plaster coat throughout."

Raul came in, gave Gene a curt nod, then smiled at

Elena and Irene. "It's Saturday, Irene. Don't feel obligated to talk shop, unless you want to."

Elena stood. "If you'll excuse me."

Irene watched her practically run out of the room, leaving her half-full plate behind. Poor Elena had been determined not to witness another fight between two people she loved. Irene gave Raul and Gene an icy look. "Elena heard you two having your 'discussion' earlier, and has had trouble handling it."

Raul's shoulders sagged slightly and the lines around his eyes deepened. "She's very sensitive."

"As you two should know by now," Irene conceded with a nod.

Raul said nothing, but took a seat at the head of the table, a full plate of food before him. "Have you finished the drawings for her greenhouse?"

Irene nodded. "They're in my office. I think you'll be pleased. I can bring them to your office after breakfast, if you'd like."

"I'd love to see the plans, if you don't mind," Raul said. "But just because you're snowed in doesn't mean you should feel pressured to do anything that's work-related."

"No problem," she assured. "Since this is for Elena, it's my pleasure."

"Could I have a look at those too when you're through, Raul?" Gene asked. "I'm glad you've decided on this. I think it's an excellent idea. Elena's needed something like this for a long time." Gene poured himself a second cup of coffee, then glanced at Irene. "I remember Cobb telling me there might be a problem if we attached the structure to the house. He felt that trying to keep the design in conformity with that of the hacienda would take quite some doing. Did you solve that in a way that's still cost-effective?"

"I've dealt with the design," she answered, "but if

expenses are a problem, it would be much cheaper to have a separate building. There're even greenhouse kits that are perfectly adequate."

"We *will* have an attached structure." Raul set his fork down and glanced at his brother, his glare lethal. "Drop it."

Gene shrugged. "I'm just trying to watch out for our interests."

"No, you've still got your mind on that damned gallery."

"And what's so bad about that!" Gene's temper flared. "At least I have a passion in my life. You exist, Raul, you don't live. I have no idea why you bother to get up in the morning sometimes."

"I have my duties to this family, which also includes working. Obviously that's a concept you'll never understand."

"I understand what it's like to do something out of love, not just because it's your obligation." His voice rose sharply. "You never have and that's what drove Reina into those depressions."

"Leave her out of this," Raul warned, standing up.

Elena ran back into the room as their angry voices rose. "Stop it! I can't take this anymore. Gene, why do you try to hurt Raul? He's never done anything to you!" Her voice broke and tears fell down her cheeks.

Raul started forward, but Gene cut in front of him. "Elenita, it's okay, it's just words." He tried to pull her into his arms for a hug, but she twisted away.

"No, it's more than just words, they hurt Raul. Stop hurting people, Gene. You've got to stop doing that. You always hurt people!"

"It's okay, Elena," Raul said gently. "I'm fine. Gene and I argue, but it's just part of being brothers."

"No, it's more. I know." She glared at Gene, tears staining her face. "You're hurting everyone, me included. I don't want to hear this anymore, and I don't want to feel this way inside. I want it to be like it was when we were kids. We all got along then."

Raul placed his arm around Elena's shoulders. "Okay, Elena. We'll try. But you shouldn't get this upset."

"It's the only way I can make you listen," she sobbed.

As Raul led her upstairs, Gene muttered an oath. "Now he ends up being the good guy with her too."

"Maybe he *is* the good guy," Irene challenged gently.

"And I'm the bad guy?"

"You're certainly a man with lots to learn about getting along with others." She stood, knowing she'd said too much, and left the dining room.

Twenty minutes later Irene went to her office, picked up the plans for the greenhouse, and walked to Raul's study. After the argument and the scene with Elena, it was quite possible neither of the men would be there, but she'd give it a try.

As she reached the open door, she saw both men inside, sitting across from each other in stony silence. Gene was pretending to read a magazine, and Raul was moving stacks of paper around his desk. The air was thick with resentment and unspoken thoughts.

She walked to Raul's desk and after he cleared some space, unrolled the plans before them. "The greenhouse would be added to the south side, and run all along that wall. With the *vigas* and old pueblo-style structure, it will look almost like an enclosed *portal*. It'll get plenty of sunlight throughout the day, since that side of the house isn't shaded, and add warmth to the house during the winter. Skylights hidden by the roof parapet would let in the northern light during the summer without ruining the hacienda's overall profile. The floors would be concrete, topped with half-bricks, and we'll be especially careful with drainage, keeping water away from the outside adobe along the foundation."

"How much of a cost overrun will this create?" Gene asked.

"None. Since we've stayed at the low end of the proposed budget, we have some latitude. This addition will simply put us closer to the high-end estimates, but won't exceed the funds already allocated to us."

Raul met Gene's gaze. "You'd try to save pennies now, when you know what this could mean to Elena?"

Something nasty sparked in Gene's eyes as he shook his head. "No, of course not. But the money spent isn't an indication of how much we love her. Being prudent with expenses is just good business. I thought that's what you've been trying to tell me all along."

Raul's expression was void of all emotion as he glanced over at Irene. "Would you give us a chance to discuss this issue in private?"

"Certainly." She retreated out of the room, eager to get away. She wasn't up to the strain of another confrontation. Walking quickly, she went to her room. At least there she'd find peace making her corn-husk dolls and looking forward to the face of the children who'd be receiving them as gifts.

The rest of the day, the house was still, but the silence was more jarring than anything else. It spoke of tensions that defied solutions.

Learning that Elena had opted for dinner in her room, Irene decided to follow suit. In truth, she was enjoying time alone to just be herself. She remained busy, scarcely aware of the passage of time as she caught up on her architectural journals and played games on her computer. When she finally glanced at the clock and saw it was half past ten, it took her by surprise.

Irene changed out of her jeans and sweater and into her nightclothes. The floor-length gown was warm and comfortable, perfect for curling up in the easy chair with her magazine. She'd just started reading an article when she heard a soft padding right outside her door. In an instant, Irene bolted out of the chair, ran to the door, and threw it open. An empty corridor greeted her. She glanced up and down the hall, but there was nothing there to account for the whisper-soft footsteps.

As she closed the door, a new plan formed in her mind. Instead of returning to the chair, she sat down right where she was standing. She'd be ready instantly next time she heard the sound. She leaned back against the wall, prepared to wait for hours if that's what it took.

Wanting to be as quiet as possible, she stayed in that one position, scarcely moving. As time ticked by, she began to feel the combined effects of the hardwood floor and boredom. She leaned back, shifting her weight from the flattened spot on her buttocks. Now that she was slightly more comfortable, her eyes started to close of their own volition when she heard the soft steps again. As the shadow began blocking the light filtering beneath the crack under the door, Irene reached for the knob and flung the door open.

# 25

**G**OTCHA!" IRENE BURST out of her room and saw a barely defined outline in the darkness at the far end of the hall. As she turned to pursue it, the shadow disappeared.

"No!" She ran to the stairs and peered down. The landing halfway down was covered in a gray half-light. She waited, her heart pounding frantically, hoping to catch a glimpse of the night stalker.

Aware suddenly of where she was standing, Irene reached over and flipped on the main stairway lights. She uttered a single expletive as three separate fixtures flooded the area, revealing an empty stairway.

Another storm passed through unexpectedly on Tuesday, and by Wednesday morning they were completely snowed in. All roads in the area were closed, and ice buildup made travel anywhere hazardous. Since the next day was Thanksgiving, everyone was understandably dejected. Fortunately the phone line wasn't down, and Raul set up a schedule so the workers could take turns talking to their families. He also made arrangements with Angela for a big Thanksgiving buffet for everyone, to be held in the *sala*.

The small amount of outside work remaining came to a temporary halt, but the craftsmen hired to do the interior work were busy. The crew was now working in the billiard room installing new flooring and repairing a load-bearing wall.

Unfortunately this meant noise and more workmen around the house, and Elena stayed in her room.

Irene was busy too, checking on details, determined not to let the pressure-cooker atmosphere inside the hacienda compromise the quality of work. She was on her way from her office to check on the *enjarradora*'s efforts in the game room when she overheard Cobb in the *sala* speaking to some of his men.

"I don't want you to spend all your time checking and rechecking everything. Now that we're snowed in, and there's no distraction, I want you boys to concentrate on picking up a little speed."

A voice from down the hall drifted into the room. "Naughty, naughty! Remember the wood-carver? If you want us to hurry, you better check with Mama Irene first."

Irene stood out of sight just beyond the doorway. The last thing she'd wanted to do was undermine Cobb's position with the men.

Cobb strode to the hall, but finding no one there, turned his attention to the two carpenters busy in front of him. "You think that's funny?"

"Don't look at us! You know *we* didn't say it," one of the men protested.

Irene waited, knowing that if she interfered in any

way now, it would be even worse. Cobb had to handle it.

"I know the crew's finding this new 'Mama' line hilarious, but I suggest you all put a lid on it. I'm still the one who hires and fires."

He started out of the room when someone whispered, "Better ask Mama about that."

Cobb spun around. His eyes searched the faces in front of him. Faced with a glower that could have cured bricks, the culprit never looked up, continuing instead to mix stucco.

"Enriquez," Cobb purred. "Would you care to put my authority to the test? You could make a good example."

"Hey, boss, I was just fooling around," he muttered. "Everybody's been saying it."

"Saying what? Enlighten me," Cobb said cynically.

"It seems there's two ways to do things around here: the Indian way or the wrong way." He shrugged. "Mama seems to have won the war."

Cobb took a step closer to the man. "Listen here, *amigo,* I'm going to let that pass this time. But if I hear any comments from you, you're history."

"Yeah, well, it was just a joke." The man adjusted his tool belt nervously. "You know that, Mr. Cobb."

"That's the only reason you're still here."

Irene stepped back out of view as Cobb strode out of the room and started down the opposite end of the hall. She wouldn't even try to talk to him now.

The sound of her steps must have made Cobb glance back. "Wait a minute, Pobikan," she heard him call to her. "We've got to talk."

She exhaled softly and waited for him to approach. "I couldn't help overhearing what happened, Cobb. That wasn't my intent when I spoke to the men. Is that what's on your mind?"

"Your office?" he snapped.

"Sure."

Cobb followed her inside and shut the door. "We're going to have a problem here very soon unless the snows stop and they can clear the roads. The men who are responsible for the exterior work haven't been able to do much except sit around. They're spending the day trying to find ways to amuse themselves while waiting for a chance to call home. Knowing they'll be missing Thanksgiving with their families isn't helping anyone's mood. Soon the fights will start, and no one will be keeping their minds on the job."

"What do you suggest we do? The weather's the weather, Thanksgiving notwithstanding. Nothing can be done about it."

"I've got a plan. For starters I'm going to start pressuring the men inside the hacienda to pick up the pace. That'll channel their energy into the work and force them to concentrate. Since you heard the exchange, you know the last thing I need is interference from you." Cobb's face was getting redder by the moment. "Serna told me you'd gone to him concerning the workers just before we found the body, and I don't like it one bit. I won't have you circumventing my authority. If you have something to say, come straight to me!" Cobb crossed his arms against his chest.

"John, my only quarrel with you is when you insist on circumventing what I want and keep trying to cut corners. I have no problem with speed as long as they keep up the quality."

"It wouldn't hurt if you put pressure on them too," Cobb added. "It might even help."

"I could, but are you sure that's the best answer? If they're on edge already, pushing them could result in the exact opposite of what we want."

"This works, I've done it before."

"But on most sites, the men go home every day, especially on holidays. This project's unusual on a variety of counts. They all know the importance of this house, and what it'll mean for the crew who works here in terms of prestige. The basic problem is that they're getting cabin fever. What we need is a way to break that tension, don't you think?"

He gave her an incredulous look. "Oh sure. Let me just go ask Raul if he has any skin flicks I can show the men on his VCR," he baited.

He was deliberately provoking her because she'd questioned his methods. She waited a moment before speaking, refusing to let him get to her. "Today, after the crew working inside is finished, I think we should sponsor a contest of skill. We'll have the men divide into teams according to their jobs. For example, the electricians can form one group, the woodworkers another, and so on. Then have them each use their knowledge and abilities to build the biggest snow Thanksgiving turkey they can in fifteen minutes. We'll give a ten-dollar bill to each member of the winning team."

"You're going to turn this into a battle between the trades? That'll segment them even more."

"No, it won't, because it'll be in the spirit of fun, and the prizes won't be much more than prestige money. It's not on-the-job competition as much as pride in their trade and the ability to pull together as a team."

"The Army used to do that in a way," he conceded. "This may actually be a good idea."

"It'll also let the men who've been cooling their heels in the trailers watching television and feeling sorry for themselves a chance to work off some steam."

"Okay, I . . ."

They heard shouts coming from down the hall. Cobb bolted to his feet and ran toward the sound. Irene followed him a second later. A Tewa man and a Hispanic were rolling around on the floor, trying to throw punches at each other. Men crowded in a loose circle around the two, shouting encouragement and offering bets on the outcome.

Cobb grabbed Serna's arm and pulled him along as he shoved his way roughly through the onlookers. "Carlos, on your feet." Cobb grabbed hold of the smaller man, who happened to be on top at that moment, and hauled him up roughly by his jacket. As the Tewa man sprang up, ready to continue the fight, Serna jumped in front of him and pushed the man back hard. "Cool it!"

"Who started this crap?" Cobb demanded. Neither man spoke. "I asked a question. What happened?"

Carlos just stared at the floor, refusing to speak. Frank Tatasawe devoted his time adjusting his shirt and belt, staring at a spot over Serna's head.

"Fine, if that's the way you want to play it. You've both just lost Friday's and Monday's work. Get out of here, and stay away from each other if you want to keep your jobs. I don't want to see either of you working until Tuesday." Cobb turned to Serna. "Find two volunteers from the men holed up in the trailers. There should be no shortage of guys willing to fill in here and help with the flooring."

Raul stood near the door as the two left the hacienda. "Irene, can I talk to you?" She nodded, and they walked away from the scene as Cobb and Serna dispersed the gathering.

Raul said nothing until they entered his study. "Listen, you've got to keep those outbreaks from happening, especially in the house. Elena's upset enough, and I'm worried about her. If you don't get along with

John, maybe you could get Serna to do something with the workers."

"I tried that once before without any success. This time, I think I have a handle on the situation. The men are going stir-crazy cooped up like they have been, so I've come up with a plan." Irene shifted in her chair and explained her idea.

"It's certainly worth a try." He reached for the corduroy jacket behind his chair and slipped it on over his pullover. "This storm has been severe enough to test the patience of a saint! I don't blame the men for getting restless."

"The weather forecast says it'll warm up in a few days."

"But it's going to take a while for the roads to dry up again." He stood by the window, watching the snow whirl across sculpted drifts. "Well, we have one thing to be grateful for. At least the accidents have stopped."

"Yes, and I'm very happy about that." She thought of the shadow she'd seen on the other side of her door, and her inability to find any sign of man or beast when she'd searched down the hall. That still made her uneasy. For a moment she considered telling Raul, then rejected the idea. He'd see it as proof that her imagination had been working overtime.

"Why don't I ask Angela to make snacks and hot cocoa for the men after the contest? We'll be providing a big Thanksgiving dinner for everyone tomorrow, but I think they could use something extra today."

"That's an excellent idea. I'll tell Cobb."

It was shortly after four when the men gathered outside. It was cold, but the wind had died down and no one complained. Irene smiled, suspecting that masculine pride was at the heart of that.

Cobb explained the contest details and saw the

men's interest spark. "There'll also be snacks inside afterward, courtesy of Mr. Mendoza." Cobb grinned as he saw from their expressions that the crew was eager to get the game under way. "Okay. You've got fifteen minutes. Go!"

The masons and roofers gathered in a huddle, discussing their strategy, but the plumbers and carpenters began to build turkey parts almost immediately, joining forces with the two electricians.

Irene stood aside, watching the competitiveness and pride in the men's faces as they worked, simultaneously monitoring what their neighbors were doing.

Raul came to stand beside her. "The plumbers' team is doing really well. That turkey's going to be fifteen feet high when they finish adding the head and feathers."

"They're packing the snow as they mold it, and that means it'll support more weight."

As the electricians on the team tried to connect a slender column of snow feathers to the body, she saw the head of the turkey sway. If it fell in the direction it was leaning, the crude sculpture would take the carpenter/roofers turkey down with it.

She started to say something, but a heartbeat later the turkey crashed, smashing into the thicker, more solid one built by the woodworkers. As turkey parts tumbled everywhere, she stared aghast at the shouting workers. "You couldn't stand it, could you?" one of the woodworkers growled, going forward. "We were going to beat you, and you knew it."

Acting on impulse, Irene made a large snowball and threw it against the woodworker's chest. "Chill out," she said with a grin. "Have a turkey egg."

He glanced down at the small globs of snow that clung to his jacket. "What the . . ."

"She's right." One of the Tewa men followed suit. "You need something to cool that temper."

Suddenly snowballs began flying back and forth. The carpenter's turkey became a fort as half a dozen men began lobbing snowballs like grenades at the workers clustered on the other side.

Raul was laughing at the mayhem when a large snowball hit him squarely in the face.

Irene's eyes widened and she smiled sheepishly. "I was aiming at Cobb," she said. "Sorry."

Raul stared so hard at her for a moment that she wondered if he'd forgotten how to play. Then he grinned, scooped up a handful of snow, and tossed it back at her.

Before long, the grounds were littered with big chunks of snow, and the air was filled with snowballs that came from all directions. Neither turkey survived.

As the battle began to subside, Irene brushed the snow from her hair, laughing and trying to catch her breath.

"You lobbed one right inside my jacket. How did you do that?" Raul asked with a shudder.

"Exceptional talent. How many times do I get to do something that nasty to my employer and still come out of it with a job?"

He waved his hand in the air. "Okay, let's call it a truce. The prize money will be donated to a Taos charity," he said. "Now let's go inside and eat!"

A cheer went around and the men streamed into the house, brushing snow off their clothing. Gene stood on the stairs staring at the men, disapproval evident on his face as water dripped onto the brick floor.

Slowly he came downstairs and approached Raul, his bloodshot eyes and unsteady gait attesting to an afternoon of heavy drinking. "You spend so much money on renovations trying to recapture the elegance this hacienda had at one time. Yet you allow anyone in here. This house has no more class than a back-alley bar in Albuquerque."

"Lighten up, Gene," Raul growled.

"You'll never be the man Dad was, but you could at least try to show a little style."

Footsteps coming down the stairs echoed loudly in the awkward silence that followed. Irene looked up and saw Elena, her face as pale as corn silk. "I've asked you two not to argue any more," she said simply, joining her brothers. Taking a plate filled with chocolate cake from Irene's hand, she turned, and in one continuous motion shoved it against Gene's face. "Next time, *listen to me!*"

Elena handed the empty plate back to Irene. Then, with monolithic dignity, she walked back up the stairs. A few seconds later, they heard a door slam.

The silence continued as chunks of chocolate cake fell off Gene's face and spilled down the front of his beige corduroy shirt.

Surprise held her for a moment, but as a piece of cake tumbled into Gene's shirt pocket, she began to laugh. It started slowly, and she tried to control it, but soon she was helpless. "Atta girl, Elena," she said.

Others began to join in, and soon the room was alive with merriment. Raul tried to keep from laughing, but as his brother wiped the frosting from his face, he couldn't resist any longer. "Gene, go upstairs and take a cold shower," he said, gasping for air. "Elena did the right thing, and we all know it."

Gene glanced around, his chocolate-covered face resembling a riverbank after spring runoff. "This is your fault, not Elena's," he told Irene. "You've been influencing her."

"Obviously in the right direction. To be honest, the

only reason I didn't do that myself was because Elena thought of it first."

Gene scowled at her, then at Raul. Wordlessly he turned and tried to go up the stairs with the same grace his sister had demonstrated. His gait, still unsteady, ruined the effect.

As he left, the men settled down to their snacks. The tension that had held them before was gone as they teased each other and consumed the steaming hot cocoa and warm cinnamon rolls. An hour later in good spirits, they drifted back to the trailers.

Irene smiled as Angela began picking up. "By Friday, after their big Thanksgiving buffet and a day off, they'll return to their jobs with renewed spirits. We did a good job here today." She glanced at Cobb. "Don't you agree?"

"Yeah, everyone came out ahead on this. Well, everyone except Gene."

Raul nodded somberly. "I never even dreamed Elena would do something like that."

Irene smiled. "She's been growing steadily as a person all along, and learning her own strengths. You haven't noticed it because you're too close to her."

Cobb left the hacienda and headed for the office trailer a few minutes later. Raul stood at the window looking at the snow that gleamed in the circle of light from the porch.

"Irene, will you go for a walk with me? It's beautiful out there with the moon reflecting off the snow." Seeing her hesitate, he added, "I'd like to talk to you about Elena."

She reached for her coat, which was draped over the back of one of the chairs. "Let's go. The fresh air will do us both good."

Feet crunching on the ice-encrusted ground, they walked up the path that led to Elena's gardens. Raul remained silent for a long time, keeping his pace slow. "This was my mother's favorite route whenever it snowed. She loved to watch the moonlight catch and play in the tree branches. She'd stay outside until she couldn't stand the cold anymore."

A slight breeze blew through the trees, and hundreds of snowflakes came fluttering down around them, shimmering like diamonds. "I'm glad I came. Sometimes I get so wrapped up in my work that I forget to stop and enjoy the little things," Irene admitted.

Raul nodded somberly. "It's like that for me also. I get too caught up in business matters. That's what Reina hated most," he added. "In that one respect, her complaints were more valid than I like to admit."

"Yes, but you always had many responsibilities, and no one to help you shoulder the load."

They started back, taking a different pathway this time. "Still, Gene was right to say that I failed her. I did."

"How?"

"She wanted a protector, a lover, and a husband. I knew that from the beginning, and thought I could be all those things to her. But other—financial— responsibilities kept pushing their way into the picture. My father died when I was twenty-two, and from that time on, the company was my responsibility. When I married Reina five years later, the company was just starting to get back into the black. It required my attention. To make a long story short, I wasn't around often enough for her to feel the love and security she desperately needed."

"You did your best; that's all anyone can ask."

"I did try, but she had a right to expect more. I knew she was high-strung when I married her and that she needed constant reassurances of love. By not nourishing her heart, I failed her on every count that mattered."

As they passed the cemetery, Raul noticed that a path had already been worn through the snow. "Someone's been here, but I can't imagine what they would have been doing."

"Let's go see where the tracks lead," Irene suggested.

After a few minutes, they came to a stop by a black granite marker with Reina's name on it. The lack of a grave took her by surprise. "She's not buried here?"

"Her body was never recovered," he answered. "Let's go back. We can finish our talk in the house where it'll be warm."

As they passed through a thick belt of trees, Irene felt a tickle at her spine. Something compelled her to look back, and as she did, she caught a glimpse of a shadow. It moved with them, but stayed just beyond the bushes. She reached casually toward Raul and touched his arm lightly.

He came out of his thoughts, but remained quiet as she placed her forefinger to her lips. Moving only slightly, she cocked her head toward the spot where the shadow was.

Raul's eyes narrowed. "Stay here," he whispered, then shot after it.

Ignoring him, Irene gave chase too, running as fast as she could in the snow. Two minutes later, she caught up with Raul. He was bent over, hands on his knees, gulping for air.

"Did you see who it was?"

He shook his head. "I wasn't even able to tell if it was a man or woman. But it wasn't an animal, that I'm sure of. This person was smart enough to keep to the brush where I wouldn't be able to find tracks to follow. Our shadow had no intention of getting caught."

The screech of an owl formed in the still air. She shuddered. "It's back."

Raul's shoulders stiffened. "Our shadow's back too," he whispered. "I'm going to try again." He waited a second, verifying its location, then whirled and sprinted after it.

Irene let Raul take the lead, but remained a few feet behind him. It was useless for her to try and cut off whoever was following them; she wasn't sure where the shadow was anymore.

Raul dodged through the trees rapidly, zigzagging around the snow-encrusted boulders on the forest floor. After five minutes he stopped, his breath forming tiny clouds in the frozen air. "It's gone again. I thought I was real close, but then it just pulled away and left us behind. You know, we saw it after we came out of the cemetery. Maybe I'm chasing a family ghost," he teased halfheartedly.

"Have you ever had one?"

"Not that I know of," Raul said. "But I prefer to think we were dealing with a ghost who vanished into thin air rather than a person who was able to elude me. Male pride, I guess."

His candor touched her. "Egos can be a burden."

"Yeah, but it can give a man a center," he said gently, "something to hold on to even when everything around him falls apart."

She wanted to ask him more about Reina. His reluctance to discuss her at any great length, coupled with the references he'd already made, had only served to intensify her need to know. She was trying to think of a way to bring the subject back up when the owl screeched again as if it were hunting. The sound was so close it sent a shiver up her spine.

"That came from up ahead. Shall we see where it's nesting?" Raul asked.

She hesitated, not really sure if she wanted to know or not. "Does it matter?"

"Are you worried?" he asked gently.

"Yes and no. It's crazy how some of these things stick with you. A part of me says that it's just a belief without foundation, but then another says the equivalent of where there's smoke there's fire. Let's face it, my people have been around for a long time. Our ways aren't necessarily wrong just because they don't mesh with the thinking of others on the outside."

"Would you rather just go back to the house?"

She hesitated, then shook her head after a second. "No. We better find out where it is in reference to the house. As your architect I have to anticipate problems, and this could become one again, unless we continue to handle it carefully."

"Let's go, then."

She followed Raul through a stand of trees, moving slowly over the snow to avoid the crunch. The owl continued calling, but the sound shifted, making it difficult to pinpoint the location. "I think it's moving toward its nest," she said.

"If it is, then it's holed up close to the house," he answered.

They approached some tall junipers about one hundred yards from the entrance. Hearing wings flapping, she looked up and saw the owl land on a branch high above them, a small rodent in its talons. Suppressing a shudder, she automatically reached for the fetish in her pocket. Irene made a fist around the small pouch, feeling the edges of the stone effigy pressing against her palm. "It's closer than it's ever been," she said.

"Yeah, it is." He rubbed his gloved hands together

for warmth. "But the work going on is mostly inside now. Maybe the men won't notice it."

"Maybe," she replied, unconvinced.

Minutes later, they entered the house. She felt instantly welcomed by the warmth and the homey scent of burning piñon coming from the kiva-style fireplaces. Her cheeks, which had been almost numb, began to tingle with life again. "If you don't mind, I think I'll say good night now. I'm really tired." She stifled a yawn.

Raul's gaze took her in slowly. "If you haven't been sleeping well, I can ask Angela to fix you one of her *remedios*. They're herbs, and probably not much different from the ones your people would use. Unlike sleeping pills, her teas don't make you feel hung over the next day."

"What makes you think I'm not sleeping?" she asked. Someone had been trying to keep her awake, but Raul's offer intimated that he was aware of the circumstances.

"You have very dark circles under your eyes."

His answer immediately brushed aside her suspicions, leaving her feeling guilty. "Don't worry. I'm exhausted tonight. Our romp through the snow did me some good. There's nothing like fresh air and exercise to help you go to sleep."

Irene went upstairs, dragging her feet with each step. She'd used up her energy reserves. Nothing would disturb her tonight; she intended to see to it.

She entered her room a moment later, locked the door, and braced it with a chair. Then, taking the small woven rug from beside her bed, she wedged it into the crack beneath the door. Not even shadows would be allowed to disrupt her rest. As she crawled between the sheets, she heard Raul coming up the stairs and walking to his room. His presence was soothing somehow. She nestled down further under the covers.

She started drifting gently to sleep when the familiar padding slowly roused her. Turning her head toward the door, she saw a shadow flicker at a corner the rug hadn't covered. Irene sighed softly and rolled over on her side. Not tonight, she'd had enough. Closing her eyes, she floated into the dark mines of sleep.

She wasn't sure when her dreamscape became alive with images, but her grandfather suddenly appeared before her, a mist shadowing his face. "The time of danger is near. You'll have to watch and remain open to the guidance of those who protect you. They *will* help, but only if your heart welcomes them."

Irene saw a giant shadow slowly materialize behind her grandfather. "Grandfather, there! Watch out!"

He appeared not to hear or notice. "Remember that the answers and knowledge you want are within you."

As his image faded, Irene felt utterly alone. The dream continued to hold her, however, unwilling to let go, though a part of her desperately wanted to come awake. Then, through her blunted senses, she heard the scream of a mountain lion pierce the night. The mournful, almost human cry jolted her awake.

Irene lay still in her bed, her heart hammering, and listened to the howl of the great cat.

# 26

**D**ESPITE THE HARDSHIPS of the storm, Thanksgiving left everyone in good spirits. The men had even been able to make it home late Saturday and spend part of the weekend with their families.

Monday morning, ready and eager to immerse herself in the work she loved, Irene glanced inside her supply box. She was nearly out of everything, including the basics—like pens and floppy disks. She glanced outside, assessing the weather. The snow flurries that had started abruptly this morning had stopped once again. The roads were still messy, but she was sure the Bronco's four-wheel drive would get her to town and back safely. If she made good time, she'd go all the way to her Santa Fe office for what was needed.

Leaving word with Angela, who insisted she take hot coffee and some burritos along, Irene started down the mountain toward Taos shortly after one. Most of the time she had to travel at an incredibly slow pace, icy spots on the road making speed hazardous. Some stretches, however, were amazingly free of everything except mud. From the presence of tracks, she could tell that others had already braved the road that day, helping clear the way.

The hour-and-a-half drive turned out to be closer to three, making her glad she'd accepted the food from Angela. Eating had helped her pass the time when she'd been forced to travel at fifteen miles an hour.

Once in town, Irene drove to the office supply store and purchased the items she needed. It was just too late to continue on to Santa Fe, especially with the roads the way they were. She was walking back to the Bronco when she noticed the public library further down the street. Surely she'd be able to dig up an article there that would tell her more about Reina.

As she placed her supplies in the back of her vehicle, she weighed the merits of her idea. It really wasn't any of her business; if Raul hadn't chosen to tell her, she had no right to seek out the information. But it certainly wouldn't hurt anyone if she were a little bit more informed. Maybe she'd even be able to help Raul work through the guilt he still harbored. She'd sensed that emotional turmoil in him as clearly as Taos Mountain appeared over the town. Surely the chance to help him would more than offset any breach she would commit by researching his past.

Her mind made up, she drove to the small building and walked inside. The newspapers had been placed in microfiche, and that made it easier. She knew the date of Reina's death, having seen it on the marker.

Because Reina had been a published poet and local celebrity, her death had garnered quite a bit of attention. The lead article reported that Raul's wife had been the victim of a boating accident off the coast of Mexico. The body had never been found. A later editorial, however, raised several questions the investigation had left unanswered. The boat had been small, so Raul must have seen or heard his wife fall overboard. Why hadn't he been able to pull her back on board? The piece also pointed out that Reina and Raul's marriage had been troubled. Public fights had taken place more than once.

A sidebar article rehashing a previous story involving the Mendoza men left no doubt that the Mendozas had been targeted by the press more than once. The feature, spotlighting teenage runaways, mentioned the disappearance of sixteen-year-old Raven Hernandez. Confidential sources reported that Raven had been involved with one of the Mendoza boys.

Although no direct mention was made, the reporter dropped enough clues to point the finger at Raul. The reporter further speculated that Raven had left because she had been rejected, therefore intimating that Raul bore some responsibility for breaking up the Hernandez family.

Angrily she thought of the damage this kind of publicity had done to Raul during his college years, and again just after his wife's death. The ultimate insult had come when the press had redone the first story to sensationalize the second. In her heart, she knew that Raven had left home of her own free will, and that he'd done nothing to harm Reina.

It was at that moment Irene realized just how much faith she'd come to have in Raul. She shut off the microfiche viewer and stood up. Although she wasn't certain exactly when it had happened, she'd given her heart to him. The intensity of emotions coursing through her let her know that she'd been hiding the truth from herself for a long time. She stood clearly in his corner now, even though he was the scion of a family traditionally considered enemies of her people.

One concern, however, overwhelmed the rest. Reina still held part of his heart, although she didn't understand the reasons behind that. It seemed the ultimate cruelty of fate. After all the years of waiting, she'd finally found the man who could have fulfilled both her fantasies and her reality. But his allegiance was to another.

As she walked outside, she realized how dark it had become, though it wasn't even six o'clock yet. She hadn't meant to stay this long. Traveling across country roads illuminated only by the moon and the headlights of the Bronco was bound to test her driving skills to the limit.

As she strode past a low adobe wall, she heard someone right behind her. Before she could react, a hand was clamped over her mouth, and she was dragged backward into the yard. Panic slammed into her with wild force. The man's arm worked around her throat, making it impossible for her to scream as he groped for her purse. Struggling to breathe, she reached backward, trying to claw at the face of her assailant. Then through the streetlight that bled its cone of yellow light onto the gathering darkness, she saw another man running toward them from down the block. "Let her go!" he yelled at the top of his voice.

Her captor dropped her quickly, and she fell onto the frozen ground, still clutching her purse. She lay dazed for a moment, struggling to catch her breath. As she started to sit up, the man who'd come to her rescue drew near.

"I don't know how to thank you," she said, getting to her feet.

"You just did." He looked her over. "Do you need a doctor?"

"No, I'm fine," she said, her voice shaky, then added, "I know you. You're Alfredo Hernandez."

He nodded. *"A sus ordenes."* She knew the Spanish phrase, "at your service." "Well, let's stop by and see the sheriff. Maybe he'll be able to catch whoever tried to mug you."

"I never even considered the possibility that this might happen."

"Just because ours is a small town doesn't mean we don't have crime. The library is a place where many passing through take shelter, though certainly the city never encourages it. I'm just glad I chose this time to go out for dinner."

The visit to the sheriff was mercifully short. She reported the attack, admitting it had all happened too quickly for her to be able to give them anything concrete. Following her instinct, however, she omitted telling the officer that she'd been someone's target for some time now.

Irene left the station shortly thereafter. Hernandez remained with her, accompanying her down the street. "You held something back," he said after they'd walked a block.

She said nothing.

"All right. It certainly isn't any of my business. But if you're going to drive all the way back to the hacienda tonight, at least stick around enough to have a bite to eat. It'll give you a chance to calm down before you tackle the roads."

"Okay. I'm not really hungry, but a snack's a good idea. A cup of coffee might also help keep me alert on the way back."

"Good. Let's go to Duke's Diner. They've got a great chocolate cream pie that goes just about perfect with coffee."

They crossed the highway and entered a small cafe filled with photos of movie cowboys. A poster of John Wayne was displayed prominently at the center of the far wall. The sounds of country-western music rose from an old-style jukebox. Still a bit on edge, she chose a booth where she could watch who came in the door. Soon the waitress came, and Hernandez ordered for both of them.

"I can't imagine a better night for you to enjoy a special treat," he said as the young woman left. "When things are going wrong, that's the time you have to be especially good to yourself."

"You're right," she conceded, hearing her own grandfather in his words. Hernandez didn't seem like the person that Gene had intimated he'd be. He was obviously sensitive to the difficulties she'd been experiencing at work. Raul's assessment was closer to the mark, if instinct served her at all. "I've seen you around the hacienda. Why do you go back there?"

She watched his eyes soften and cloud with emotions. Then in an instant, as if abruptly aware of the lapse, he brought himself under control. She waited, not interrupting his silence.

"After my daughter ran off, I sank into a depression I very nearly couldn't escape. Then my wife left and I retreated into a bottle. That combination almost finished me. It took years for me to be able to find my way out of the hole I'd dug for myself." His words were as soft as falling leaves. "Now, finally, I'm back on my feet, with a business and an office down the street. My visits to the hacienda were my way of proving that I've put the past behind me, and I have. I didn't feel angry anymore when I walked around the place. Instead, I was at peace again. None of what happened was really the Mendozas' fault. It's just that for a long time it was easier to blame them."

"You've had to face some very tough times, but you've come through it. That takes a great deal of courage."

"Courage? No. Stubbornness is more like it. But let's not dwell on the past anymore." He smiled. "Career-wise, this must be a very exciting time for you. John Cobb and I have been friends for years, and he's been showing me the progress you've made with the renovation. It's turning out beautifully."

"Thank you for saying that." She stirred her coffee absently. "Strange that Cobb never mentioned you to me," she said, wondering exactly how much Hernandez knew about the accidents.

"Don't blame *him* for that. I asked him not to. I thought it would upset the Mendozas. As it was, maybe I just made things worse."

She shook her head. "No, it's all right. We've had some trouble at the site and everyone was a bit jumpy for a while. But that's been handled now. Your presence did raise some questions, but Raul never believed that you had anything to do with the problems."

"You have no idea how much that means to me. The past is finally behind me now," he answered, his voice taut with emotion. "I've started up my architectural and contractor work again, and I'm prospering."

They finished their coffee and pie in silence. Finally Irene glanced at her watch. "Now I really have to be going back."

He dropped a few bills on the table. "I'll walk you to your car and then get back to my office." He fell into step beside her as they crossed to the library's parking lot.

For the life of her, she couldn't imagine this man, as nice as he was, being friends with someone like John Cobb. "If you want to drop by and look at how the restoration's going inside, I'm sure Raul wouldn't mind."

"Thanks." He cleared his throat. "I'll make sure I'm more open about my visits from now on. I'm sorry if I gave anyone reason for concern. That was exactly what I was trying to avoid."

Saying a quick good-bye, she slipped behind the wheel and started the long drive back. There was much to like about Alfredo Hernandez. The man had suffered a great deal, but he'd made it. He was one of life's survivors. But in a way, those people were the most dangerous. They knew they could make it no matter how much hurt they were forced to endure. And they seldom showed mercy, knowing others could take it as they had. The thought momentarily occurred to her that maybe he hadn't just "happened by" on the way to dinner.

Still, something inside her said that Hernandez was okay. She remembered her grandfather and what he'd taught her. He'd always maintained that every individual had a role to play in the larger scheme of things. He'd used their tribe as an example, pointing to the two major religious groups, the Summer People and the Winter People. Although each faction had its own duties to fulfill, individual members had to make his or her unique contribution before the rituals could accomplish the good intended.

The significance of those teachings was too much a part of her to brush aside now. It was inappropriate to pass judgment on someone until the role that person played in the overall pattern was determined. As she drove up the graveled road toward the hacienda, she knew that by neither condemning nor accepting Alfredo Hernandez, she'd done the right thing.

It took Irene three hours to make the return journey. The traffic-worn snow had frozen over to ice again shortly after sunset. By the time she reached the hacienda, she was surprised to see Raul waiting for her at the courtyard gate. She hastened her steps, worried by the look on his face. "Has something happened?"

Raul started to pull her into his arms, but stopped, hearing Angela behind him opening the front door of the house. Instead, he reached for her hand and held it for a moment. "We were scared to death. We kept waiting for you, but it's been forever, even taking the roads into account. Then the sheriff phoned and told us what happened to you earlier. He'd wanted permission to stop by tomorrow so you could sign one of the crime reports. We didn't know what to think after that! We were about to go out looking for you."

"I'm so sorry you worried! I never expected the sheriff to call here."

"You should have telephoned one of us . . . Me," he added, his voice a whisper. "Why didn't you?"

"There was no need . . ." she started, then clamped her mouth shut. She was only making things worse.

"Maybe that's the real problem between us," he said, quietly enough for only her to hear. "You don't need anyone. I thought I was that way too, but I was wrong." Turning, he walked back to the house.

Elena greeted her at the door a minute later. "I tried to tell Raul you'd be okay, but he wouldn't listen." Annoyance came through in her voice. "He wasn't interested in anyone but you. He's still upset. He just walked right by me without saying anything."

Irene sighed. Things were going from bad to worse, and she had no idea how to stop the progression. "Elena, sometimes if you're really worried about one thing, your mind shuts off everything else. I'm sure he didn't mean to hurt your feelings."

"It's not *his* fault. It's yours." Her eyes were as cold and impenetrable as the darkness outside. "For a while I thought you'd be a friend, but I was wrong. All you've done is bring strangers and trouble. My brothers fight more than ever, and it's usually over you or what you're doing to our home. I wish you would just go back to the pueblo and leave us alone!"

Irene watched Elena run upstairs. Her throat felt so tight she could scarcely breathe. Tears stung her eyes, but she managed to keep them from falling down her cheeks by not blinking.

Angela cleared her throat, letting Irene know she was standing there. "It's okay, she'll be all right. It's just that she's not used to having Mr. Raul be short with her. Are you hungry? Can I get you something to eat or drink?"

"No, thanks," she managed, struggling to keep her voice steady. "I'm going to go upstairs to bed. I've just about had it today."

Irene walked upstairs slowly, and as she reached her door, she stopped trying to contain her tears. Pain and frustration tore into her with overwhelming intensity. When she'd accepted the job, her goals had been to fulfill herself as an architect and build the reputation she needed to help her people. She'd never thought she'd be bringing this kind of chaos to those living in the house she'd come to restore.

She stripped quickly, allowing her clothing to fall into a heap on the floor, and crawled into bed.

Sleep came soon, but rest eluded her as nightmares filled her with horrific visions. Ancient supernaturals that brought evil in their wake, ragged woman, *w'itsa kwiyo,* and *pineto kwiyo,* mean old man, chilled her soul. Like a spider crawling through her brain, the threatening images intensified, using fears hidden in the deepest recesses of her mind against her. Her terror grew with each new vista that unfolded until she sat up, jolted awake, a scream forming at the back of her throat.

Shivers spreading through her, she slowly nestled back down into the covers. Her body was covered with perspiration, but she had to swallow to aid the dryness on her throat. She shifted restlessly, but finding a comfortable position seemed impossible.

Time passed slowly as an eternity of darkness stretched out before her. When she finally noted the first rays of sunlight streaming through her window, she welcomed them with relief. Things would be better today, she assured herself, getting up.

Irene walked to the shower feeling both sweaty and cold. The terrors of the night still lingered at the edges of her mind. Refusing to dwell on it, she tried to divert herself by concentrating on the delights of Angela's breakfast cinnamon rolls waiting downstairs. Her stomach rumbled noisily.

Reaching for the shampoo, Irene turned toward the small shelf beneath the frosted glass pane. Her breath suddenly lodged in her throat as fear clawed into her. An undefinable shape, much too large to be a bird, loomed outside a few feet away from her second-story window.

# 27

DESPERATE FOR A clearer look, Irene tried to open the window a crack, but it was jammed. By the time she managed to slide it open a few inches, the figure seemed to have moved out of her field of vision. All she could see now were branches from one of the tall pines beside the house. Assuring herself that she'd only seen a raccoon or some other harmless creature whose image had been distorted by the frosted glass, she finished bathing.

Despite her logical assertions that nothing would have been simply looming there that high off the ground, she felt uneasy. With a towel wrapped turban style around her head, she walked into the bedroom and started rummaging through drawers for something to wear. It was warm in her room, but the bleakness outside heralded a nasty and cold day.

She pulled a sweater from the drawer, then turned to search for a pair of slacks she'd hung in the closet.

Seeing the closet door open a slit, she stopped suddenly. She had a habit of always shutting doors and drawers; it had been her mother's pet peeve and ingrained in her as far back as she could remember.

She turned sideways and struggled to stay calm. She slipped her sweater on, then the dirty jeans she'd left on the floor. She considered calling out for help right then, but first she wanted to make sure this wasn't a new trick. She'd lost enough credibility in front of Raul.

She came up with a quick plan. Moving away from the closet, she noiselessly opened the door to her room, then crossed to the desk. Knowing the intruder could see her now, she furtively slipped a letter opener from the top drawer into her sleeve, then started casually in the direction of the window. Irene took a few steps, then stopped abruptly and flung the closet door open.

A man in jeans and a brown jacket, wearing a dark blue ski mask, crouched inside. Her gesture had taken him by surprise, and for a second he didn't move.

"Get out of there," she said, pointing the tip of the letter opener toward him menacingly. "And take off the ski mask. If you try anything, you'll leave this room leaking blood like a sieve."

He laughed and started toward her. "Yeah?"

"Try me," she said, holding her ground, although her hand was now shaking badly.

She held his brown-eyed gaze, hoping he wouldn't call her bluff.

He suddenly feinted a move to the left, then dodged right the moment she reacted. Pushing her hard, he bolted through the doorway into the hall. Irene was hurled against the armoire, sending the tiny potted rose that adorned the top crashing to the floor. The chest continued on over onto its side, its resounding crash vibrating through the room.

As she struggled to her feet, she heard Elena scream. Irene bolted toward the door, but before she could reach it, Elena burst into the room. "What happened Irene, are you okay?"

"Did you see him?" Irene asked, rushing past her. She reached the stairs, then glanced down. No one was there. She felt torn between disappointment and relief.

Elena waited halfway down the hall staring wide-eyed at her, but saying nothing. Her silence frightened Irene more than anything else could have. "Talk to me Elena, please! Do you know who that was?"

"No," she answered quickly.

"But you saw him." She saw Elena nod.

Entering her room again, Irene walked to the window. She'd left it open a crack, enjoying fresh air while she slept. Now, as she pulled the curtains back wide and glanced outside, she realized the figure she'd seen while taking a shower had not been a four-footed animal. She studied the sturdy pine branch that nearly touched her window and saw where bark had been chipped loose, and needles had been torn off, denuding areas. This was how he'd gained entry.

Irene turned to talk to Elena and saw her standing by the closet, her eyes riveted on something that had fallen to the floor. A small metal hip flask lay by one of Irene's shoes.

Irene picked it up by the metal strap that held the cap in place and set it down on one of the chairs. As she glanced at Elena, she saw her trying to edge out of the room. "Wait, Elena, don't go."

Elena avoided her gaze. "I don't want to talk about the man."

"All right. Then just listen." She told her what had happened, then continued. "This man didn't hurt me, but he's sick. Chances are he'll do this to one of the other women next. If you know anything, please tell me. We'll go to Raul . . ."

"Raul left for Albuquerque early this morning, and Gene won't be back until later this afternoon," she said, her voice rising. "Do you think that man is going to come back again?"

She cursed herself for not phrasing things a little differently. "I don't think we're in any immediate danger. I scared him as much as he scared me," she added gently.

"You might have, but I sure didn't," she answered.

"What do you mean?" Seeing the reluctance on Elena's face, she softened her tone. "Are you afraid to tell me?"

Elena nodded. "He could hurt me."

"No, not if we stop him first, and that's exactly what I intend to do." She grasped Elena's shoulders and sought her eyes. "Listen to me, Elena. People like that man thrive on fear. They want you to be afraid, because that's a way to control you. Tell me what you know, and we'll both make sure this man doesn't bother anyone again."

"I don't know who he is," Elena repeated. "One night after the construction started, he hid in my closet and watched me undress. I saw him in my mirror and I started to scream, but he grabbed me hard. I was so scared! I couldn't even breathe because his hand was over my nose and my mouth."

"Did he touch you or hurt you?" She tried to keep the edge out of her voice, but didn't quite manage.

Elena's eyes brimmed over with tears. "He touched me," she shuddered, "and he said terrible things. He said that if I told anyone, he'd be back to do all those things to me. He said that I needed a man to show me what I'd been missing."

Rage filled Irene, and she was surprised that she was able to manage a gentle smile. "What did he look like? Was it the same man you saw leaving my room?"

"I never saw his face clearly. All I know is that there was a funny mark on the back of his hand. It was tiny, but I remember seeing it and staring, trying not to think of where he was touching me."

Irene pushed back the bitterness that gushed to her mouth, stinging her throat. The construction effort was all part of what she'd brought to this home. Now she had to face the possibility it had caused lasting harm to the one person who'd be least able to cope with it. "What kind of mark?"

"It was a patch of dark brown, shaped a little like a tulip." She pointed to a spot right between her thumb and forefinger. "There."

Cobb appeared at the open doorway, glanced inside, then stopped. "Hey, I heard all the racket. Is everything okay with you two?"

Irene hesitated only a second. They had to act fast, and Cobb was her best chance. She had to trust him on this; there was no other choice. She highlighted the actions of the intruder who'd hidden in her closet, and described the man as best she could. She then added Elena's description of the birthmark, alluding to the incident that had preceded hers. Last of all, she showed him the flask.

Cobb turned to Elena, but before he could say anything, she rushed out of the room in tears. His face turned red and ugly. "Did he hurt her?"

Irene explained succinctly, and saw the muscles in his jaw start to twitch. "Do you know who the guy is?" she asked.

"Yeah, and I'll take care of it," Cobb said, going to the door.

She slipped on her boots and ran after him. "Wait a second!"

He didn't slow down, but she managed to catch up with him at the courtyard gate. "Remember Carlos, the guy who got treed when he saw the mountain lion?" Cobb answered at last. "He has a birthmark like the one Elena described to you, and that's his flask you found. He always said it was filled with cough medicine. Sometimes it was."

Irene hurried along beside Cobb as he strode across the snowy grounds, heading straight for the trailer Carlos occupied. He banged loudly on the door. A moment later another Hispanic worker answered. "It's early, Cobb. What's going on?" He looked as if he'd just awakened.

"Where's Carlos?"

"I dunno. He drove off a few minutes ago."

"Then it'll be easy to catch him," Cobb said, turning to Irene. "He has a beat-up sedan with slicks for tires, so he'll have to creep along."

"Yeah, man, except he left his car and took one of the company's pickups. Serna must have given him the keys," the Hispanic man added.

Serna poked his head out of the adjacent trailer's kitchen window. "What's going on, and what's this about Carlos?"

Cobb explained things quickly. "I want him."

Serna spat out an oath, then emerged at the door. "That *hijo de puta* conned me out of one of our trucks, I'm going after him." The two men ran to one of the pickups just as Carlos' roommate came out of the trailer with three other workers.

"We'll follow in our trucks," one of them yelled.

"Hold it," Irene protested, thinking of the road conditions and the possible results of a chase. "You can't . . ."

Realizing she was talking to herself, she ran to the parking area. With the speed the vehicles took off, it was impossible for her to do anything except pray no one would be hurt in an accident.

Ed Reyes, the crane operator, who had overheard Cobb's charges against Carlos, came and stood beside her. "You can't blame them, you know. Carlos didn't just dishonor the Mendozas, he dishonored the entire crew. They wouldn't be worth much as men if they let him get away."

"But with the roads as bad as they are, someone could be killed."

"At the moment they're more worried about what they'll tell their families once the news gets out. None of them would be able to look at themselves in the mirror if they let Carlos get away now."

The possibility that Elena would soon become the main subject of gossip in Taos made her ill. Somehow she had to get hold of Raul. Maybe there was still a way to protect Elena from this. Raul's standing in the community might at least help restrain some of the gossip.

She ran back to the house in search of Angela. The woman, alert to what had happened, was just coming out of Elena's room.

"How is she?" Irene asked quickly.

"Not good. She's afraid."

"That Carlos will come back?"

"Yes, and that people will start asking her all kinds of embarrassing questions."

Elena stepped out of her room and stood in the doorway. Tearstains were on her cheeks. "It already happened with Mr. Cobb. I knew what he was going to ask. That's why I ran to my room. People have always stared and felt sorry for me. That's why I hated going into town. Now it'll be even worse."

Her heart went out to Elena. People could be cruel without ever realizing it. Pity could sometimes do more damage than a physical injury. "Elena, I'm going to do all I can to protect your privacy. Don't lose faith in me completely."

Elena's downcast expression didn't change. Silently she turned and went back into her room, closing the door.

Irene walked down the stairs with Angela. "I need to get hold of Raul right away. How can I do that?"

"By turning around," she heard a familiar voice coming from the sitting room.

Raul's face was lined with worry. "What's going on here? Where did everybody go? I only saw a few vehicles when I drove in."

"Let's go to your study," Irene suggested. "I need to talk to you privately." Once the door was closed, she told him the story without inflection, relating only the facts as she knew them. Yet her efforts to stem the reaction she'd feared in Raul turned out to be useless.

A white-hot rage gripped him and he rose from his chair, his fists clenched so tightly his knuckles turned a pearly color. "I'd like to get my hands on that bastard." His eyes blazed. "How is Elena taking it?" He listened to her account, then responded. "She won't be dragged into this, if I have to pull every connection this family has ever had." Anger energized him, and as he paced she had the vision of a rodeo bull about to erupt from the chute.

"Several of the men went after him, but I don't know what that's going to accomplish. They might end up making things worse."

"Maybe, but if I'd been here, I'd have gone with them." He stopped and looked at her. "This family has a checkered past, but we've never turned our back on the community. That has won us some loyalty. The man who did this won't slip through our fingers. I can guarantee it."

"Maybe my testimony will be enough to convict him and Elena won't have to be dragged into it. It's the damage gossip can cause that worries me the most."

"My family's standing should curb some of that, and Elena has no enemies. I think the community will help us protect her." He paused, then looked toward the door. "I have to go see if Elena needs me."

"Why don't you give her a little more time first? Seeing you might make her think she's expected to explain, and that's just going to upset her all over again. She's afraid of questions, you know. Let her work with her plants for a while. That'll give her a chance to get herself together."

"All right. I'll wait until lunch. But if she hasn't come down by then, I'm going to see her anyway."

A knock sounded at the door, and a moment later Cobb stepped inside the room. Raul faced the man squarely. "Well?"

"Carlos won't be causing any problems for anyone here again," he said flatly.

The finality in his tone made her chest tighten. "So, there was a car accident," Irene concluded. "Was anyone else hurt?"

Cobb glanced at Raul, holding his gaze for a second, then looked back at her. "Carlos was banged up pretty bad. But no, no one else."

"He should have known better than to make a run for it," Irene said, her words as cold as sleet. "Even a truck with snow tires has its limitations on roads like these."

Cobb shrugged. "The truck's okay. It just has a few dents."

She gave him a puzzled look. "So you're saying it wasn't a serious accident?"

"Only for Carlos. He won't be up and around for a while." He glanced back at Raul. "I want you to know just how sorry the men are for what happened. There's no way to undo the harm this scumbag has done, but we had a long talk with him, and he understands how we feel. Nothing like that will ever happen again."

Irene stared at Cobb knowing something had just transpired between the men, but uncertain of what it was. After Cobb left the room, she glanced at Raul. "I missed something here. What happened to Carlos?"

"My guess is that he's been admitted to the county hospital as an accident victim."

"The others put him there, or took him there?" she whispered.

"We'll never know, and you can be sure that Carlos will never speak about it." Seeing the horrified look on her face, he continued. "Pressing charges would have meant having to put Elena through things she may never have been able to handle. Both of you, through no fault of your own, would have been stigmatized." The tension left his shoulders, and the lines around his face eased and disappeared. "It's primitive justice, Irene, but fitting."

She leaned back in her chair. "Send Carlos his final wages at the hospital, along with his belongings. You don't want him to have a reason to return here," she said.

"Count on it. Neither one of you will ever be exposed to that man again." Raul returned to his chair and sank into the cushions.

"You're exhausted," she said quietly. Darkly shadowed eye sockets and the fixity of his look attested to his weariness.

"I haven't been to bed yet. I drove all night so I could get back sooner. I've been very worried about Elena." He rubbed his face with one hand. "After lunch, I'll talk to her, and if she needs counseling I'll make sure she gets the best." His eyes met hers in a raw, unguarded look. "I don't like to think what might have happened to my sister if you hadn't been around. I'm very grateful to you." He shook his head, as if frustrated by his choice of words. "But my feelings are more than that. I've enjoyed your friendship, and all that it's meant. There have been times when it's been tested, but it's held, though I wasn't always sure it would."

"Neither was I." She felt as if an invisible hand were drawing them together. Tender, loving feelings were slowly sealing the rift that history had placed in their path.

"Yet what I feel for you goes much deeper than friendship." His words resonated with gentle conviction. "When you were late coming back, and I thought something had happened to you, I nearly lost my mind. I kept thinking I'd let you slip through my fingers without fighting to win you or even telling you what was in my heart." He moved to her side, and taking her hand, lifted her out of the chair.

"It's not a matter of fighting for me," she said in a quiet voice. "A woman chooses whether or not to surrender her heart."

He gathered her into his arms. "What I see in your face when you look at me and when I hold you, surely that's love," he coaxed softly.

"It doesn't matter what we choose to call it. It isn't enough to form a lasting relationship." The words tore at her heart.

"I don't believe that. We've both fought hard against what we're feeling. Yet despite everything, it endured."

His words went straight to her heart. She was an

adult woman, levelheaded in almost every way, but the lure of what he offered was magnetic.

He kissed her softly, letting his tongue slip between her lips to mate with hers. When she didn't struggle or try to pull away, he deepened his kiss, fueling the greed they both felt.

He whispered her name over and over again, and a part of her heart sang. It felt good to hear him call to her in such a wonderful raw voice. It assured her that it was she he wanted, and that she wasn't a substitute or the object of a basic need.

When he swept her up into his arms, carrying her across the room, she buried her head against his shoulder. A second later, he lowered her onto the couch and started to undress her, then with an embarrassed look suddenly stopped. "I have nothing to protect you with."

"I . . ."

"No. It means I'll have to carry you to my room. I have what I need there." He smiled.

"What if someone sees?"

"Elena's in her room. Gene's not coming back till later today, and Angela will be in the kitchen for hours. We won't be disturbed."

He scooped her up with an ease that melted her insides and carried her to the door. As he bent down slightly, she reached out and turned the knob for him, opening it. "Thanks," he murmured. He edged sideways to maneuver out, but miscalculated, and her head struck the door frame. "I'm so sorry!"

"I'm okay. It's just a minor concussion," she teased. "But I've got a better idea. Rather than risk having us both hospitalized by the time we get upstairs, why don't I just walk with you?"

He set her down, chagrined. "So much for the grand, passionate romantic scene."

"Romance doesn't always make sense," she said simply. "But it doesn't matter. It's the feelings behind it that count." Need that went beyond pleasure guided her now. She wanted to share the purest of life's joys with this man whom she'd come to love.

He gave her hand a gentle squeeze. "It's been a long time for me," he said slowly.

Sensing his insecurity, she pressed his hand against her face and brushed it with a kiss. "We're taught to be patient, but there are times I neither want that nor expect it."

He gave her a quirky half-smile, then led her into his room. Closing the door, he turned to face her. For a long moment he was content to gaze into her eyes. Then slowly he moved toward her and undressed her, enjoying the coppery smoothness his efforts revealed.

Naked before him, she allowed his gaze to take her in. "My turn now," she whispered. As she began to undress him, a button popped off his silk shirt and landed across the room.

"Oh, phooey!" She turned to locate it, but he pulled her back into his arms with a tiny smile.

"It's not important. Forget about it," he whispered. He bent to kiss her, drawing her tongue gently into his mouth until she trembled.

When he eased his hold a moment later, need guided her fingers into acting with more finesse. She slipped his shirt away from his shoulders, her gaze feasting on his muscular, hair-roughened chest. Unable to resist the temptation, she kissed his nipples, teasing them with the hardened tip of her tongue.

He shuddered and a long rumble seemed to come from the depths of his soul. "How did you know I'd like that?" he said, pulling her closer to him.

She suckled him, enjoying the way he responded to

her. "I'm attuned to you in ways I wasn't even aware of."

After a long while, she stopped and moved back, unbuckling his belt so she could finish undressing him. With shaking hands, she drew down his pants and saw his body tense to an impossible state.

"Come kiss me again," he said, guiding her onto his bed.

She wrapped her arms around his neck and pulled his mouth down to hers. The desire to invade and stake her own claim on him made her aggressive.

The sweet intrusion of her tongue shattered his restraint. He kissed her hard, the male need to possess her pounding through him. He was aware of everything about her, from the soft sighs that came from the back of her throat to the instinctive way her hips moved against him. Shifting slightly, he slid his hand down the center of her body and slipped his fingers inside her warmth. When the intimacy of that caress made her gasp, he took full advantage of it, ravaging her with his kiss as he continued to stroke her.

She felt the tiny explosions his fingers triggered all throughout her body. When he finally drew away, she didn't think she'd ever move again.

"You're ready for me now," he said, reaching toward the nightstand for what he needed to protect her.

No, she wasn't ready for more; she was very nearly dead. Yet when he covered her body with his own and entered her, she found energy reserves she hadn't suspected were there.

His penetration was tender, his strokes deep and rhythmic. Then urgency and passion led to a wildness neither could control. As he thrust down hard on her, she moved in counterpoise, whimpering for more. He drove into her again and again. Her body, flushed and desperate, engulfed him in fire. From the edges of sanity, he heard her final moan of surrender, and with a cry of male triumph, he followed her over the edge.

A while afterward, satisfied to the point of catatonia, she stirred in his arms and smiled up at him lazily.

"I'm glad you're not asleep," he said. "It's early and I can think of so many wonderful ways to start a new day."

Shortly after noon, she headed outside. She had no regrets about what had happened between Raul and her, but now she'd have to make the most of discretion. There was no way she'd allow herself to become the object of the crew's jokes.

The day was cloudy, but the gray sameness that seemed to lie over everything didn't dampen her own good spirits. She strolled at a leisurely pace toward Cobb's trailer, enjoying the cool breeze. But then as she went past a thick belt of trees, her mood was suddenly shattered. Out of the corner of her eye, she caught a flicker of movement. She managed to see only the barest glimpse of a shadow, but it was enough to let her know someone was dogging her footsteps.

She'd hoped, and had desperately wanted to believe, that with Carlos out of the way, all their troubles would be resolved. Her heart sank as the reality of her situation hit her. Carlos had been one factor in the problems that had plagued her at *Casa de Encanto,* but the threat to her remained.

Anger gave her the incentive to burst through her fears. She'd had enough of being the victim. This time the prey was about to teach the hunter a lesson he wouldn't soon forget.

# 28

RENE STARTED BACK toward the house. Although it was cloudy, the weather had warmed considerably and the snow was rapidly melting. As she walked, the shadowy shape stayed with her, just out of her line of vision, but never far behind. She suppressed a shudder. It was as if the person was waiting for the right moment to strike, but gauging her abilities first. To show fear was to play into his hands. She threw her shoulders back, determined not to give him more of an advantage than he already had. She walked around to the rear of the hacienda, prepared to put her plan into action. It was a trick her grandfather had once played on her in jest, but now would prove to be her shadow's undoing.

Irene carefully propped a ladder beside the hacienda's wall and climbed up to the pueblo-style roof, pretending to study the workmanship. As she walked around the large chimneys and "swamp coolers," a

type of evaporative air-conditioning used in the Southwest, she allowed herself a grim smile. The shadow
had followed her up. He was quiet as a mouse, but she
had him now. Moving quickly, she scrambled down
the ladder, then removed it from the side of the building. There was no way he'd ever get down now without help.

Irene ran into the house to get Raul. She had the last
piece of the puzzle. The threats to her, and the accidents around the hacienda, would finally be explained.
Most important of all, the identity of the culprit would
at last be revealed.

She found Raul in the kitchen, holding a plate filled
with guacamole and tortilla chips. He offered her
some. "The guacamole is freshly made. It's extra
spicy, but I think you'll like the flavor."

"Not now, there's no time. You have to come outside with me, quickly." She hurried him along as she
explained.

"Way to go!" Raul said, hearing what she'd accomplished. "Now let's go find out who he is and what he's
been hoping to gain. I've got to admit I'm tired of
guessing games, and chasing that antelope of a man
through the snow."

Raul replaced the ladder, then yelled up. "You
might as well come down. Otherwise, I may be inclined to let you stay up there all night, and you'll
probably freeze to death."

They waited expectantly, listening, but heard no
footsteps and could see no one moving around above.
Irene glanced at Raul and gave him a quizzical look.
"Should I get some of the workers and have him
hauled down off there?"

He shook his head and yelled a warning. "This is
your last chance. We can do this nicely, or the hard
way."

Still no sounds. Impatient, Irene started to go up the ladder. "I'm going to find out who he is. I'm tired of waiting."

"No, wait!" Before Raul was able to complete the last word, she was already above his reach. Raul cursed softly and followed. "Will you hold on a minute?"

She stood on the last rung, glanced around, then finished climbing up. "There's no one here," she said, her stomach flip-flopping. "Or else he's hiding behind something."

"If he followed you to the roof, he has to still be around." Raul hoisted himself over the parapet and walked around. The massive evaporative cooler and a few thick chimneys were the only places that could shelter and hide someone. He examined each one carefully, making a wide circle around them. The metal covers on the coolers were still screwed into place, so no one could be inside them, and fires were going in the fireplaces below. Hiding inside a chimney under those circumstances was impossible. "We're the only ones here. Maybe you mistook the shadow you saw."

"I didn't." She felt like screaming in rage. Once again she'd been made to look like a fool. "Can you think of some way he could have climbed down?"

Raul studied the north end of the roof. "Would this *canale* support a man's weight?" He pointed to the drain half a step below him. Water from melted snow cascaded down to the ground from it in a steady stream.

She nodded. "It's set in adobe that's strong enough for that. But where could he have gone from there?"

"If he was agile, he might have been able to leap to the branch."

It was a ten-foot jump to the pine branch, and the

drop was close to thirty feet. "It would take a desperate man, or a very brave and lucky one."

"Maybe all three," he shrugged, "because that's the only way he could have found a way off this roof without the ladder."

Irene jammed her hands into her pockets. "Raul, do you believe me?"

He turned and faced her squarely. "Yes, I do. There was a time when I couldn't have brought myself to admit anything that undermined the image of this hacienda. But you and I are past the point where we have to worry about keeping up appearances."

Irene smiled, relief sweeping over her. "I'm glad to hear you say that."

They made their way down and looked for tracks. The snow was almost melted except on the north side. Still, they were unable to find any marks that couldn't be explained away. Finally, when it started to rain, they went back inside the house. "Have you told Elena that Carlos won't be coming back?"

He nodded. "But you know, I'm not sure she understood. She turned beet-red, ran into the bathroom, and locked herself in. I had Angela go up and talk to her. She assured me that all Elena needs is a chance to relax. Apparently she was humiliated by the thought that I'd learned what had been done to her." His voice hardened. "Carlos was lucky that it was the men who caught up to him, and not me." Rage shook him and for a moment he could barely contain the intensity.

"It's over now. Both you and Elena have to put it behind you. Hatred like that is corrosive. It'll eat through you and rip apart your humanity."

"I hate to see her living in fear, and hiding out in her room like she used to."

"She blames me for the problems the crew have created here, you know, and for the dissension between you and Gene. She thinks I've brought misery to your household."

"She might blame you, but those feelings don't stem from anger or hatred. It's just that Elena is as protective of me as I am of her. She wants me to be happy, and equates that to the same things that make her happy. Security and a stable environment are everything to her. Without that, she's lost."

"I think you're underestimating her. She's become much stronger these past few months. In my opinion, the old Elena is gone. She'll never go back to being the way she was. Keep in mind that she came to my aid though she was terrified, and even seeing Carlos in the hall didn't stop her."

"That's a very good point. Maybe Elena has grown up more than I realized."

"Let's go see her together. She knows I shared in the trouble she faced, so my presence might help make her feel less embarrassed."

Elena was just stepping out of her room when Raul and Irene came up. "I was coming to look for you two. Would you like to come into my room? I need to talk."

Raul glanced at Irene, curiosity more than worry on his features. "Sure, Elenita, wherever you're comfortable." They walked in and sat down on a small sofa opposite Elena, who was on her bed.

Elena looked at Irene first. "I hated you at first for bringing so many strangers here. But then I started to like you. You weren't bad, but bad things followed you. That's why I thought you should leave."

"Elenita, it wasn't her fault," Raul said, but Elena shook her head.

"The problem was that I'd never learned how not to be afraid. I was scared of going into town, scared of being around strangers. Then I started watching you, and even when terrible things were happening, you didn't stay in your room. You knew how not to be scared. And then when that awful man was in your room, you got angry and wanted to fight back. You didn't run. I got angry too, because I wasn't like that."

"You don't have to worry. He's gone," Irene said.

"Good, but it doesn't matter now. I don't want to worry or hide anymore. I want to 'be useful.' I want to be more like other people."

"Elena, remember when you said you wanted to grow even more flowers?" Irene looked at Raul, who nodded. "I think it's time you knew about the surprise your brother's planned for you."

Elena looked at Raul. "What is it?"

Raul smiled. "We're going to build you a greenhouse, Elena. You can have all the plants you want in there. You can sell them or give them away. Whatever would make you happy."

Elena's smile was radiant, and she jumped to her feet excitedly. "I'd like to do both. Sell enough to buy more, and also give some away to the hospital. They like my plants. And I could grow Christmas flowers, and all kinds of things! I could 'be useful.' Where are you going to put my greenhouse?"

"Along the south wall. It'll look like another *portal,* except enclosed. There'll be big skylights, and it will face toward the winter sun so you can have sunshine even in winter."

"Let's go outside. You can show me exactly what I'll be looking at, and how big it'll be!"

Raul glanced out the window. "I think it's still raining out there now, Elenita. It's melting all the leftover snow and making it real muddy in places. We can show you the plans if you like, but why don't we at least wait until it stops raining to go out? We have all afternoon."

"Oh, it's only rain! We can bundle up in our raincoats and carry an umbrella."

Raul saw the eagerness in her face, and his resolve melted like the snow outside. "All right. Let's go get our coats."

Elena led the way out of the room. As Raul waited for Irene to follow her, she couldn't resist teasing him. "Such firm resolve!"

"Oh, be quiet," he growled. "I never claimed to be tough as nails."

They'd just retrieved raincoats and an umbrella from the closet when Gene stepped out of the sitting room, holding a mug of cocoa. "Where are you all going? It's raining!"

"We're going to show Elena where the greenhouse will be constructed," Irene answered.

Gene smiled, placed the mug down, and retrieved his coat from the closet too. "This is one trip that's worth getting wet for."

When they reached the south side of the house, Irene began to explain. "It'll be attached to the house, but the outside walls will be wood frame and stucco. Visually we can make it appear the same as adobe, though. With the brick floors we plan to install, it's going to look much like a *portal* that's covered with windows on three sides."

Raul stepped off the dimensions, delighted to see Elena happy. "It's going to be very large. Much more so than anything you've ever had, including the outside garden."

Elena walked the area Raul had stepped off. "It'll be wonderful," she said at last. As her gaze wandered over the grounds, her eyebrows knitted together. "That piñon . . . when it gets taller it's going to shade my greenhouse. It'll ruin the plants that need the sun."

"We'll have it dug up," Raul said.

"No, you can't kill it."

Gene placed a hand on her shoulder. "I'll personally dig it up and replant it elsewhere as soon as it stops raining. How's that?"

Elena stepped forward and pointed to a spot in the yard. "Will you put it by that big boulder? It'll get lots of light there." As Gene nodded, she relaxed. "Then that's okay. But if I'm going to have lots of plants, I'm going to need *big* watering cans. Otherwise, I'll spend all my time going back and forth to the house."

Raul laughed. "There'll be a door leading to the greenhouse through the sitting room. But we'll make sure you have a water supply inside your greenhouse, Elenita. You can use a hose, instead."

Raul glanced at Irene, and she nodded. "It's no big problem to extend the plumbing out here. Well, providing the ground below is clear of any large boulders. Otherwise we can just put in a separate line from the well, though that might take a little longer. I'll have to talk to Cobb about that."

"Good." Gene shuddered. "It's settled. Now let's go back inside. I'm starting to freeze out here."

They returned to the house, glad to reach the warmth once again. Slipping out of their wet gear, they walked to the *sala* where Cobb stood inspecting the finished adobe plastering job. Raul glanced around. "This room is magnificent," he said, running his hand over the thick wall. Once we get everything back in here, it's going to look the way I envisioned, with old-style elegance." He glanced at Cobb, then Irene. "I think this deserves a glass of champagne."

"I agree," Irene said, her eyes taking in the room with pride.

They adjourned to the sitting room, and while Gene made a fire to take the chill out of the air, Raul went to the kitchen. He returned, holding a chilled bottle of

Krug's rosé, a rich, luscious champagne. "I've been saving this for a special occasion—like this," he said.

Angela came in with champagne glasses on a tray and set them on the table before him. Moments later, Raul filled the glasses, then passed them around.

Elena took a sip, then smiled eagerly at Raul. "Now can we talk about my greenhouse?"

Raul laughed, and told Cobb what they wanted done. Irene quickly filled in the pertinent details.

Cobb smiled at Elena. "I'll make it top priority. I'll probe the ground tomorrow and make sure there are no boulders or outcrops in the way. We're dealing with mountain soil here, so it'll be hit-or-miss. If the route's clear, I'll put in new water and sewage lines. Barring major problems, by tomorrow afternoon we can have things staked out, and maybe even start with some of the trenching."

Elena clapped her hands together, then ran up to Raul and threw her arms around his neck. "This is the best gift ever. Better than Christmas or even my birthday."

Gene, having set aside his champagne in favor of cocoa, waved to get her attention. "I'll transplant that tree, just like I promised too, Elena. It'll keep growing, just in a new place."

Elena managed a smile. "Thanks," she murmured.

They sat beside the fireplace for the next thirty minutes, the comfortable warmth of the room enveloping them. Finally the sounds of the rain stopped and the sun poked through the clouds.

"I better get back to work." Cobb stood. "I've got to check the crew schedules. I want to make sure everything is ready for the extensive interior work coming up."

Gene stood up slowly. "Well, I promised I'd move

that tree. I might as well get to it," he said, grinning at Elena.

She nodded. "That would be nice."

As he left the room, Elena turned to Raul. "Thanks for doing this for me. I'm very happy right now."

"As you should be always," Raul said, kissing her on the cheek.

"I'm going to go upstairs and look through my catalogs. Now that I'll have more room, I'll be able to order lots of new things."

As Elena left, Raul glanced at Irene. "If you have some time, will you bring the greenhouse drawings in here and go over them with me one more time?"

"No problem." She returned a few minutes later. They stood behind the large corner table, the blueprints rolled out. As Raul made modification suggestions, she indicated them on the plans. A slightly altered design began to take shape over the next few hours. "You do have some of your family's artistic talent too," she conceded when they were both satisfied with the results. "These changes really made a nice difference in the overall appearance."

"I was inside a greenhouse like that once, with the thick *vigas* crisscrossing the ceilings, curved windows, and a dark red brick floor. It gave it a very traditional look."

"We'll also make sure the stucco is a good match to the adobe. No one will ever know the difference."

Gene came in a moment later, covered in mud. "Thank God that piñon wasn't any bigger than it was, and that the ground was soft."

"You look like you've been through trench warfare," Raul said with a chuckle.

"Hey, the pine didn't want to be moved. What can I say?" Gene wiped the mud from his cheek with a handkerchief. "I hope she's pleased. I put it by the rock just like she asked. I try hard to get her to like me, but you've always been her favorite."

"It's only because you're less predictable," Raul explained, "and that makes her uneasy." He poured some brandy into three glasses, took one, and offered the others to Gene and Irene.

Gene stared at the amber fluid in the glass. "She's never really said anything to me, but I know she hates my drinking."

"So do I," Raul answered. "But you've cut down. I've noticed you drinking cocoa instead of wine lately. That's a good sign."

"It's a time of renewal not only for the hacienda but for all of us." He glanced at Irene, then at Raul as he set the brandy down, untouched. "I'm thinking of moving out for a while."

"Why now when the renovation is more than halfway completed? Soon we'll be able to really enjoy it." Raul gave his brother a puzzled look.

"This house is more you than it ever was me, Raul. That's especially true now. I'm not passing judgment on the work, or on you, I'm stating a fact. I need to make a fresh start, and I can't do that here. I'll return someday when I can come back as your equal, not as the younger brother who stands in your shadow." He stood up, and met his brother's surprised look. "We all have to grow up sometime; it just takes some of us longer than others."

"Have you come up with any job prospects?" Raul asked.

"I never thought I'd be working for someone else, but I've made a few calls and have some possibilities. There are art dealers in Taos and Santa Fe who could use a man experienced in bronze casting. I'm going to be setting up some interviews." Gene smiled modestly.

"If you'll excuse me now, I think it's a good time to update my résumé."

Raul watched him leave. As Gene's footsteps faded up the stairs, Raul downed the rest of his brandy in one gulp. "I never thought I'd see the day," he said. "But maybe it's also time for me to start reaching out for the kind of future I want too."

He shifted on the couch until he faced Irene and then reached for her hand. "Irene, my marriage was a disaster; there was much truth in the accusations Gene leveled at me. I failed Reina completely. I married her knowing what she wanted, catering to her fantasies, and then broke her heart by not delivering what she expected. After my father died, the family business was all-important. It consumed me. I needed to get it back on steady ground."

He looked at her hand, aware of how small it looked nestled inside his. Tenderness filled him. More than anything he wanted her to understand. "It was a test of my abilities as a businessman and a man to do what my father had entrusted to me as the elder son. I also carried the responsibility of making sure that Elena would always be provided for. Without our company, I couldn't have done that. All that spelled divided loyalties."

She nodded slowly. "Tell me this: how did Reina die?" she asked, needing to hear it from him. "You've never wanted to talk about that. All I really know is what I managed to learn from newspapers at the library." Seeing the startled look on his face, she placed her hand over his. "I care deeply for you, and my heart required the answers you wouldn't give me. In my place, would you have done differently?"

Raul shook his head. "I don't blame you. The reason I never spoke about it was because that was my greatest failure." He paused, and glanced pensively across the room. "We'd gone to Mexico on what was supposed to have been a second honeymoon. We both knew that unless we rekindled what we'd had it would disintegrate, tearing us into pieces along with it. But instead of finding love, all we did was argue. We'd both been hurt badly, and those scars were too fresh to brush aside. One night, we rented a boat and went out to see the coastline. Reina started drinking heavily and told me she'd made plans to leave me as soon as we got back. She was going to go to Los Angeles and live there. She was tired of the hacienda, of me, and of the laid-back life-style in Taos and Santa Fe."

Irene could feel the pain that lay just beyond his words. "It must have been incredibly difficult for you."

His gaze was unfocused and he continued as if he hadn't heard her words. "By then I was heading back to the shore because the wind was coming up. I wasn't about to argue with her while she was drunk. That made her even angrier. Then the waves started to pick up. She was already unsteady on her feet, so I reached out to keep her from falling. She acted as if I'd struck her. She was totally out of control. She yanked free and climbed out onto the bow, fully dressed." Naked sorrow shone in his eyes. "She was screaming at me, telling me that I couldn't strong-arm her into doing anything. As if I actually would," he added bitterly.

"She didn't know you very well," Irene observed rhetorically.

"She never tried. Reina swore she'd jump into the ocean if I touched her again. Do you have any idea what that does to a man? My wife was willing to commit suicide rather than allow me to touch her." He stood, walked to the window, and stared out into the gathering shadows of night.

Irene walked up to him and placed a hand on his

arm. His body was shaking; she could feel the vibrations beneath her fingers. "She was drunk, and she was looking for a way to force you to react to her. When you wouldn't, she increased the pressure."

Raul exhaled softly. "She was hysterical, and I knew I had to get her to come down from the bow. I tried to guide her away from the edge, but she jerked away. That's when she lost her balance and fell overboard. I heard a loud thump, and realized she must have bumped her head or hit the propeller as the boat went by." He covered his face with one hand and remained silent for a few moments before continuing. "I turned the boat around right away, and went back to where I thought she'd fallen in. I kicked off my shoes and dove in, determined to find her though the waters were pitch-black. The boat's lights weren't much help, but I kept diving until I thought my lungs would burst. I finally crawled up on the boat and called in a Mayday. Then I dove back in and continued swimming around, looking and diving."

"Did they dispatch search teams?"

He nodded wearily. "Several, but the riptide was incredibly strong. Even though I tried to compensate, it carried me away from the boat. By the time they pulled me out of the water I was exhausted. I very nearly drowned trying to swim back to the boat. The next day the diving teams also gave up the search. They concluded Reina had washed out to sea." He returned around to face her, his eyes narrowed with pain. "An investigation followed. There was talk, and the rumor that I'd been directly responsible for her death. But without witnesses, the police were forced to rule Reina's death an accident."

"You did all you could for her; that's all anyone can do." She heard someone coming down the stairs and hoped they wouldn't be interrupted. The footsteps continued down the hall, going outside.

"Yes, I accept that now, but for a long time, I blamed myself. It tore me apart. Of course, Reina's death devastated Gene, and he's never forgiven me."

They sat in front of the fireplace side by side for a long time, neither speaking. Raul finally placed a hand on her shoulder, then moved it slowly to cup her neck. "Having you in my life has been like letting the sun back in. To face my feelings for you, I've had to come to terms with my past. I've always been a one-woman man."

Firelight danced in his eyes, making them gleam with a single-minded intensity that was almost frightening. His hand on her neck was warm, infusing her with a different kind of strength. She knew that the choice was hers to make. There were other factors in her life that she owed allegiance and respect to: the collective past of her tribe; her aunt and her mother, who had raised her; the memory of her grandfather. But she suddenly realized there was another factor she hadn't considered: what she owed herself.

"This house now has your mark on it too," he started, "like . . ."

He stopped speaking abruptly as a dull thump sounded somewhere in the yard. He listened, signaling for her to remain quiet. More thuds followed.

Raul went to his desk drawer and retrieved a flashlight. "Maybe our prowler has returned. Call the sheriff's department, I'm going to go take a look."

Irene dialed, made her report, then dashed outside. The beam of the flashlight cut through the darkness ahead. She was running toward it when Raul spun around in a fighting stance. "I told you to stay inside."

"No, you didn't," she answered, matching his whisper. "You told me to call the sheriff's office, and I did."

"Go back in. I'll take care of this."

"Very brave, but not very bright. One of us can always run for help if the other's clobbered."

He exhaled softly. "I don't have time to argue, but your faith in my fighting ability is less than inspiring."

"We'll worry about your ego later," she whispered. "Right now I'd rather have you in one piece."

"Ah, if you're worried about my body, then I forgive you," he said, then signaled for her to grow still.

She smirked. He *would* give her a line like that just when she couldn't reply!

Through the circle of trees ahead a small light was shining on the ground. Raul turned off his own flashlight and waited for his vision to adjust to the faint rays of moonlight that peered between the clouds. They heard a soft scuffling sound next, then a terror-filled scream splintered the night.

# 29

I T'S ELENA!" RAUL started running toward the south side of the house.

He'd gone about thirty yards when he saw Elena struggling to break free from a man who was holding her. The stocking mask distorting his features made him seem more like an apparition from hell.

Elena's movements were desperate, like those of a terrified rabbit in the clutches of a wolf. Rage gave him extra speed, but before Raul could reach them, Elena broke free and ran toward the woods. The man fled.

"I'll get the guy," Raul yelled back at Irene. "Find Elena!"

He heard Irene veer away into the darkness, but his eyes remained focused on the figure running away. He wouldn't lose him. As he dodged around a large rock resting on an unfamiliar mound of dirt, his foot struck something hard. He stumbled forward, dropping his flashlight. Suddenly the ground gave way beneath him. He fell hard, crashing into the side of some kind of shallow pit, his face in the mud.

He brushed away the muck, trying to collect his thoughts as he sat up. Damn it to hell! This hadn't been here before. He was still in the garden, yet he was in a hole that was at least three feet deep and four feet wide.

As the full moon peeked out from behind a cloud, illuminating the grounds, he took a look around. There was a shovel about half a foot from the hole, undoubtedly what he'd tripped over. The newly planted piñon Gene had relocated was to his left. But unless he missed his guess, he was standing right at the spot Elena had wanted the tree moved to. The boulder she'd pointed to was the one he'd tried to avoid, the one now on the mound of dirt. Dissatisfied with Gene's job, had she come out to dig it up and move it herself?

Raul took a step to retrieve his flashlight and felt something crunch underfoot. He aimed the light down and saw a tattered remnant of cloth wound around his boot. As he pulled it free, a skull rose up out of the loose dirt with it, the jaw opening in a silent scream. He dropped the cloth as if it were a hot coal, and jumped back, trying to swallow back his disgust.

Heart pounding, he tried to steady the wildly jitter-bugging flashlight in his hand. Through the remaining strands of what he speculated had once been a laundry bag used to contain the body, he could see a woman's belt and a high-heel shoe. Raul stepped aside quickly, realizing he was standing on the skeleton. That's when the beam of his flashlight fell upon a small gold object hanging loosely from the cadaver's neck vertebrae. He reached down and turned the familiar locket over. Gently scraping away the encrusted dirt, he uncovered an initial, the letter "R."

Raul jumped out of the hole, his breathing heavy as he struggled for air clean of death's smell. Dear heaven, this was what Elena had stumbled on when she'd tried to replant the piñon! But who was the man who'd intercepted her?

He glanced toward the forest where both Elena and Irene had disappeared, panning the light from left to right. He couldn't hear or see either of them. Fear shot through him, and he bolted into the wooded area to find them. Not daring to call out and risk having them reveal their positions to an enemy, he searched in silence.

Uncertainty mocked his courage, undermining his ability to think clearly. In near desperation, he circled back to the clearing near the garden. That's when he saw Irene walking back toward the house, the few lights along the *portal* making identification possible without using his flashlight. His heart sank as he noted that Elena wasn't with her.

Raul ran up to Irene, who turned as she heard him coming. "You couldn't find Elena?" he asked.

She shook her head. "I'm a good runner, but your sister is as fast as a jackrabbit when she's frightened. One second she was there, the next she was gone."

Raul told her about the body Elena had uncovered, and the man in the stocking mask. "From the locket, I believe she found Raven Hernandez's grave."

Irene stared at Raul in shock. "Elena finds Raven's skeleton, then she's attacked. It's like a horror movie come to life. She must be in a total panic. We've got to find her."

He exhaled loudly. "Elena knows these woods well, even at night. We used to play hide-and-seek at all hours. She'll make it to a safe spot."

"We should still get a search party together and

comb the woods for her. She could freeze to death out here."

"I doubt she's outside anymore," Raul said. "My guess is she probably circled back to the house and is hiding there."

"Even so, we need help finding her. We can't be sure how much the person who attacked her knows about the layout of the house or about Elena."

Raul and Irene jogged back to the house. "I'll go upstairs and get Gene and Cobb," Raul said. "They can alert the crew. Why don't you find Angela? She knows practically all of Elena's hiding spots."

"I know it's an off chance," Irene suggested, "but while you're upstairs, check my room as well as hers."

Raul ran to the second floor and Irene hurried to Angela's room. She was awake, reading a book. Irene quickly related what she knew.

"If Elena got away from him, she'll be okay," Angela said with so much conviction it sounded more like a prayer. "But we better get started because we're not going to find much help around here now. Most of the men left after work to go into town. With the roads passable, they were eager to leave and spend the time with their families."

"Then you and I have to split up so we can cover more ground."

"I'll go check her dressing room closet. When she was small, she'd lock herself in there and curl up in one of the corners whenever something frightened her."

As Irene searched through the big house, she wondered about Hernandez and if this news would make the burden he carried easier to bear. Raven's absence had not been connected to anything he'd done or failed to do. Though her fate had been tragic, it had clearly been beyond his control.

Irene heard Raul moving upstairs, doors opening

and closing in unison with his footsteps. An unsettling thought began forming in her mind as she recalled Elena's attitude toward Raven. Elena had been very jealous of Raven's interest in Raul, and when younger Elena had probably been far more temperamental. Was it possible that the young woman and the girl had fought, and that had led to a terrible accident? She thought of Elena's anxiousness around Gene and wondered if Gene might have learned or witnessed something on that order. If he had, she was certain that he would have kept it a secret and done whatever he'd felt necessary to protect his sister, even burying Raven's body.

"Neither Elena, Gene, nor Cobb is up there," Raul said. "If you'll continue looking here in the house, I'll have as many of the crew I can find start searching the grounds. They can come and get one of us if they find Elena."

Angela came out and rushed up the stairs. "I'd like to look inside all the upstairs closets." She glanced at Raul and Irene. "You won't mind?"

"Check wherever you want," Raul answered.

Irene nodded. "Elena's the only priority now."

While Angela continued searching upstairs, Irene went downstairs to the cellar where Elena had hidden once before. After peering into every nook and cranny, she went back to the ground floor. Irene searched the laundry room and the closets inside the kitchen, feeling certain Elena would pick someplace small and sheltered, but her efforts proved fruitless.

Irene was virtually certain there were no hidden rooms or other closed-in spaces that she'd missed; she practically knew the hacienda by heart. Frustrated, she walked to her office, intending to check the house plans again just in the off chance there was some detail she'd forgotten. If she hadn't, then she'd join the others outside.

As she walked inside her office and flipped on the light switch, she felt a blast of icy air knifing through her sweater. The window was open only a few inches, but the wind was biting cold. Cursing her habit of wanting fresh air no matter what the weather, she walked across the room. As she slammed the window down, she heard a scuttling sound directly behind her.

Irene spun around, aware of the startled cry that came from between her filing cabinet and the wall. "Elena?"

Irene advanced slowly and warily until she recognized the familiar figure huddled tightly against the wall. "Elena, it's okay. It's just me, Irene."

Elena tried to scoot even further away, but trapped in the corner there was nowhere else for her to go. "Go away." Her voice was whisper-thin.

"You're safe here in my office," Irene said gently. "You knew that; that's why you came here. And now you're not alone anymore." She held out her hand.

Elena tentatively reached for it, then slowly came out, mud and water still covering her jacket. "I was so scared," she sobbed. "I didn't want him to hurt me! He looked so ugly! He had something tight over his face, and everything was smudged in like when you press your face against a window."

The stocking mask Raul had mentioned. To have someone disguised like that attack you after you'd just uncovered a grave would have been enough to terrify even the bravest person. "What happened, Elena?"

"I didn't want to hurt Gene's feelings, but he planted the tree in the wrong spot. When it grew, it might have still shaded my greenhouse, so I decided to go out while it was dark and move it myself. I was afraid he'd get mad if he saw me digging it up. With the ground soft from the rain, I knew I could do it. I know how to dig."

"That's when you uncovered the grave?"

Elena nodded grimly. "I didn't know what it was at first, but I was curious, so I shined my flashlight on it and dug a little deeper. Then I heard a sound behind me. Before I could turn around, he grabbed me and started to pull me away. I screamed and fought back, but he was too strong."

"Don't worry, Raul will find him."

"It won't matter," Elena said in a barely audible whisper. "I know who it was."

"Elena, if you think you know, you have to tell me right now. We have to catch this man."

She shook her head. "I'm not sure I should."

"You have to! This person could be dangerous."

"No, he's not. He's just afraid."

"You can't possibly know that!"

"But I do." Elena stared at the floor.

"Elena, please, trust me!"

"I do," she said softly, and glanced up at last. "Okay. Maybe if I tell you, you'll know what the best thing is to do. I sure don't."

"I will," Irene answered, unable to suppress the uneasiness she felt.

"I recognized him almost right away from his cologne and his watch. He tried to disguise his voice when he told me to be quiet, but it didn't work." The muscle at the corner of her mouth pulsed frantically as her eyes filled with tears. "It was my brother Gene."

Irene ran a hand through her hair, trying desperately to absorb this new information. There were two possibilities. Gene could have gone to the grave site to keep his sister from uncovering her own secret. Or perhaps his motive had been more direct. Gene could have been Raven's murderer.

Irene remembered the movie Elena had told her about. Her descriptions had been so vivid. If Elena had seen Gene kill the girl, it seemed entirely likely that she would have turned the memory into a movie filled with strangers in order to deal with it.

Irene sat in the chair closest to Elena. "I know that must have been hard to tell me. It's natural for you to want to protect Gene. Even though you're not as close to him as you are to Raul, he's still your brother."

Elena nodded. "Poor Gene. He's always wanted to be Raul, but he's stuck being himself, kinda like I am." She paused and wiped a tear from her face. "But it's worse for Gene. He's always tried so hard, but people just like Raul better. It happened even with Reina."

"And with Raven Hernandez?"

"Yes," Elena said in a hushed whisper. "Raven would come over to see Raul. Sometimes she'd use me as an excuse, but sometimes she'd use Gene. I tried to tell him, but he wouldn't listen. Since they were both the same age, he thought Raven had really started liking him."

"Sometimes pride makes it impossible to accept the truth." She looked directly at Elena. "Did Gene finally learn what Raven was doing?"

"I . . . don't know."

"Elena, you don't have to be afraid of telling me anything."

"I'm not afraid; I'm just not sure. Sometimes I remember things that I don't think happened. I get everything mixed up."

"What is it you remember?"

"I think I saw Gene and Raven having a fight once." She curled up in the seat, huddling in an almost fetal position. "When I was trying to get him to let go of me, I just remembered. I'd been sitting in the window, looking down into the garden. Raven was laughing at Gene for something and he got mad. He grabbed her like he did me, only he ripped her dress all up. She started screaming at him, and he pushed part of her sleeve into her mouth to keep her from yelling. Or maybe that was the movie I saw." She exhaled and shrugged. "I just don't know."

"Don't worry, Elena. Everyone gets confused sometimes." More than ever, she now felt she was right. The movie had been Elena's way of coping. Seeing her brother forcing himself on a girl must have been impossible for her to handle.

Hearing someone coming down the hall, Irene glanced behind her. Raul walked stiffly into the office, but before Irene could say a word, she saw the barrel of a shotgun pointed at his back. A second later, Gene stepped inside, holding the weapon.

Gene was dressed in old clothes, mud caked on his feet and hands. "Let's go," he ordered, looking at Irene and Elena. "To the basement. Now!"

"Do as he says," Raul said, reaching out to a frightened Elena and taking her hand gently.

Irene led the way across the back hall and then down the stairs. "This is pointless. We already know the story, Gene. You killed Raven during a fight, then carried her body to the shed and buried her there. Then the gardener had the misfortune of discovering the body, so you killed him too. And since the man was larger and heavier, you buried him in the grave Raven had occupied, and took her body to a new grave some distance away."

"You're smart, Irene, but it's too late. By the time you manage to get out of the basement, I'll be long gone." He glanced at Raul. "Give me your wallet."

Raul slowly handed Gene the billfold. "Now you want to rob me too?"

"I don't want your money, even though part of it

should be mine." Gene gave the hand-tooled leather wallet to Elena. "Go upstairs and wedge this in the bottom of the cellar door so no one can open it from the outside. And be quick about it. You wouldn't want anything to happen to Raul." There was an infinite sadness in his gaze as he looked at his sister.

"You're going to hide in here with us?" Irene asked. "What's the point in that?"

"I'm not waiting around. I just don't want Angela to stumble on to us before I'm finished. I don't want to hurt any of you, so my only option is to leave you here bound and gagged. By the time you work the ropes loose, I'll be long gone."

Elena started up the stairs, then gave Irene an almost imperceptible wink.

Realizing Elena had a plan, Irene prepared herself to act quickly. She turned to look at Raul, hoping to alert him, when out of the corner of her eye a flicker of movement caught her attention. A shadow had appeared on one side of the open door.

Raul stood rock-still, but something in his expression told her that he'd also seen it. They were about to get help, she felt it in her bones, but she wasn't sure exactly what was going to happen next.

"Elena, don't waste time!" Gene clipped. "Don't make me do something we'll all regret."

Elena rushed up the last few steps. Then suddenly she ducked out the door, slammed it shut, and turned off the light. The basement became encased in tomblike darkness.

"Don't you move!" She heard Gene's voice in front of her. Disregarding his order, Irene reached to her right, fumbling for a jar of preserves she'd had an eye on. She threw the jar an instant later where Gene had been standing, and ducked fast.

There was a thud and a grunt. Then the shotgun

went off with an ear-shattering roar, simultaneously illuminating the area like a strobe light. In the immediate darkness that followed she heard the sound of footsteps stumbling hastily up the stairs. Abruptly the door was flung open, and light streamed into the basement.

Raul, right behind his brother, ran past the switch and flipped the light back on. Irene stood up, and saw where the buckshot had gouged out a double handful of wooden flooring. Her legs felt rubbery but, gathering her courage, she went up the stairs quickly.

Elena met Irene at the top of the stairs. "Did I do all right?"

"You did just fine." She glanced up and down the hall. "Was Angela around here?"

"I haven't seen anyone except Gene, and Raul as he ran after him down the hall," Elena said excitedly.

Just then, Raul's voice boomed from the direction of the billiard room. "Gene's outside. I'm going after him."

"He's still armed," Irene yelled, racing toward the sound of his voice.

"So am I."

A second later, she caught up to Raul. He had a shotgun, and was feeding shells into the magazine as he walked toward the open front door. "Stay inside the house," he growled. "I'll handle my brother. He won't hurt me."

"Then why take the gun?" she challenged.

"It's just a way of getting his attention long enough for me to talk to him."

"You realize that he was probably behind the accidents that took place during construction. He's quite willing to gamble with lives. Your brother's extremely dangerous."

"If you believe that, then don't come with me." He

glanced back but she remained half a step behind him. "I don't think he ever intended to hurt anyone." Raul continued to the gate, searching the moonlit ground for Gene's footprints. "He was probably trying to discourage any work that might involve digging, because he didn't want the bodies to be found." Raul slowed, and pointed to the ground. "He came this way," he whispered. "I recognize his boot prints."

Moving silently, they followed the trail that led them toward the family cemetery. Staying within the outcropping of trees that afforded them cover, they looked out among the graves for signs of Gene.

Near Reina's marker they heard a faint rustle behind them.

"Drop it, Raul. I don't want to shoot you or anyone else, but I'm not going to jail." Gene waited until Raul placed the shotgun on the ground before rising from where he'd been sitting, hidden under the boughs of a thick spruce. "Just leave me alone, and I'll get out of your life."

"You're my brother; I don't want you out of my life."

"The way things stand, we don't have a choice."

"Yes, you do," Irene said, turning around completely to face Gene. His face was pale and frightened, much like she imagined her own appeared. "Give yourself up."

"No, I can't do that. I'll just make sure you two can't tell the police who to look for right away, and that'll buy me the time I need. I think it's likely Cobb will get blamed if you two disappear for a while, and in fact, I'm counting on it. I figure that even if Elena decides to say something to the police, they probably won't pay serious attention to her. Then, by the time they locate where I've left you tied up, and discover

Cobb's not responsible, I'll be out of the country. They'll never catch me then."

"At first I thought it *was* Cobb," Irene began, stalling for time. "I'd overheard a conversation he had with one of the women workers, and I knew he was being blackmailed. I figured she'd found out he was responsible for the accidents. But then other evidence came up, and that pointed to you. The cops are trained to find answers fast, so they'll figure it out too. Then they'll go after you, and you'll spend the rest of your life looking over your shoulder, wondering when they'll catch up. Is that the way you want to live?"

"Think about it, Gene. Irene's telling you the truth."

"If I turn myself in, I may not live anyway. New Mexico still has the death penalty."

"They're not going to execute you for something that happened years ago when you were sixteen. Our lawyer will use the fact you surrendered to the authorities to support your case. It's your only chance," Raul pleaded. "You've thrown enough of your life away hiding from your past."

"Fear of getting caught has haunted me through the years like a second shadow. At first I thought that no one would ever know. But right after Raven's death, Elena started acting scared around me. I realized that Elena had probably been sitting in the window when I'd killed Raven and had witnessed everything. I was scared out of my mind. She was twenty-two and older than Raul, but she had the temperament of a ten-year-old. I kept waiting for her to blurt it out. When she didn't say anything I figured that she'd forgotten or blocked it out."

"She had," Irene answered. "She couldn't cope with the reality of what she'd seen, so she remembered it as a movie."

"I can forgive you for everything except putting Elena through this just to save yourself." Angrily, Raul took a step forward, reaching for his brother's gun barrel.

"Raul, don't!" Gene stepped back fast, pointing the muzzle at Raul's chest.

"No!" Irene jumped into the line of fire, hoping to stop the confrontation, but Gene didn't lower the shotgun.

At that instant, the deafening scream of a mountain lion hidden in the bush a few feet away rose in the air. The cry, so cold and full of fury, pierced Irene like a needle through the marrow.

A powerful form stepped out from the shadows and bared its ivory fangs. Serpentine tendrils of light fastened on the jagged points. As the cougar advanced with graceful strength, moonlight bathed him in an unearthly glow.

# 30

SEEING GENE'S EYES intent on the ethereal
beast, Irene lunged for the barrel and yanked the
shotgun out of his hands. Raul immediately tackled
his brother, sending Gene to the ground as Irene spun
around to deal with the creature. She turned in a complete circle, but it had vanished inexplicably.

The sound of a fist striking flesh brought Irene's
mind back to the confrontation at her feet. Raul had
grabbed Gene's shirt with one hand, holding him
down while warding off Gene's futile punches with his
forearm. Then Gene kicked Raul off and rolled away,
cursing savagely.

Irene swung the shotgun around and fired a shot
into the air. The blast startled both men and they
froze, giving her the second she needed. "Get away
from him, Gene, now!" Irene pointed the smoking
muzzle at Gene, simultaneously raising the shotgun
stock to her shoulder.

His eyes grew large as he saw Irene start to take careful aim at his face. "Don't let her shoot me, Raul. She wants an excuse to pull the trigger." Gene stumbled back, covering his face with his arms in a futile attempt to ward off the shotgun pellets he anticipated any second.

"You certainly gambled with *my* life, didn't you?" she said bitterly.

Raul stood up. "What are you going to do?" he asked calmly.

She kept the gun trained on Gene for several more seconds, moving her aim first to his heart, then back to his head. Finally she forced her body to relax slightly. "He's your brother. Do you want to hold the shotgun on him?"

"I'll get my own." Raul walked over to where Gene had forced him to drop the other weapon. As he picked up the shotgun, he studied the ground where the mountain lion had been. "Where did it go?"

"You tell me," she said with a shrug, not taking her eyes off Gene, who was rock-still.

As Raul approached, Irene shifted the gun and reached down to feel the mountain lion fetish in the pocket of her slacks. It felt almost hot.

"That damn cougar," Gene muttered, rubbing his jaw where Raul's fist had struck him. "Was it for real?" he whispered.

"I'm not sure, but we all saw it," Raul said hesitantly.

Irene said nothing. She wasn't ready to try and explain what had happened. The answers wouldn't have made things any easier on either of the men.

She pointed the barrel of the gun back at Gene, figuring the threat would carry more effectively if it came from her. "Let's go back to the house. Move."

Gene cursed softly, but did as she asked. "Maybe it

was something straight from one of your legends," he grumbled cynically.

"Does it matter? It appeared at just the right time, and that's enough for me." Silently she marveled at the protection she'd received. It really made no difference at all to her whether or not the animal had been real.

Gene entered the house moments later, and Irene guided him forward to the sitting room. While Raul called their family attorney, Gene sat down, a defeated, crestfallen expression frozen on his face. "I did everything I could to disrupt the construction. Right from the start, I tried to spook you and the other Indian workers with that witch doll. Then when I realized that none of my 'accidents' were going to accomplish anything, I tried to move the gardener's body. But every time I started, someone would come outside. The workers' trailers weren't too far from there. One time I even went out in the middle of the night, but the noise from my shovel must have woken up one of the guys. He came out to investigate."

"And later you couldn't plant the tree where Elena wanted because the body was already there."

He nodded. "When I heard her leave the house, I suspected she was going to try and do the job herself. I took a stocking from her room, pulled it over my face, and went after her. I'd hoped to get Elena safely out of the way, so I could move the body quickly. Only she recognized me, and then Raul came up, and everything fell apart."

"Why didn't you just let the body be discovered? Elena's recollections wouldn't have been enough to convict you."

"Once Raven's body was found, it would have been very easy to check up on other things. For instance, people had seen us together earlier that day."

"Gene, we have to drive down to the sheriff's office together," Raul said, interrupting them. "Jim Montoya's partner will represent you. He's familiar with criminal law, and will meet us there. Will you come with me freely?"

Gene nodded slowly. "Yeah, it's time for some personal renovation, so this family can get a fresh start."

Irene stood by the door, watching the two brothers as they entered Raul's sedan. They'd fought each other most of their lives, but now they were together. Perhaps some good was finally starting to come from all the trouble at the hacienda.

Elena walked up and stood behind her. "Gene will be gone for a long time, won't he?"

Irene nodded. "That's my guess, yes."

"And you? What happens to you and Raul now?"

"Nothing," she answered. "I'll finish my work here and then go back to the pueblo. We each have our own lives."

Elena said nothing for a minute. "When two plants are set close in the ground for a long time, their roots get so entangled that they're practically one. When you try to separate them, you can damage the plants a lot. Sometimes one of them even dies." She glanced at Irene, raised her eyebrows in question, then turned and went back upstairs.

Irene thought about Elena's words. Though simply stated, the meaning had been powerfully clear. The thought of completing the job filled her with a regret so intense all she could feel was a dull ache in her chest.

Serna caught up to her in her office the following morning. "Mr. Mendoza wants Carlos' final check delivered to the hospital. He doesn't want Carlos around here for any reason whatsoever; not that I blame him. But there's a problem. The bookkeeper just called and she doesn't have a time sheet for him. Cobb's going to be gone till later this afternoon, and I don't know squat about the payroll." He glanced at a work crew carrying table saws into the house. "Can you look through the payroll books and see if you can come up with something? I've got to supervise those guys, or there's no telling what condition everything will be in by the time they get through."

"I'll take care of it. It shouldn't be too difficult to figure his earnings."

Irene went to Cobb's trailer and found the weekly time sheets. They'd been stuffed in a pouch inside a ledger-style notebook. As she searched for the one with Carlos' name, she noticed there were two sets of time sheets, and all the Indians' surnames seemed to be on a different page. As she stared at the numbers, flipping pages back and forth, confusion gave way to outrage. She stood immobile, the numbers swimming before her eyes as her anger mounted. Hands shaking, she tucked the ledger under her arm and walked straight to Raul's office.

"That's why he was being blackmailed," Irene said, showing Raul the figures. "He's been paying the Indian workers at a lower rate than he used for the Hispanic and Anglo workers."

"Then he's going to have to make up the difference, even if it comes from his own pocket," Raul said flatly.

They were busy trying to come up with the exact dollar amount Cobb would owe when they heard a knock. Cobb stood at the doorway. "I just got back. Serna said you wanted to see me." Cobb looked at Raul.

"Come in." Raul gestured for Cobb to take a seat.

As Cobb saw his ledger open on Raul's desk, he

snapped his head around to look at Irene. His eyes blazed with undisguised hatred. "That's your doing, isn't it? Who gave you permission to go into my trailer and take whatever you wanted?"

She told him about her conversation with Serna and the circumstances that had prompted her search. "When I found the time sheets, I realized what you'd been doing." She handed him a sheet of paper. "That's the amount of total back pay you owe the Indian workers."

Cobb glanced at the figure, then cursed under his breath. "You don't expect me to come up with this right now, do you?"

Raul's face was set in hard lines that offered no compromise. "Would you rather spend it on a lawyer trying to stay out of jail?"

"I'll have to sell everything I own, including my pickup."

"That's your problem. I know that the proper funds were allocated by the company that employs you. What did you do with their money?"

"I bought things I needed," Cobb muttered. "Until you stuck your nose in it, no one had any reason to complain. They were happy enough just to be working."

Irene disclosed the conversation she'd overheard in the trailer. "I realize now what that was about. Someone else found out and decided to blackmail you. Who was she?"

"Janna. I've been paying her to keep her mouth shut. And now that I have to pay the workers too, I'm going to end up losing everything I own."

"Tough," Irene answered calmly. "And by the way, you have until quitting time today to pack your things and get out. You're no longer working here."

Cobb glanced at Raul. "She can't do that. We have a contract."

"Which you've violated through your illegal activity. I have more lawyers than you have excuses, so don't fight it. Just leave. You're lucky we don't have you thrown in jail right now."

"And what about the rest of my salary?" Cobb demanded.

"It'll be withheld as back pay for the workers who are entitled to it."

After watching Cobb storm out of the study, Raul glanced at Irene. "I should have listened to you right from the start."

"Finally we're in complete agreement on a subject!"

He smiled, then grew serious. "You're going to need to find yourself a new contractor, since there's a lot of work, including the greenhouse, to be finished by Christmas."

"I know who's perfect for the job—Alfredo Hernandez."

He nodded slowly. "I also owe him a debt of gratitude for coming to your rescue," he added. "I'll give him a call."

# EPILOGUE

IRENE ENTERED THE *sala* and found Raul sitting on the couch admiring the eight-foot-tall blue spruce he'd brought in for the approaching holiday. According to his family's custom, it would be decorated Christmas Eve, before the *Noche Buena* feast.

"The renovation is now officially completed," she announced. "And three days ahead of our deadline, I might add."

He forced a smile. "Shall we take one last tour together?" Sadness engulfed him like a cold wind through the hollow of his bones.

They walked around slowly, studying and admiring the results of months of painstaking work. The hand-carved rails on the stairway, the newly polished wood flooring, the smooth finish on the adobe walls, all attested to a job well done.

As their hour-long walk ended, Raul stood outside in the crisp winter afternoon, gazing at *Casa de Encanto* proudly.

"Is it what you expected?" Irene asked.

"More. It has elegance and style, and like everything you've touched in this home, it almost sings with new life."

Elena brushed by them, a handful of gardening catalogs in her hand. "Angela just brought the mail! I've found lots of new places to order from!"

Raul chuckled as Elena rushed inside the house. "You may have to expand that greenhouse soon."

"Anytime you need an architect, just give me a call. I'll never be too busy," she said, trying desperately to keep her voice from trembling. She'd never been very adept at saying good-bye.

Raul pulled Irene back against him, his arms enfolding her gently. "*Casa de Encanto* bears your mark in so many ways. It's become your home too; can't you feel it calling?" he whispered. "You're a part of life here now. And you're a part of me."

A feeling of rightness enveloped her as she acknowledged the truth her heart had known all along. The past mattered only if it created a foundation solid enough to build from. But without the willingness to risk, nothing was ever gained. She remembered her grandfather's words and silently thanked him.

She started to turn around to face Raul when the flicker of a shadow caught her eye. She smiled seeing the vague outline of a mountain lion on the rough ground. There was beauty in the shadow she'd come to know as a friend.

"Come on, let's go inside," she said, knowing three would cross the entrance doors. "It's time to celebrate what we have created together."